Angela Carter was born in 1940. She published her first novel, *Shadow Dance*, in 1965. Her second novel, *The Magic Toyshop*, won the John Llewellyn Rhys Prize in 1967 (Virago, 1981), and her third, *Several Perceptions*, won the Somerset Maugham Award in 1968. *Heroes and Villains* was published in 1969, *Love* in 1971, *The Infernal Desire Machines of Dr Hoffman* in 1972 and *The Passion of New Eve* in 1977 (Virago, 1982). *Nights at the Circus* was joint winner of the James Tait Black Memorial Prize for 1985. Angela Carter has also published three collections of short stories, *Fireworks* (1974), *The Bloody Chamber*, which was received with great acclaim in 1979 and won the Cheltenham Festival of Literature Award, and *Black Venus* (1985); and two works of non-fiction, *The Sadeian Woman: An Exercise in Cultural History* (Virago, 1979) and *Nothing Sacred* (Virago, 1982), a collection of her journalism from *New Society* and elsewhere. She also wrote, with Neil Jordan, the script for the film *The Company of Wolves* (1984). Angela Carter lives in London.

Wayward Girls and Wicked Women is a collection of nineteen stories, widely ranging in time and place, in which women, for once, make the running. Some triumph, others are defeated; all of them take the law into their own hands and all of them make a virtue of not being *nice*. Here is a world of adventuresses and schemers who refuse to be limited by society's expectations or culture's taboos.

WAYWARD GIRLS & WICKED WOMEN

An anthology of stories edited by

ANGELA CARTER

Published by VIRAGO PRESS Limited 1986
41 William IV Street, London WC2N 4DB

Collection, Introduction and Notes © Angela Carter 1986

British Library Cataloguing in Publication Data

Wayward girls and wicked women: an anthology
    of stories.
    1. Short stories, English   2. English
    fiction—20th century
    I. Carter, Angela, *1940–*
    823'.01'08 [FS]   PR1309.S5

    ISBN 0-86068-574-8
    ISBN 0-86068-579-9 Pbk

Typeset by Rowland Phototypesetting Ltd
Bury St Edmunds, Suffolk, and printed by litho
by Anchor Brendon of Tiptree, Essex

CONTENTS

ACKNOWLEDGEMENTS

Permission to reproduce the following stories is gratefully acknowledged: 'The Last Crop' from *Woman in a Lampshade*, Elizabeth Jolley by Penguin Books Australia Ltd; 'The Débutante', translated by Angela Carter, from *La Débutante, Contes et Pieces*, Leonora Carrington by Flammarion, France; 'The Gloria Stories' from *Cventos*, Rocky Gámez by Kitchen Table Press, USA; 'Life' from *The Collector of Treasures*, Bessie Head by Heinemann Educational Books Ltd, London; 'A Guatemalan Idyll' from *Plain Pleasures*, Jane Bowles by Peter Owen Ltd, London and from *The Collected Works of Jane Bowles*, copyright © 1946, 1949, 1966 by Jane Bowles, by Farrar Straus and Giroux Inc, USA: 'The Young Girl' from *The Collected Katherine Mansfield*, Katherine Mansfield; 'Case History', 'A Room of His Own' and 'Legend' from *Feminist Fables*, Suniti Namjoshi by Sheba, London; 'The Rainy Moon', translated by Antonia White, from *The Collected Stories of Colette* edited by Robert Phelps, Colette by Secker & Warburg Ltd, London and by Farrar Straus and Giroux Inc, USA; 'Wedlock' from *Keynotes and Discords*, George Egerton by Virago Press Ltd, London; 'Violet' from *Tea with Mr Rochester and Other Stories*, Frances Towers by John Johnson Ltd, London; 'The Plums' from *Our Sister Killjoy*, Ama Ata Aidoo by Longman Group Ltd, Harlow; 'A Woman Young and Old' from *The Little Disturbances of Man*, Grace Paley by Virago Press Ltd, London and by Viking Penguin Inc, USA; 'The Long Trial', translated by David K. Bruner, from *Les Corps et le Temps*, Andrée Chedid by Flammarion, France; 'The Loves of Lady Purple' from *Fireworks*, Angela Carter; 'The Earth' from *Smoke and Other Early Stories*, Djuna Barnes by Virago Press Ltd, London and Sun & Moon

INTRODUCTION

Angela Carter

'WAYWARD Girls and Wicked Women': the title of this collection is, of course, ironic. Very few of the women in these stories are guilty of criminal acts, although all of them have spirit and one or two of them, to my mind, are, or have the potential to be, *really* evil. The horrid adolescent in Katherine Mansfield's 'The Young Girl', for example, selfish, vain, rude to her mother, uncivil to strangers, beastly to her little brother. (Though Katherine Mansfield herself, who was an adventuress in a mild way and boasted the reputation of a wayward girl in her own lifetime, emerges here as narrator as a woman of such transparent good faith that small boys instinctively trust her to stand them expensive ice-creams.)

Most of the variously characterized girls and women who inhabit these stories, however, would seem much, much worse if men had invented them. They would be predatory, drunken hags; confidence tricksters; monstrously precocious children; liars and cheats; promiscuous heartbreakers. As it is, they are all presented as if they were perfectly normal. On the whole, women writers are kind to women.

Perhaps too kind. Women, it is true, commit far fewer crimes than men in the first place; we do not have the same opportunities to do so. But, from the evidence of the fiction we write, we find it very hard to blame ourselves even for those we do commit. We tend to see the extenuating circumstances, so that it is difficult to apportion blame, impossible to judge – or, indeed, to acknowledge responsibility and then take up the terrible burden of remorse as it is summed up in Samuel Beckett's phrase, 'my crime is my punishment'.

I cannot think of any woman in any work of fiction written by a woman who is taken to this final revelation of moral horror. We forgive; we don't judge.

Of the women in these stories, only one would qualify on Dostoevskian terms – the heroine of George Egerton's story, 'Wedlock'. 'Wedlock' is written in the harshest kind of documentary realism; it is almost too harrowing for fiction, so that one guesses its origin might be in a newspaper cutting. And it turns out that there are extenuating circumstances for what at first would seem a crime for which there is no explanation, for which there could be no forgiveness – extenuating circumstances of the most heart-rending kind, so that the reader is gripped with pity.

George Egerton finally absolves her heroine but in the oddest way: she makes her go mad. The woman, it turns out, did not know what she was doing. Nor will she ever know. At the end of the story, mad, she believes herself happy for the first time since the story began. In a rather horrible way, her crime is not her punishment but the instrument of her reward.

What happens to the wandering holy man in the Moroccan village in Andrée Chedid's story, 'The Long Trial', is an event of a different order; it is less of a murder than a triumph over history.

But, on the whole, morality as regards woman has nothing to do with ethics; it means sexual morality and nothing but sexual morality. To be a wayward girl usually has something to do with pre-marital sex; to be a wicked woman has something to do with adultery. This means it is far easier for a woman to lead a blameless life than it is for a man; all she has to do is to avoid sexual intercourse like the plague. What hypocrisy!

Therefore I have been careful to select bad girls who are not sexual profligates. The heroine of my own story, 'The Loves of Lady Purple', *is* sexually profligate in a thoroughly reprehensible manner, but, then, she isn't real. She is a puppet, and a man made her, and made up her entire biography as a *femme fatale*, and willed her into being because he wanted so much for her to exist, and if she destroys him the very minute she comes to life, then it is his own silly fault for thinking such dreadful things in the first place.

Life in Bessie Head's marvellous story is thought to be bad, even wicked, not because she distributes her sexual favours but because she charges money for them, and, by doing so, disrupts the easy-going harmony of her village and transforms its most intimate relations into cash transactions. She imports the twentieth century into the timeless African village and she is made to suffer for it, by a man who thinks he has the right to do so because he loves her.

If you don't play by the rules but try to start a new game, you will not necessarily prosper, nor will the new game necessarily be an improvement on the old one. But this does not mean it is not worth trying.

Most of the women in these stories, even if they do not prosper exceedingly, at least contrive to evade the victim's role by the judicious use of their wits, and they share a certain cussedness, a bloodymindedness, even though their stories are told in an enormous variety of ways, and come from all over the world.

The mother in Elizabeth Jolley's 'The Last Crop' is one of the few female con-men in fiction. The voracious and crazed women in Jane Bowles's 'A Guatemalan Idyll' are the type of women with whom one would least like one's son or brother to get involved. It would seem that the young woman in Colette's 'The Rainy Moon' is trying to dispose of her husband, possibly by occult means, and that she has been moved by no nobler motive than that of spite.

Frances Towers' Violet is also not averse to a little domestic witchery, verging – were her tale not told with such a light touch – towards the genuinely wicked. Vernon Lee's story concerns a bored wife who prefers a ghost to her husband; of course she knows no good can come of it, but does that stop her? Of course not. Leonora Carrington's débutante sends a hyena in her place to her own coming out ball, with predictably disastrous consequences. The under-age heroine of Grace Paley's 'A Woman Young and Old' is a positive menace to young men. But – what must one do to be *good*? Jamaica Kincaid's mother has some suggestions. While Suniti Namjoshi's bittersweet fables suggest that nothing a woman can do will, in the final analysis, ever be *really* right.

But then, again, Ama Ata Aidoo's Ghanaian student in Europe in 'The Plums' is thoroughly in the right; uncommonly clear-sighted, clear-sighted enough, and with sufficient of the necessary virulent self-respect, to find herself labelled 'bad' if she doesn't watch out all the time. 'The Plums' comes from a book with the title *Our Sister Killjoy: Reflections from a Black-Eyed Squint*.

All the stories I have chosen are reflections in some kind of squinting, oblique, penetrating vision. (Some of them are also very funny.)

And all these disparate women have something else in common – a certain sense of self-esteem, however tattered. They know they are worth more than that which fate has allotted them. They are prepared to plot and scheme; to snatch; to battle; to burrow away from within, in order to get their hands on that little bit extra, be it of love, or money, or vengeance, or pleasure, or respect. Even in defeat, they are not defeated; like Aunt Liu in the final story in the book, they are women 'who know about life'.

THE LAST CROP
Elizabeth Jolley

IN HOME SCIENCE I had to unpick my darts as Hot Legs said they were all wrong and then I scorched the collar of my dress because I had the iron too hot.

'It's the right side too!' Hot Legs kept moaning over the sink as she tried to wash out the scorch. And then the sewing-machine needle broke and there wasn't a spare, that made her really wild and Peril Page cut all the notches off her pattern by mistake and that finished everything.

'I'm not ever going back there.' I took some bread and spread the butter thick, Mother never minded how much butter we had even when we were short of things. Mother was sitting at the kitchen table when I got home, she was wondering what to get my brother for his tea and she didn't say anything, so I said again, 'I'm finished with that place. I'm not going back.' So that was the two of us, my brother and me both leaving school before we should have, and he kept leaving jobs, one after the other, sometimes not even waiting for his pay.

'Well I s'pose they would have asked you to leave before the exam,' was all she said, which was what my brother said once on another occasion and, at the time, she had nearly killed him for saying what he said about the school not wanting expected failures to stay on.

'Whatever shall I get for him?' she said.

'What about a bit of lamb's fry and bacon,' I suggested and I spread more bread, leaving school so suddenly had made me hungry. She brightened up then and, as she was leaving to go up the terrace for her shopping, she said, 'You can come with me tomorrow and help me to get through quicker.'

So the next day I went to South Heights with her to clean these very posh apartments. Luxury all the way through, one place even has a fur-lined toilet. Mother doesn't like it as it clogs up the vacuum cleaner.

'Let's weigh ourselves,' I said when mother had had a quick look to see how much washing up there was.

'Just look at the mess,' she said. 'I really must get into the stove and the fridge today somehow I've been slipping lately.' She preferred them to eat out, which they did mostly.

'It's bringing the girls in that makes the mess,' she complained. 'Hair everywhere and panty hose dripping all over and grease on the stove. Why they want to cook beats me!'

'Let's weigh ourselves,' I got on the little pink scales.

'I'm bursting,' Mother said.

'Well weigh yourself before and after.'

'Whatever for!'

'Just for the interest,' I said and when I got off the scales I banged my head on the edge of the bathroom cupboard which is made all of looking glass.

'Really these expensive places!' Mother rubbed my head. 'All inconvenience not even a back door! Mind you, if there was a back door you'd step out and fall twenty-four floors to your death. And another thing, the washing machines drain into the baths. For all the money these places cost you can smell rubbish as soon as you enter the building and all day you can hear all the toilets flushing.'

Funnily enough her weight was no different after she'd been to the toilet and we worked like mad as Mother had some people coming into number eleven for a few hours.

'I want to get it nice for them,' she gave me the key to go down ahead of her. 'I'll be finished here directly and I'll come down.' As I left she called me, 'Put some sheets in the freezer, the black ones, and see the bathroom's all nice and lay those photography magazines and the scent spray out on the bedside table.' She felt people had a better time in cold sheets. 'There's nothing worse than being all boiled up in bed,' she said.

Mother's idea came to her first when she was in jail the second time, it was after she had borrowed Mrs Lady's car to take my brother on a little holiday for his health. It was in the jail, she told me afterwards, she had been struck forcibly by the fact that people had terrible dull lives with nothing to look forward to and no tastes of the pleasures she felt sure we were on this earth to enjoy.

'They don't ever get no pleasure,' she said to me. 'Perhaps the pictures now and then but that's only looking at other people's lives.' So she made it her business to get places in South Heights and quite soon she was cleaning several of the luxury apartments there.

She had her own keys and came and went as her work demanded and as she pleased.

'It's really gas in there,' she used one of my words to try and describe the place. And then bit by bit she began to let people from down our street, and other people too as the word spread, taste the pleasures rich people took for granted in their way of living. While the apartments were empty, you know, I mean while the people who lived there were away to their offices or to the hairdressers or to golf or horse riding or on business trips and the things rich people are busy with, she let other people in.

First, it was the old man who lived on the back verandah of our corner grocery store and then the shop keeper himself.

'They've been very deprived,' Mother said. She let them into Mr Baker's ground floor flat for an hour once a week while she brushed and folded Mr Baker's interesting clothes and washed his dishes. She admired Mr Baker though she had never seen him and she cherished his possessions for him. She once said she couldn't work for people if she didn't love them.

'How can you love anyone you never seen?' I asked.

'Oh I can see all about them all I need to know, even their shirt sizes and the colours of their socks tells you a lot,' she said. And then she said love meant a whole lot of things like noticing what people spent their money on and what efforts they made in their lives like buying bread and vegetables or books or records. All these things touched her she said. 'Even their pills are interesting,' she said. 'You can learn a lot about people just by looking in their bathroom cupboards.'

The first time I went with her I broke an ash tray, I felt terrible and showed her the pieces just when we were leaving. She wrote a note for Mr Baker, she enjoyed using his green biro and scrawled all over a piece of South Heights note paper.

'Very sorry about the ash tray, will try to find suitable replacement.' She put the broken pieces in an honest little heap by the note.

'Don't worry,' she said to me. 'Old Baldpate up in the penthouse has a whole cupboard of things she never uses, she's even got a twenty-four-piece dinner service; you don't see many of those these days. We'll find something there. Easy. She owes Mr Baker polish and an hour of his electric clothes drier so it'll all come straight.' She was forever borrowing things from one person for another and then paying them back from one to the other all without any of them knowing a thing about it.

As I was saying the old men came in once a week and had coffee served them on a tray with a thimble of French brandy and they sat in the bedroom, which was papered all over with nude arms and legs and bodies, they sat in armchairs in there as this had the best view of the swimming pool and they could watch the girls. There were always a lot of pretty girls around at South Heights with nothing to do except lie around and sunbake.

One of Mother's troubles was her own liking for expensive things, she didn't know why she had expensive tastes. She often sat at our kitchen table with a white dinner napkin on her lap.

'Always remember, they are napkins, only common people call them serviettes,' she said and she would show me how to hold a knife with the palm of the hand over the handle. 'It's very important,' she said. Anyway there she sat, dinner napkin and all, and she would eat an avocado pear before bawling at me to go down the road to get our chips.

'I just hope they had a nice time,' Mother said when we cleaned up in number eleven that afternoon. 'It's terrible to be young and newly married living in her big family the way they have to. I'll bet they haven't got a bed to themselves in that house let alone a room. All that great family around them the whole time! A young couple need to be on their own. They'll have had a bit of peace and quiet in here.' Mother looked with approval at the carpeted secluded comfort of the apartment she'd let this young couple have for a morning.

'There's no need for young people to get babies now unless they really want to so I hope they've used their common sense and modern science,' Mother went on, she always talked a lot when she was working. She said when I wasn't with her she pulled faces at herself in all the mirrors and told herself off most of the time.

'Babies,' she said. 'Is all wind and wetting and crying for food and then sicking it up all over everything and no sooner does a baby grow up it's all wanting. Wanting and wanting this and that, hair and clothes and records and shoes and money and more money. And, after one baby there's always another and more wetting and sicking. Don't you ever tell me you haven't been warned!'

She washed out the black sheets and stuck them in the drier.

'Open the windows a bit,' she said to me. 'There's a smell of burned toast and scented groins in here. Young people always burn their toast, they forget about it with all that kissing. We'll get the place well aired before the Blacksons come home or they'll wonder what's been going on.'

On the way home Mother kept wondering whatever she could get for my brother's tea and she stood in the supermarket thinking and thinking and all she could come up with was fish fingers and a packet of jelly beans.

Somehow my brother looked so tall in the kitchen.

'You know I always chunder fish!' He was in a terrible mood. 'And I haven't eaten sweets in years!' He lit a cigarette and went out without any tea.

'If only he'd eat,' Mother sighed. She worried too much about my brother, the door slamming after him upset her and she said she wasn't hungry.

'If only he'd eat and get a job and live,' she said. 'That's all I ask.'

Sometimes at the weekends I went with Mother to look at Grandpa's valley. It was quite a long bus ride, we had to get off at the twenty-nine-mile peg, cross the Medulla Brook and walk up a country road with scrub and bush on either side till we came to some cleared acres of pasture which was the beginning of her father's land. She struggled through the wire fence hating the mud and the raw country air. She cursed out loud the old man for hanging on to the land and she cursed the money that was buried in the sodden meadows of cape weed and stuck fast in the outcrops of granite high up on the slopes where dead trees held up their gaunt arms, pitiful as if begging for something from the sky, she cursed the place because nothing could grow among their exposed gnarled boots as the topsoil had washed away. She cursed the pig styes built so solidly years ago of corrugated iron and old railway sleepers of jarrah, useful for nothing now but so indestructible they could not be removed.

She couldn't sell the land because Grandpa was still alive in a Home for the Aged and he wanted to keep the farm though he couldn't do anything with it. Even sheep died there. They either starved or got drowned depending on the time of year. It was either drought or flood, never anything happily between the two extremes.

There was a house there, weatherboard, with a wide wooden verandah all round it high off the ground. It could have been pretty and nice.

'Why don't we live there?' I asked her once.

'How could any of us get to work,' Mother said. 'It's too far from anywhere.'

And my brother said to her, 'It's only you as has to get to work,' and I thought Mother would kill him, she called him a good for nothing lazy slob.

'You're just nothing but a son of a bitch!' she screamed. He turned his eyes up till just the white showed.

'Well Dear Lady,' he said making his voice all furry and thick as if he'd been drinking. 'Dear Lady,' he said, 'if I'm the son of a bitch then you must be a bitch!' and he looked so like an idiot standing there we had to see the funny side and we roared our heads off.

The house was falling apart. The tenants were feckless, Mother suspected the man was working at some other job really. The young woman was mottled all over from standing too close to the stove and her little boys were always in wetted pants. They, the whole family, all had eczema. When a calf was born there it could never get up; that was the kind of place it was.

Every weekend Mother almost wept with the vexation of the land which was not hers and she plodded round the fences hating the scrub and the rocks where they invaded.

When we went to see Grandpa he wanted to know about the farm as he called it, and Mother tried to think of things to tell him to please him. She didn't say that the fence posts were crumbling away and that the castor-oil plants had taken over the yard so you couldn't get through to the barn.

There was an old apricot tree in the middle of the meadow, it was as big as a house and a terrible burden to us to get the fruit at the right time.

'Don't take that branch!' Mother screamed. 'I want it for the Atkinsons.' Grandpa owed those people some money and it made Mother feel better to give them apricots as a present. She liked to take fruit to the hospital too so that Grandpa could keep up his pride and self respect a bit.

In the full heat of the day I had to pick with an apron tied round me, it had big deep pockets for the fruit. I grabbed at the green fruit when I thought Mother wasn't looking and pulled it off, whole branches whenever I could, so it wouldn't be there to be picked later.

'Not them!' Mother screamed from the ground. 'Them's not ready yet. We'll have to come back tomorrow for them.'

I lost my temper and pulled off the apron full of fruit and hurled it down but it caught on a dumb branch and hung there laden and quite out of reach either from up the tree where I was or from the ground.

'Wait! Just you wait till I get hold of you!' Mother roared and pranced round the tree and I didn't come down till she had calmed down and by that time we had missed our bus and had to thumb a lift which is not so easy now as it used to be. On the edge of the little township the road seemed so long and desolate and seemed to lead nowhere and, when it got dark, all the dogs barked as if they were insane and a terrible loneliness came over me then.

'I wish we were home,' I said as cars went by without stopping.

'Wait a minute,' Mother said and in the dark she stole a

piece of rosemary off someone's hedge. 'This has such a lovely fragrance,' she crushed it in her rough fingers and gave it to me to smell. 'Someone'll pick us up soon, you'll see,' she comforted.

One Sunday in the winter it was very cold but Mother thought we should go all the same. I had such a cold and she said, 'The country air will do you good,' and then she said, 'if it don't kill you first.' The cuckoo was calling and calling.

'Listen!' Mother said. 'That bird really sings up the scale,' and she tried to whistle like the cuckoo but she kept laughing and of course you can't whistle if you're laughing.

We passed some sheep huddled in a natural fold of furze and long withered grass, all frost-sparkled, the blackened trunk of a burnt and fallen tree made a kind of gateway to the sheep.

'Quick!' Mother said. 'We'll grab a sheep and take a bit of wool back to Grandpa.'

'But they're not our sheep.'

'Never mind!' And she was over the burnt tree in among the sheep before I could stop her. The noise was terrible. In all the commotion she managed to grab some wool.

'It's terrible dirty and shabby,' she complained, pulling at the shreds with her cold fingers. 'I don't think I've ever seen such miserable wool,' she said.

All that evening she was busy with the wool. She put it on the kitchen table.

'How will Modom have her hair done this week?' she addressed it. She tried to wash and comb it to make it look better. She put it on the table again and kept walking round and talking to it and looking at it from all sides of the table. Talk about laugh, she had me in fits, I was laughing till I ached.

'Let me put it round one of your curlers,' she said at last.

But even after being on a roller all night it still didn't look anything at all.

'I'm really ashamed of the wool,' Mother said.

'But it isn't ours.'

'I know but I'm ashamed all the same,' she said.

So at Mr Baker's she went in the toilet and cut a tiny bit off the white carpet, from the back part where it wouldn't show. It was so soft and silky, she wrapped it carefully in a piece of foil and in the evening we went to visit Grandpa. He was sitting with his poor paralysed legs under his tartan rug and the draughts board was set up beside him, he always had the black ones, but the other old men in the room had fallen asleep so he had no one to play a game with.

'Here's a bit of the wool clip Dad,' Mother said bending over and giving him a kiss. His whole face lit up.

'That's nice of you to bring it, really nice,' and he took the little corner of nylon carpet out of its wrapping.

'It's very good, deep and soft,' his old fingers stroked the smooth silkiness, he smiled at Mother as she searched his face for traces of disapproval or disappointment.

'They do wonderful things with sheep these days Dad,' she said.

'They do indeed,' he said, and all the time his fingers were feeling the bit of carpet.

'Are you pleased Dad?' she asked him anxiously. 'You are pleased aren't you?'

'Oh yes I am,' he assured her.

I thought I saw a moment of disappointment in his eyes, but the eyes of old people often look full of tears.

Mother was so tired, she was half asleep by the bed but she played three games of draughts and let him win them all and I watched the telly in the dinette with the night nurse. And then we really had to go as Mother had a full day ahead of her at the Heights, not so much work but a lot of arrangements and she would need every bit of her wits about her she said as we hurried home.

On the steps I tripped and fell against her.

'Ugh! I felt your bones!' Really she was so thin it hurt to bang into her.

'Well what d'you expect me to be, a boneless wonder? How-ever could I walk if I didn't have bones to hold me up!'

The situation was terrible, really it was. Mother had such a hard life, for one thing, she was a good quick worker and she could never refuse people and so had too many jobs to get through as well as the other things she did. And the place where we lived was so ugly and cramped and squalid. She longed for a nice home with better things and she longed, more than anything, for my brother to get rid of what she called his deep unhappiness, she didn't know how he had got it but it was the reason for all his growling and his dislike of good food, she longed too for him to have some ambition or some aim in his life, she was always on about it to me.

Why wouldn't the old man agree to selling his land, it couldn't do him any good to keep it. His obstinacy really forced her to wishing he would die. She never said that to me but I could feel what she must be wishing because I found myself wishing him to die, every night I wished it, and whoever really wanted to wish someone to death!

It was only that it would sort things out a bit for us.

Next day we had to be really early as, though she had only one apartment to clean, she'd arranged a little wedding reception, with a caterer, in the penthouse. The lady who owned it, Baldpate Mother called her, had gone away on a trip for three months and during this time Mother had been able to make very good use of the place.

'They're a really splendid little set of rooms,' Mother said every time we went there. Once she tried on one of Baldpate's wigs it was one of those blue grey really piled-up styles and she looked awful. She kept making faces at herself in the mirror.

'I'm just a big hairy eagle in this,' she said. And when she put on a bathing cap later, you know, one of those meant to look like the petals of a flower she looked so mad I nearly died!

Baldpate was so rich she'd had a special lift put up the side of the building to have a swimming pool made after the South Heights had been built. Right up there on top of everything she had her own swimming pool.

'It makes me dizzy up here,' Mother said. 'Is my back hair all right?' I said it was, she was always asking about her back hair, it was awful but I never said so because what good would it have done. She never had time for her hair.

'Some day I'm going to write a book,' Mother said. 'We were setting out the glasses and silver forks carefully on the table by the window. Far below was the blue river and the main road with cars, like little coloured beetles, aimlessly crawling to and fro.

'Yes, I'm going to write this book,' she said. 'I want it brought out in paperjacks.'

'Paperbacks you mean.'

'Yes, like I said, paperjacks, with a picture on the front of a girl with her dress ripped off and her tied to a post in the desert and all the stories will have expensive wines in them and countries in Europe and the names of famous pictures and buildings and there will be wealthy people with expensive clothes and lovely jewels very elegant you know but doing and saying terrible things, the public will snap it up. I'll have scenes with people eating and making love at the same time. Maybe they'll want to make a film of it, it's what people want. It's called supply and demand.'

'That's a good title.'

She thought a moment. 'I hadn't thought of a title.' She had to interrupt her dream as the caterer arrived with his wooden trays of curried eggs and meat balls, and the guests who had got away quickly from the wedding were beginning to come in. Mother scattered frangipani blossoms made of plastic all over the rooms and, as soon as the bridal couple and their folks came in, we began serving.

'People really eat on these occasions,' Mother whispered to me. She really liked to see them enjoying themselves. 'Where else could they have such a pretty reception in such a nice place for the price.' She had even put out Baldpate's thick towels and she sent a quiet word round that any guest who would like to avail themselves of the facilities was welcome to have a shower, they were welcome to really enjoy the bathroom and there was unlimited hot water.

'Show them how to work those posh taps,' she whispered to me. 'They probably have never ever seen a bathroom like this one.' And smiling all over her face, she was a wonderful hostess everyone said so, she went on handing drinks and food to the happy guests.

In the middle of it all when Mother was whispering to me, 'It takes all the cheapness out of their lives to have an occasion like this and it's not hurting anybody at all. Even sordid things are all right if you have the right surroundings and don't hurt anyone –' she was interrupted by the doorbell ringing and ringing.

'Oh my Gawd!' Mother's one fear, the fear of being discovered, gripped. 'Open the balcony!' she pushed me to the double doors. 'This way to see the lovely view,' her voice rose over the noise of talking and laughing and eating. 'Bring your ice-cream and jelly out here and see the world.' She flung her arm towards the sky and came back in and hustled them all out onto the narrow space around the penthouse pool.

'No diving in,' she joked. 'Not in your clothes, anyhow.' She left me with the bewildered wedding and dashed to the door. I strained to listen trying to look unconcerned but I was that nervous. Baldpate could have come home sooner than she was expected and however would we explain about all these people in her penthouse. I couldn't hear a thing and my heart was thumping so I thought I would drop dead in front of everyone.

In a little while though Mother was back.

'A surprise guest brings luck to a wedding feast!' she announced and she drew all the people back inside for the champagne.

The surprise guest enjoyed herself very much. Mother had quite forgotten that she had told old Mrs Myer from down the bottom of our street that she could come any time to soak her feet and do her washing in the penthouse and she had chosen this day for both these things. One or two of the guests washed a few of their clothes as well to try out the machines.

'There's nothing so nice as clean clothes,' Mother said and then she proposed a special toast.

'Absent friend!' She was thinking lovingly of Baldpate she said to me. 'Absent friend!' And soon all the champagne was gone.

'Is my nose red?' she whispered to me anxiously during the speeches. Her nose was always red and got more so after wine of any sort or if she was shouting at my brother. She would really go for him and then ask him if her nose was red as if he cared. We could never see why she bothered so much.

'No,' I said.

'Oh! That's such a relief!' she said.

We were ages clearing up. Mother was terribly tired but so pleased with the success of the day. She seemed to fly round the penthouse singing and talking.

'Get this straight,' she said to me, 'one human being can't make another human being do anything. But if you are a mother this is the one thing you've got to do. Babies eat and sick and wet and sit up and crawl and walk and talk but after that you just got to make your children do the things they have to do in this world and that's why I got to keep shouting the way I do and, believe me, it's really hard!'

'Yes,' I said to her and then for some reason I began to cry. I really howled out loud. I knew I sounded awful bawling like that but I couldn't help it.

'Oh! I've made you work too hard!' Mother was so kind she made me sit down on the couch and she switched on the telly and made us both a cup of cocoa before we went home.

Grandpa was an old man and though his death was expected it was unexpected really and of course everything was suddenly changed. Death is like that. Mother said it just seemed like in five minutes, all at once, she had eighty-seven acres to sell. And there was the house too. Mother had a lot to do, she didn't want to let down the people at the South Heights so she turned up for work as usual and we raced through the apartments.

As it was winter there wasn't anything for old Fred and the Grocer to watch at the pool so Mother put on Mr Baker's record player for them and she let them wear the headphones. Luckily there were two sets, and you know how it is when you have these headphones on you really feel you are singing with the music, it's like your head is in beautiful cushions of voices and the music is right in your brain.

'Come and listen to them, the old crabs!' Mother beckoned to me, we nearly died of laughing hearing them bleating and moaning thinking they were really with those songs, they sounded like two old lost sheep.

'They're enjoying themselves, just listen!' I thought Mother would burst out crying she laughed herself silly behind the lounge room door.

'I'm so glad I thought of it,' she said. 'Whatever you do don't let them see you laughing like that!'

Mother decided she would sell the property by herself as she didn't want any agent to get his greasy hands on any percent of that land. There was a man interested to buy it, Mother had kept him up her sleeve for years. I think he was an eye surgeon, Oscar Harvey, Mother said he should have a dance band with a name like that. Well Doctor Harvey wanted the valley he had said so ages ago and Mother was giving him first refusal.

We all three, Mother and myself and my brother, went out at the weekend to tidy things up a bit and to make sure those tenants didn't go off with things which had been Grandpa's and were now Mother's.

I don't think I ever noticed the country as being so lovely before, always I complained and wanted to go home as soon as I got there, but this time it was different. The birds were making a lot of noise.

'It's really like music,' Mother said. The magpies seemed to stroke the morning with their voices and we went slowly along the top end of the wet meadow.

'Summer land it's called,' Mother explained. And then suddenly we heard this strange noise behind us. And there was my brother running and running higher up on the slope, running like he was mad! And he was shouting and that was the noise we had heard. We didn't recognize his voice, it was like a man's, this voice shouting filling the valley. We hadn't ever seen him run like that before either, his thin arms and legs were flying in all directions and his voice lifted up in the wind.

'I do believe he's laughing!' Mother stood still sinking into the mud without noticing it. Tears suddenly came out of her eyes as she watched him. 'I think he's happy!' she said. 'He's happy!' she couldn't believe it. And I don't think I've ever seen her look so happy in her life before. We walked on up to the house. The tenant was at the side of the shed and he had just got the big tractor going and it had only crawled to the doorway, like a sick animal, and there it had stopped and he was supposed to get a firebreak made before the sale could go through.

My brother was nowhere to be seen but then I saw his thin white fingers poking through the castor oil plants in the yard.

'Halp!' and his fingers clutched the leaves and the air and then disappeared again. 'Halp! Halp!'

'He's stuck!' Mother was laughing, she pushed through the overgrown yard and my brother kept partly appearing and disappearing pretending he was really caught and she pulled at him and lost her balance and fell, both of them laughing like idiots. Funny I tell you it was a scream and for once I didn't feel cold there.

Mother and I started at once on the house sweeping and cleaning. They had repaired a few things and it was not as bad as she expected, there were three small rooms and quite a big kitchen. Grandpa had never lived there, he had only been able to buy the land late in life and had gone there weekends. He had always longed for the country.

'He was always on about a farm,' Mother said, she explained how he wanted to live here and was putting it all in order bit by bit when he had the stroke and after that of course he couldn't be there as it needed three people to move him around and whatever could he do out there paralysed like he was and then all those sad years in the hospital.

'It's not bad in here,' Mother said. 'It's nice whichever way you look out from these little windows and that verandah all round is really something! We'll sit there a bit later when we've finished.'

My brother came in, he was really keen about getting new fencing posts and wire and paint, he kept asking her, 'How about I paint the house?'

'Oh the new owner can do that,' Mother said, her head in the wood stove, she was trying to figure out the flues and how to clean them.

'Well, what if I paint the sheds then?' He seemed really interested. As she was busy she took no notice so he went off outside again.

Then we heard the tractor start up rattling and scraping over the rocks as it started up the slope to get into the scrub part which needed clearing to keep in with the regulations. Mother went out on to the verandah to shake the mats.

'Come and look!' she called me. And there was my brother driving the tractor looking proud and as if he knew exactly what to do.

'He's like a prince on that machine!' Mother was pleased. Of course he clowned a bit as he turned, pretending to fall off, once he stopped and got off as if he had to push the great thing. He hit the rocks and made a terrible noise and the tenant just stood there staring at him.

'It's been years since the tractor got up there,' he said to Mother.

We really had a wonderful day and, on the bus going back, my brother fell asleep he was so unused to the fresh air his nose and ears were bright red and Mother kept looking at him and she was very quiet and I knew she was thinking and thinking.

Next day my brother went out there by himself to try to get all the firebreaks finished, the agreement couldn't be signed till they were done also the fencing posts. Before he left he told Mother what to order and have sent out there, he suddenly seemed to know all about everything. The change in him was like a miracle, he was even quite nice to me.

As well as seeing to the sale there was Grandpa's funeral and Mother said he had to have a headstone and she came up with an inscription at the stone mason's.

'"It is in vain that ye rise thus early and eat the bread of care; for He giveth his Beloved Sleep."'

I stared at her.

'I didn't know you knew the Bible.'

'I don't,' Mother said. 'It was in this morning's paper in that little square "text for today" or something like it and I think it's really beautiful and it's so suitable. I wouldn't mind having it for myself but as I'm still after the bread of care and not as yet the "Beloved" I'm putting it for Grandpa.'

There was no trouble about the price of the property. This Dr Harvey really wanted it, he had asked about the valley years ago, once when we were there, stopping his car just too late to prevent it from getting bogged at the bottom end of the track, and

Mother had to say it wasn't for sale though, at the time, she said she would have given her right arm to be able to sell it but she promised him she'd let him know at once if she could ever put it on the market. We had to leave then for our bus and so were not able to help him get his car out of the mud. As he wasn't there by the next weekend we knew he must have got himself out somehow.

'You might as well come with me,' Mother said to me on the day the papers had to be signed. 'It won't do you any harm to learn how business is carried out, the best way to understand these things is to see for yourself.'

My brother had already gone by the early bus to the valley. Now that the property was ours in the true sense it seemed he couldn't be there enough even though it was about to belong to someone else. Mother watched him run off down our mean little street and she looked so thoughtful.

The weatherboard house at the top of the sunlit meadow kept coming into my mind too and I found I was comparing it all the time with the terrible back landing where our room and kitchen was. Having looked out of the windows of the cottage I realized how we had nothing to look at at home except the dustbins and people going by talking and shouting and coughing and spitting and hurrying all the time, having the same rushed hard life Mother had. Of course the money from the sale would make all the difference to Mother's life so I said nothing, she didn't say much except she seemed to argue with herself.

'Course the place means nothing, none of us ever came from there or lived there even.' I could hear her muttering as we walked.

No one can do anything with property, it doesn't matter how many acres it is, if you haven't any money, of course Mother needed the money so I didn't say out loud, 'Wouldn't it be lovely to live out there for a bit'. I guessed my brother was feeling the same though he never said anything but I saw him reading a bit of an old poultry magazine he must have picked up at the barber's place. As a little boy he never played much, Mother always said he stopped playing too soon. But he would often bring in a stray cat and beg to keep it and play with it and stroke it with a fondness we never saw him show any other way and he would walk several streets to a place where a woman had some fowls in her backyard and he would stand ages looking at them through a broken fence picket, perhaps some of Grandpa's farming blood was in him. I wondered if Mother was thinking the same things as I was but the next thing was we were in the lawyer's office. The doctor was there too, very nicely dressed. I could see Mother look at his well-laundered shirt with approval. The room was brown and warm and comfortable, all polished wood and leather and a window high up in the wall let in the sunshine so it came in a kind of dust-dancing spotlight on the corner of the great big desk.

I feel I will never forget that room for what happened there changed our lives in a way I could never even have dreamed of.

Well, we all sat down and I tried to listen as the lawyer spoke and read. It all sounded foreign to me. Acres I knew and roods and perches that was Hot Legs all over again, same with the hundreds and thousands of dollars, it was a bit like school and I began to think of clothes I would like and how I would have my hair. The lawyer was sorting pages. I gave up trying to follow things like 'searching the title', 'encumbered and unencumbered land', instead I thought about some kneeboots and a black coat with white lapels, fur I thought it was, and there was a little white round hat to go with it.

They were writing their names in turn on different papers, all of them busy writing.

'Here,' said the lawyer, Mr Rusk his name was, 'and here,' he pointed with his white finger for Mother to know where to put her name.

Mother suddenly leaned forward, 'I'm a little bit faint,' she said. Oh I was scared! I nudged her.

'Don't you faint here in front of them!' I was that embarrassed.

Mr Rusk asked the secretary to fetch a glass of water.

'Thank you my dear,' Mother sipped the water. I was a bit afraid I can tell you as I don't think ever in my life had I seen Mother drink cold water straight like that.

'All right now?' Dr Harvey, the owner of so much money and

now the owner of the lovely valley, looked at Mother gently. He really was a gentleman and a kind one too, I could see that.

'You see,' Mother said suddenly and her nose flushed up very red the way it does when she is full of wine or angry with my brother or, as it turned out in this case, when she had an idea. 'You see,' she said to the doctor, 'Dad longed to live in that house and to be in the valley. All his life he wished for nothing but having his farm, it was something in his blood and it meant everything to him and as it so happened he was never able to have his wish. Having waited so long for the valley yourself,' she went on to the doctor, 'You will understand and, loving the land as you do, you will understand how I feel now. I feel,' she said, 'I feel if I could be in the valley and live in the house and plant one crop there and just be there till it matures I feel Dad, your Grandpa,' she turned to me, 'I feel he would rest easier in his last resting place.' They looked at Mother and she looked back at them.

The doctor smiled kindly. 'Well,' he said, oh he was a generous man all right, he had just paid the whole price Mother asked. 'I don't see any harm in that.'

'It's not in the agreement,' Mr Rusk was quite annoyed but the doctor waved his hand to quieten old Rusk's indignation.

'It's a gentlemen's agreement,' and he came over and shook hands with Mother.

'That's the best sort,' Mother smiled up at him under her shabby brown hat.

Then the lawyer and the doctor had a bit of an argument and in the end the lawyer agreed to add in writing for them to sign that we could live in the house and be in the valley till the maturity of just one last crop.

'I wish your crop well,' the doctor came round the desk and shook hands with Mother again.

'Thank you,' Mother said.

'It's all settled and signed,' Mother told my brother in the evening. The few days of working in the country seemed to have changed him, he looked strong and sun tanned and, for once, his eyes had a bit of expression in them, usually he never revealed anything of himself by a look or a word except to be disagreeable. Mother always excused him saying the world wasn't the right place for him and his terrible mood was because he couldn't explain this to himself or to anyone and because he couldn't explain it he didn't know what to do about it. I thought he looked sad in his eyes even though we had had a bit of a spend for our tea we had ham off the bone and vanilla slices.

She told him how we could be there for one last crop.

'I'll paint the house then.'

'Good idea!' Mother said. 'We'll get the paint but we needn't rush, we can take our time getting things. We'll need a vehicle of some kind.'

'You haven't got your licence,' I said to my brother. Any other time he would have knocked me into next week for saying that.

'I'll get my test,' he said quietly.

'There's no rush,' Mother said.

'But one crop isn't very long.'

'It's long enough,' Mother said, she spent the evening studying catalogues she had picked up on the way home and she wrote a letter which she took out to post herself.

Mother was sorry to let down the people at the South Heights so badly but after the gentlemen's agreement everything seemed to happen differently and it was a bit of a rush for her. Already in her mind she was planning.

'We'll have the whole street out to a barbecue once the weather changes,' she said. 'They can come out on the eleven o'clock bus and walk up through the bottom paddocks. It'll be a little taste of pleasure, a bit different, there's nothing like a change for people even for one day, it's as good as a holiday.'

The first night at the cottage seemed very quiet.

'I expect we'll get used to it,' Mother said. I meant to wake up and see the place as the sun came through the bush but I slept in and missed the lot.

Bit by bit Mother got things, oh it was lovely going out to spend, choosing new things like a teapot and some little wooden chairs which Mother wanted because they were so simple.

And then her crop came. The carter set down the boxes, they

were like baskets only made of wood with wooden handles, he set them down along the edge of the verandah. They were all sewn up in sacking and every one was labelled with our name, and inside these boxes were a whole lot of tiny little seedlings, hundreds of them. When the carter had gone my brother lifted out one of the little plastic containers; I had never seen him doing anything so gently.

'What are they?'

'They're our crop. The last crop.'

'Yes I know but what are they?'

'Them? Oh they're a jarrah forest,' Mother said.

We looked at her.

'But that will take years and years to mature,' my brother said.

'I know,' she seemed unconcerned but the way her nose was going red I knew she was as excited about the little tiny seedling trees as we were. She of course had the idea already, it had to come upon us, the surprise of it I mean and we had to get over it.

'But what about Dr Harvey?' Somehow I could picture him pale and patient beside his car out on the lonely road which went through his valley looking longingly at his house and his meadows and his paddocks and at his slopes of scrub and bush.

'Well there's nothing in the gentlemen's agreement to say he can't come on his land whenever he wants to and have a look at us,' Mother said. 'We'll start planting tomorrow,' she said. 'We'll pick the best places and then clear the scrub and the dead stuff away as we go along. I've got full instructions as to how it's done.' She looked at her new watch. 'It's getting a bit late, I'll go for chips,' she said. 'I suppose I'll have to go miles for them from here.' She followed us into the cottage to get her purse. 'You'll be able to do your schooling by correspondence,' she said. 'I might even take a course myself!' It was getting dark quickly. 'Get a good fire going,' she said.

We heard her drive down the track and, as she turned onto the road, we heard her crash the gears. My brother winced, he couldn't bear machinery to be abused but he agreed with me that she probably couldn't help it as it's been quite a while since she had anything to drive.

THE DÉBUTANTE

Leonora Carrington

WHEN I was a débutante, I often went to the zoo. I used to go there so often that I knew the animals better than the girls of my own set. In fact, I went to the zoo every day in order to get away from society. The animal that I got to know best was a young hyena. She got to know me, too; I taught her French and she taught me her language in return. So we passed many a pleasant hour.

My mother arranged a ball in my honour for the first of May; the very thought kept me awake at night; I have always detested balls, above all those held in my own honour.

I paid a visit to the hyena very early in the morning on the first of May. 'What a bore!' I said to her. 'I must go to my ball this evening.'

'You're in luck,' she said. 'I'd love to go. I don't know how to dance but at least I could make conversation.'

'There's going to be lots to eat,' I said. 'I've seen trucks full of stuff driving up to the house.'

'And here you are complaining!' said the hyena disgustedly. 'I get just the one meal a day and it's pigshit.'

I had such a brilliant idea I almost burst out laughing. 'You could go instead of me.'

'We don't look enough like each other or I would, too,' said the hyena rather sadly.

'Listen,' I said, 'nobody sees well in the twilight; nobody will notice you in the crowd if you are a bit disguised. Anyway, you are about the same size as me. You are my only friend. I beg you.'

She thought about it, I knew she wanted to say yes.

'Done,' she announced suddenly.

As it was so early, there weren't many keepers there. I opened the cage quickly and a few seconds later we were in the street. I took a taxi and everybody was asleep at home. In my room, I took out the dress I was supposed to wear that evening. It was a bit long and the hyena had trouble walking on the high heels of my shoes. Her hands were too hairy to look like mine so I found her some gloves. When the sun arrived in my room she walked all round it several times more or less straight. We were so preoccupied that my mother, who came to say good morning, almost opened the door before the hyena hid under my bed. 'There is a bad smell in your room,' said my mother as she opened the window, 'take a bath perfumed with my new salts before this evening.'

'Yes, of course,' I said.

She did not stay long, I think the smell was too strong for her.

'Don't be late for breakfast,' said my mother as she left my room.

The most difficult thing was, how to disguise her face. We pondered for hours and hours; she rejected all my proposals. At last she said, 'I think I know the answer. Do you have a maid?'

'Yes,' I said, perplexed.

'Well, then, listen. Ring for the maid and when she comes in we'll pounce on her and tear off her face; I shall wear her face instead of mine this evening.'

'That isn't practical,' I said. 'She will probably die when she doesn't have a face any more; somebody is sure to find the body and we'll go to prison.'

'I'm hungry enough to eat her,' replied the hyena.

'What about the bones?'

'Those, too. Is it settled?'

'Only if you promise to kill her before you tear her face off, otherwise it will hurt her too much.'

'It's all the same to me.'

Rather nervously I rang for Marie, the maid. I would never have done it if I hadn't hated balls so much. When Marie came in, I turned my face to the wall so as not to see. I admit it was soon over. A brief cry and it was all done. While the hyena was eating, I looked out of the window.

After a few minutes, she said, 'I can't eat any more; there are still the two feet left but if you've got a little bag, I'll finish them off later.'

'You'll find a bag embroidered with fleur de lys in the chest-of-drawers. Empty out the handkerchiefs and take it.'

She did what I told her. Then she said, 'Turn around and see how pretty I am!'

The hyena was looking at herself in the mirror and admiring Marie's face. She had eaten all round the face very carefully so that only what she needed remained. 'You've been really neat,' I said. Towards evening, when the hyena was all dressed up, she announced, 'I feel I'm in very good form. I think I'm going to be a big hit this evening.'

When we'd been hearing the music from below for some time, I said to her: 'Go down now and remember not to go near my mother, she'd be sure to know it wasn't me. I don't know anybody apart from her. Good luck!' I gave her a kiss as she left but she smelled very strong. Night had fallen. Exhausted by the emotions of the day, I picked up a book and relaxed beside the open window. I remember I was reading *Gulliver's Travels* by Jonathan Swift. After about an hour came the first sign of bad luck. A bat came in through the window uttering little cries. I am terribly frightened of bats. My teeth chattering, I hid behind a chair. Hardly was I on my knees before the beating of wings was drowned by a loud noise at my door. My mother came in, white with fury. She said, 'We had just sat down at table when the thing that was in your place leapt up and cried out; 'I smell a bit strong, eh? Well, as for me, *I* don't eat cakes!' Then she snatched off her face and ate it. One big jump and she vanished out of the window.'

from
THE GLORIA STORIES

Rocky Gámez

EVERY child aspires to be something when she grows up. Sometimes these aspirations are totally ridiculous, but coming from the mind of a child they are forgiven and given enough time, they are forgotten. These are normal little dreams from which life draws its substance. Everyone has aspired to be something at one time or another; most of us have aspired to be *many* things. I remember wanting to be an acolyte so badly I would go around bobbing in front of every icon I came across whether they were in churches or private houses. When this aspiration was forgotten, I wanted to be a kamikazi pilot so I could nosedive into the church that never allowed girls to serve at the altar. After that I made a big transition. I wanted to be a nurse, then a doctor, then a burlesque dancer, and finally I chose to be a school-teacher. Everything else was soon forgiven and forgotten.

My friend Gloria, however, never went beyond aspiring to be one thing, and one thing only. She wanted to be a man. Long after I had left for college to learn the intricacies of being an educator, my youngest sister would write to me long frightening letters in which she would say that she had seen Gloria barrelling down the street in an old Plymouth honking at all the girls walking down the street. One letter said that she had spotted her in the darkness of a theatre making out with another girl. Another letter said that she had seen Gloria coming out of a cantina with her arms hooked around two whores. But the most disturbing one was when she said that she had seen Gloria at a 7-11 store, with a butch haircut and what appeared to be dark powder on the sides of her face to imitate a beard.

I quickly sat down and wrote her a letter expressing my

concern and questioning her sanity. A week later I received a fat letter from her. It read:

Dear Rocky,

Here I am, taking my pencil in my hand to say hello and hoping that you are in the best of health, both physically and mentally. As for me, I am fine, thanks to Almighty God.

The weather in the Valley is the shits. As you have probably read or heard on the radio we had a hurricane named Camille, a real killer that left many people homeless. Our house is still standing, but the Valley looks like Venice without gondolas. As a result of the flooded streets, I can't go anywhere. My poor car is under water. But that's all right. I think the good Lord sent us a killer storm so that I would sit home and think seriously about my life, which I have been doing for the last three days.

You are right, my most dearest friend, I am not getting any younger. It is time that I should start thinking about what to do with my life. Since you left for school, I have been seeing a girl named Rosita, and I have already asked her to marry me. It's not right to go around screwing without the Lord's blessings. As soon as I can drive my car I'm going to see what I can do about this.

Your sister is right, I have been going around with some whores, but now that I have met Rosita, all that is going to change. I want to be a husband worthy of her respect, and when we have children, I don't want them to think that their father was a no good drunk.

You may think I'm crazy for talking about being a father, but seriously Rocky, I think I can. I never talked to you about anything so personal as what I'm going to say, but take it from me, it's true. Every time I do you-know-what, I come just like a man. I know you are laughing right now, but Rocky, it is God's honest truth. If you don't believe me, I'll show you someday. Anyhow it won't be long until you come home for Christmas. I'll show you and I promise you will not laugh and call me an idiot like you always do.

In the meantime since you are now close to the University library you can go and check it out for yourself. A woman can become a father if nature has given her enough come to penetrate inside a woman. I bet you didn't know that. Which goes to prove that you don't have to go to college to learn everything.

That shadow on my face that your sister saw was not charcoal or anything that I rubbed on my face to make it look like beard. It is the real thing. Women can grow beards, too, if they shave their faces every day to encourage it. I really don't give a damn if you or your sister think it looks ridiculous. I like it, and so does Rosita. She thinks I'm beginning to look a lot like Sal Mineo, do you know who he is?'

Well, Rocky, I think I'll close for now. Don't be too surprised to find Rosita pregnant when you come in Christmas. I'll have a whole case of Lone Star for me and a case of Pearl for you. Till then I remain your best friend in the world.

> *Love, Gloria*

I didn't go home that Christmas. A friend of mine and I were involved in a serious automobile accident a little before the holidays and I had to remain in the hospital. While I was in traction with almost every bone in my body shattered, one of the nurses brought me another letter from Gloria. I couldn't even open the envelope to read it, and since I thought I was on the brink of death, I didn't care at all when the nurse said she would read it to me. If this letter contained any information that would shock the nurse, it wouldn't matter anyway. Death is beautiful insofar as it brings absolution, and once you draw your last breath, every peccadillo is forgiven.

'Yes,' I nodded to the matronly nurse, 'you may read my letter.'

The stern-looking woman found a comfortable spot at the foot of my bed and, adjusting her glasses over her enormous nose, began to read.

Dear Rocky,

Here I am taking my pencil in my hand to say hello, hoping you are in the best of health, both physically and mentally. As for me, I am fine thanks to Almighty God.

The nurse paused to look at me and smiled in a motherly way. 'Oh, that sounds like a very sweet person!'

I nodded.

The weather in the Valley is the shits. It has been raining since Thanksgiving and here it is almost the end of December and it's still raining. Instead of growing a prick I think I'm going to grow a tail, like a tadpole. Ha, ha, ha!

The matronly nurse blushed a little and cleared her throat. 'Graphic, isn't she?'

I nodded again.

Well, Rocky, not much news around this asshole of a town except that Rosita and I got married. Yes, you heard right, I got married. We were married in St Margaret's Church, but it wasn't the type of wedding you are probably imagining. Rosita did not wear white, and I did not wear a tuxedo like I would have wanted to.

The nurse's brow crinkled into two deep furrows. She picked up the envelope and turned it over to read the return address and then returned to the letter with the most confused look I have ever seen in anybody's face.

Let me explain. Since I wrote you last, I went to talk to the priest in my parish and confessed to him what I was. In the beginning he was very sympathetic and he said that no matter what I was, I was still a child of God. He encouraged me to come to mass every Sunday and even gave me a box of envelopes so that I could enclose my weekly tithe money. But then when I asked him if I could marry Rosita in his church, he practically threw me out.

The nurse shook her head slowly and pinched her face tightly. I wanted to tell her not to read anymore, but my jaws were wired so tight I couldn't emit a comprehensible sound. She mistook my effort for a moan and continued reading and getting redder and redder.

He told me that I was not only an abomination in the eyes of God, but a lunatic in the eyes of Man. Can you believe that? First

I am a child of God, then when I want to do what the church commands in Her seventh sacrament, I'm an abomination. I tell you, Rocky, the older I get, the more confused I become.

But anyway, let me go on. This did not discourage me in the least. I said to myself, Gloria, don't let anybody tell you that even if you're queer, you are not a child of God. You are! And you got enough right to get married in church and have your Holy Father sanctify whatever form of love you wish to choose.

The nurse took out a small white hanky from her pocket and dabbed her forehead and upper lip.

So, as I walked home having been made to feel like a turd, or whatever it is abomination means, I came upon a brilliant idea. And here's what happened. A young man that works in the same slaughter house that I do invited me to his wedding. Rosita and I went to the religious ceremony which was held in your home-town, and we sat as close to the altar rail as we possibly could, close enough where we could hear the priest. We pretended that she and I were the bride and groom kneeling at the rail. When the time came to repeat the marriage vows, we both did, in our minds, of course, where nobody could hear us and be shocked. We did exactly as my friend and his bride did, except kiss, but I even slipped a ring on Rosita's finger and in my mind said, 'With this ring, I wed thee.'

Everything was like the real thing, Rocky, except that we were not dressed for the occasion. But we both looked nice. Rosita wore a beautiful lavender dress made out of dotted Swiss material. Cost me $5.98 at J. C. Penny. I didn't want to spend that much money on myself because Lord knows how long it will be until I wear a dress again. I went over to one of your sisters' house, the fat one, and asked if I could borrow a skirt. She was so happy to know that I was going to go to church and she let me go through her closet and choose anything I wanted. I chose something simple to wear. It was a black skirt with a cute little poodle on the side. She went so far as to curl my hair and make it pretty. Next time you see me, you'll agree that I do look like Sal Mineo.

The nurse folded the letter quietly and stuffed it back inside the envelope, and without a word disappeared from the room, leaving nothing behind but the echoing sound of her running footsteps.

After my release from the hospital, I went back to the Valley to recuperate from the injuries received in the accident. Gloria was very happy that I was not returning to the University for the second semester. Although I wasn't exactly in any condition to keep up with her active life, I could at least serve as a listening post in that brief period of happiness she had with Rosita.

I say brief because a few months after they got married, Rosita announced to Gloria that she was pregnant. Gloria took her to the doctor right away, and when the pregnancy was confirmed, they came barrelling down the street in their brand new car to let me be the first to know the good news.

Gloria honked the horn outside and I came limping out of the house. I had not met Rosita until that day. She was a sweet-looking little person with light brown hair, who smiled a lot. A little dippy in her manner of conversing, but for Gloria, who wasn't exactly the epitome of brilliance, she was all right.

Gloria was all smiles that day. Her dark brown face was radiant with happiness. She was even smoking a cigar and holding it between her teeth on the corner of her mouth.

'Didn't I tell you in one of my letters that it could be done?' She smiled. 'We're going to have a baby!'

'Oh, come on, Gloria, cut it out!' I laughed.

'You think I'm kidding?'

'I *know* you're kidding!'

She reached across Rosita who was sitting in the passenger seat of the car and grabbed my hand and laid it on Rosita's stomach. 'There's the proof!'

'Oh, shit, Gloria, I don't believe you!'

Rosita turned and looked at me, but she wasn't smiling. 'Why don't you believe her?' she wanted to know.

'Because it's biologically impossible. It's . . . absurd.'

'Are you trying to say that it's crazy for me to have a baby?'

I shook my head. 'No, that's not what I meant.'

Rosita got defensive. I moved away from the car and leaned on my crutches, not knowing how to respond to this woman because I didn't even know her at all. She began trying to feed me all this garbage about woman's vaginal secretions being as potent as the ejaculations of a male and being quite capable of producing a child. I backed off immediately, letting her talk all she wanted. When she finished talking, and she thought she had fully convinced me, Gloria smiled triumphantly and asked, 'What do you got to say now, Rocky?'

I shook my head slowly. 'I don't know. I just don't know. Your woman is either crazy or a damn good liar. In either case, she scares the hell out of me.'

'Watch your language, Rocky,' Gloria snapped. 'You're talking to my wife.'

I apologized and made an excuse to go back into the house. But somehow Gloria knew that I had limped away with something in my mind. She went and took Rosita home, and in less than an hour, she was back again, honking outside. She had a six-pack of beer with her.

'All right, Rocky, now that we're alone, tell me what's on your mind.'

I shrugged my shoulders. 'What can I tell you? You're already convinced that she's pregnant.'

'She is!' Gloria explained. 'Dr Long told me so.'

'Yes, but that's not what I'm trying to tell you.'

'What are you trying to tell me?'

'Will you wait until I go inside the house and get my biology book. There's a section in it on human reproduction that I'd like to explain to you.'

'Well, all right, but you'd better convince me or I'll knock you off your crutches. I didn't appreciate you calling Rosita a liar.'

After I explained to Gloria why it was biologically impossible that she could have impregnated Rosita, she thought for a long silent moment and drank most of the beer she had brought. When I saw a long tear streaming down her face, I wanted to use one of my crutches to hit myself. But then, I said to myself, 'What are friends for if not to tell us when we're being idiots?'

Gloria turned on the engine to her car. 'Okay, Rocky, git outta my car! I should've known better than come killing my ass to tell you something nice in my life. Ever since I met you, you've done nothing but screw up my life. Get out. The way I feel right now I could easily ram up one of them crutches up your skinny ass, but I'd rather go home and kill that fucking Rosita.'

'Oh, Gloria, don't do that! You'll go to jail. Making babies is not the most important thing in the world. What's important is the trying. And just think how much fun that is as opposed to going to the electric chair.'

'Git outta the car *now*!'

I did.

LIFE

Bessie Head

In 1963, when the borders were first set up between Botswana and South Africa, pending Botswana's independence in 1966, all Botswana-born citizens had to return home. Everything had been mingled up in the old colonial days, and the traffic of people to and fro between the two countries had been a steady flow for years and years. More often, especially if they were migrant labourers working in the mines, their period of settlement was brief, but many people had settled there in permanent employment. It was these settlers who were disrupted and sent back to village life in a mainly rural country. On their return they brought with them bits and pieces of a foreign culture and city habits which they had absorbed. Village people reacted in their own way; what they liked, and was beneficial to them, they absorbed – for instance, the faith-healing cult churches which instantly took hold like wildfire; what was harmful to them, they rejected. The murder of Life had this complicated undertone of rejection.

Life had left the village as a little girl of ten years old with her parents for Johannesburg. They had died in the meanwhile, and on Life's return, seventeen years later, she found, as was village custom, that she still had a home in the village. On mentioning that her name was Life Morapedi, the villagers immediately and obligingly took her to the Morapedi yard in the central part of the village. The family yard had remained intact, just as they had left it, except that it looked pathetic in its desolation. The thatch of the mud huts had patches of soil over them where the ants had made their nests; the wooden poles that supported the rafters of the huts had tilted to an angle as their base had been eaten through by the ants. The rubber hedge had grown to a disproportionate size and enclosed the yard in a gloom of shadows that kept out the sunlight. Weeds and grass of many seasonal rains entangled themselves in the yard.

Life's future neighbours, a group of women, continued to stand near her.

'We can help you to put your yard in order,' they said kindly. 'We are very happy that a child of ours has returned home.'

They were impressed with the smartness of this city girl. They generally wore old clothes and kept their very best things for special occasions like weddings, and even then those best things might just be ordinary cotton prints. The girl wore an expensive cream costume of linen material, tailored to fit her tall, full figure. She had a bright, vivacious, friendly manner and laughed freely and loudly. Her speech was rapid and a little hysterical but that was in keeping with her whole personality.

'She is going to bring us a little light,' the women said among themselves, as they went off to fetch their work tools. They were always looking 'for the light' and by that they meant that they were ever alert to receive new ideas that would freshen up the ordinariness and everydayness of village life.

A woman who lived near the Morapedi yard had offered Life hospitality until her own yard was set in order. She picked up the shining new suitcases and preceded Life to her own home, where Life was immediately surrounded with all kinds of endearing attentions – a low stool was placed in a shady place for her to sit on; a little girl came shyly forward with a bowl of water for her to wash her hands; and following on this, a tray with a bowl of meat and porridge was set before her so that she could revive herself after her long journey home. The other women briskly entered her yard with hoes to scratch out the weeds and grass, baskets of earth and buckets of water to re-smear the mud walls, and they had found two idle men to rectify the precarious tilt of the wooden poles of the mud hut. These were the sort of gestures people always offered, but they were pleased to note that the newcomer seemed to have an endless stream of money which she flung around generously. The work party in her yard would suggest that the meat of a goat, slowly simmering in a great iron pot, would help the work to move with a swing, and Life would immediately produce the money to purchase the goat and also tea, milk, sugar, pots of porridge or anything the workers expressed a preference for, so that those two weeks of making Life's yard beautiful for her seemed like one long wedding-feast; people usually only ate that much at weddings.

'How is it you have so much money, our child?' one of the women at last asked, curiously.

'Money flows like water in Johannesburg,' Life replied, with her gay and hysterical laugh. 'You just have to know how to get it.'

The women received this with caution. They said among themselves that their child could not have lived a very good life in Johannesburg. Thrift and honesty were the dominant themes of village life and everyone knew that one could not be honest and rich at the same time; they counted every penny and knew how they had acquired it – with hard work. They never imagined money as a bottomless pit without end; it always had an end and was hard to come by in this dry, semi-desert land. They predicted that she would soon settle down – intelligent girls got jobs in the post office sooner or later.

Life had had the sort of varied career that a city like Johannesburg offered a lot of black women. She had been a singer, beauty queen, advertising model, and prostitute. None of these careers were available in the village – for the illiterate women there was farming and housework; for the literate, teaching, nursing, and clerical work. The first wave of women Life attracted to herself were the farmers and housewives. They were the intensely conservative hard-core centre of village life. It did not take them long to shun her completely because men started turning up in an unending stream. What caused a stir of amazement was that Life was the first and the only woman in the village to make a business out of selling herself. The men were paying her for her services. People's attitude to sex was broad and generous – it was recognized as a necessary part of human life, that it ought to be available whenever possible like food and water, or else one's life would be extinguished or one would get dreadfully ill. To prevent these catastrophes from happening, men and women generally had quite a lot of sex but on a respectable and human level, with financial considerations coming in as an afterthought. When the news spread around that this had now become a business in Life's yard, she attracted to herself a second wave of women – the beer-brewers of the village.

The beer-brewing women were a gay and lovable crowd who had emancipated themselves some time ago. They were drunk every day and could be seen staggering around the village, usually with a wide-eyed, illegitimate baby hitched on to their hips. They also talked and laughed loudly and slapped each other on the back and had developed a language all their own:

'Boyfriends, yes. Husbands, uh, uh, no. Do this! Do that! We want to rule ourselves.'

But they too were subject to the respectable order of village life. Many men passed through their lives but they were all for a time steady boyfriends. The usual arrangement was:

'Mother, you help me and I'll help you.'

This was just so much eye-wash. The men hung around, lived on the resources of the women, and during all this time they would part with about two rand of their own money. After about three months a tally-up would be made:

'Boyfriend,' the woman would say, 'love is love and money is money. You owe me money.' And he'd never be seen again, but another scoundrel would take his place. And so the story went on and on. They found their queen in Life and like all queens, they set her activities apart from themselves; they never attempted to extract money from the constant stream of men because they did not know how, but they liked her yard. Very soon the din and riot of a Johannesburg township was duplicated, on a minor scale, in the central part of the village. A transistor radio blared the day long. Men and women reeled around drunk and laughing and food and drink flowed like milk and honey. The people of the surrounding village watched this phenomenon with pursed lips and commented darkly:

'They'll all be destroyed one day like Sodom and Gomorrah.'

Life, like the beer-brewing women, had a language of her own too. When her friends expressed surprise at the huge quantities of steak, eggs, liver, kidneys, and rice they ate in her yard – the sort of food they too could now and then afford but would not dream of purchasing – she replied in a carefree, off-hand way: 'I'm used to handling big money.' They did not believe it; they were too solid to trust to this kind of luck which had such shaky foundations, and as though to offset some doom that might be just around the corner they often brought along their own scraggy, village chickens reared in their yards, as offerings for the day's round of meals. And one of Life's philosophies on life, which they were to recall with trembling a few months later, was: 'My motto is: live fast, die young, and have a good-looking corpse.' All this was said with the bold, free joy of a woman who had broken all the social taboos. They never followed her to those dizzy heights.

A few months after Life's arrival in the village, the first hotel with its pub opened. It was initially shunned by all the women and even the beer-brewers considered they hadn't fallen *that* low yet – the pub was also associated with the idea of selling oneself. It became Life's favourite business venue. It simplified the business of making appointments for the following day. None of the men questioned their behaviour, nor how such an unnatural situation had been allowed to develop – they could get all the sex they needed for free in the village, but it seemed to fascinate them that they should pay for it for the first time. They had quickly got to the stage where they communicated with Life in short-hand language:

'When?' And she would reply: 'Ten o'clock.' 'When?' 'Two o'clock.' 'When?' 'Four o'clock,' and so on.

And there would be the roar of cheap small talk and much buttock slapping. It was her element and her feverish, glittering, brilliant black eyes swept around the bar, looking for everything and nothing at the same time.

Then one evening death walked quietly into the bar. It was Lesego, the cattle-man, just come in from his cattle-post, where he had been occupied for a period of three months. Men built up their own, individual reputations in the village and Lesego's was one of the most respected and honoured. People said of him: 'When Lesego has got money and you need it, he will give you what he has got and he won't trouble you about the date of payment . . .' He was honoured for another reason also – for the clarity and quiet indifference of his thinking. People often found difficulty in sorting out issues or the truth in any debatable matter. He had a way of keeping his head above water, listening to an argument and always pronouncing the final judgement: 'Well, the truth about this matter is . . .' He was also one of the most successful cattle-men with a balance of seven thousand rand in the bank, and whenever he came into the village he lounged around and gossiped or attended village kgotla meetings, so that people had a saying: 'Well, I must be getting about my business. I'm not like Lesego with money in the bank.'

As usual, the brilliant radar eyes swept feverishly around the bar. They did the rounds twice that evening in the same manner, each time coming to a dead stop for a full second on the thin, dark, concentrated expression of Lesego's face. There wasn't any other man in the bar with that expression; they all had sheepish, inane-looking faces. He was the nearest thing she had seen for a long time to the Johannesburg gangsters she had associated with – the same small, economical gestures, the same power and control. All the men near him quietened down and began to consult with him in low earnest voices; they were talking about the news of the day which never reached the remote cattle-posts. Whereas all the other men had to approach her, the third time her radar eyes swept round he stood his ground, turned his head slowly, and then jerked it back slightly in a silent command:

'Come here.'

She moved immediately to his end of the bar.

'Hullo,' he said, in an astonishingly tender voice and a smile flickered across his dark, reserved face. That was the sum total of Lesego, that basically he was a kind and tender man, that he liked women and had been so successful in that sphere that he took his dominance and success for granted. But they looked at each other from their own worlds and came to fatal conclusions – she saw in him the power and maleness of the gangsters; he saw the freshness and surprise of an entirely new kind of woman. He had left all his women after a time because they bored him, and like all people who live an ordinary humdrum life, he was attracted to that undertone of hysteria in her.

Very soon they stood up and walked out together. A shocked silence fell upon the bar. The men exchanged looks with each other and the way these things communicate themselves, they knew that all the other appointments had been cancelled while Lesego was there. And as though speaking their thoughts aloud, Sianana, one of Lesego's friends, commented, 'Lesego just wants to try it out like we all did because it is something new. He won't stay there when he finds out that it is rotten to the core.'

But Sianana was to find out that he did not fully understand his friend. Lesego was not seen at his usual lounging-places for a week and when he emerged again it was to announce that he was to marry. The news was received with cold hostility. Everyone talked of nothing else; it was as impossible as if a crime was being committed before their very eyes. Sianana once more made himself the spokesman. He waylaid Lesego on his way to the village kgotla:

'I am much surprised by the rumours about you, Lesego,' he said bluntly. 'You can't marry that woman. She's a terrible fuck-about!'

Lesego stared back at him steadily, then he said in his quiet, indifferent way, 'Who isn't here?'

Sianana shrugged his shoulders. The subtleties were beyond him; but whatever else was going on it wasn't commercial, it was human, but did that make it any better? Lesego liked to bugger up an argument like that with a straightforward point. As they walked along together Sianana shook his head several times to indicate that something important was eluding him, until at last, with a smile, Lesego said, 'She has told me all about her bad ways. They are over.'

Sianana merely compressed his lips and remained silent.

Life made the announcement too, after she was married, to all her beer-brewing friends: 'All my old ways are over,' she said. 'I have now become a woman.'

She still looked happy and hysterical. Everything came to her too easily, men, money, and now marriage. The beer-brewers were not slow to point out to her with the same amazement with which they had exclaimed over the steak and eggs, that there were many women in the village who had cried their eyes out over Lesego. She was very flattered.

Their lives, at least Lesego's, did not change much with marriage. He still liked lounging around the village; the rainy season had come and life was easy for the cattle-men at this time because there was enough water and grazing for the animals. He wasn't the kind of man to fuss about the house and during this time he only made three pronouncements about the household. He took control of all the money. She had to ask him for it and state what it was to be used for. Then he didn't like the transistor radio blaring the whole day long.

'Women who keep that thing going the whole day have nothing in their heads,' he said.

Then he looked down at her from a great height and commented finally and quietly: 'If you go with those men again, I'll kill you.'

This was said so indifferently and quietly, as though he never really expected his authority and dominance to encounter any challenge.

She hadn't the mental equipment to analyse what had hit her, but something seemed to strike her a terrible blow behind the head. She instantly succumbed to the blow and rapidly began to fall apart. On the surface, the everyday round of village life was deadly dull in its even, unbroken monotony; one day slipped easily into another, drawing water, stamping corn, cooking food. But within this there were enormous tugs and pulls between people. Custom demanded that people care about each other, and all day long there was this constant traffic of people in and out of each other's lives. Someone had to be buried; sympathy and help were demanded for this event – there were money loans, new-born babies, sorrow, trouble, gifts. Lesego had long been the king of this world; there was, every day, a long string of people, wanting something or wanting to give him something in gratitude for a past favour. It was the basic strength of village life. It created people whose sympathetic and emotional responses were always fully awakened, and it rewarded them by richly filling in a void that was one big, gaping yawn. When the hysteria and cheap rowdiness were taken away, Life fell into the yawn; she had nothing inside herself to cope with this way of life that had finally caught up with her. The beer-brewing women were still there; they still liked her yard because Lesego was casual and easy-going and all that went on in it now – like the old men squatting in corners with gifts: 'Lesego, I had good luck with my hunting today. I caught two rabbits and I want to share one with you . . .' – was simply the Tswana way of life they too lived. In keeping with their queen's new status, they said:

'We are women and must do something.'

They collected earth and dung and smeared and decorated Life's courtyard. They drew water for her, stamped her corn, and things looked quite ordinary on the surface because Lesego also liked a pot of beer. No one noticed the expression of anguish that had crept into Life's face. The boredom of the daily round was almost throttling her to death and no matter which way she looked, from the beer-brewers to her husband to all the people who called, she found no one with whom she could communicate what had become an actual physical pain. After a month of it, she was near collapse. One morning she mentioned her agony to the beer-brewers: 'I think I have made a mistake. Married life doesn't suit me.'

And they replied sympathetically, 'You are just getting used to it. After all it's a different life in Johannesburg.'

The neighbours went further. They were impressed by a marriage they thought could never succeed. They started saying that one never ought to judge a human being who was both good and bad, and Lesego had turned a bad woman into a good woman which was something they had never seen before. Just as they were saying this and nodding their approval, Sodom and Gomorrah started up all over again. Lesego had received word late in the evening that the new born calves at his cattle-post were dying, and early the next morning he was off again in his truck.

The old, reckless wild woman awakened from a state near death with a huge sigh of relief. The transistor blared, the food flowed again, the men and women reeled around dead drunk. Simply by their din they beat off all the unwanted guests who nodded their heads grimly. When Lesego came back they were going to tell him this was no wife for him.

Three days later Lesego unexpectedly was back in the village. The calves were all anaemic and they had to be brought in to the vet for an injection. He drove his truck straight through the village to the vet's camp. One of the beer-brewers saw him and hurried in alarm to her friend.

'The husband is back,' she whispered fearfully, pulling Life to one side.

'Agh,' she replied irritably.

She did dispel the noise, the men, and the drink, but a wild anger was driving her to break out of a way of life that was like death to her. She told one of the men she'd see him at six o'clock. At about five o'clock Lesego drove into the yard with the calves. There was no one immediately around to greet him. He jumped out of the truck and walked to one of the huts, pushing open the door. Life was sitting on the bed. She looked up silently and sullenly. He was a little surprised but his mind was still distracted by the calves. He had to settle them in the yard for the night.

'Will you make some tea,' he said. 'I'm very thirsty.'

'There's no sugar in the house,' she said. 'I'll have to get some.'

Something irritated him but he hurried back to the calves and his wife walked out of the yard. Lesego had just settled the calves when a neighbour walked in, he was very angry.

'Lesego,' he said bluntly, 'we told you not to marry that woman. If you go to the yard of Radithobolo now you'll find her in bed with him. Go and see for yourself that you may leave that bad woman!'

Lesego stared quietly at him for a moment, then at his own pace as though there were no haste or chaos in his life, he went to the hut they used as a kitchen. A tin full of sugar stood there. He turned and found a knife in the corner, one of the large ones he used for slaughtering cattle, and slipped it into his shirt. Then at his own pace he walked to the yard of Radithobolo. It looked deserted, except that the door of one of the huts was partially open and one closed. He kicked open the door of the closed hut and the man within shouted out in alarm. On seeing Lesego he sprang cowering into a corner. Lesego jerked his head back indicating that the man should leave the room. But Radithobolo did not run far. He wanted to enjoy himself so he pressed himself into the shadows of the rubber hedge. He expected the usual husband-and-wife scene – the irate husband cursing at the top of his voice; the wife, hysterical in her lies and self-defence. Only Lesego walked out of the yard and he held in his hand a huge, blood-stained knife. On seeing the knife Radithobolo immediately fell to the ground in a dead faint. There were a few people on the footpath and they shrank into the rubber hedge at the sight of that knife.

Very soon a wail arose. People clutched at their heads and began running in all directions crying yo! yo! yo! in their shock. It was some time before anyone thought of calling the police. They were so disordered because murder, outright and violent, was a most uncommon and rare occurrence in village life. It seemed that only Lesego kept cool that evening. He was sitting quietly in his yard when the whole police force came tearing in. They looked at him in horror and began to thoroughly upbraid him for looking so unperturbed.

'You have taken a human life and you are cool like that!' they said angrily. 'You are going to hang by the neck for this. It's a serious crime to take a human life.'

He did not hang by the neck. He kept that cool, head-above-water indifferent look, right up to the day of his trial. Then he looked up at the judge and said calmly, 'Well, the truth about this matter is, I had just returned from the cattle-post. I had had trouble with my calves that day. I came home late and being thirsty, asked my wife to make me tea. She said there was no sugar in the house and left to buy some. My neighbour, Mathata, came in after this and said that my wife was not at the shops but in the yard of Radithobolo. He said I ought to go and see what she was doing in the yard of Radithobolo. I thought I would check up about the sugar first and in the kitchen I found a tin full of it. I was sorry and surprised to see this. Then a fire seemed to fill my heart. I thought that if she was doing a bad thing with Radithobolo as Mathata said, I'd better kill her because I cannot understand a wife who could be so corrupt . . .'

Lesego had been doing this for years, passing judgement on all aspects of life in his straightforward, uncomplicated way. The judge, who was a white man, and therefore not involved in Tswana custom and its debates, was as much impressed by Lesego's manner as all the village men had been.

'This is a crime of passion,' he said sympathetically, 'so there are extenuating circumstances. But it is still a serious crime to take a human life so I sentence you to five years' imprisonment . . .'

Lesego's friend, Sianana, who was to take care of his business affairs while he was in jail, came to visit Lesego still shaking his head. Something was eluding him about the whole business, as though it had been planned from the very beginning.

'Lesego,' he said, with deep sorrow, 'why did you kill that fuck-about? You had legs to walk away. You could have walked away. Are you trying to show us that rivers never cross here? There are good women and good men but they seldom join their lives together. It's always this mess and foolishness . . .'

A song by Jim Reeves was very popular at that time: *That's What Happens When Two Worlds Collide*. When they were drunk, the beer-brewing women used to sing it and start weeping. Maybe they had the last word on the whole affair.

A GUATEMALAN IDYLL

Jane Bowles

WHEN the traveller arrived at the pension the wind was blowing hard. Before going in to have the hot soup he had been thinking about, he left his luggage inside the door and walked a few blocks in order to get an idea of the town. He came to a very large arch through which, in the distance, he could see a plain. He thought he could distinguish figures seated around a far-away fire, but he was not certain because the wind made tears in his eyes.

'How dismal,' he thought, letting his mouth drop open. 'But never mind. Brace up. It's probably a group of boys and girls sitting around an open fire having a fine time together. The world is the world, after all is said and done, and a patch of grass in one place is green the way it is in any other.'

He turned back and walked along quickly, skirting the walls of the low stone houses. He was a little worried that he might not be able to recognize the door of his pension.

'There's not supposed to be any variety in the USA,' he said to himself. 'But this Spanish architecture beats everything, it's so monotonous.' He knocked on one of the doors, and shortly a child with a shaved head appeared. With a strong American accent he said to her: 'Is this the Pension Espinoza?'

'*Sí*!' The child led him inside to a fountain in the centre of a square *patio*. He looked into the basin and the child did too.

'There are four fish inside here,' she said to him in Spanish. 'Would you like me to try and catch one of them for you?'

The traveller did not understand her. He stood there uncomfortably, longing to go to his room. The little girl was still trying to get hold of a fish when her mother, who owned the pension, came out and joined them. The woman was quite fat, but her face was small and pointed, and she wore glasses attached by a gold chain to her dress. She shook hands with him and asked him in fairly good English if he had had a pleasant journey.

'He wants to see some of the fish,' explained the child.

'Certainly,' said Señora Espinoza, moving her hands about in the water with dexterity. 'Soon now, soon now,' she said, laughing as one of the fish slipped between her fingers.

The traveller nodded. 'I would like to go to my room,' he said.

The American was a little dismayed by his room. There were four brass beds in a row, all of them very old and a little crooked.

'God!' he said to himself. 'They'll have to remove some of these beds. They give me the willies.'

A cord hung down from the ceiling. On the end of it at the height of his nose was a tiny electric bulb. He turned it on and looked at his hands under the light. They were chapped and dirty. A barefoot servant girl came in with a pitcher and a bowl.

In the dining-room calendars decorated the walls, and there was an elaborate cut-glass carafe on every table. Several people had already begun their meal in silence. One little girl was speaking in a high voice.

'I'm not going to the band concert tonight, Mama,' she was saying.

'Why not?' asked her mother with her mouth full. She looked seriously at her daughter.

'Because I don't like to hear music. I hate it!'

'Why?' asked her mother absently, taking another large mouthful of her food. She spoke in a deep voice like a man's. Her head, which was set low between her shoulders, was covered with black curls. Her chin was heavy and her skin was dark and coarse; however, she had very beautiful blue eyes. She sat with her legs apart, with one arm lying flat on the table. The child bore no resemblance to her mother. She was frail, with stiff hair of the peculiar light colour that is often found in mulattos. Her eyes were so pale that they seemed almost white.

As the traveller came in, the child turned to look at him.

'Now there are nine people eating in this pension,' she said immediately.

'Nine,' said her mother. 'Many mouths.' She pushed her plate aside wearily and looked up at the calendar beside her on the wall. At last she turned around and saw the stranger. Having already finished her own dinner, she followed the progress of his meal with interest. Once she caught his eye.

'Good appetite,' she said, nodding gravely, and then she watched his soup until he had finished it.

'My pills,' she said to Lilina, holding her hand out without turning her head. To amuse herself, Lilina emptied the whole bottle into her mother's hand.

'Now you have your pills,' she said. When Señora Ramirez realized what had happened, she dealt Lilina a terrible blow in the face, using the hand which held the pills, and thus leaving them sticking to the child's moist skin and in her hair. The traveller turned. He was so bored and at the same time disgusted by what he saw that he decided he had better look for another pension that very night.

'Soon,' said the waitress, putting his meat in front of him, 'the musician will come. For fifty cents he will play you all the songs you want to hear. One night would not be time enough. *She* will be out of the room by then.' She looked over at Lilina, who was squealing like a stuck pig.

'Those pills cost me three *quetzales* a bottle,' Señora Ramirez complained. One of the young men at a nearby table came over and examined the empty bottle. He shook his head.

'A barbarous thing,' he said.

'What a dreadful child you are, Lilina!' said an English lady, who was seated at quite a distance from everybody else. All the diners looked up. Her face and neck were quite red with annoyance. She was speaking to them in English.

'Can't you behave like civilized people?' she demanded.

'You be quiet, you!' The young man had finished examining the empty pill bottle. His companions burst out laughing.

'OK, girl,' he continued in English. 'Want a piece of chewing gum?' His companions were quite helpless with laughter at his last remark, and all three of them got up and left the room. Their guffaws could be heard from the *patio* where they had grouped around the fountain, fairly doubled up.

'It's a disgrace to the adult mind,' said the English lady. Lilina's nose had started to bleed, and she rushed out.

'And tell Consuelo to hurry in and eat her dinner,' her mother called after her. Just then the musician arrived. He was a small man and he wore a black suit and a dirty shirt.

'Well,' said Lilina's mother. 'At last you came.'

'I was having dinner with my uncle. Time passes, Señora Ramirez! *Gracias a Dios!*'

'*Gracias a Dios* nothing! It's unheard-of having to eat dinner without music.'

The violinist fell into a chair, and, bent over low, he started to play with all his strength.

'Waltzes!' shouted Señora Ramirez above the music. 'Waltzes!' She looked petulant and at the same time as though she were about to cry. As a matter of fact, the stranger was quite sure that he saw a tear roll down her cheek.

'Are you going to the band concert tonight?' she asked him; she spoke English rather well.

'I don't know. Are you?'

'Yes, with my daughter Consuelo. If the unfortunate girl ever gets here to eat her supper. She doesn't like food. Only dancing. She dances like a real butterfly. She has French blood from me. She is of a much better type than the little one, Lilina, who is always hurting; hurting me, hurting her sister, hurting her friends. I hope that God will have pity on her.' At this she really did shed a tear or two, which she brushed away with her napkin.

'Well, she's young, yet,' said the stranger. Señora Ramirez agreed heartily.

'Yes, she is young.' She smiled at him sweetly and seemed quite content.

Lilina meanwhile was in her room, standing over the white bowl in which they washed their hands, letting the blood drip into it. She was breathing heavily like someone who is trying to simulate anger.

'Stop that breathing! You sound like an old man,' said her sister Consuelo, who was lying on the bed with a hot brick on her

stomach. Consuelo was small and dark, with a broad flat face
and an unusually narrow skull. She had a surly nature, which is
often the case when young girls do little else but dream of a lover.
Lilina, who was a bully without any curiosity concerning the
grown-up world, hated her sister more than anyone else she
knew.

'Mama says that if you don't come in to eat soon she will hit
you.'

'Is that how *you* got that bloody nose?'

'No,' said Lilina. She walked away from the basin and her eye
fell on her mother's corset which was lying on the bed. Quickly
she picked it up and went with it into the *patio*, where she threw
it into the fountain. Consuelo, frightened by the appropriation
of the corset, got up hastily and arranged her hair.

'Too much upset for a girl of my age,' she said to herself,
patting her stomach. Crossing the *patio* she saw Señorita Córdoba walking along, holding her head very high as she slipped
some hairpins more firmly into the bun at the back of her neck.
Consuelo felt like a frog or a beetle walking behind her. Together
they entered the dining-room.

'Why don't you wait for midnight to strike?' said Señora
Ramirez to Consuelo. Señorita Córdoba, assuming that this
taunt had been addressed to her, bridled and stiffened. Her eyes
narrowed and she stood still. Señora Ramirez, a gross coward,
gave her a strange idiotic smile.

'How is your health, Señorita Córdoba?' she asked softly, and
then feeling confused, she pointed to the stranger and asked him
if he knew Señorita Córdoba.

'No, no; he does not know me.' She held out her hand stiffly to
the stranger and he took it. No names were mentioned.

Consuelo sat down beside her mother and ate voraciously, a
sad look in her eye. Señorita Córdoba ordered only fruit. She sat
looking out into the dark *patio*, giving the other diners a view of
the nape of her neck. Presently she opened a letter and began to
read. The others all watched her closely. The three young men
who had laughed so heartily before were now smiling like idiots,
waiting for another such occasion to present itself.

The musician was playing a waltz at the request of Señora

Ramirez, who was trying her best to attract again the attention of the stranger. 'Tra-la-la-la,' she sang, and in order better to convey the beauty of the waltz she folded her arms in front of her and rocked from side to side.

'Ay, Consuelo! It is for her to waltz,' she said to the stranger. 'There will be many people in the *plaza* tonight, and there is so much wind. I think that you must fetch my shawl, Consuelo. It is getting very cold.'

While awaiting Consuelo's return she shivered and picked her teeth.

The traveller thought she was crazy and a little disgusting. He had come here as a buyer for a very important textile concern. Having completed all his work, he had for some reason decided to stay on another week, perhaps because he had always heard that a vacation in a foreign country was a desirable thing. Already he regretted his decision, but there was no boat out before the following Monday. By the end of the meal he was in such despair that his face wore a peculiarly young and sensitive look. In order to buoy himself up a bit, he began to think about what he would get to eat three weeks hence, seated at his mother's table on Thanksgiving Day. They would be very glad to hear that he had not enjoyed himself on this trip because they had always considered it something in the nature of a betrayal when anyone in the family expressed a desire to travel. He thought they led a fine life and was inclined to agree with them.

Consuelo had returned with her mother's shawl. She was dreaming again when her mother pinched her arm.

'Well, Consuelo, are you coming to the band concert or are you going to sit here like a dummy? I daresay the Señor is not coming with us, but *we* like music, so get up, and we will say goodnight to this gentleman and be on our way.'

The traveller had not understood this speech. He was therefore very much surprised when Señora Ramirez tapped him on the shoulder and said to him severely in English: 'Good night, Señor. Consuelo and I are going to the band concert. We will see you tomorrow at breakfast.'

'Oh, but I'm going to the band concert myself,' he said, in a panic lest they leave him with a whole evening on his hands.

Señora Ramirez flushed with pleasure. The three walked down the badly lit street together, escorted by a group of skinny yellow dogs.

'These old grilled windows are certainly very beautiful,' the traveller said to Señora Ramirez. 'Old as the hills themselves, aren't they?'

'You must go to the capital if you want beautiful buildings,' said Señora Ramirez. 'Very new and clean they are.'

'I should think,' he said, 'that these old buildings were your point of interest here, aside from your Indians and their native costumes.'

They walked on for a little while in silence. A small boy came up to them and tried to sell them some lollipops.

'Five *centavos*,' said the little boy.

'Absolutely not,' said the traveller. He had been warned that the natives would cheat him, and he was actually enraged every time they approached him with their wares.

'Four *centavos* . . . three *centavos* . . .'

'No, no, no! Go away!' The little boy ran ahead of them.

'I would like a lollipop,' said Consuelo to him.

'Well, why didn't you say so, then?' he demanded.

'No,' said Consuelo.

'She does not mean no,' explained her mother. 'She can't learn to speak English. She has clouds in her head.'

'I see,' said the traveller. Consuelo looked mortified. When they came to the end of the street, Señora Ramirez stood still and lowered her head like a bull.

'Listen,' she said to Consuelo. 'Listen. You can hear the music from here.'

'Yes, Mama. Indeed you can.' They stood listening to the faint *marimba* noise that reached them. The traveller sighed.

'Please, let's get going if we *are* going,' he said. 'Otherwise there is no point.'

The square was already crowded when they arrived. The older people sat on benches under the trees, while the younger ones walked round and round, the girls in one direction and the boys in the other. The musicians played inside a kiosk in the centre of the square. Señora Ramirez led both Consuelo and the stranger into the girls' line, and they had not been walking more than a minute before she settled into a comfortable gait, with an expression very much like that of someone relaxing in an armchair.

'We have three hours,' she said to Consuelo.

The stranger looked around him. Many of the girls were barefoot and pure Indian. They walked along holding tightly to one another, and were frequently convulsed with laughter.

The musicians were playing a formless but militant-sounding piece which came to many climaxes without ending. The drummer was the man who had just played the violin at Señora Espinoza's pension.

'Look!' said the traveller excitedly. 'Isn't that the man who was just playing for us at dinner. He must have run all the way. I'll bet he's sweating some.'

'Yes, it is he,' said Señora Ramirez. 'The nasty little rat. I would like to tear him right off his stand. Remember the one at the Grand Hotel, Consuelo? He stopped at every table, Señor, and I have never seen such beautiful teeth in my life. A smile on his face from the moment he came into the room until he went out again. This one looks at his shoes while he is playing, and he would like to kill us all.'

Some big boys threw confetti into the traveller's face.

'I wonder,' he asked himself. 'I wonder what kind of fun they get out of just walking around and around this little park and throwing confetti at each other.'

The boys' line was in a constant uproar about something. The broader their smiles became, the more he suspected them of plotting something, probably against him, for apparently he was the only tourist there that evening. Finally he was so upset that he walked along looking up at the stars, or even for short stretches with his eyes shut, because it seemed to him that somehow this rendered him a little less visible. Suddenly he caught sight of Señorita Córdoba. She was across the street buying lollipops from a boy.

'Señorita!' He waved his hand from where he was, and then joyfully bounded out of the line and across the street. He stood panting by her side, while she reddened considerably and did not know what to say to him.

Señora Ramirez and Consuelo came to a standstill and stood like two monuments, staring after him, while the lines brushed past them on either side.

Lilina was looking out of her window at some boys who were playing on the corner of the street under the street light. One of them kept pulling a snake out of his pocket; he would then stuff it back in again. Lilina wanted the snake very much. She chose her toys according to the amount of power or responsibility she thought they would give her in the eyes of others. She thought now that if she were able to get the snake, she would perhaps put on a little act called 'Lilina and the Viper', and charge admission. She imagined that she would wear a fancy dress and let the snake wriggle under her collar. She left her room and went out of doors. The wind was stronger than it had been, and she could hear the music playing even from where she was. She felt chilly and hurried toward the boys.

'For how much will you sell your snake?' she asked the oldest boy, Ramón.

'You mean Victoria?' said Ramón. His voice was beginning to change and there was a shadow above his upper lip.

'Victoria is too much of a queen for you to have,' said one of the smaller boys. 'She is a beauty and you are not.' They all roared with laughter, including Ramón, who all at once looked very silly. He giggled like a girl. Lilina's heart sank. She was determined to have the snake.

'Are you ever going to stop laughing and begin to bargain with me? If you don't I'll have to go back in, because my mother and sister will be coming home soon, and they wouldn't allow me to be talking here like this with you. I'm from a good family.'

This sobered Ramón, and he ordered the boys to be quiet. He took Victoria from his pocket and played with her in silence. Lilina stared at the snake.

'Come to my house,' said Ramón. 'My mother will want to know how much I'm selling her for.'

'All right,' said Lilina. 'But be quick, and I don't want them with us.' She indicated the other boys. Ramón gave them orders to go back to their houses and meet him later at the playground near the Cathedral.

'Where do you live?' she asked him.

'Calle de las Delicias number six.'

'Does your house belong to you?'

'My house belongs to my Aunt Gudelia.'

'Is she richer than your mother?'

'Oh, yes.' They said no more to each other.

There were eight rooms opening onto the *patio* of Ramón's house, but only one was furnished. In this room the family cooked and slept. His mother and his aunt were seated opposite one another on two brightly painted chairs. Both were fat and both were wearing black. The only light came from a charcoal fire which was burning in a brazier on the floor.

They had bought the chairs that very morning and were consequently feeling light-hearted and festive. When the children arrived they were singing a little song together.

'Why don't we buy something to drink?' said Gudelia, when they stopped singing.

'Now you're going to go crazy, I see,' said Ramón's mother. 'You're very disagreeable when you're drinking.'

'No, I'm not,' said Gudelia.

'Mother,' said Ramón. 'This little girl has come to buy Victoria.'

'I have never seen you before,' said Ramón's mother to Lilina.

'Nor I,' said Gudelia. 'I am Ramón's aunt, Gudelia. This is my house.'

'My name is Lilina Ramirez. I want to bargain for Ramón's Victoria.'

'Victoria,' they repeated gravely.

'Ramón is very fond of Victoria and so are Gudelia and I,' said his mother. 'It's a shame that we sold Alfredo the parrot. We sold him for far too little. He sang and danced. We have taken care of Victoria for a long time, and it has been very expensive. She eats much meat.' This was an obvious lie. They all looked at Lilina.

'Where do you live, dear?' Gudelia asked Lilina.

'I live in the capital, but I'm staying now at Señora Espinoza's pension.'

'I meet her in the market every day of my life,' said Gudelia. 'Maria de la Luz Espinoza. She buys a lot. How many people has she staying in her house? Five, six?'

'Nine.'

'Nine! Dear God! Does she have many animals?'

'Certainly,' said Lilina.

'Come,' said Ramón to Lilina. 'Let's go outside and bargain.'

'He loves that snake,' said Ramón's mother, looking fixedly at Lilina.

The aunt sighed. 'Victoria . . . Victoria.'

Lilina and Ramón climbed through a hole in the wall and sat down together in the midst of some foliage.

'Listen,' said Ramón. 'If you kiss me, I'll give you Victoria for nothing. You have blue eyes. I saw them when we were in the street.'

'I can hear what you are saying,' his mother called out from the kitchen.

'Shame, shame,' said Gudelia. 'Giving Victoria away for nothing. Your mother will be without food. I can buy my own food, but what will your mother do?'

Lilina jumped to her feet impatiently. She saw that they were getting nowhere, and unlike most of her countrymen, she was always eager to get things done quickly.

She stamped back into the kitchen, opened her eyes very wide in order to frighten the two ladies, and shouted as loud as she could: 'Sell me that snake right now or I will go away and never put my foot in this house again.'

The two women were not used to such a display of rage over the mere settlement of a price. They rose from their chairs and started moving about the room to no purpose, picking up things and putting them down again. They were not quite sure what to do. Gudelia was terribly upset. She stepped here and there with her hand below her breast, peering about cautiously. Finally she slipped out into the *patio* and disappeared.

Ramón took Victoria out of his pocket. They arranged a price and Lilina left, carrying her in a little box.

Meanwhile Señora Ramirez and her daughter were on their way home from the band concert. Both of them were in a bad humour. Consuelo was not disposed to talk at all. She looked angrily at the houses they were passing and sighed at everything her mother had to say.

'You have no merriment in your heart,' said Señora Ramirez. 'Just revenge.' As Consuelo refused to answer, she continued. 'Sometimes I feel that I am walking along with an assassin.'

She stopped still in the street and looked up at the sky. '*Jesus Maria!*' she said. 'Don't let me say such things about my own daughter.' She clutched at Consuelo's arm.

'Come, come. Let us hurry. My feet ache. What an ugly city this is!'

Consuelo began to whimper. The word assassin had affected her painfully. Although she had no very clear idea of an assassin in her mind, she knew it to be a gross insult and contrary to all usage when applied to a young lady of breeding. It so frightened her that her mother had used such a word in connection with her, that she actually felt a little sick to her stomach.

'No, Mama, no!' she cried. 'Don't say that I am an assassin. Don't!' Her hands were beginning to shake, and already the tears were filling her eyes. Her mother hugged her and they stood for a moment locked in each other's arms.

Maria, the servant, was standing near the fountain looking into it when Consuelo and her mother arrived at the pension. The traveller and Señorita Córdoba were seated together having a chat.

'Doesn't love interest you?' the traveller was asking her.

'No . . . no . . .' answered Señorita Córdoba. 'City life, business, the theatre . . .' She sounded somewhat half-hearted about the theatre.

'Well, that's funny,' said the traveller. 'In my country most young girls are interested in love. There are some, of course, who are interested in having a career, either business or the stage. But I've heard tell that even these women deep down in their hearts want a home and everything that goes with it.'

'So?' said Señorita Córdoba.

'Well, yes,' said the traveller. 'Deep down in your heart

don't you always hope the right man will come along some day?'

'No . . . no . . . no . . . Do you?' she said absent-mindedly.

'Who, me? No.'

'No?'

She was the most preoccupied woman he had ever spoken with.

'Look, Señoras,' said Maria to Consuelo and her Mother. 'Look what is floating around in the fountain! What is it?'

Consuelo bent over the basin and fished around a bit. Presently she pulled out her mother's pink corset.

'Why, Mama,' she said. 'It's your corset.'

Señora Ramirez examined the wet corset. It was covered with muck from the bottom of the fountain. She went over to a chair and sat down in it, burying her face in her hands. She rocked back and forth and sobbed very softly. Señora Espinoza came out of her room.

'Lilina, my sister, threw it into the fountain,' Consuelo announced to all present.

Señora Espinoza looked at the corset.

'It can be fixed. It can be fixed,' she said, walking over to Señora Ramirez and putting her arms around her.

'Look, my friend. My dear little friend, why don't you go to bed and get some sleep? Tomorrow you can think about getting it cleaned.'

'How can we stand it? Oh, how can we stand it?' Señora Ramirez asked imploringly, her beautiful eyes filled with sorrow. 'Sometimes,' she said in a trembling voice, 'I have no more strength than a sparrow. I would like to send my children to the four winds and sleep and sleep and sleep.'

Consuelo, hearing this, said in a gentle tone: 'Why don't you do so, Mama?'

'They are like two daggers in my heart, you see?' continued her mother.

'No, they are not,' said Señora Espinoza. 'They are flowers that brighten your life.' She removed her glasses and polished them on her blouse.

'Daggers in my heart,' repeated Señora Ramirez.

'Have some hot soup,' urged Señora Espinoza. 'Maria will make you some – a gift from me – and then you can go to bed and forget all about this.'

'No, I think I will just sit here, thank you.'

'Mama is going to have one of her fits,' said Consuelo to the servant. 'She does sometimes. She gets just like a child instead of getting angry, and she doesn't worry about what she is eating or when she goes to sleep, but she just sits in a chair or goes walking and her face looks very different from the way it looks at other times.' The servant nodded, and Consuelo went in to bed.

'I have French blood,' Señora Ramirez was saying to Señora Espinoza. 'I am very delicate for that reason – too delicate for my husband.'

Señora Espinoza seemed worried by the confession of her friend. She had no interest in gossip or in what people had to say about their lives. To Señora Ramirez she was like a man, and she often had dreams about her in which she became a man.

The traveller was highly amused.

'I'll be damned!' he said. 'All this because of an old corset. Some people have nothing to think about in this world. It's funny, though, funny as a barrel of monkeys.'

To Señorita Córdoba it was not funny. 'It's too bad,' she said. 'Very much too bad that the corset was spoiled. What are you doing here in this country?'

'I'm buying textiles. At least, I was, and now I'm just taking a little vacation here until the next boat leaves for the United States. I kind of miss my family and I'm anxious to get back. I don't see what you're supposed to get out of travelling.'

'Oh, yes, yes. Surely you do,' said Señorita Córdoba politely. 'Now if you will excuse me I am going inside to do a little drawing. I must not forget how in this peasant land.'

'What are you, an artist?' he asked.

'I draw dresses.' She disappeared.

'Oh, God!' thought the traveller after she had left. 'Here I am, left alone, and I'm not sleepy yet. This empty *patio* is so barren and so uninteresting, and as far as Señorita Córdoba is concerned, she's an iceberg. I like her neck though. She has a neck like a swan, so long and white and slender, the kind of neck you dream about girls having. But she's more like a virgin than a swan.' He turned around and noticed that Señora Ramirez was still sitting in her chair. He picked up his own chair and carried it over next to hers.

'Do you mind?' he asked. 'I see that you've decided to take a little night air. It isn't a bad idea. I don't feel like going to bed much either.'

'No,' she said. 'I don't want to go to bed. I will sit here. I like to sit out at night, if I am warmly enough dressed, and look up at the stars.'

'Yes, it's a great source of peace,' the traveller said. 'People don't do enough of it these days.'

'Would you not like very much to go to Italy?' Señora Ramirez asked him. 'The fruit trees and the flowers will be wonderful there at night.'

'Well, you've got enough fruit and flowers here, I should say. What do you want to go to Italy for? I'll bet there isn't as much variety in the fruit there as here.'

'No? Do you have many flowers in your country?'

The traveller was not able to decide.

'I would like really,' continued Señora Ramirez, 'to be some-where else — in your country or in Italy. I would like to be somewhere where the life is beautiful. I care very much whether life is beautiful or ugly. People who live here don't care very much. Because they do not think.' She touched her finger to her forehead. 'I love beautiful things: beautiful houses, beautiful gardens, beautiful songs. When I was a young girl I was truly wild with happiness — doing and thinking and running in and out. I was so happy that my mother was afraid I would fall and break my leg or have some kind of accident. She was a very religious woman, but when I was a young girl I could not remember to think about such a thing. I was up always every morning before anybody except the Indians, and every morning I would go to market with them to buy food for all the houses. For many years I was doing this. Even when I was very little. It was very easy for me to do anything. I loved to learn English. I had a professor and I used to get on my knees in front of my father that the professor would stay longer with me every day. I was walking in the parks when my sisters were sleeping. My eyes were so big.' She made a circle with two fingers. 'And shiny like two diamonds, I was so excited all the time.' She churned the air with her clenched fist. 'Like this,' she said. 'Like a storm. My sisters called me wild Sofia. At the same time they were calling me wild Sofia, I was in love with my uncle, Aldo Torres. He never came much to the house before, but I heard my mother say that he had no more money and we would feed him. We were very rich and getting richer every year. I felt very sorry for him and was thinking about him all the time. We fell in love with each other and were kissing and hugging each other when nobody was there who could see us. I would have lived with him in a grass hut. He married a woman who had a little money, who also loved him very much. When he was married he got fat and started joking a lot with my father. I was glad for him that he was richer but pretty sad for myself. Then my sister Juanita, the oldest, married a very rich man. We were all very happy about her and there was a very big wedding.'

'You must have been broken-hearted though about your uncle Aldo Torres going off with someone else, when you had befriended him so much when he was poor.'

'Oh, I liked him very much,' she said. Her memory seemed suddenly to have failed her and she did not appear to be interested in speaking any longer of the past. The traveller felt disturbed.

'I would love to travel,' she continued, 'very, very much, and I think it would be very nice to have the life of an actress, without children. You know it is my nature to love men and kissing.'

'Well,' said the traveller, 'nobody gets as much kissing as they would like to get. Most people are frustrated. You'd be surprised at the number of people in my country who are frustrated and good-looking at the same time.'

She turned her face toward his. The one little light bulb shed just enough light to enable him to see into her beautiful eyes. The tears were still wet on her lashes and they magnified her eyes to such an extent that they appeared to be almost twice their normal size. While she was looking at him she caught her breath.

'Oh, my darling man,' she said to him suddenly. 'I don't want to be separated from you. Let's go where I can hold you in my arms.' The traveller was feeling excited. She had taken hold of his hand and was crushing it very hard.

'Where do you want to go?' he asked stupidly.

'Into your bed.' She closed her eyes and waited for him to answer.

'All right. Are you sure?'

She nodded her head vigorously.

'This', he said to himself, 'is undoubtedly one of those things that you don't want to remember next morning. I'll want to shake it off like a dog shaking water off its back. But what can I do? It's too far along now. I'll be going home soon and the whole thing will be just a soap bubble among many other soap bubbles.'

He was beginning to feel inspired and he could not understand it, because he had not been drinking.

'A soap bubble among many other soap bubbles,' he repeated to himself. His inner life was undefined but well controlled as a rule. Together they went into his room.

'Ah,' said Señora Ramirez, after he had closed the door behind them, 'this makes me happy.'

She fell onto the bed sideways, like a beaten person. Her feet stuck out into the air, and her heavy breathing filled the room. He realized that he had never before seen a person behave in this manner unless sodden with alcohol, and he did not know what to do. According to all his standards and the standards of his friends she was not a pleasant thing to lie beside.

She was unfastening her dress at the neck. The brooch with which she pinned her collar together she stuck into the pillow behind her.

'So much fat,' she said. 'So much fat.' She was smiling at him very tenderly. This for some reason excited him, and he took off his own clothing and got into bed beside her. He was as cold as a clam and very bony, but being a truly passionate woman she did not notice any of that.

'Do you really want to go through with this?' he said to her, for he was incapable of finding new words for a situation that was certainly unlike any other he had ever experienced.

She fell upon him and felt his face and his neck with feverish excitement.

'Dear God!' she said. 'Dear God!' They were in the very act of making love. 'I have lived twenty years for this moment and I cannot think that heaven itself could be more wonderful.'

The traveller hardly listened to this remark. His face was hidden in the pillow and he was feeling the pangs of guilt in the very midst of his pleasure. When it was all over she said to him: 'That is all I want to do ever.' She patted his hands and smiled at him.

'Are you happy, too?' she asked him.

'Yes, indeed,' he said. He got off the bed and went out into the *patio*.

'She was certainly in a bad way,' he thought. 'It was almost like death itself.' He didn't want to think any further. He stayed outside near the fountain as long as possible. When he returned she was up in front of the bureau trying to arrange her hair.

'I'm ashamed of the way I look,' she said. 'I don't look the way I feel.' She laughed and he told her that she looked perfectly all right. She drew him down onto the bed again. 'Don't send me back to my room,' she said. 'I love to be here with you, my sweetheart.'

The dawn was breaking when the traveller awakened next morning. Señora Ramirez was still beside him, sleeping very soundly. Her arm was flung over the pillow behind her head.

'Lordy,' said the traveller to himself. 'I'd better get her out of here.' He shook her as hard as he could.

'Mrs Ramirez,' he said. 'Mrs Ramirez, wake up. Wake up!' When she finally did wake up, she looked frightened to death. She turned and stared at him blankly for a little while. Before he noticed any change in her expression, her hand was already moving over his body.

'Mrs Ramirez,' he said. 'I'm worried that perhaps your daughters will get up and raise a hullabaloo. You know, start whining for you, or something like that. Your place is probably in there.'

'What?' she asked him. He had pulled away from her to the other side of the bed.

'I say I think you ought to go into your room now the morning's here.'

'Yes, my darling, I will go to my room. You are right.' She sidled over to him and put her arms around him.

'I will see you later in the dining-room, and look at you and look at you, because I love you so much.'

'Don't be crazy,' he said. 'You don't want anything to show in your face. You don't want people to guess about this. We must be cold with one another.'

She put her hand over her heart.

'Ay!' she said. 'This cannot be.'

'Oh, Mrs Ramirez. Please be sensible. Look, you go to your room and we'll talk about this in the morning . . . or, at least, later in the morning.'

'Cold I cannot be.' To illustrate this, she looked deep into his eyes.

'I know, I know,' he said. 'You're a very passionate woman. But my God! Here we are in a crazy Spanish country.'

He jumped from the bed and she followed him. After she had put on her shoes, he took her to the door.

'Good-bye,' he said.

She couched her cheek on her two hands and looked up at him. He shut the door.

She was too happy to go right to bed, and so she went over to the bureau and took from it a little stale sugar Virgin which she broke into three pieces. She went over to Consuelo and shook her very hard. Consuelo opened her eyes, and after some time asked her mother crossly what she wanted. Señora Ramirez stuffed the candy into her daughter's mouth.

'Eat it, darling,' she said. 'It's the little Virgin from the bureau.'

'Ay, Mama!' Consuelo sighed. 'Who knows what you will do next? It is already light out and you are still in your clothes. I am sure there is no other mother who is still in her clothes now, in the whole world. Please don't make me eat any more of the Virgin now. Tomorrow I will eat some more. But it is tomorrow, isn't it? What a mix-up. I don't like it.' She shut her eyes and tried to sleep. There was a look of deep disgust on her face. Her mother's spell was a little frightening this time.

Señora Ramirez now went over to Lilina's bed and awakened her. Lilina opened her eyes wide and immediately looked very tense, because she thought she was going to be scolded about the corset and also about having gone out alone after dark.

'Here, little one,' said her mother. 'Eat some of the Virgin.'

Lilina was delighted. She ate the stale sugar candy and patted her stomach to show how pleased she was. The snake was asleep in a box near her bed.

'Now tell me,' said her mother. 'What did you do today?' She had completely forgotten about the corset. Lilina was beside herself with joy. She ran her fingers along her mother's lips and then pushed them into her mouth. Señora Ramirez snapped at the fingers like a dog. Then she laughed uproariously.

'Mama, please be quiet,' pleaded Consuelo. 'I want to go to sleep.'

'Yes, darling. Everything will be quiet so that you can sleep peacefully.'

'I bought a snake, Mama,' said Lilina.

'Good!' exclaimed Señora Ramirez. And after musing a little while with her daughter's hand in hers, she went to bed.

In her room Señora Ramirez was dressing and talking to her children.

'I want you to put on your *fiesta* dresses,' she said, 'because I am going to ask the traveller to have lunch with us.'

Consuelo was in love with the traveller by now and very jealous of Señorita Córdoba, who she had decided was his sweetheart. 'I daresay he has already asked Señorita Córdoba to lunch,' she said. 'They have been talking together near the fountain almost since dawn.'

'*Santa Catarina!*' cried her mother angrily. 'You have the eyes of a madman who sees flowers where there are only cow turds.' She covered her face heavily with a powder that was distinctly violet in tint, and pulled a green chiffon scarf around her shoulders, pinning it together with a brooch in the form of a golf club. Then she and the girls, who were dressed in pink satin, went out into the *patio* and sat together just a little out of the sun. The parrot was swinging back and forth on his perch and singing. Señora Ramirez sang along with him; her own voice was a little lower than the parrot's.

> '*Pastores, pastores, vamos a Belen*
> *A ver a Maria y al niño tambien.*'

She conducted the parrot with her hand. The old Señora, mother of Señora Espinoza, was walking round and round the *patio*. She stopped for a moment and played with Señora Ramirez's seashell bracelet.

'Do you want some candy?' she asked Señora Ramirez.

'I can't. My stomach is very bad.'

'Do you want some candy?' she repeated. Señora Ramirez smiled and looked up at the sky. The old lady patted her cheek.

'Beautiful,' she said. 'You are beautiful.'

'Mama!' screamed Señora Espinoza, running out of her room. 'Come to bed!'

The old lady clung to the rungs of Señora Ramirez's chair like a tough bird, and her daughter was obliged to pry her hands open before she was able to get her away.

'I'm sorry, Señora Ramirez,' she said. 'But when you get old, you know how it is.'

'Pretty bad,' said Señora Ramirez. She was looking at the traveller and Señorita Córdoba. They had their backs turned to her.

'Lilina,' she said. 'Go and ask him to have lunch with us . . . go. No, I will write it down. Get me a pen and paper.'

'Dear,' she wrote, when Lilina returned. 'Will you come to have lunch at my table this afternoon? The girls will be with me, too. All the three of us send you our deep affection. I tell Consuelo to tell the maid to move the plates all to the same table. Very truly yours, Sophia Piega de Ramirez.'

The traveller read the note, acquiesced, and shortly they were all seated together at the dining-room table.

'Now this is really stranger than fiction,' he said to himself. 'Here I am sitting with these people at their table and feeling as though I had been here all my life, and the truth of the matter is that I have only been in this pension about fourteen or fifteen hours altogether – not even one day. Yesterday I felt that I was on a Zulu island, I was so depressed. The human animal is the funniest animal of them all.'

Señora Ramirez had arranged to sit close beside the stranger, and she pressed her thigh to his all during the time that she was eating her soup. The traveller's appetite was not very good. He was excited and felt like talking.

After lunch Señora Ramirez decided to go for a walk instead of taking a *siesta* with her daughters. She put on her gloves and took with her an umbrella to shield her from the sun. After she had walked a little while she came to a long road, completely desolate save for a few ruins and some beautiful tall trees along the way. She looked about her and shook her head at the thought of the terrible earthquake that had thrown to the ground this city, reputed to have been once the most beautiful city in all the Western hemisphere. She could see ahead of her, way at the road's end, the volcano named Fire. She crossed herself and bit her lips. She had come walking with the intention of dreaming of her lover, but the thought of this volcano which had erupted many centuries ago chased all dreams of love from her mind. She saw in her mind the walls of the houses caving in, and the roofs falling on the heads of the babies . . . and the mothers, their skirts covered with mud, running through the streets in despair.

'The innocents,' she said to herself. 'I am sure that God had a perfect reason for this, but what could it have been? *Santa Maria*, but what could it have been! If such a disorder should happen again on this earth, I would turn completely to jelly like a helpless idiot.'

She looked again at the volcano ahead of her, and although nothing had changed, to her it seemed that a cloud had passed across the face of the sun.

'You are crazy', she went on, 'to think that an earthquake will again shake this city to the earth. You will not be going through such a trial as these other mothers went through because everything now is different. God doesn't send such big trials any more, like floods over the whole world, and plagues.'

She thanked her stars that she was living now and not before. It made her feel quite weak to think of the women who had been forced to live before she was born. The future too, she had heard, was to be very stormy because of wars.

'Ay!' she said to herself. 'Precipices on all sides of me!' It had not been such a good idea to take a walk, after all. She thought again of the traveller, shutting her eyes for a moment.

'*Mi amante! Amante querido!*' she whispered; and she remembered the little books with their covers lettered in gold, books about love, which she had read when she was a young girl, and without the burden of a family. These little books had made the ability to read seem like the most worthwhile and delightful talent to her. They had never, of course, touched on the coarser aspects of love, but in later years she did not find it strange that it was for such physical ends that the heroes and heroines had been pining. Never had she found any difficulty in associating nosegays and couplets with the more gross manifestations of love.

She turned off into another road in order to avoid facing the volcano, constantly ahead of her. She thought of the traveller without really thinking of him at all. Her eyes glowed with the pleasure of being in love and she decided that she had been very stupid to think of an earthquake on the very day that God was making a bed of roses for her.

'Thank you, thank you,' she whispered to Him, 'from the bottom of my heart. Ah!' She smoothed her dress over her bosom. She was suddenly very pleased with everything. Ahead she noticed that there was a very long convent, somewhat ruined, in front of which some boys were playing. There was also a little pavilion standing not far away. It was difficult to understand why it was so situated, where there was no formal park, nor any trees or grass – just some dirt and a few bushes. It had the strange static look of a ship that has been grounded. Señora Ramirez looked at it distastefully; it was a small kiosk anyway and badly in need of a coat of paint. But feeling tired, she was soon climbing up the flimsy steps, red in the face with fear lest she fall through to the ground. Inside the kiosk she spread a newspaper over the bench and sat down. Soon all her dreams of her lover faded from her mind, and she felt hot and fretful. She moved her feet around on the floor impatiently at the thought of having to walk all the way home. The dust rose up into the air and she was obliged to cover her mouth with her handkerchief.

'I wish to Heaven', she said to herself, 'that he would come and carry me out of this kiosk.' She sat idly watching the boys playing in the dirt in front of the convent. One of them was a good deal taller than the others. As she watched their games, her head slumped forward and she fell asleep.

No tourists came, so the smaller boys decided to go over to the main square and meet the buses, to sell their lollipops and picture postcards. The oldest boy announced that he would stay behind.

'You're crazy,' they said to him. 'Completely crazy.'

He looked at them haughtily and did not answer. They ran down the road, screaming that they were going to earn a thousand *quetzales*.

He had remained behind because for some time he had noticed that there was someone in the kiosk. He knew even from where he stood that it was a woman because he could see that her dress was brightly coloured like a flower garden. She had been sitting there for a long time and he wondered if she were not dead.

'If she is dead,' he thought, 'I will carry her body all the way into town.' The idea excited him and he approached the pavilion with bated breath. He went inside and stood over Señora Ramirez, but when he saw that she was quite old and fat and obviously the mother of a good rich family he was frightened and all his imagination failed him. He thought he would go away, but then he decided differently, and he shook her foot. There was no change. Her mouth which had been open, remained so, and she went on sleeping. The boy took a good piece of the flesh on her upper arm between his thumb and forefinger and twisted it very hard. She awakened with a shudder and looked up at the boy perplexed.

His eyes were soft.

'I awakened you', he said, 'because I have to go home to my house, and you are not safe here. Before, there was a man here in the bandstand trying to look under your skirt. When you are asleep, you know, people just go wild. There were some drunks here too, singing an obscene song, standing on the ground, right under you. You would have had red ears if you had heard it. I can tell you that.' He shrugged his shoulders and spat on the floor. He looked completely disgusted.

'What is the matter?' Señora Ramirez asked him.

'Bah! This city makes me sick. I want to be a carpenter in the capital, but I can't. My mother gets lonesome. All my brothers and sisters are dead.'

'Ay!' said Señora Ramirez. 'How sad for you! I have a beautiful house in the capital. Maybe my husband would let you be a carpenter there, if you did not have to stay with your mother.'

The boy's eyes were shining.

'I'm coming back with you,' he said. 'My uncle is with my mother.'

'Yes,' said Señora Ramirez. 'Maybe it will happen.'

'My sweetheart is there in the city,' he continued. 'She was living here before.'

Señora Ramirez took the boy's long hand in her own. The word sweetheart had recalled many things to her.

'Sit down, sit down,' she said to him. 'Sit down here beside me. I too have a sweetheart. He's in his room now.'

'Where does he work?'

'In the United States.'

'What luck for you! My sweetheart wouldn't love him better than she loves me, though. She wants me or simply death. She says so any time I ask her. She would tell the same thing to you if you asked her about me. It's the truth.'

Señora Ramirez pulled him down onto the bench next to her. He was confused and looked out over his shoulder at the road. She tickled the back of his hand and smiled up at him in a coquettish manner. The boy looked at her and his face seemed to weaken.

'You have blue eyes,' he said.

Señora Ramirez could not wait another minute. She took his head in her two hands and kissed him several times full on the mouth.

'Oh, God!' she said. The boy was delighted with her fine

clothes, her blue eyes and her womanly ways. He took Señora Ramirez in his arms with real tenderness.

'I love you,' he said. Tears filled his eyes and because he was so full of a feeling of gratitude and kindness, he added: 'I love my sweetheart and I love you too.'

He helped her down the steps of the kiosk, and with his arm around her waist he led her to a sequestered spot belonging to the convent grounds.

The traveller was lying on his bed, consumed by a feeling of guilt. He had again spent the night with Señora Ramirez, and he was wondering whether or not his mother would read this in his eyes when he returned. He had never done anything like this before. His behaviour until now had never been without precedent, and he felt like a two-headed monster, as though he had somehow slipped from the real world into the other world, the world that he had always imagined as a little boy to be inhabited by assassins and orphans, and children whose mothers went to work. He put his head in his hands and wondered if he could ever forget Señora Ramirez. He remembered having read that the careers of many men had been ruined by women who because they had a certain physical stranglehold over them made it impossible for them to get away. These women, he knew, were always bad, and they were never Americans. Nor, he was certain, did they resemble Señora Ramirez. It was terrible to have done something he was certain none of his friends had ever done before him, nor would do after him. This experience, he knew, would have to remain a secret, and nothing made him feel more ill than having a secret. He liked to imagine that he and the group of men whom he considered to be his friends, discoursed freely on all things that were in their hearts and in their souls. He was beginning to talk to women in this free way, too – he talked to them a good deal, and he urged his friends to do likewise. He realized that he and Señora Ramirez never spoke, and this horrified him. He shuddered and said to himself: 'We are like two gorillas.'

He had been, it is true, with one or two prostitutes, but he had never taken them to his own bed, nor had he stayed with them longer than an hour. Also, they had been curly-headed blonde American girls recommended to him by his friends.

'Well,' he told himself, 'there is no use making myself into a nervous wreck. What is done is done, and anyway, I think I might be excused on the grounds that: one, I am in a foreign country which has sort of put me off my balance; two, I have been eating strange foods that I am not used to, and living at an unusually high altitude for me; and, three, I haven't had my own kind to talk to for three solid weeks.'

He felt quite a good deal happier after having enumerated these extenuating conditions, and he added: 'When I get onto my boat I shall wave goodbye to the dock, and say good riddance to bad rubbish, and if the boss ever tries to send me out of the country, I'll tell him: "Not for a million dollars!"' He wished that it were possible to change pensions, but he had already paid for the remainder of the week. He was very thrifty, as, indeed, it was necessary for him to be. Now he lay down again on his bed, quite satisfied with himself but soon he began to feel guilty again, and like an old truck horse, laboriously he went once more through the entire process of reassuring himself.

Lilina had put Victoria into a box and was walking in the town with her. Not far from the central square there was a dry-goods shop owned by a Jewish woman. Lilina had been there several times with her mother to buy wool. She knew the son of the proprietress, with whom she often stopped to talk. He was very quiet, but Lilina liked him. She decided to drop in at the shop now with Victoria.

When she arrived, the boy's mother was behind the counter stamping some old bolts of material with purple ink. She saw Lilina and smiled brightly.

'Enrique is in the *patio*. How nice of you to come and see him. Why don't you come more often?' She was very eager to please Lilina, because she knew the extent of Señora Ramirez's wealth and was proud to have her as a customer.

Lilina went over to the little door that led into the *patio* behind the shop, and opened it. Enrique was crouching in the dirt beside the washtubs. She was surprised to see that his head was wrapped in bandages. From a distance the dirty bandages gave the effect of a white turban.

She went a little nearer, and saw that he was arranging some marbles in a row.

'Good morning, Enrique,' she said to him.

Enrique recognized her voice, and without turning his head, he started slowly to pick up the marbles one at a time and put them into his pocket.

His mother had followed Lilina into the *patio*. When she saw that Enrique, instead of rising to his feet and greeting Lilina, remained absorbed in his marbles, she walked over to him and gave his arm a sharp twist.

'Leave those damned marbles alone and speak to Lilina,' she said to him. Enrique got up and went over to Lilina, while his mother, bending over with difficulty, finished picking up the marbles he had left behind on the ground.

Lilina looked at the big, dark red stain on Enrique's bandage. They both walked back into the store. Enrique did not enjoy being with Lilina. In fact, he was a little afraid of her. Whenever she came to the shop he could hardly wait for her to leave.

He went over now to a bolt of printed material which he started to unwind. When he had unwound a few yards, he began to follow the convolutions of the pattern with his index finger. Lilina, not realizing that his gesture was a carefully disguised insult to her, watched him with a certain amount of interest.

'I have something with me inside this box,' she said after a while.

Enrique, hearing his mother's footsteps approaching, turned and smiled at her sadly.

'Please show it to me,' he said.

She lifted the lid from the snake's box and took it over to Enrique.

'This is Victoria,' she said.

Enrique thought she was beautiful. He lifted her from her box and held her just below the head very firmly. Then he raised his arm until the snake's eyes were on a level with his own.

'Good morning, Victoria,' he said to her. 'Do you like it here in the store?'

This remark annoyed his mother. She had slipped down to the other end of the counter because she was terrified of the snake.

'You speak as though you were drunk,' she said to Enrique. 'That snake can't understand a word you're saying.'

'She's really beautiful,' said Enrique.

'Let's put her back in the box and take her to the square,' said Lilina. But Enrique did not hear her, he was so enchanted with the sensation of holding Victoria.

His mother again spoke up. 'Do you hear Lilina talking to you?' she shouted. 'Or is that bandage covering your ears as well as your head?'

She had meant this remark to be stinging and witty, but she realized herself that there had been no point to it.

'Well, go with the little girl,' she added.

Lilina and Enrique set off toward the square together. Lilina had put Victoria back into her box.

'Why are we going to the square?' Enrique asked Lilina.

'Because we are going there with Victoria.'

Six or seven buses had converged in one of the streets that skirted the square. They had come from the capital and from other smaller cities in the region. The passengers who were not going any farther had already got out and were standing in a bunch talking together and buying food from the vendors. One lady had brought with her a cardboard fan intended as an advertisement for beer. She was fanning not only herself, but anyone who happened to come near her.

The bus drivers were racing their motors, and some were trying to move into positions more advantageous for departing. Lilina was excited by the noise and the crowd. Enrique, however, had sought a quiet spot, and was now standing underneath a tree. After a while she ran over to him and told him that she was going to let Victoria out of her box.

'Then we'll see what happens,' she said.

'No, no!' insisted Enrique. 'She'll only crawl under the buses and be squashed to death. Snakes live in the woods or in the rocks.'

Lilina paid little attention to him. Soon she was crouching on the edge of the kerbstone, busily unfastening the string around Victoria's box.

Enrique's head had begun to pain him and he felt a little ill. He wondered if he could leave the square, but he decided he did not have the courage. Although the wind had risen, the sun was very hot, and the tree afforded him little shade. He watched Lilina for a little while, but soon he looked away from her, and began to think instead about his own death. He was certain that his head hurt more today than usual. This caused him to sink into the blackest gloom, as he did whenever he remembered the day he had fallen and pierced his skull on a rusty nail. His life had always been precious to him, as far back as he could recall, and it seemed perhaps even more so now that he realized it could be violently interrupted. He disliked Lilina; probably because he suspected intuitively that she was a person who could fall over and over again into the same pile of broken glass and scream just as loudly the last time as the first.

By now Victoria had wriggled under the buses and been crushed flat. The buses cleared away, and Enrique was able to see what had happened. Only the snake's head, which had been severed from its body, remained intact.

Enrique came up and stood beside Lilina. 'Now are you going home?' he asked her, biting his lip.

'Look how small her head is. She must have been a very small snake,' said Lilina.

'Are you going home to your house?' he asked her again.

'No. I'm going over by the cathedral and play on the swings. Do you want to come? I'm going to run there.'

'I can't run,' said Enrique, touching his fingers to the bandages. 'And I'm not sure that I want to go over to the playground.'

'Well,' said Lilina. 'I'll run ahead of you and I'll be there if you decide to come.'

Enrique was very tired and a little dizzy, but he decided to follow her to the playground in order to ask her why she had allowed Victoria to escape under the buses.

When he arrived, Lilina was already swinging back and forth.

He sat on a bench near the swings and looked up at her. Each time her feet grazed the ground, he tried to ask her about Victoria, but the question stuck in his throat. At last he stood up, thrust his hands into his pockets, and shouted at her.

'Are you going to get another snake?' he asked. It was not what he had intended to say. Lilina did not answer, but she did stare at him from the swing. It was impossible for him to tell whether or not she had heard his question.

At last she dug her heel into the ground and brought the swing to a standstill. 'I must go home,' she said, 'or my mother will be angry with me.'

'No,' said Enrique, catching hold of her dress. 'Come with me and let me buy you an ice.'

'I will,' said Lilina. 'I love them.'

They sat together in a little store, and Enrique bought two ices.

'I'd like to have a swing hanging from the roof of my house,' said Lilina. 'And I'd have my dinner and my breakfast served while I was swinging.' This idea amused her and she began to laugh so hard that her ice ran out of her mouth and over her chin.

'Breakfast, lunch and dinner and take a bath in the swing,' she continued. 'And make *pipi* on Consuelo's head from the swing.'

Enrique was growing more and more nervous because it was getting late, and still they were not talking about Victoria.

'Could I swing with you in your house?' he asked Lilina.

'Yes. We'll have two swings and you can make *pipi* on Consuelo's head, too.'

'I'd love to,' he said.

His question seemed more and more difficult to present. By now it seemed to him that it resembled more a declaration of love than a simple question.

Finally he tried again. 'Are you going to buy another snake?' But he still could not ask her why she had been so careless.

'No,' said Lilina. 'I'm going to buy a rabbit.'

'A rabbit?' he said. 'But rabbits aren't as intelligent or as beautiful as snakes. You had better buy another snake like Victoria.'

'Rabbits have lots of children,' said Lilina. 'Why don't we buy a rabbit together?'

Enrique thought about this for a while. He began to feel almost lighthearted, and even a little wicked.

'All right,' he said. 'Let's buy two rabbits, a man and a woman.' They finished their ices and talked together more and more excitedly about the rabbits.

On the way home, Lilina squeezed Enrique's hand and kissed him all over his cheeks. He was red with pleasure.

At the square they parted, after promising to meet again that afternoon.

It was a cloudy day, rather colder than usual, and Señora Ramirez decided to dress in her mourning clothes, which she always carried with her. She hung several strands of black beads around her neck and powdered her face heavily. She and Consuelo began to walk slowly around the *patio*.

Consuelo blew her nose. 'Ay, Mama,' she said. 'Isn't it true that there is a greater amount of sadness in the world than happiness?'

'I don't know why you are thinking about this,' said her mother.

'Because I have been counting my happy days and my sad days. There are many more sad days, and I am living now at the best age for a girl. There is nothing but fighting, even at balls. I would not believe any man if he told me he liked dancing better than fighting.'

'This is true,' said her mother. 'But not all men are really like this. There are some men who are as gentle as little lambs. But not so many.'

'I feel like an old lady. I think that maybe I will feel better when I'm married.' They walked slowly past the traveller's door.

'I'm going inside,' said Consuelo suddenly.

'Aren't you going to sit in the *patio*?' her mother asked her.

'No, with all those children screaming and the chickens and the parrot talking and the white dog. And it's such a terrible day. Why?'

Señora Ramirez could not think of any reason why Consuelo

should stay in the *patio*. In any case she preferred to be there alone if the stranger should decide to talk to her.

'What white dog?' she said.

'Señora Espinoza has bought a little white dog for the children.'

The wind was blowing and the children were chasing each other around the back *patio*. Señora Ramirez sat down on one of the little straight-backed chairs with her hands folded in her lap. The thought came into her mind that most days were likely to be cold and windy rather than otherwise, and that there would be many days to come exactly like this one. Unconsciously she had always felt that these were the days preferred by God, although they had never been much to her own liking.

The traveller was packing with the vivacity of one who is in the habit of making little excursions away from the charmed fold to return almost immediately.

'Wow!' he said joyfully to himself. 'I sure have been giddy in this place, but the bad dream is over now.' It was nearly bus time. He carried his bags out to the *patio*, and was confused to find Señora Ramirez sitting there. He prompted himself to be pleasant.

'Señora,' he said, walking over to her. 'It's good-bye now till we meet again.'

'What do you say?' she asked.

'I'm taking the twelve o'clock bus. I'm going home.'

'Ah! You must be very happy to go home.' She did not think of looking away from his face. 'Do you take a boat?' she asked, staring harder.

'Yes. Five days on the boat.'

'How wonderful that must be. Or maybe it makes you sick.' She put her hand over her stomach.

'I have never been seasick in my life.'

She said nothing to this.

He backed against the parrot swinging on its perch, and stepped forward again quickly as it leaned to bite him.

'Is there anyone you would like me to look up in the United States?'

'No. You will be coming back in not such a long time?'

'No, I don't think I will come back here again. Well . . .' He put out his hand and she stood up. She was fairly impressive in her black clothes. He looked at the beads that covered her chest.

'Well, good-bye, Señora. I was very happy to have met you.'

'*Adios*, Señor, and may God protect you on your trip. You will be coming back maybe. You don't know.'

He shook his head and walked over to the Indian boy standing by his luggage. They went out into the street and the heavy door closed with a bang. Señora Ramirez looked around the *patio*. She saw Señorita Córdoba move away from the half-open bedroom door where she had been standing.

THE YOUNG GIRL

Katherine Mansfield

IN HER BLUE dress, with her cheeks lightly flushed, her blue, blue eyes, and her gold curls pinned up as though for the first time – pinned up to be out of the way for her flight – Mrs Raddick's daughter might have just dropped from this radiant heaven. Mrs Raddick's timid, faintly astonished, but deeply admiring glance looked as if she believed it, too; but the daughter didn't appear any too pleased – why should she? – to have alighted on the steps of the Casino. Indeed, she was bored – bored as though Heaven had been full of casinos with snuffy old saints for *croupiers* and crowns to play with.

'You don't mind taking Hennie?' said Mrs Raddick. 'Sure you don't? There's the car, and you'll have tea and we'll be back here on this step – right here – in an hour. You see, I want her to go in. She's not been before, and it's worth seeing. I feel it wouldn't be fair to her.'

'Oh, shut up, mother,' said she wearily. 'Come along. Don't talk so much. And your bag's open; you'll be losing all your money again.'

'I'm sorry, darling,' said Mrs Raddick.

'Oh, *do* come in! I want to make money,' said the impatient voice. 'It's all jolly well for you – but I'm broke!'

'Here – take fifty francs, darling, take a hundred!' I saw Mrs Raddick pressing notes into her hand as they passed through the swing doors.

Hennie and I stood on the steps a minute, watching the people. He had a very broad, delighted smile.

'I say,' he cried, 'there's an English bulldog. Are they allowed to take dogs in there?'

'No, they're not.'

'He's a ripping chap, isn't he? I wish I had one. They're such fun. They frighten people so, and they're never fierce with their – the people they belong to.' Suddenly he squeezed my arm. 'I say, *do* look at that old woman. Who is she? Why does she look like that? Is she a gambler?'

The ancient, withered creature, wearing a green satin dress, a black velvet cloak and a white hat with purple feathers, jerked slowly, slowly up the steps as though she were being drawn up on wires. She stared in front of her, she was laughing and nodding and cackling to herself; her claws clutched round what looked like a dirty boot-bag.

But just at that moment there was Mrs Raddick again with – *her* – and another lady hovering in the background. Mrs Raddick rushed at me. She was brightly flushed, gay, a different creature. She was like a woman who is saying 'goodbye' to her friends on the station platform, with not a minute to spare before the train starts.

'Oh, you're here, still. Isn't that lucky! You've not gone. Isn't that fine! I've had the most dreadful time with – her,' and she waved to her daughter, who stood absolutely still, disdainful, looking down, twiddling her foot on the step, miles away. 'They won't let her in. I swore she was twenty-one. But they won't believe me. I showed the man my purse; I didn't dare to do more. But it was no use. He simply scoffed . . . And now I've just met Mrs MacEwen from New York, and she just won thirteen thousand in the *Salle Privée* – and she wants me to go back with her while the luck lasts. Of course I can't leave – her. But if you'd –'

At that 'she' looked up; she simply withered her mother. 'Why can't you leave me?' she said furiously. 'What utter rot! How dare you make a scene like this? This is the last time I'll come out with you. You really are too awful for words.' She looked her mother up and down. 'Calm yourself,' she said superbly.

Mrs Raddick was desperate, just desperate. She was 'wild' to go back with Mrs MacEwen, but at the same time . . .

I seized my courage. 'Would you – do you care to come to tea with – us?'

'Yes, yes, she'll be delighted. That's just what I wanted, isn't it darling? Mrs MacEwen . . . I'll be back here in an hour . . . or less . . . I'll –'

Mrs R. dashed up the steps. I saw her bag was open again.

So we three were left. But really it wasn't my fault. Hennie looked crushed to the earth, too. When the car was there she wrapped her dark coat round her – to escape contamination. Even her little feet looked as though they scorned to carry her down the steps to us.

'I am so awfully sorry,' I murmured as the car started.

'Oh, I don't *mind*,' said she. 'I don't *want* to look twenty-one. Who would – if they were seventeen! It's' – and she gave a faint shudder – 'the stupidity I loathe, and being stared at by fat old men. Beasts!'

Hennie gave her a quick look and then peered out of the window.

We drew up before an immense palace of pink-and-white marble with orange-trees outside the doors in gold-and-black tubs.

'Would you care to go in?' I suggested.

She hesitated, glanced, bit her lip, and resigned herself. 'Oh well, there seems nowhere else,' said she. 'Get out, Hennie.'

I went first – to find the table, of course – she followed. But the worst of it was having her little brother, who was only twelve, with us. That was the last, final straw – having that child, trailing at her heels.

There was one table. It had pink carnations and pink plates with little blue tea-napkins for sails.

'Shall we sit here?'

She put her hand wearily on the back of a white wicker chair.

'We may as well. Why not?' said she.

Hennie squeezed past her and wriggled on to a stool at the end. He felt awfully out of it. She didn't even take her gloves off. She lowered her eyes and drummed on the table. When a faint violin sounded she winced and bit her lip again. Silence.

The waitress appeared. I hardly dared to ask her. 'Tea – coffee? China tea – or iced tea with lemon?'

Really she didn't mind. It was all the same to her. She didn't really want anything. Hennie whispered, 'Chocolate!'

But just as the waitress turned away she cried out carelessly, 'Oh, you may as well bring me a chocolate, too.'

While we waited she took out a little, gold powder-box with a mirror in the lid, shook the poor little puff as though she loathed it, and dabbed her lovely nose.

'Hennie,' she said, 'take those flowers away.' She pointed with her puff to the carnations, and I heard her murmur, 'I can't bear flowers on a table.' They had evidently been giving her intense pain, for she positively closed her eyes as I moved them away.

The waitress came back with the chocolate and the tea. She put the big, frothing cups before them and pushed across my clear glass. Hennie buried his nose, emerged, with, for one dreadful moment, a little trembling blob of cream on the tip. But he hastily wiped it off like a little gentleman. I wondered if I should dare draw her attention to her cup. She didn't notice it – didn't see it – until suddenly, quite by chance, she took a sip. I watched anxiously; she faintly shuddered.

'Dreadfully sweet!' said she.

A tiny boy with a head like a raisin and a chocolate body came round with a tray of pastries – row upon row of little freaks, little inspirations, little melting dreams. He offered them to her. 'Oh, I'm not at all hungry. Take them away.'

He offered them to Hennie. Hennie gave me a swift look – it must have been satisfactory – for he took a chocolate cream, a coffee éclair, a meringue stuffed with chestnut and a tiny horn filled with fresh strawberries. She could hardly bear to watch him. But just as the boy swerved away she held up her plate.

'Oh well, give me *one*,' said she.

The silver tongs dropped one, two, three – and a cherry tartlet. 'I don't know why you're giving me all these,' she said, and nearly smiled. 'I shan't eat them; I couldn't!'

I felt much more comfortable. I sipped my tea, leaned back, and even asked if I might smoke. At that she paused, the fork in her hand, opened her eyes and really did smile. 'Of course,' said she. 'I always expect people to.'

But at that moment a tragedy happened to Hennie. He speared

his pastry horn too hard, and it flew in two, and one half spilled on the table. Ghastly affair! He turned crimson. Even his ears flared, and one ashamed hand crept across the table to take what was left of the body away.

'You *utter* little beast!' said she.

Good heavens! I had to fly to the rescue. I cried hastily, 'Will you be abroad long?'

But she had already forgotten Hennie. I was forgotten, too. She was trying to remember something . . . She was miles away.

'I – don't – know,' she said slowly, from that far place.

'I suppose you prefer it to London. It's more – more –'

When I didn't go on she came back and looked at me, very puzzled. 'More – ?'

'*Enfin* – gayer,' I cried, waving my cigarette.

But that took a whole cake to consider. Even then, 'Oh well, that depends!' was all she could safely say.

Hennie had finished. He was still very warm.

I seized the butterfly list off the table. 'I say – what about an ice, Hennie? What about tangerine and ginger? No, something cooler. What about a fresh pineapple cream?'

Hennie strongly approved. The waitress had her eye on us. The order was taken when she looked up from her crumbs.

'Did you say tangerine and ginger? I like ginger. You can bring me one.' And then quickly, 'I wish that orchestra wouldn't play things from the year One. We were dancing to that all last Christmas. It's too sickening!'

But it was a charming air. Now that I noticed it, it warmed me.

'I think this is rather a nice place, don't you, Hennie?' I said.

Hennie said: 'Ripping!' He meant to say it very low, but it came out very high in a kind of squeak.

Nice? This place? Nice? For the first time she stared about her, trying to see what there was . . . She blinked; her lovely eyes wondered. A very good-looking elderly man stared back at her through a monocle on a black ribbon. But him she simply couldn't see. There was a hole in the air where he was. She looked through and through him.

Finally the little flat spoons lay still on the glass plates. Hennie looked rather exhausted, but she pulled on her white gloves again. She had some trouble with her diamond wrist-watch; it got in her way. She tugged at it – tried to break the stupid little thing – it wouldn't break. Finally, she had to drag her glove over. I saw, after that, she couldn't stand this place a moment longer, and, indeed, she jumped up and turned away while I went through the vulgar act of paying for the tea.

And then we were outside again. It had grown dusky. The sky was sprinkled with small stars; the big lamps glowed. While we waited for the car to come up she stood on the step, just as before, twiddling her foot, looking down.

Hennie bounded forward to open the door and she got in and sank back with – oh – such a sigh!

'Tell him,' she gasped, 'to drive as fast as he can.'

Hennie grinned at his friend the chauffeur. '*Allie veet!*' said he. Then he composed himself and sat on the small seat facing us.

The gold powder-box came out again. Again the poor little puff was shaken; again there was that swift, deadly-secret glance between her and the mirror.

We tore through the black-and-gold town like a pair of scissors tearing through brocade. Hennie had great difficulty not to look as though he were hanging on to something.

And when we reached the Casino, of course Mrs Raddick wasn't there. There wasn't a sign of her on the steps – not a sign.

'Will you stay in the car while I go and look?'

But no – she wouldn't do that. Good heavens, no! Hennie could stay. She couldn't bear sitting in a car. She'd wait on the steps.

'But I scarcely like to leave you,' I murmured. 'I'd very much rather not leave you here.'

At that she threw back her coat; she turned and faced me; her lips parted. 'Good heavens – why! I – I don't mind it a bit. I – I like waiting.' And suddenly her cheeks crimsoned, her eyes grew dark – for a moment I thought she was going to cry. 'L – let me, please,' she stammered, in a warm, eager voice. 'I like it. I love waiting! Really – really I do! I'm always waiting – in all kinds of places . . .'

Her dark coat fell open, and her white throat – all her soft young body in the blue dress – was like a flower that is just emerging from its dark bud.

THREE FEMINIST FABLES

Suniti Namjoshi

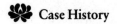 Case History

AFTER the event Little R. traumatized. Wolf not slain. Forester is wolf. How else was he there exactly on time? Explains this to mother. Mother not happy. Thinks that the forester is extremely nice. Grandmother dead. Wolf not dead. Wolf marries mother. R. not happy. R. is a kid. Mother thinks wolf is extremely nice. Please to see shrink. Shrink will make it clear that wolves on the whole are extremely nice. R. gets it straight. Okay to be wolf. Mama is a wolf. She is a wolf. Shrink is a wolf. Mama and shrink, and forester also, extremely uptight.

A Room of His Own

THE fifth time around things were different. He gave her instructions, he gave her the keys (including the little one) and rode off alone. Exactly four weeks later he reappeared. The house was dusted, the floors were polished and the door to the little room hadn't been opened. Bluebeard was stunned.

'But weren't you curious?' he asked his wife.

'No,' she answered.

'But didn't you want to find out my innermost secrets?'

'Why?' said the woman.

'Well,' said Bluebeard, 'it's only natural. But didn't you want to want to know who I really am?'

'You are Bluebeard and my husband.'

'But the contents of the room. Didn't you want to see what is inside that room?'

'No,' said the creature, 'I think you're entitled to a room of your own.'

This so incensed him that he killed her on the spot. At the trial he pleaded provocation.

 Legend

ONCE upon a time there was a she-monster. She lived submerged 20,000 feet under the sea, and was only a legend, until one day the scientists got together to fish her out. They hauled her ashore and loaded her on trucks and finally set her down in a vast amphitheatre where they began their dissection. It soon became evident that the creature was pregnant. They alerted security and sealed all the doors, being responsible men and unwilling to take chances with the monster's whelps, for who could know what damage they might do if unleashed on the world. But the she-monster died with her litter of monsters buried inside her. They opened the doors. The flesh of the monster was beginning to smell. Several scientists succumbed to the fumes. They did not give up. They worked in relays and issued gas masks. At last the bones of the creature were scraped quite clean, and they had before them a shining skeleton. The skeleton may be seen at the National Museum. It bears the legend: 'The Dreaded She-Monster. The fumes of this creature are noxious to men.'

Inscribed underneath are the names of the scientists who gave their lives to find this out.

THE RAINY MOON
Colette

'Oh, I can manage that,' the withered young girl told me. 'Yes certainly, I can bring you each set of pages as I type them as you'd rather not trust them to the post.'

'Can you? That would be kind of you. You needn't trouble to come and collect my manuscript, I'll bring it to you in batches as I go along. I go out for a walk every morning.'

'It's so good for the health,' said Mademoiselle Barberet.

She gave a superficial smile and pulled one of the two little sausages of gold hair, threaded with white, that she wore tied on the nape with a black ribbon bow, forward again into its proper place, over her right shoulder, just below the ear. This odd way of doing her hair did not prevent Mademoiselle Barberet from being perfectly correct and pleasant to look at from her pale blue eyes to her slender feet, from her delicate, prematurely aged mouth to her frail hands whose small bones were visible under the transparent skin. Her freshly ironed linen collar and her plain black dress called for the accessories of a pair of those glazed cotton over-sleeves that were once the badge of writers. But typists, who do not write, do not wear their sleeves out below the elbows.

'You're temporarily without your secretary, Madame?'

'No. The girl who used to type my manuscripts has just got married. But I don't possess a secretary. I shouldn't know what to do with a secretary, you see. I write everything by hand. And, besides, my flat is small, I should hear the noise of the typewriter.'

'Oh! I do understand, I do understand,' said Mademoiselle Barberet. 'There's a gentleman I work for who only writes on the right-hand half of the pages. For a little while, I took over the typing for Monsieur Henri Duvernois who would never have anything but pale yellow paper.'

She gave a knowing smile that lumped together and excused all the manias of scribblers and, producing a file – I noticed she matched the cardboard to the blue of my paper – she neatly put away the sixty or so pages I had brought.

'I used to live in this neighbourhood once. But I can't recognize anything any more. It's all straightened out and built up; even the street's disappeared or changed its name. I'm not wrong, am I, Mademoiselle?'

Mademoiselle Barberet removed her spectacles, out of politeness. Her blue eyes were then unable to see me and her aimless gaze was lost in the void.

'Yes, I believe so,' she said, without conviction. 'You must be right.'

'Have you lived here long?'

'Oh, yes,' she said emphatically.

She fluttered her lashes as if she were lying.

'I think that, in the old days, a row of houses opposite hid the rise.'

I got up to go over to the window and passed out of the circle of light that the green-shaded lamp threw over the table. But I did not see much of the view outside. The lights of the town made no breaches in the blue dusk of evening that falls early, in February. I pushed up the coarse muslin curtain with my forehead and rested my hand on the window catch. Immediately, I was conscious of the faint, rather pleasant giddiness that accompanies dreams of falling and flying. For I was clutching in my hand the peculiar hasp, the little cast-iron mermaid, whose shape my palm had not forgotten after all these years. I could not prevent myself from turning round in an abrupt, questioning way.

Not having resumed her glasses, Mademoiselle Barberet noticed nothing. My enquiring gaze went from her civil, short-sighted face to the walls of the room, almost entirely covered with gloomy steel engravings framed in black, coloured reproductions of Chaplin – the fair-haired woman in the black velvet collar – and Henner, and even, a handicraft rare nowadays, thatchwork frames which young girls have lost the art of fashioning out of tubes of golden straw. Between an enlarged photograph and a sheaf of bearded rye, a few square inches of wallpaper remained bare; on it I could make out roses whose colour had almost gone, purple convolvulus faded to grey and tendrils of bluish foliage, in short, the ghost of a bunch of flowers, repeated a hundred times all over the walls, that it was impossible for me not to recognize. The twin doors, to right and left of the blind fireplace where a stove was fitted, promptly became intelligible and, beyond their closed panels, I revisualized all I had long ago left.

Behind me, I became unpleasantly conscious that Mademoiselle Barberet must be getting bored, so I resumed our conversation.

'It's pretty, this outlook.'

'Above all, it's light, for a first floor. You won't mind if I put your pages in order, Madame, I notice there's a mistake in the sequence of numbers. The three comes after the seven and I can't see the eighteen.'

'I'm not in the least surprised, Mademoiselle Barberet. Yes, do sort them out, do . . .'

'Above all, it's light.' Light, this mezzanine floor, where, at all times of the year, almost at all times of the day, I used to switch on a little chandelier under the ceiling-rose? On that same ceiling there suddenly appeared a halo of yellow light. Mademoiselle Barberet had just turned on a glass bowl, marbled to look like onyx, that reflected the light up on to the ceiling-rose, the same icing-sugar ceiling-rose under which, in other days, a branch of gilded metal flowered into five opaline blue corollas.

'A lot of mistakes, Mademoiselle Barberet? Especially a lot of crossings-out.'

'Oh, I work from manuscripts much more heavily corrected than this. The carbon copy, shall I do it in purple or black?'

'In black. Tell me, Mademoiselle . . .'

'My name's Rosita, Madame. At least, it's nicer than Barberet.'

'Mademoiselle Rosita, I'm going to abuse your kindness. I see that I've brought you the whole of my text up to date and I haven't a rough copy. If you could type page sixty-two for me, I could take it away with me so as to get my sequence right.'

'Why, of course, Madame. I'll do it at once. It'll only take me seven minutes. I'm not boasting, but I type fast. Do please sit down.'

All that I wanted to do was just that, to stay a few minutes longer and find in this room the traces, if any, of my having lived here; to make sure I was not mistaken, to marvel at the fact that a wallpaper, preserved by the shade, should not, after all these years, be in tatters. 'Above all, it's light.' Evidently the sanitary authorities or perhaps just some speculative builder had razed all the bank of houses that, in the old days, hid the slope of one of Paris's hills from my unwitting eyes.

To the right of the fireplace – in which a little wood stove, flanked by its provision of sticks, tarred road-blocks and old packing-case staves, was snoring discreetly – I could see a door and, to the left, a door exactly like it. Through the one on the right, I used to enter my bedroom. The one on the left led into the little hall, which ended in a recess I had turned into a bathroom by installing a slipper-bath and a geyser. Another room, very dark and fairly large, which I never used, served as a boxroom. As to the kitchen . . . That minute kitchen came back to my memory with extraordinary vividness; in winter, its old-fashioned blue-tiled range was touched by a ray of sun that glided as far as the equally old-world cooking-stove, standing on very tall legs and faintly Louis Quinze in design. When I could not, as they say, stick it any more, I used to go into the kitchen. I always found something to do there; polishing up the jointed gas-pipe, running a wet cloth over the blue procelain tiles, emptying out the water of faded flowers and rubbing the vase clear again with a handful of coarse, damp salt.

Two good big cupboards, of the jam-cupboard type; a cellar that contained nothing but a bottle-rack, empty of bottles.

'I'll have finished in one moment, Madame.'

What I most longed to see again was the bedroom to the right of the fireplace, *my* room, with its solitary square window, and the old-fashioned bed-closet whose doors I had removed. That marvellous bedroom, dark on one side, light on the other! It would have suited a happy, clandestine couple, but it had fallen to my lot when I was alone and very far from happy.

'Thank you so much. I don't need an envelope, I'll fold up the page and put it in my bag.'

The front door, slammed to by an impetuous hand, banged. A sound is always less evocative than a smell, yet I recognized that one and gave a start, as Mademoiselle Barberet did too. Then a second door, the door of my bathroom – was shut more gently.

'Mademoiselle Rosita, if I've got through enough work, you'll see me again on Monday morning round about eleven.'

Pretending to make a mistake, I went towards the right of the fireplace. But, between the door and myself, I found Mademoiselle Barberet, infinitely attentive.

'Excuse me. It's the one the other side.'

Out in the street, I could not help smiling, realizing that I had run heedlessly down the stairs without making a single mistake and that my feet, if I may risk the expression, still knew the staircase by heart. From the pavement, I studied my house, unrecognizable under a heavy make-up of mortar. The hall, too, was well-disguised and now, with its dado of pink and green tiles, reminded me of the baleful chilliness of those mass-produced villas on the Riviera. The old dairy on the right of the entrance now sold banjos and accordions. But, on the left, the 'Palace of Dainties' remained intact, except for a coat of cream paint. Pink sugared almonds in bowls, redcurrant balls in full glass jars, emerald peppermints and beige caramels . . . And the slabs of coffee cream and the sharp-tasting orange crescents . . . And those lentil-shaped sweets, wrapped in silver paper, like worm-pills, and flavoured with aniseed. At the back of the shop I recognized too, under their coat of new paint, the hundred little drawers with protruding navels, the low-carved counter and all the charming woodwork of shops that date from the Second Empire, the old-fashioned scales whose shining copper pans danced under the beam like swings.

I had a sudden desire to buy those squares of liquorice called 'Pontefract cakes' whose flavour is so full-bodied that, after them, nothing seems eatable. A mauve lady of sixty came forward to serve me. So this was all that survived of her former self, that handsome blonde proprietress who had once been so fond of sky-blue. She did not recognize me and, in my confusion, I asked her for peppermint creams which I cannot abide. The following Monday, I would have the opportunity of coming back for the little Pontefract cakes that give such a vile taste to fresh eggs, red wine and every other comestible.

To my cost, I have proved from long experience that the past is a far more violent temptation to me than the craving to know the future. Breaking with the present, retracing my steps, the sudden apparition of a new, unpublished slice of the past is accompanied by a shock utterly unlike anything else and which I cannot lucidly describe. Marcel Proust, gasping with asthma amid the bluish haze of fumigations and the shower of pages dropping from him one by one, pursued a bygone and completed time. It is neither the true concern nor the natural inclination of writers to love the future. They have quite enough to do with being incessantly forced to invent their characters' future which, in any case, they draw up from the well of their own past. Mine, whenever I plunge into it, turns me dizzy. And when it is the turn of the past to emerge unexpectedly, to raise its dripping mermaid's head into the light of the present and look at me with delusive eyes long hidden in the depths, I clutch at it all the more fiercely. Besides the person I once was, it reveals to me the one I would have liked to be. What is the use of employing occult means and occult individuals in order to know that person better? Fortune-tellers and astrologers, readers of tarot cards and palmists are not interested in my past. Among the figures, the swords, the cups and the coffee-grounds my past is written in three sentences. The seeress briskly sweeps away bygone 'ups and downs' and a few vague 'successes' that have had no marked results, then hurriedly plants on the whole the plaster rose of a today shorn of mystery and a tomorrow of which I expect nothing.

Among fortune-tellers, there are very few whom our presence momentarily endows with second sight. I have met some who went triumphantly backwards in time, gathering definite, blindingly true, pictures from my past, then leaving me shipwrecked amidst a fascinating welter of dead people, children from the past, dates and places, leapt, with one bound, into my future: 'In three years, in six years, your situation will be greatly improved.' Three years! Six years! Exasperated, I forgot them and their promises too.

But the temptation persists, along with a definite itch, to which I do not yield, to climb three floors or work a shaky lift, stop on a landing and ring three times. You see, one day, I might hear my own footsteps approaching on the other side of the door and my own voice asking me rudely: 'What is it?' I open the door to myself and, naturally, I am wearing what I used to wear in the old days, something in the nature of a dark pleated tartan skirt and a high-collared shirt. The bitch I had in 1900 puts up her hackles and shivers when she sees me double . . . The end is missing. But as good nightmares go, it's a good nightmare.

For the first time in my life, I had just, by going into Mademoiselle Barberet's flat, gone back into my own home. The coincidence obsessed me during the days that followed my visit. I looked into it and I discovered something ironically interesting about it. Who was it who had suggested Mademoiselle Barberet to me? None other than my young typist who was leaving her job to get married. She was marrying a handsome boy who was 'taking', as they say, a gymnasium in the district of Grenelle and whom she had been anxious I should meet. While he was explaining to me, thoroughly convinced of my passionate interest, that, nowadays, a gymnasium in a working-class district was a goldmine, I was listening to his slight provincial accent. 'I come from B . . . like all my family,' he mentioned, in passing. 'And like the person who was responsible for certain searing disappointments in my life,' I added mentally. Disappointments in love, naturally. They are the least worthy of being brought back to mind but, sometimes, they behave just like a cut in which a fragment of hair is hidden; they heal badly.

This second man from B . . . had vanished, having fulfilled his obligations towards me which consisted of flinging me back, for unknown ends, into a known place. He had struck me as gentle; as slightly heavy, like all young men made tired and drowsy by injudicious physical culture. He was dark, with beautiful southern eyes, as the natives of B . . . often are. And he carried off the passionate young girl, thin to the point of emaciation, who had been typing my manuscripts for three years and crying over them when my story ended sadly.

The following Monday, I brought Mademoiselle Rosita the meagre fruit – twelve pages – of work that was anything but a labour of love. There was no motive whatever for being in a hurry to have two typed copies of a bad first draft, none except the pleasure and the risk of braving the little flat of long ago. 'Worth doing just this once more,' I told myself, 'then I'll put my mind on other things.' Nevertheless, my remembering hand searched the length of the door-jamb for the pretty beaded braid, my pretentious bell-pull of the old days, and found an electric push-button.

An unknown person promptly opened the door, answered me only with a nod and showed me into the room with two windows where Mademoiselle Barberet joined me.

'Have you worked well, Madame? The bad weather hasn't had too depressing an effect on you?'

Her small, cold hand had hurriedly withdrawn from mine and was pulling forward the two sausage-curls tied with black ribbon and settling them in their proper place on her right shoulder, nestling in her neck.

She smiled at me with the tempered solicitude of a well-trained nurse or a fashionable dentist's receptionist or one of those women of uncertain age who do vague odd jobs in beauty-parlours.

'It's been a bad week for me, Mademoiselle Rosita. What's more, you'll find my writing difficult to read.'

'I don't think so, Madame. A round hand is seldom illegible.'

She looked at me amiably; behind the thick glasses, the blue of her eyes seemed diluted.

'Just imagine, when I arrived, I thought I must have come to the wrong floor, the person who opened the door to me . . .'

'Yes. That's my sister,' said Mademoiselle Barberet as if, by satisfying my indiscreet curiosity, she hoped to prevent it from going any further.

But when we are in the grip of curiosity, we have no shame.

'Ah! That's your sister. Do you work together?'

Mademoiselle Barberet's transparent skin quivered on her cheekbones.

'No, Madame. For some time now, my sister's health has needed looking after.'

This time, I did not dare insist further. For a few moments more I lingered in my drawing-room that was now an office, taking in how much lighter it was. I strained my ear in vain for anything that might echo in the heart of the house or in the depths of myself and I went away, carrying with me a romantic burden of conjectures. The sister who was ill – and why not melancholy mad? Or languishing over an unhappy love-affair? Or struck with some monstrous deformity and kept in the shade? That is what I'm like when I let myself go.

During the following days, I had no leisure to indulge my wild fancies further. At that particular time F.-I. Mouthon had asked me to write a serial-novelette for *Le Journal*. Was this intelligent, curly-haired man making his first mistake? In all honesty, I had protested that I should never be able to write the kind of serial that would have been suitable for the readers of a big daily paper. F.-I. Mouthon, who seemed to know more about it than I did myself, had winked his little elephant's eye, shaken his curly forehead, shrugged his heavy shoulders and – I had sat down to write a serial-novelette for which you will look in vain among my works. Mademoiselle Barberet was the only person who saw the first chapters before I tore them up. For, in the long run, I turned out to be right; I did not know how to write a serial-novelette.

On my return from my second visit to Mademoiselle Barberet, I re-read the forty typed pages.

And I swore to peg away at it, as they say, like the very devil, to deprive myself of the flea-market and the cinema and even of lunch in the Bois . . . This, however, did not mean Armenonville or even the Cascade, but pleasant impromptu picnics on the grass, all the better if Annie de Pène, a precious friend, came with me. There is no lack of milder days, once we are in February. We would take our bicycles, a fresh loaf stuffed with butter and sardines, two 'delicatessen' sausage-rolls we bought at a pork butcher's near La Muette and some apples, the whole secured with string to a water-bottle in a wicker jacket, filled with white wine. As to coffee, we drank that at a place near the station at Auteuil, very black, very tasteless but piping hot and syrupy with sugar.

Few memories have remained as dear to me as the memory of those meals without plates, cutlery or cloth, of those expeditions on two wheels. The cool sky, the rain in drops, the snow in flakes, the sparse, rusty grass, the tameness of the birds. These idylls suited a certain state of mind, far removed from happiness, frightened yet obstinately hopeful. By means of them, I have succeeded in taking the sting out of an unhappiness that wept small, restrained tears, a sorrow without great storms, in short a love-affair that began just badly enough to make it end still worse. Does one imagine those periods, during which anodynes conquer an illness one believed serious at the time, fade easily from one's memory? I have already compared them, elsewhere, to the 'blanks' that introduce space and order between the chapters of a book. I should very much like – late in life, it is true – to call them 'merciful blanks', those days in which work and sauntering and friendship played the major part, to the detriment of love. Blessed days, sensitive to the light of the external world, in which the relaxed and idle senses made chance discoveries. It was not very long after I had been enjoying this kind of holiday that I made the acquaintance of Mademoiselle Barberet.

It was – and for good reason – three weeks before I went to see her again. Conceiving a loathing for my serial-novelette every time I tried to introduce 'action', swift adventure and a touch of the sinister into it, I had harnessed myself to short stories for *La Vie Parisienne*. It was therefore with a new heart and a light step that I climbed the slopes of her part of Paris, which shall be nameless. Not knowing whether Mademoiselle Barberet liked 'Pontefract cakes' I bought her several small bunches of snow-drops, that had not yet lost their very faint perfume of orange-flowers, squeezed tight together in one big bunch.

Behind the door, I heard her little heels running forward over the uncarpeted wooden floor. I recognize a step more quickly than a shape, a shape more quickly than a face. It was bright out-of-doors and in the room with the two windows. Between the photographic enlargements, the 'studies' of woodland land-scapes, and the straw frames with red ribbon bows, the February sun was consuming the last faint outlines of my roses and blue convolvulus on the wallpaper.

'*This* time, Mademoiselle Rosita, I haven't come empty-handed! Here are some little flowers for you and here are two short stories, twenty-nine pages of manuscript.'

'It's too much, Madame, it's too much . . .'

'It's the length they have to be. It takes thirteen closely written pages, a short story for *La Vie Parisienne*.'

'I was talking of the flowers, Madame.'

'They're not worth mentioning. And you know, on Monday, I've a feeling I'm going to bring you . . .'

Behind her spectacles, Mademoiselle Barberet's eyes fixed themselves on me, forgetting to dissemble the fact that they were red, bruised, filled with bitter water and so sad that I broke off my sentence. She made a gesture with her hand, and murmured:

'I apologize. I have worries . . .'

Few women keep their dignity when they are in tears. The withered young girl in distress wept simply, decently controlling the shaking of her hands and her voice. She wiped her eyes and her glasses and gave me a kind of smile with one side of her mouth.

'It's one of those days . . . it's because of the child, I mean of my sister.'

'She's ill, isn't she?'

'In one sense, yes. She has no disease,' she said emphatically. 'It's since she got married. It's changed her character. She's so rough with me. Of course all marriages can't turn out well, one knows that.'

I am not very fond of other people's matrimonial troubles, they bear an inevitable resemblance to my own personal dis-appointments. So I was anxious to get away at once from the sorrowing Barberet and the unhappily married sister. But, just as I was leaving her, a little blister in the coarse glass of one of the window-panes caught a ray of sun and projected on to the opposite wall the little halo of rainbow colours I used once to call the 'rainy moon'. The apparition of that illusory planet shot me back so violently into the past that I remained standing where I was, transfixed and fascinated.

'Look, Mademoiselle Rosita. How pretty that is.'

I put my finger on the wall, in the centre of the little planet ringed with seven colours.

'Yes,' she said. 'We know that reflection well. Just fancy, my sister's frightened of it.'

'Frightened? What do you mean, frightened? Why? What does she say about it?'

Mademoiselle smiled at my eagerness.

'Oh! You know . . . silly things, the sort that nervous children imagine. She says it's an omen. She calls it her sad little sun, she says it only shines to warn her something bad is going to happen. Goodness knows what else. As if the refraction of a prism really could influence . . .'

Mademoiselle Barberet gave a superior smile.

'You're right,' I said weakly. 'But those are charming poetic fancies. Your sister is a poet without realizing it.'

Mademoiselle Barberet's blue eyes were fixed on the place where the rainbow-coloured ghost had been before a passing cloud had just eclipsed it.

'The main thing is she's a very unreasonable young woman.'

'She lives in the other . . . in another part of the flat?'

Mademoiselle Barberet's gaze switched to the closed door on the right of the fireplace.

'Another part, you could hardly call it that. They chose . . . Her bedroom and dressing-room are separate from my bedroom.'

I nodded 'Yes, yes,' as my thorough acquaintance with the place gave me the right to do.

'Is your sister like you to look at?'

I made myself gentle and spoke tonelessly as one does to people asleep so as to make them answer one from the depths of their slumber.

'Like me? Oh dear, no! To begin with, there's a certain difference of age between us, and she's dark. And then, as to character, we couldn't be less alike in every way.'

'Ah! She's dark . . . One of these days you must let me meet her. There's no hurry! I'm leaving you my manuscript. If you don't see me on Monday . . . Would you like me to settle up with you for the typing you've already done?'

Mademoiselle Barberet blushed and refused, then blushed and accepted. And, although I stopped in the hall to make some unnecessary suggestion, no sound came from my bedroom and nothing revealed the presence of the dark sister.

'She calls it her sad little sun. She says that it foretells something bad. Whatever can I have bequeathed to that reflection, that looks like a planet in a ring of haze, where the red is never anywhere but next to the purple? In the old days, when the wind was high and the sky cloudy, it would keep vanishing, reappearing, fading away again, and its caprices would distract me for a moment from my state of suspense, of perpetual waiting.'

I admit that, as I descended the slope of the hill, I gave myself up to excitement. The play of coincidences shed a false, un-hoped-for light on my life. Already I was promising myself that the 'Barberet story' would figure in a prominent place in the fantastic gallery we secretly furnish and which we open more readily to strangers than to our near ones; the gallery reserved for premonitions, for the phenomena of mistaken identity, for visions and predictions. In it I had already lodged the story of the woman with the candle, the story of Jeanne D.; the story of the woman who read the tarot pack and of the little boy who rode on horseback.

In any case, the Barberet story, barely even roughly sketched, was already acting for me as a 'snipe's bandage'. That is what I used to call, and still call, a particular kind of unremarkable and soothing event that I liken to the dressing of wet clay and bits of twig, the marvellous little splint the snipe binds round its foot when a shot has broken it. A visit to the cinema, provided the films are sufficiently mediocre, counts as a snipe's bandage. But, on the contrary, an evening in the company of intelligent friends who know what it is to be hurt and are courageous and disillusioned, undoes the bandage. Symphonic music generally tears it off, leaving me flayed. Poured out by a steady, indifferent voice, pronouncements and predictions are compresses and camomile-tea to me.

'I'm going to tell the Barberet story to Annie de Pène,' I mentally began. And then I told nothing at all. Would not Annie's subtle ear and those lively bronze eyes of hers have weighed up and condemned everything in my narrative that revealed no more than the craving to go over old ground again, to deck out what was over and done with in a new coat of paint? 'That window, Annie, where a young woman whose man has left her, spends nearly all her time waiting, listening – just as I did long ago.'

I said nothing to Annie. It is as well for a toy to be played with in solitude, if something or other about its colour, about its acid varnish, about a chance distortion of its shadow, warns one it may be dangerous. But I went off and translated the 'Barberet story' into commonplace language for the benefit of the woman who came by the day to 'make and mend' for me, a stout brunette who was relaxing after singing in operetta in Oran by sewing and ironing for other people. In order to listen to me, Marie Mallier stopped crushing gathers under a cruel thumb-nail, blew into her thimble and waited, her needle poised.

'And then what happened?'

'That's the end.'

'Oh,' said Marie Mallier. 'It seemed to me more like a beginning.'

The words enchanted me. I read into them the most romantic omen and I swore to myself I would not delay another moment in making the acquaintance of the dark, unhappily married sister who lived in my gloomy bedroom and was frightened of my 'rainy moon'.

Those tugs on my sleeve, those little presents fate has offered me might have given me the power of escaping from myself, sloughing my skin and emerging in new, variegated colours. I believe they might have succeeded, had I not lacked the society and influence of someone for whom there is hardly any difference between what really happens and what does not, between fact and possibility, between an event and the narration of it.

Much later on, when I came to know Francis Carco I realized

that he would, for example, have interpreted my stay at Bella-Vista and my meeting with the Barberets with an unbridled imagination. He would have plucked out of them the catastrophic truth, the element of something unfinished, something left suspended that spurs imagination and terror to a gallop; in short, their poetry. I saw, years afterwards, how a poet makes use of tragic embellishment and lends a mere news item the fascination of some white, inanimate face behind a pane.

Lacking a companion with a fiery imagination, I clung to a rational view of things, notably of fear and of hallucination. This was a real necessity, as I lived alone. On some nights, I would look very carefully round my little flat; I would open my shutters to let the nocturnal light play on the ceiling while I waited for the light of day. The next morning, my concierge, when she brought me my coffee, would silently flourish the key she had found in the lock, on the outside. Most of the time I gave no thought to perils that might come from the unknown and I treated ghosts with scant respect.

That was how, the following Monday, I treated a window in the Barberet flat which I had entered at the same moment as a March wind with great sea pinions that flung all the papers on the floor. Mademoiselle Rosita put both hands over her ears, and shrieked 'Ah!' as she shut her eyes. I gripped the cast-iron mermaid with a familiar hand and closed the window with one turn of my wrist.

'At the very first go!' exclaimed Mademoiselle Barberet admiringly. 'That's extraordinary! I hardly ever manage to . . . Oh, goodness, all these typed copies flying about! Monsieur Vandérem's novel! Monsieur Pierre Veber's short story! This wind! Luckily I'd put your text back in its folder . . . Here's the top copy, Madame, and the carbon. There are several traces of india rubber. If you'd like me to re-do some of the scratched pages, it'll be a pleasure to me, tonight after dinner.'

'Find yourself more exciting pleasures, Mademoiselle Rosita. Go the cinema. Do you like the cinema?'

The avidity of a small girl showed in her face, accentuating the fine wrinkles round the mouth.

'I adore it, Madame! We have a very good local cinema, five

francs for quite good seats, that shows splendid films. But, at this moment, I can't possibly . . .'

She broke off and fixed her gaze on the door to the right of the fireplace.

'Is it still your sister's health? Couldn't her husband take on the job of . . .'

In spite of myself, I imitated her prudish way of leaving her sentences unfinished. She flushed and said hastily:

'Her husband doesn't live here, Madame.'

'Ah! he doesn't live . . . And she, what does she do? Is she waiting for him to come back?'

'I . . . Yes, I think so.'

'All the time?'

'Day and night.'

I stood up abruptly and began to pace the room, from the window to the door, from the door to the far wall, from the far wall to the fireplace; the room where once *I* had waited – day and night.

'That's stupid!' I exclaimed. 'That's the last thing to do. Do you hear me, the very last!'

Mademoiselle Barberet mechanically pulled out the spiral of hair that caressed her shoulder and her withered angel's face followed my movement to and fro.

'If *I* knew her, that sister of yours, I'd tell her straight to her face that she's chosen the worst possible tactics. They couldn't be more . . . more idiotic.'

'Ah, I'd be only too glad, Madame, if you'd tell her so! Coming from you, it would have far more weight than from me. She makes no bones about making it plain to me that old maids have no right to speak on certain topics. In which she may well be mistaken, moreover . . .' Mademoiselle Barberet lowered her eyes and gave a little resentful toss of her chin.

'A fixed idea isn't always a good idea. She's in there, with her fixed idea. When she can't stand it any more, she goes downstairs. She says she wants to buy some sweets. She says: "I'm going to telephone." To other people! As if she thought I was deceived for a moment!'

'You're not on the telephone?'

I raised my eyes to the ceiling. A little hole in the moulded cornice still showed where the telephone wire had passed through it. When *I* was in this place, I had the telephone. I could beg and implore without having to bother to go outside.

'Not yet, Madame. We're going to have it put in, of course.'

She blushed, as she did whenever there was a question of money or of lack of money, and seemed to make a desperate resolve.

'Madame, since you think as I do that my sister is wrong to be so obstinate, if you have two minutes . . .'

'I have two minutes.'

'I'll go and tell my sister.'

She went out through the hall instead of opening the door on the right of the fireplace. She walked gracefully, carried on small, arched feet. Almost at once, she came back, agitated and with red rims to her eyelids.

'Oh! I don't know how to apologize. She's terrible. She says "Not on your life" and "What are you sticking your nose in for?" and "I wish to goodness everyone would shut up." She says nothing but rude things.'

Mademoiselle Barberet blew her distress into her handkerchief, rubbed her nose and became ugly, as if on purpose. I had just time to think: 'Really, I'm being unnecessarily tactful with these females,' before I turned the handle of the right-hand door which recognized me and obeyed me without a sound. I did not cross the threshold of *my* room whose half-closed shutters filled it with a faintly green dusk. At the far end of the room, on a divan-bed that seemed not to have moved from the place I had chosen for it in the old days, a young woman, curled up like a gun-dog, raised the dim oval of her face in my direction. For a second, I had that experience only dreams dare conjure up; I saw before me, hostile, hurt, stubbornly hoping, the young self I should never be again, whom I never ceased disowning and regretting.

But there is nothing lasting in any touch of the fabulous we experience outside sleep. The young myself stood up, spoke and was no longer anything more than a stranger, the sound of whose voice dissipated all my precious mystery.

'Madame . . . But I told my sister – Really, Rosita, whatever are you thinking of? My room's untidy, I'm not well. You must understand, Madame, why I couldn't ask you to come in.'

She had only taken two or three steps towards me. In spite of the gloom, I could make out that she was rather short, but upright and self-assured. As a cloud outside uncovered the sun, the construction of her face was revealed to me, a straight, firm nose, strongly marked brows, a little Roman chin. It is a double attraction when well-modelled features are both youthful and severe.

I made myself thoroughly amiable to this young woman who was throwing me out.

'I understand perfectly, Madame. But do realize that your sister's only crime was to imagine I might be of some use to you. She made a mistake. Mademoiselle Rosita, it'll be all right, won't it, to fetch the typescript as usual, next Monday?'

The two sisters did not notice the ease with which I found the curtained door at the far end of the room, crossed the dark little hall and shut myself out. Downstairs, I was joined by Rosita.

'Madame, Madame, you're not angry?'

'Not in the very least. Why should I be. She's pretty, your sister. By the way, what's her name?'

'Adèle. But she likes to be called Délia. Her married name is Essendier, Madame Essendier. Now she's heartbroken, she'd like to see you.'

'Very well then! She shall see me on Monday,' I conceded with dignity.

As soon as I was alone, the temptation to be entrapped in this snare of resemblances lost its power; the strident glare of the Rue des Martyrs at midday dissipated the spell of the bedroom and the young woman curled up 'day and night'. On the steep slope, what quantities of chickens with their necks hanging down, small legs of mutton displayed outside shops, fat sausages, enamelled beer-mugs with landscapes on them, oranges piled up in formation like cannon-balls for ancient artillery, withered apples, unripe bananas, anaemic chicory, glutinous wads of dates, daffodils, pink 'milanese' panties, camiknickers encrusted with imitation Chantilly, little bags of ingredients for home-made stomach remedies, mercerized lisle stockings. What a number of postiches – they used to call them 'chichés' – of ties sold in threes, of shapeless housewives, of blondes in down-at-heel shoes and brunettes in curling-pins, of mother-of-pearl smelts, of butcher-boys with fat, cherubic faces. All this profusion, which had not changed in the least, awakened my appetite and vigorously restored me to reality.

Away with these Barberets! That chit of a girl with no manners was a sniveller, a lazy slut who must have driven her husband's patience beyond all bounds. Caught between a prim, fussy old maid and a jealous young wife, what a charming life for a man!

Thus, wandering along and gazing at the shops, did I indict Madame Délia Essendier, christened Adèle . . . '*Adèle . . . T'es belle* . . .' Standing in front of a sumptuous Universal Provision Store, I hummed the silly, already hoary song, as I admired the oranges between the tumbled rice and the sweating coffee, the red apples and the split green peas. Just as in Nice one longs to buy the entire flower market, here I would have liked to buy a whole stall of eatables, from the forced lettuces to the blue packets of semolina. '*Adèle . . . T'es belle* . . .' I hummed.

'If you ask *me*,' said an insolent-eyed local girl, right under my nose, 'I'd say *The Merry Widow* was a lot more up-to-date than that old thing.'

I did not reply, for this strapping blonde with her hair curled to last a week, planted solidly on her feet and sugared with coarse powder, was, after all, speaking for the whole generation destined to devour my own.

All the same I was not old and, above all, I did not look my real age. But a private life that was clouded and uncertain, a solitude that bore no resemblance to peace had wiped all the life and charm out of my face. I have never had less notice taken of me by men than during those particular years whose date I dissemble here. It was much later on that they treated me again to the good honest offensive warmth of their looks, to that genial concupiscence which will make an admirer, when he ought to be kissing your hand, give you a friendly pinch on the buttock.

The following Monday, on a sultry March morning when the

sky was a whitish blue and Paris, dusty and surprised, was spilling her overflow of jonquils and anemones into the streets, I walked limply up the steep slope of Montmartre. Already the wide-open entrances to the blocks of flats were ejecting the air that was colder inside than out, along with the carbonic smell of stoves that had been allowed to go out. I rang the bell of Mademoiselle Rosita's flat; she did not answer it and I joyfully welcomed the idea that she might be out, busy buying a pale escalope of veal or some ready-cooked sauerkraut . . . To salve my conscience, I rang a second time. Something brushed faintly against the door and the parquet creaked.

'Is that you, Eugène?' asked the voice of Mademoiselle Barberet.

She spoke almost in a whisper and I could hear her breathing at the level of the keyhole.

As if exculpating myself, I cried:

'It's me, Mademoiselle Rosita! I'm bringing some pages of manuscript . . .'

Mademoiselle Barberet gave a little 'Ah!' but did not open the door at once. Her voice changed and she said in mincing tones:

'Oh, Madame, what can I have been thinking of. I'll be with you in a moment.'

A safety-bolt slid in its catch and the door was half-opened.

'Be very careful, Madame, you might stumble . . . My sister's on the floor.'

She could not have spoken more politely and indifferently had she said: 'My sister's gone out to the post.' I did, in fact, stumble against a body lying prone, with its feet pointing skywards and its hands and face mere white blurs. The sight of it threw me into a state of cowardice which I intensely dislike. Drawing away from the body stretched out on the floor, I asked, to give the impression of being helpful:

'What's the matter with her? Would you like me to call someone?'

Then I noticed that the sensitive Mademoiselle Rosita did not seem to be greatly perturbed.

'It's a fainting fit . . . a kind of dizziness that isn't serious. Let me just get the smelling-salts and a wet towel.'

She was already running off. I noticed she had forgotten to turn the light on and I had no trouble in finding the switch to the right of the front-door. A ceiling-light in the form of a plate with a crinkled border feebly lit up the hall and I bent down over the prostrate young woman. She was lying in an extremely decent attitude, with her skirt down to her ankles. One of her bent arms, whose hand lay palm upwards, beside her ear, seemed to be commanding attention, and her head was slightly averted on her shoulders. Really, a very pretty young woman, taking refuge in a sulky swoon. I could hear Mademoiselle Rosita in the bedroom, opening and shutting a drawer, slamming the door of a cupboard.

And I found the seconds drag heavily as I stared at the tubular umbrella-stand, at the cane table; in particular, at the door-curtain of Algerian design that roused a regret in my heart for a rather pretty strip of leafy tapestry that used to hang there in the old days. As I looked down at the motionless young woman, I realized, from a narrow gleam between her eyelids, that she was secretly watching me. For some reason, I felt disagreeably surprised, as if by some practical joke. I bent over this creature who was shamming a faint and applied another approved remedy for swoons – a good, hard, stinging slap. She received it with an offended snarl and sat up with a jerk.

'Well! So you're better?' cried Rosita, who was arriving with a wet towel and a litre of salad vinegar.

'As you see, Madame slapped my hands,' said Délia coldly. 'You'd never have thought of that, would you? Help me to get up, please.'

I could not avoid giving her my arm. And, supporting her thus, I entered the bedroom she had practically asked me to leave.

The room reverberated with the noises of the street that came up through the open window. There was just the same contrast I remembered so well between the cheerful noises and the mournful light. I guided the young pretender to the divan-bed.

'Rosita, perhaps you'd have the charity to bring me a glass of water?'

I began to realize that the two sisters adopted a bitter, bantering tone whenever they spoke to each other. Rosita's small steps went off towards the kitchen and I prepared to leave her younger sister's bedside. But, with an unexpected movement, Délia caught hold of my hand, then clasped her arms round my knees and wildly pressed her head against them.

You must remember that, at that period of my life, I was still childless and that friendship, for me, wore the guise of undemonstrative, off-hand, unemotional comradeliness. You must also take into account that, for many months, I had been starved of the coarse, invigorating bread of physical contact. A kiss, a good warm hug, the fresh touch of a child or anyone young had remained so long out of my reach that they had become distant, almost forgotten joys. So this unknown young woman's outburst, her surge of tears and her sudden embrace stunned me. Rosita's return found me standing just where I was and the imploring arms unloosed their grip.

'I let the tap run for two minutes,' explained the elder sister. 'Madame, how can I apologize . . .'

I suddenly resented Mademoiselle Barberet's air of businesslike alacrity; her two ringlets bobbed on her right shoulder and she was slightly out of breath.

'Tomorrow morning,' I interrupted, 'I've got to buy some remnants in the Saint-Pierre market. So I could come and collect the typed copies and you can give me news of . . . this . . . young person. No, stay where you are. I know the way.'

What stirred just now in the thicket? No, it isn't a rabbit. Nor a grass snake. Nor a bird, that travels in shorter spurts. Only lizards are so agile, so capable of covering a long distance fast, so reckless . . . It's a lizard. That large butterfly flying in the distance – I always had rather bad eyesight – you say it's a Swallowtail? No, it's a Large Tortoiseshell. Why? Because the one we're looking at glides magnificently as only the Large Tortoiseshell can, and the Swallowtail has a flapping flight. 'My husband, such a placid man . . .' a friend of mine used to tell me. She did not see that he sucked his tongue all day long. She thought he was eating chewing-gum, not differentiating between the chewing of gum and the nervous sucking of the tongue. Personally, I thought that this man had cares on his mind or else that the presence of his wife exasperated him.

Ever since I had made the acquaintance of Délia Essendier I had found myself 'recapping' in this way lessons I had learnt from my instinct, from animals, children, nature and my disquieting fellow human beings. It seemed to me that I needed more than ever to know of my own accord, without discussing it with anyone, that the lady going by has a left shoe that pinches her, that the person I am talking to is pretending to drink in my words but not even listening to me, that a certain woman who hides from herself the fact that she loves a certain man, cannot stop herself from following him like a magnet whenever he is in the room, but always turning her back to him. A dog with evil intentions sometimes limps out of nervousness.

Children, and people who retain some ingenuous trait of childhood, are almost indecipherable, I realize that. Nevertheless, in a child's face, there is just one revealing, unstable area, a space comprised between the nostril, the eye and the upper lip, where the waves of secret delinquency break on the surface. It is as swift and devastating as lightning. Whatever the child's age, that little flash of guilt turns the child into a ravaged adult. I have seen a serious lie distort a little girl's nostril and upper lip like a hare-lip . . .

'Tell me, Délia . . .'

. . . but on Délia's features nothing explicit appeared. She took refuge in a smile – for me – or in bad temper directed against her elder sister, or else she entered into a sombre state of waiting, installing herself in it as if at the window of a watch-tower. She would half-sit, half-lie on her divan-bed, that was covered with a green material printed with blue nasturtiums – the last gasps of the vogue for 'Liberty' fabrics – clutching a big cushion against her, propping her chin on it, and scarcely ever moving. Perhaps she was aware that her attitude suited her often cantankerous beauty.

'But tell me, Délia, when you got married, didn't you have a presentiment that . . .'

Propped up like that, with her skirt pulled down to her ankles, she seemed to be meditating, rather than waiting. Since profound meditation is not concerned with being expressive, Délia Essendier never turned her eyes to me, even when she was speaking. More often than not, she looked at the half-open window, the reservoir of air, the source of sounds, a greenish aquarium in the shade of the green and blue curtains. Or else she stared fixedly at the little slippers with which her feet were shod. I, too, in the old days, used to buy those little heelless slippers of imitation silk brocade, adorned with a flossy pompon on the instep. In those days they cost thirteen francs seventy-five and their poor material soon tarnished. The young voluntary recluse I saw before me did not bother herself with shoes. She was only half a recluse, going out in the morning to buy a squirrel's provisions, a provender of fresh bread, dry nuts, eggs and apples, and the little meat that sufficed for the appetite of the two sisters.

'Didn't you tell me, Délia . . .'

No. She had told me nothing. Her brief glance accused me of imagining things, of having no memory. What was I doing there, in a place which ought to have been forbidden ground for me, at the side of a woman young enough to give no indication of being a wife and who manifested neither virtues nor nobility of mind nor even as much intelligence as any lively, gentle animal? The answer, I insist, is that this was a period in my life which motherhood and happy love had not yet enriched with their marvellous commonplace.

People might already have taken me to task for my choice of associates – those who tried to got an extremely poor reception – and my friends might have been surprised, for example, to find me pacing up and down the Avenue du Bois in the company of a shabby groom who brought and took away the horses hired out by a riding-school. A former jockey who had been unlucky and come down in the world and who looked like an old glove. But he was a mine of information on everything to do with horses and dogs, diseases, remedies, fiery beverages that would kill or cure, and I liked his meaty conversation even though he did teach me too much about the way animals are 'made-up' to get a better price for them. For example, I would gladly have been dispensed from knowing that they pour sealing-wax into a French bull-dog's ears if it has slightly limp auricles . . . The rest of his expert knowledge was fascinating.

With less fundamental richness, Marie Mallier had considerable charm. If any of my circle had decided to be captious about all the things Marie Mallier did in the course of what she broadly described as 'touring in Operetta', I would not have stood for it. Reduced to accepting all and sundry, the only transgressions Marie Mallier really enjoyed were the unprofitable delights of sewing and ironing. For the spice of an occupation, generally considered innocent, can be more exciting than many a guilty act performed out of necessity.

'To make a darn so that the corners don't pucker and all the little loops on the wrong side stand out nice and even,' Marie Mallier used to say. 'It makes my mouth water like cutting a lemon!' Our vices are less a matter of yielding to temptation than of some obsessive love. Throwing oneself passionately into helping some unknown woman, founding hopes on her that would be discouraged by the wise affection of our friends, wildly adopting a child that is not ours, obstinately ruining ourselves for a man whom we probably hate, such are the strange manifestations of a struggle against ourselves that is sometimes called disinterestedness, sometimes perversity. When I was with Délia Essendier, I found myself once again as vulnerable, as prone to giving presents out of vanity as a schoolgirl who sells her books to buy a rosary, a ribbon or a little ring and slips them, with a shy note, into the desk of a beloved classmate.

Nevertheless, I did not love Délia Essendier and the beloved classmate I was seeking, who was she but my former self, that sad form stuck, like a petal between two pages, to the walls of an ill-starred refuge.

'Délia, haven't you got a photograph of your husband here?'

Since the day when her arms had clasped my knees, Délia had made no other mute appeal to me except, when I stood up to go, a gesture to hold me back by the hand, the gesture of an awkward young girl who has not learnt how to grip or offer a palm frankly. All she did was to pull on my fingers and hurriedly let them go, as if out of sulkiness, then turn away towards the window that was nearly always open. Following the suggestion of her gaze, it was I who would go over to the window and stare at the passers-by or rather at their lids for, in those days, all men wore hats. When the entrance down below swallowed up a man with a long stride, dressed in a blue overcoat, in spite of myself I would count the seconds and reckon the time it would take a visitor in a hurry to cross the hall, walk up to our floor and ring the bell. But no one would ring and I would breathe freely again.

'Your husband, does he write to you, Délia?'

This time, the reticent young person whom I continued to ask tactless questions, whether she left them unanswered or not, scanned me with her insulting gaze. But I was long past the stage of taking any notice of her disdain, and I repeated:

'Yes, I'm asking if your husband writes to you sometimes?'

My question produced a great effect on Rosita, who was walking through the bedroom. She stopped short, as if waiting for her sister's reply.

'No,' said Délia at last. 'He doesn't write to me and it's just as well he doesn't. We've nothing to say to each other.'

At this, Rosita opened her mouth and her eyes in astonishment. Then she continued her light-footed walk and, just before she disappeared, raised both her hands to her ears. This scandalized gesture revived my curiosity which, at times, died down. I must also admit that, going back to the scene of my unhappy, fascinating past, I found it shocking that Délia – Délia and not myself – should be lying on the divan-bed, playing at taking off and putting on her little slippers, while I, tired of an uncomfortable seat, got up to walk to and fro, to push the table closer to the window as if by accident, to measure the space once filled by a dark cupboard.

'Délia, was it you who chose this wallpaper?'

'Certainly not. *I'd* have liked a flowered paper, like the one in the living-room.'

'What living-room?'

'The big room.'

'Ah! yes. It isn't a living-room, because you don't live in it. I should be more inclined to call it the workroom because your sister works in it.'

Now that the days were growing longer, I could make out the colour of Délia's eyes – round her dilated pupils there was a ring of dark grey-green – and the whiteness of her skin, like the complexion of southern women who are uniformly pale from head to foot. She threw me a look of obstinate mistrust.

'My sister can work just as well in a living-room if she chooses.'

'The main thing is that she works, isn't it?' I retorted.

With a kick, she flung one of her slippers a long way away.

'*I* work too,' she said stiffly. 'Only nobody sees what I do. I wear myself out, oh! I wear myself out. In there . . . In there . . .'

She was touching her forehead and pressing her temples. With slight contempt, I looked at her idle woman's hands, her delicate fingers, long, slim and turned up at the tips, and her fleshy palms. I shrugged my shoulders.

'Fine work, a fixed idea! You ought to be ashamed, Délia.'

She gave way easily to tempers typical of an ill-bred schoolgirl with no self-control.

'I don't only just think!' she screamed. 'I . . . I work in my own way! It's all in my head!'

'Are you planning a novel?'

I had spoken sarcastically but Délia, quite unaware of this, was flattered and calmed down.

'Oh! Well, not exactly so . . . it's a bit like a novel, only better.'

'What is it you call better than a novel, my child?'

For I allowed myself to call her that when she seemed to be pitchforked into a kind of brutal, irresponsible childishness. She always flinched at the word and rewarded me with an angry, lustrous glance, accompanied by an ill-tempered shrug.

'Ah, I can't tell you that,' she said in a self-important voice.

She went back to fishing cherries out of a newspaper cornet. She pinched the stones between her fingers and aimed at the open window. Rosita passed through the room, busy on some errand, and scolded her sister without pausing in her walk.

'Délia, you oughtn't to throw the stones out into the street.'

What was I doing there, in that desert? One day, I brought some better cherries. Another day, having brought Rosita a manuscript full of erasures, I said:

'Wait. Could I re-do this page on . . . on a corner of a table, doesn't matter where. There, look, that'll do very well. Yes, yes, I can see well enough there. Yes, I've got my fountain-pen.'

Leaning on a rickety one-legged table, I received, from the left, the light of the solitary window and, from the right, the attention of Délia. To my amazement, she set to work with a needle. She was doing the fine beadwork that was all the rage at the moment for bags and trimmings.

'What a charming talent, Délia.'

'It isn't a talent, it's a profession,' said Délia in a tone of disgust.

But she was not displeased, I think, to devote herself under my eyes to work that was as graceful as a charming pastime. The needles, fine as steel hairs, the tiny multicoloured beads, the canvas net, she manipulated them all with the deftness of a blind person, still half-recumbent on a corner of the divan-bed. From the neighbouring room came the choppy chatter of the type-writer, the jib of its little carriage at every line, and its crystalline bell. What was I doing, in that desert? It was not a desert. I forsook my own three small, snug rooms, my books, the scent I sprayed about, my lamp. But one cannot live on a lamp, on a perfume, on pages one has read and re-read. I had moreover friends and good companions; I had Annie de Pène, who was better than the best of them. But, just as delicate fare does not stop you from craving for saveloys, so tried and exquisite friendship does not take away your taste for something new and dubious.

With Rosita, with Délia, I was insured against the risk of making confidences. My hidden past climbed the familiar stairs with me, sat secretly beside Délia, rearranged furniture on its old plan, revived the colours of the 'rainy moon' and sharpened a weapon once used against myself.

'Is it a profession you chose yourself, Délia?'

'Not exactly. In January, this year, I took it up again because it means I can work at home.'

She opened the beak of her fine scissors.

'It's good for me to handle pointed things.'

There was a gravity about her, like the gravity of a young

madwoman, that oddly suited Délia. I thought it unwise to encourage her further than by a questioning glance.

'Pointed things,' she reiterated. 'Scissors, needles, pins . . . It's good.'

'Would you like me to introduce you to a sword-swallower, a knife-thrower and a porcupine?'

She deigned to laugh and that chromatic laugh made me sorry she was not happy more often. A powerful feminine voice in the street called out the greengrocer's cry.

'Oh, it's the cherry cart,' murmured Délia.

Without taking time to put on my felt hat, I went down bareheaded and bought a kilo of white-heart cherries. Running to avoid a motor-car, I bumped into a man who had stopped outside *my* door.

'Another moment, Madame, and your cherries . . .'

I smiled at this passer-by, who was a typical Parisian, with a lively face, a few white threads in his black hair and fine, tired eyes that suggested an engraver or printer. He was lighting a cigarette, without taking his eyes off the first-floor window. The lighted match burnt his fingers; he let it drop and turned away.

A cry of pleasure – the first I had ever heard from Délia's lips – greeted my entrance, and the young woman pressed the back of my hand against her cheek. Feeling oddly rewarded, I watched her eating the cherries and putting the stalks and stones into the lid of a box of pins. Her expression of greed and selfishness did not deprive her of the charm that makes us feel tender towards violent children, withdrawn into their own passions and refusing to condescend to be pleasant.

'Just imagine, Délia, down there on the pavement . . .'

She stopped eating, with a big cherry bulging inside her cheek.

'What, down there on the pavement?'

'There's a man looking up at your windows. A very charming man, too.'

She swallowed her cherry and hastily spat out the stone.

'What's he like?'

'Dark, a face . . . well, pleasant . . . white hairs in his black hair. He's got red-brown stains on his finger-tips, they're the fingers of a man who smokes too much.'

As she tucked her slipperless feet under her again with a sudden movement, Délia scattered all her fragile needlework tools on the floor.

'What day is it today? Friday, isn't it? Yes, Friday.'

'Is he your Friday lover? Have you got one for all the days of the week?'

She stared full in my face with the insulting glare adolescents reserve for anyone who treats them as 'big babies'.

'You know everything, don't you?'

She rose to pick up her embroidery equipment. As she flourished a delicate little antique purse she was copying against the light, I noticed her hands were trembling. She turned towards me with a forced playfulness.

'He's nice, isn't he, my Friday lover? D'you think he's attractive?'

'I think he's attractive, but I don't think he looks well. You ought to look after him.'

'Oh! I look after him all right, you needn't worry about *him*.'

She began to laugh crazily, so much so that she brought on a fit of coughing. When she had stopped laughing and coughing, she leant against a piece of furniture as if overcome with giddiness, staggered and sat down.

'It's exhaustion,' she muttered.

Her black hair, which had come down, fell no lower than her shoulders. Combed up on her temples and revealing her ears, it looked like an untidy little girl's and accentuated the regularity of her profile and its childish, inexorable cast.

'It's exhaustion.' But what exhaustion? Due to an unhealthy life? No unhealthier than my own, as healthy as that of all women and girls who live in Paris. A few days earlier Délia had touched her forehead and clutched her temples: 'It's there I wear myself out . . . And there . . .' Yes, the fixed idea; the absent man, the faithless Essendier. No matter how much I studied that perfect beauty – if you scanned it carefully, there was not a flaw in Délia's face – I searched it in vain for any expression of suffering, in other words, of love.

She remained seated, a little out of breath, with her slender pointed scissors dangling over her black dress from a metal chain. My scrutiny did not embarrass her, but, after a few moments, she stood up like someone getting on her way again and reproaching herself for having lingered too long. The change in the light and in the street-noises told me the afternoon was over and I got myself ready to leave. Behind me, irreproachably slim, with her muted fairness, stood Mademoiselle Rosita. For some time, I had lost the habit of looking at her; she struck me as having aged. It struck me too that, through the wide-open door, she had probably heard us joking about the Friday lover. At the same instant, I realized that, in frequenting the Barberet sisters for no reason, I left the elder sister out in the cold. My intercourse with her was limited to our brief professional conversations and to polite nothings, observations about the weather, the high cost of living and the cinema. For Mademoiselle Rosita would never have allowed herself to ask any question that touched on my personal life, on my obvious freedom of a woman who lived alone. But how many days was it since I had displayed the faintest interest in Rosita? I felt embarrassed by this, and, as Délia was making her way to the bathroom, I meditated being 'nice' to Rosita. An exemplary worker, endowed with sterling virtues and even with natural distinction, who types Vandérem's manuscripts and Arthur Bernède's novelettes and my own crossed-out and interlined pages deserved a little consideration.

With her hands clasped palm to palm, her two little ringlets on her right shoulder, she was waiting patiently for me to go. As I went up to her, I saw she was paying not the slightest heed to me. What she was staring at was Délia's back as she left the room. Her eyes, of a middling blue, were hardened; they never left the short, slightly Spanish figure of her sister and the black hair that she was putting up with a careless hand. And, as we take our interior shocks and shudders for divination, I thought as I walked down the hill, whose houses were already rosy at the top: 'But it's in the depths of this prim, colourless Rosita that I must find the answer to this little enigma brooding between the divan and the solitary window of a bedroom where a young woman is pretending, out of sheer obstinacy and jealousy, to relive a moment of my own life. The stubborn young woman very likely has few clues to the little enigma. If she knew more about it, she would never tell me. Her mystery, or her appearance of mystery, is a gratuitous gift; she might just as well have had a golden strand in her black hair or a mole on her cheek.'

Nevertheless, I continued walking along the pavements where, now that it was June, the concierges sitting out on their chairs, the children's games and the flight of balls obliged one to perform a kind of country-dance, two steps forward, two steps back, swing to the right and turn . . . The smell of stopped-up sinks, in June, dominates the exquisite pink twilights. By contrast I quite loved my western district that echoed like an empty corridor. A surprise awaited me in the form of a telegram: Sido, my mother, was arriving on the morrow and was staying in Paris three days. After this particular one, she only made a single last journey away from her own surroundings.

While she was there, there was no question of the Barberet young ladies. I am not concerned here to describe her stay. But her exacting presence recalled my life to dignity and solicitude. In her company, I had to pretend to be almost as young as she was, to follow her impulsive flights. I was terrified to see her so very small and thin, feverish in her enchanting gaiety and as if hunted. But I was still far from admitting the idea that she might die. Did she not insist, the very day she arrived, on buying pansy-seeds, hearing a comic opera and seeing a collection bequeathed to the Louvre? Did she not arrive bearing three pots of raspberry-and-currant jam and the first roses in bud wrapped up in a damp handkerchief, and had she not made me a barometer by sewing weather-predicting wild oats on to a square of cardboard?

She abstained, as always, from questioning me about my most intimate troubles. The sexual side of my life inspired her, I think, with great and motherly repugnance. But I had to keep guard over my words and my face and to beware of her look which read right through the flesh she had created. She liked to hear the news of my men and women friends, and of any newly formed acquaintances. I omitted however to tell her the Barberet story.

Sitting opposite me at the table, pushing away the plate she had not emptied, she questioned me less about what I was writing than about what I wanted to write. I have never been subjected to any criticism that resembled Sido's for, while believing in my vocation as a writer, she was dubious about my career. 'Don't forget that you have only one gift,' she used to say. 'But what is one gift? One gift has never been enough for anyone.'

The air of Paris intoxicated her as if she had been a young girl from the provinces. When she left, I put her on her slow train, anxious about letting her travel alone, yet happy to know that, a few hours later, she would be in the haven of her little home where there were no comforts but also no dangers.

After her departure, everything seemed to me unworthy of pursuit. The wholesome sadness, the pride, the other good qualities she had instilled into me could not be more than ephemeral, I had already lived away from her too long. Yet, when she had gone, I took up my place again in the deep embrasure of my window and once more switched on my green-shaded daylight lamp. But I was impelled by necessity, rather than by love, of doing a good piece of work. And I wrote until it was time to travel by métro up the hill whose slope I liked to descend on foot.

Mademoiselle Rosita opened the door to me. By chance, she exclaimed 'Ah!' at the sight of me, which checked a similar exclamation of surprise on my own lips. In less than a fortnight, my withered young girl had become a withered old maid. A little charwoman's bun replaced the bow and the two ringlets; she was wearing a bibbed apron tied round her waist. She mechanically fingered her right shoulder and stammered:

'You've caught me not properly dressed. I've been dreadfully rushed these last days.'

I shook her dry, delicate hand which melted away in mine. A rather common scent, mingled with the smell of a frying-pan in which cooking-oil is being heated, revived my old memory of the little flat and of the younger sister.

'Are you keeping well? And your sister too?'

She jerked her shoulders in a way that signified nothing definite. I added, with involuntary pride:

'You understand, I've had my mother with me for a few days.

And how's Délia getting on? Still working hard? Can I go and say how d'you do to her?'

Mademoiselle Rosita lowered her head as sheep do when they are mustering up their courage to fight.

'No, you can't. That is to say you can, but I don't see why you should go and say how d'you do to a murderess.'

'What did you say?'

'To a murderess. *I* have to stay here. But you, what have *you* got to do with a murderess?'

Even her manner had changed. Mademoiselle Rosita remained polite but she used a tone of profound indifference to utter words that could have been considered monstrous. I could not even see her familiar little white collar; it was replaced by a piece of coarse sky-blue machine embroidery.

'But, Mademoiselle, I couldn't possibly have guessed. I was bringing you . . .'

'Very good,' she said promptly. 'Will you come in here?'

I went into the big room, just as in the days when Mademoiselle Rosita used adroitly to bar one from entering Délia's bedroom. I unpacked my manuscript in the intolerable glare of the unshaded windows and gave instructions as if to a stranger. Like a stranger, Rosita listened, and said: 'Very good . . . Exactly . . . One black and one purple . . . It'll be finished Wednesday.' The frequent, unnecessary interjections – 'Madame . . . Yes, Madame . . . Oh! Madame . . .' had vanished from her replies. In her conversation too, she had cut out the ringlets.

As in the days of my first curiosity, I kept my patience at first, then suddenly lost it. I hardly lowered my voice, as I asked Mademoiselle Barberet point blank:

'Whom has she killed?'

The poor girl, taken by surprise, made a small despairing gesture and leant against the table with both hands.

'Ah! Madame, it's not done yet, but he's going to die.'

'Who?'

'Why, her husband, Eugène.'

'Her husband? The man she was waiting for day and night? I thought he had left her?'

'Left her, that's easier said than done. They didn't get on but you mustn't think the fault was on his side, very far from it. He's a very nice boy indeed, Eugène is, Madame. And he's never stopped sending my sister something out of what he earns, you know. But she – *she's* taken it into her head to revenge herself.'

In the increasing confusion that was overtaking Rosita Barberet, I thought I could detect the disorder of a mind in which the poison of an old love was at work. The commonplace, dangerous rivalry between the pretty sister and the faded sister. A strand of hair, escaped from Rosita's perfunctorily scraped-up bun, became, in my eyes, the symbol of a madwoman's vehemence. The 'rainy moon' gleamed in its seven colours on the wall of my former refuge, now given over to enemies in process of accusing each other, fighting each other.

'Mademoiselle Rosita, I do beg you. Aren't you exaggerating a little? This is a very serious accusation, you realize.'

I did not speak roughly, for I am frightened of harmless lunatics, of people who deliver long monologues in the street without seeing us, of purple-faced drunks who shake their fists at empty space and walk zigzag. I wanted to take back my manuscript, but the roll of papers had been grabbed by Rosita and served to punctuate her sentences. She spoke violently, without raising her voice:

'I definitely mean, revenge herself, Madame. When she realized he did not love her any more, she said to herself: "I'll get you." So she cast a spell on him.'

The word was so unexpected that it made me smile and Rosita noticed it.

'Don't laugh, Madame. Anyone would think you really didn't know what you were laughing about.'

A metallic object fell, on the other side of the door, and Rosita gave a start.

'Well! right, so it's the scissors now,' she said, speaking to herself.

She must have read on my face something like a desire to be elsewhere, and tried to reassure me.

'Don't be afraid. She knows quite well that you're here, but if you don't go into her room, she won't come into this one.'

'I'm not afraid,' I said sharply. 'What has she given him? A drug?'

'She's convoked him. Convoking, do you know what that is?'

'No . . . that's to say I've got some vague idea, but I don't know all the . . . the details.'

'Convoking is summoning a person by force. That poor Eugène . . .'

'Wait!' I exclaimed in a low voice. 'What's he like, your brother-in-law? He's not a dark young man who's got white hairs among his black ones? He looks rather ill, he's got the complexion of people who have a cardiac lesion? Yes? Then it was him I saw about . . . say two weeks ago.'

'Where?'

'Down there, in the street. He was looking up at the window of my . . . the window of Délia's bedroom. He looked as if he were waiting. I even warned Délia she had a lover under her window . . .'

Rosita clasped her hands.

'Oh! Madame! And you didn't tell me! A whole fortnight!'

She let her arms fall and hang limp over her apron. Her light eyes held a reproach, which, to me, seemed quite meaningless. She looked at me without seeing me, her spectacles in her hand, with an intense, unfocused, gaze.

'Mademoiselle Rosita, you don't really mean to say you're accusing Délia of witchcraft and black magic?'

'But indeed I am, Madame! What she is doing is what they call convoking, but it's the same thing.'

'Listen, Rosita, we're not living in the Middle Ages now . . . Think calmly for a moment . . .'

'But I am thinking calmly, Madame. I've never done anything else! This thing she's doing, she's not the only one who's doing it. It's quite common. Mark you, I don't say it succeeds every time. Didn't you know anything about it?'

I shook my head and the other faintly shrugged her shoulders, as if to indicate that my education had been seriously lacking. A clock somewhere struck midday and I rose to go. Absorbed in her own thoughts, Rosita followed me to the door out of mechanical politeness. In the dark hall, the plate-shaped ceiling-light chiselled her features into those of a haggard old lady.

'Rosita,' I said, 'if your sister's surprised I didn't ask to see her . . .'

'She won't be surprised,' she said, shaking her head. 'She's far too occupied in doing evil.'

She looked at me with an irony of which I had not believed her capable.

'And besides, you know, this is not a good moment to see her. She's not at all pretty, these days. If she were, it really wouldn't be fair.'

Suddenly, I remembered Délia's extraordinary words: 'It's good for me to touch pointed things, scissors, pins.' Overcome by the excitement of passing on baleful news, I bent over and repeated them in Rosita's ear. She seized the top of my arm, in a familiar way, and drew me out on to the landing.

'I'll bring you back your typed pages tomorrow evening about half-past six or seven. Make your escape, *she'll* be asking me to get her lunch.'

I did not savour the pleasure I had anticipated, after leaving Rosita Barberet. Yet, when I thought over the extravagance, the ambitiousness of this anecdote which aspired to be a sensational news item, I found that it lacked only one thing, guilelessness. A want of innocence spoilt its exciting colour, all its suggestion of old women's gossip and brewings of mysterious herbs and magic potions. For I do not care for the picturesque when it is based on feelings of black hatred. As I returned to my own neighbourhood, I compared the Barberet story with 'the story of the Rue Truffaut' and found the latter infinitely pleasanter with its circle of worthy women in the Batignolles district who, touching hands round a dinner table, conversed with the great beyond and received news of their dead children and their departed husbands. They never enquired my name because I had been introduced by the local hairdresser and they slipped me a warning to mistrust a lady called X. It so happened that the advice was excellent. But the principal attraction of the meeting lay in the darkened room, in the table-cloth bordered with a bobble-fringe that matched the one on the curtains, in the spirit of a young sailor, an invisible and mischievous ghost who haunted it on regular days, and shut himself up in the cupboard in order to make all the cups and saucers rattle. 'Ah! *that* chap . . .' the stout mistress of the house would sigh indulgently.

'You let him get away with anything, Mamma,' her daughter (the medium) would say reproachfully. 'All the same, it would be a pity if he broke the blue cup.'

At the end of the séance, these ladies passed round cups of pale, tepid tea. What peace, what charm there was in being entertained by these hostesses whose social circle relied entirely on an extra-terrestrial world! How agreeable I found her too, that female bone-setter, Mademoiselle Lévy, who undertook the care of bodies and souls and demanded so little money in exchange! She practised massage and the laying on of hands in the darkest depths of pallid concierges' lodges, in variety artistes' digs in the Rue Biot and dressing-rooms in the music-halls of La Fauvette. She sewed beautiful Hebrew characters into sachets and hung them round your neck: 'You can be assured of its efficaciousness, it is prepared by the hands of innocence.' And she would display her beautiful hands, softened by creams and unguents, and add: 'If things don't go better tomorrow, when I go away, I can light a candle for you to Our Lady of Victories. *I'm* on good terms with everyone.'

Certainly, in the practices of innocent, popular magic, I was not such a novice as I had wished to appear in the eyes of Mademoiselle Barberet. But, in frequenting my ten- or twenty-franc sibyls, all I had done was to amuse myself, to listen to the rich but limited music of old, ritual words, to abandon my hands into hands so foreign to me, so worn smooth by contact with other human hands, that I benefited from them for a moment as I might have done from immersing myself in a crowd or listening to some voluble, pointless story. In short, they acted on me like a pain-killing drug, warranted harmless to children . . .

Whereas these mutual enemies, the Barberets . . . A blind alley, haunted by evil designs, was this what had become of the little flat where once I had suffered without bitterness, watched over by my rainy moon?

And so I reckoned up everything in the realm of the inexplicable that I owed to some extent to obtuse go-betweens, to vacant creatures whose emptiness reflects fragments of destinies, to modest liars and vehement visionaries. Not one of these women had done me any harm, not one of them had frightened me. But these two sisters, so utterly unlike . . .

I had had so little for lunch that I was glad to go and dine at a modest restaurant whose proprietress was simply known as 'that fat woman who knows how to cook'. It was rare for me not to meet under its low ceilings one of those people one calls 'friends' and who are sometimes, in fact, affectionate. I seem to remember that, with Count d'Adelsward de Fersen, I crowned my orgy – *bœuf à l'ancienne* and cider – by spending two hours at the cinema. Fersen, fair-haired and coated with brick-red sun-tan, wrote verses and did not like women. But he was so cut out to be attractive to all females that one of them exclaimed at the sight of him: 'Ah! What waste of a good thing!' Intolerant and well-read, he had a quick temper and his exaggerated flamboyance hid a fundamental shyness. When we left the restaurant, Gustave Téry was just beginning his late dinner. But the founder of *L'Œuvre* gave me no other greeting than some buffalo-like glares, as was his habit whenever he was swollen with polemic fury and imagined he was being persecuted. Spherical, light on his feet, he entered like a bulky cloud driven by a gale. Either I am mistaken or else, that night, everyone I ran into, the moment I recognized them, showed an extraordinary tendency to move away and disappear. My last meeting was with a prostitute who was eyeing the pedestrians at the corner of the street, about a hundred steps from the house where I lived. I did not fail to say a word to her, as well as to the wandering cat who was keeping her company. A large, warm moon, a yellow June moon, lit up my homeward journey. The woman, standing on her short shadow, was talking to the cat Mimine. She was only interested in meteorology or, at least, so one would have imagined from her rare words. For six months I had seen her in a shapeless coat and a cloche hat, with a little military plume, that hid the top of her face.

'It's a mild night,' she said, by way of greeting. 'But you mustn't imagine it's going to last, the mist is all in one long sheet over the stream. When it's in big separate puffs like bonfires, that means fine weather. So you're back again, on foot, as usual?'

I offered her one of the cigarettes Fersen had given me. She remained faithful to the district longer than I did, with her shadow crouched like a dog at her feet, this shepherdess without a flock who talked about bonfires and thought of the Seine as a stream. I hope that she has long been sleeping, alone for ever more, and dreaming of hay-lofts, of dawns crisp with frosted dew, of mists clinging to the running water that bears her along with it.

The little flat I occupied at that time was the envy of my rare visitors. But I soon knew that it would not hold me for long. Not that its three rooms — let's say two-and-a-half rooms — were inconvenient, but they thrust into prominence single objects that, in other surroundings, had been one of a pair. Now I only possessed one of the two beautiful red porcelain vases, fitted up as a lamp. The second Louis Quinze armchair held out its slender arms elsewhere for someone else to rest in. My square book-case waited in vain for another square book-case and is still waiting for it. This series of amputations suffered by my furniture distressed no one but myself, and Rosita Barberet did not fail to exclaim: 'Why, it's a real nest!' as she clasped her gloved hands in admiration. A low shaft of sunlight — Honnorat had not yet finished serving his time as a page, and seven on the Charles X clock meant that it was a good seven hours since noon — reached my writing-table, shone through a small carafe of wine, and touched, on its way, a little bunch of those June roses that are sold by the dozen, in Paris, in June.

I was pleased to see that she was once again the prim, neat Rosita, dressed in black with her touch of white lingerie at the neck. Fashion at that time favoured little short capes held in place by tie-ends that were crossed in front and fastened at the back of the waist. Mademoiselle Barberet knew how to wear a Paris hat, which means a very simple hat. But she seemed to have definitely repudiated the two little ringlets over one shoulder. The brim of her hat came down over the sad snail-shaped bun, symbol of all renouncements, on the thin, greying nape and the face it shaded was wasted with care. As I poured out a glass of

Lunel for Rosita, I wished I could also offer her lipstick and powder, some form of rejuvenating make-up.

She began by pushing away the burnt-topaz-coloured wine and the biscuits.

'I'm not accustomed to it, Madame, I only drink water with a dash of wine in it or sometimes a little beer.'

'Just a mouthful. It's a wine for children.'

She drank a mouthful, expostulated, drank another mouthful and yet another, making little affected grimaces because she had not learnt to be simple, except in her heart. Between times, she admired everything her short-sightedness made it impossible for her to see clearly. Soon she had one red cheek and one pale cheek and some little threads of blood in the whites of her eyes, round the brightened blue of the iris. All this would have made a middle-aged woman look younger but Mademoiselle Barberet was only a girl, still young and withered before her time.

'It's a magic potion,' she said, with her typical smile that seemed set in inverted commas.

Continuing, as if she were speaking a line in a play, she sighed: 'Ah! if that poor Eugène . . .'

By this, I realized that her time was limited and I wanted to know how long she had.

'Has your sister gone out? She's not waiting for you?'

'I told her I was bringing you your typescript and that I was also going to look in on Monsieur Vandérem and Monsieur Lucien Muhlfeld so as to make only one journey of it. If she's in a hurry for her dinner, there's some vegetable soup left over from yesterday, a boiled artichoke and some stewed rhubarb.'

'In any case, the little restaurant on the right as you go down your street . . .'

Mademoiselle Barberet shook her head.

'No. She doesn't go out. She doesn't go out any more.' She swallowed a drop of wine left in the bottom of her glass, then folded her arms in a decided way on my work-table, just opposite me. The setting sun clung for a moment to all the features of her half-flushed, half-pale face, to a turquoise brooch that fastened her collar. I wanted to come to her aid and spare her the preamble.

'I have to admit, Rosita, that I didn't quite understand what you were saying to me yesterday.'

'I realized that,' she said, with a little whinny. 'At first I thought you were making fun of me. A person as well-read as you are ... To put it in two words instead of a hundred, Madame, my sister is in process of making her husband die. On my mother's memory, Madame, she is killing him. Six moons have already gone by, the seventh is coming, that's the fatal moon, this unfortunate man knows that he's doomed, besides he's already had two accidents, from which he's entirely recovered, but all the same it's a handicap that puts him in a state of less resistance and makes the task easier for *her*.'

She would have exceeded the hundred words in her first breath, had not her haste and, no doubt, the warmth of the wine slightly choked her. I profited by her fit of coughing to ask:

'Mademoiselle Rosita, just one question. Why should Délia want to make her husband die?'

She threw up her hands in a disclaiming gesture of impotence.

'Ah, as to that ... you may well hunt for the real reason! All the usual reasons between a man and a woman! And you don't love me any more and I still love you, and you wish I were dead and come back I implore you, and I'd like to see you in hell.'

She gave a brutal 'Hah!' and grimaced.

'My poor Rosita, if all couples who don't get on resorted to murder ...'

'But they do resort to it,' she protested. 'They make no bones about resorting to it!'

'You see very few cases reported in the papers.'

'Because it's all done in private, it's a family affair. Nine times out of ten, no one gets arrested. It's talked about a little in the neighbourhood. But just you see if you can find any traces! Fire-arms, poisons, that's all out-of-date stuff. My sister knows that all right. What about the woman who keeps the sweet-shop just below us, whatever's *she* done with her husband? And the milkman at Number 57, rather queer isn't it that he's gone and lost his second wife too?'

Her refined, high-class saleslady's vocabulary had gone to pieces and she had thrust out her chin like a gargoyle. With a flip of her finger, she pushed back her hat which was pinching her forehead. I was as shocked as if she had pulled up her skirt and fastened her suspenders without apologizing. She uncovered a high forehead, with sloping temples, which I had never seen so nakedly revealed, from whence I imagined there was to be a burst of confidences and secrets that might or might not be dangerous. Behind Rosita, the window was turning pink with the last faint rose reflection of daylight. Yet I dared not switch on my lamp at once.

'Rosita,' I said seriously, 'are you in the habit of saying . . . what you've just said to me . . . to just anybody?'

Her eyes looked frankly straight into mine.

'You must be joking, Madame. Should I have come so far if I'd had anyone near me who deserved to be trusted?'

I held out my hand, which she grasped. She knew how to shake hands, curtly and warmly, without prolonging the pressure.

'If you believe that Délia is doing harm to her husband, why don't you try to counteract that harm? Because *you*, at least it seems so to me, wish nothing but good to Eugène Essendier.'

She gazed at me dejectedly.

'But I can't, Madame! Love would have to have passed between Eugène and me. And it hasn't passed between us! It's never passed, never, never!'

She pulled a handkerchief out of her bag and wept, taking care not to wet her little starched neck-piece. I thought I had understood everything. 'Now we have it, jealousy of course.' Promptly Rosita's accusations and she herself became suspect, and I turned on the switch of my lamp.

'That doesn't mean I must go, Madame?' she asked anxiously.

'Of course not, of course not,' I said weakly.

The truth was that I could hardly bear the sight, under the strong rays of my lamp, of her red-eyed face and her hat tipped backwards like a drunken woman's. But Rosita had hardly begun to talk.

'Eugène has never even thought of wanting me,' she said humbly. 'If he had wanted me, even just once, I'd be in a position to fight against her, you understand.'

'No. I don't understand. I've everything to learn, as you see. Do you really attribute so much importance to the fact of having . . . having belonged to a man?'

'And you? Do you really attribute so little to it?'

I decided to laugh.

'No, no, Rosita, I'm not so frivolous, unfortunately. But, all the same, I don't think it constitutes a bond, that it sets a seal on you.'

'Well, you're mistaken, that's all. Possession gives you the power to summon, to convoke, as they say. Have you really never "called" anyone?'

'Indeed I have,' I said laughing. 'I must have hit on someone deaf. I didn't get an answer.'

'Because you didn't call hard enough, for good or evil. My sister, *she* really does call. If you could see her. She's unrecognizable. Also she's up to some pretty work, I can assure you.'

She fell silent, and, for a moment, it was quite obvious she had stopped thinking of me.

'But, Eugène himself, couldn't you warn him?'

'I have warned him. But Eugène, he's a sceptic. He told me he'd had enough of one crack-brained woman and that the second crack-brained woman would do him a great favour if she'd shut up. He's got pockets under his eyes and he's the colour of butter. From time to time he coughs, but not from the chest, he coughs because of palpitations of the heart. He said to me: "All I can do for you is to lend you *Fantomas*. It's just your cup of tea." That just shows,' added Mademoiselle Barberet, with a bitter smile. 'That just shows how the most intelligent men can argue like imbeciles, seeing no difference between fantastic made-up stories and things as real as this . . . as such deadly machinations.'

'But what machinations, will you kindly tell me?' I exclaimed.

Mademoiselle Barberet unfolded her spectacles and put them on, wedging them firmly in the brown dints that marked either side of her transparent nose. Her gaze became focused, taking on new assurance and a searching expression.

'You know,' she murmured, 'that it is never too late to

summon? You have quite understood that one can *summon* for good and for evil?'

'I know it now that you have told me.'

She pushed my lamp a little to one side and leant over closer to me. She was hot and nothing is so unbearable to me as the human smell except when – very rarely indeed – I find it intoxicating. Moreover, the wine to which she was not accustomed kept repeating and her breath smelt of it. I wanted to stand up but she was already talking.

There are things that are written down nowhere, except by clumsy hands in school exercise books, or on thin grey-squared paper, yellowed at the edges, folded and cut into pages and sewn together with red cotton; things that the witch bequeathed to the bone-setter, that the bone-setter sold to the love-obsessed woman, that the obsessed one passed on to another wretched creature. All that the credulity and the sullied memory of a pure girl can gather in the dens that an unfathomable city harbours between a brand-new cinema and an espresso-bar, I heard from Rosita Barberet, who had learnt it from the vaunts of widows who had willed the deaths of the husbands who had deserted them, from the frenzied fantasies of lonely women.

'You say a name, nothing but the name, the name of the particular person, a hundred times, a thousand times. No matter how far away they are, they will hear you in the end. Without eating or drinking, as long as you can possibly keep it up, you say the name, nothing else but the name. Don't you remember one day when Délia nearly fainted? I suspected at once. In our neighbourhood there are heaps of them who repeated the name . . .'

Whisperings, an obtuse faith, even a local custom, were these the forces and the magic philtres that procured love, decided life and death, removed that lofty mountain, an indifferent heart?

'. . . One day when you rang the bell, and my sister was lying behind the door . . .'

'Yes, I remember . . . You asked me: "Is that you, Eugène?"'

'She'd said to me: "Quick, quick, he's coming. I can feel it, quick, he must tread on me as he comes in, it's essential!" But it was you.'

'It was only me.'

'She'd been lying there, believe me or not, for over two hours. Soon after that, she took to pointed things again, Knives, scissors, embroidery needles. That's very well known, but it's dangerous. If you haven't enough strength, the points can turn against you. But do you imagine *that one* would ever lack strength? If I lived the life she does, I should have been dead by now. *I've* got nothing to sustain me.'

'Has she, then?'

'Of course she has. She hates. That nourishes her.'

That Délia, so young, with her rather arrogant beauty, her soft cheek that she laid against my hand. That was the same Délia who played with twenty little glittering thunderbolts that she intended to be deadly, and she used their sharp points to embroider beaded flowers.

'. . . But she's given up embroidering bags now. She's taken to working with needles whose points she's contaminated.'

'What did you say?'

'I said, she's contaminated them by dipping them in a mixture.'

And Rosita Barberet launched out into the path, strewn with nameless filth, into which the practice of base magic drags its faithful adherents. She pursued that path without blenching, without omitting a word, for fastidiousness is not a feminine virtue. She would not allow me to remain ignorant of one thing to which her young sister stooped in the hope of doing injury, that same sister who loved fresh cherries . . . So young, with one of those rather short bodies a man's arms clasp so easily, and, beneath that black, curly hair, the pallor that a lover longs to crimson.

Luckily, the narratress branched off and took to talking only about death, and I breathed again. Death is not nauseating. She discoursed on the imminent death of this unfortunate Eugène, which so much resembled the death of the husband of the woman in the sweet-shop! And then there was the chemist, who had died quite black.

'You must surely admit, Madame, that the fact of a chemist

being fixed like that by his wife, that really is turning the world upside down!'

I certainly did admit it. I even derived a strange satisfaction from it. What did I care about the chemist and the unlucky husband of the woman who kept the sweet-shop? All I was waiting for now from my detailed informant was one final picture: Délia arriving at the cross-roads where, amidst the vaporous clouds produced by each one's illusion, the female slaves of the cloven-footed one meet for the sabbath.

'Yes, indeed. And where does the devil come in, Rosita?'

'What devil, Madame?'

'Why the devil pure and simple, I presume. Does your sister give him a special name?'

An honest amazement was depicted on Rosita's face and her eyebrows flew up to the top of her high forehead.

'But, Madame, whatever trail are you off on now. The devil, that's just for imbeciles. The devil, just imagine . . .'

She shrugged her shoulders, and, behind her glasses, threw a withering glance at discredited Satan.

'The devil! Admitting he existed, he'd be just the one to mess it all up!'

'Rosita, you remind me at this moment of the young woman who said: "God, that's all hooey! . . . But no jokes in front of me about the Blessed Virgin!"'

'Everyone's got their own ideas, Madame. Good heavens! It's ten to eight! It was very kind of you to let me come,' she sighed in a voice that did not disguise her disappointment.

For I had offered her neither help nor connivance. She pulled down her hat – at last – over her forehead. I remembered, just in time, that I had not paid her for her last lot of work.

'A drop of Lunel before you go, Mademoiselle Rosita?'

Involuntarily, by calling her 'Mademoiselle' again, I was putting her at a distance. She swallowed the golden wine in one gulp and I complimented her.

'Oh, I've got a good head,' she said.

But, as she had folded up her spectacles again, she searched round for me with a vague eye, and, as she went out, she bumped against the door-post, to which she made a little apologetic bow.

As soon as she had gone, I opened the window to its fullest extent to let in the evening air. Mistaking the feeling of exhaustion her visit had given me for genuine tiredness, I made the error of going to bed early. My dreams showed the effects of it and, through them, I realized I was not yet rid of the two enemy sisters nor of another memory. I kept relapsing into a nightmare in which I was now my real self, now identified with Délia. Half-reclining, like her on *our* divan-bed, in the dark part of our room, I 'convoked' with a powerful summons, with a thousand repetitions of his name, a man who was not called Eugène . . .

Dawn found me drenched with those abundant tears we rain in sleep and that go on flowing after we are awake and can no longer track them to their source. The thousand-times repeated name grew dim and lost its nocturnal power. In my own mind, I said farewell to it and thrust its echo back into the little flat where I had taken pleasure in suffering. And I abandoned that flat to those other women, to their stifled, audacious, incantation-ridden lives where witchcraft could be fitted in between the daily task and the Saturday cinema, between the little wash-tub and the frying steak.

When the short night was ended, I promised myself that never again would I climb the Paris hill with the steep, gay streets. Between one day and the next, I turned Rosita's furtive charm, her graceful way of putting down her slender feet when she walked and the two little ringlets that fluttered on her shoulder, into a memory. With that Délia who did not want to be called Adèle, I had a little more trouble. All the more so, as, after the lapse of a fortnight, I took to running into her by pure chance. Once she was rummaging in a box of small remnants near the entrance of a big shop, and three days later she was buying spaghetti in an Italian grocer's. She looked pale and diminished, like a convalescent who is out too soon, pearly under the eyes, and extremely pretty. A thick, curled fringe covered her forehead to the eyebrows. Something indescribable stirred in the depths of myself and spoke in her favour. But I did not answer.

Another time, I recognized only her walk, seeing her from the back. We were walking along the same pavement and I had to slow down my step so as not to overtake her. For she was advancing by little, short steps, then making a pause, as if out of breath, and going on again. Finally, one Sunday when I was returning with Annie de Pène from the flea-market and, loaded with treasure such as milk-glass lamps and Rubelles plates, we were having a rest and drinking lemonade, I caught sight of Délia Essendier. She was wearing a dress whose black showed purplish in the sunlight, as happens with re-dyed fabrics. She stopped not far from us in front of a fried-potato stall, bought a large bag of chips and ate them with gusto. After that, she stayed standing for a moment, with an air of having nothing to do. The shape of the hat she was wearing recalled a Renaissance 'béguine's', and cupping Délia's little Roman chin was the white crêpe band of a widow.

WEDLOCK

George Egerton

TWO bricklayers are building a yellow brick wall to the rear of one of a terrace of new jerry-built houses in a genteel suburb. At their back is the remains of a grand old garden. Only the unexpired lease saves it from the clutch of the speculator. An apple-tree is in full blossom, and a fine elm is lying on the grass, sawn down, as it stood on the boundary of a 'desirable lot'; many fair shrubs crop up in unexpected places, a daphne-mezereum struggles to redden its berries amid a heap of refuse thrown out by the caretakers; a granite urn, portions of a deftly carven shield, a mailed hand and a knight's casque, relics of some fine old house demolished to accommodate the ever-increasing number of the genteel, lie in the trampled grass. The road in front is scarcely begun, and the smart butchers' carts sink into the soft mud and red brick-dust, broken glass, and shavings; yet many of the houses are occupied, and the unconquerable London soot has already made some of the cheap 'art' curtains look dingy. A brass plate of the 'Prudential Assurance Company' adorns the gate of Myrtle House; 'Collegiate School for Young Ladies' that of Evergreen Villa. Victoria, Albert and Alexandria figure in ornamental letters over the stained-glass latticed square of three pretentious houses, facing Gladstone, Cleopatra and Lobelia. The people move into 26 to the ring of carpenters' hammers in 27, and 'go carts', perambulators, and half-bred fox terriers impede the movements of the men taking in the kitchen boiler to 28.

One of the men, a short, wiry-looking man of fifty, with grizzled sandy hair and a four days' growth of foxy beard on his sharp chin, is whistling 'Barbara Allen' softly as he pats down a brick and scrapes the mortar neatly off the joinings. The other, tall and swarthy, a big man with a loose mouth and handsome wicked eyes and a musical voice, is looking down the lane-way leading to a side street.

''Ere she comes, the lydy wot owns this 'ere desirable abode. I want 'er to lend me a jug. Wo-o-a hup, missis! Blind me tight if she ain't as boozed as they makes 'em! Look at 'er, Seltzer; ain't she a beauty, ain't she a sample of a decent bloke's wife! She's a fair sickener, she iz. Hy, 'old 'ard! She dunno where she are!' with a grin.

But the woman, reeling and stumbling up the lane, neither hears nor sees; she is beyond that. She feels her way to the back-yard door of the next house, and, rocking on her feet, tries to find the pocket of her gown. She is much under thirty, with a finely-developed figure. Her gown is torn from the gathers at the back and trails down, showing her striped petticoat; her jacket is of good material, trimmed with silk, but it is dusty and lime-marked. Her face is flushed and dirty; her light golden-brown fringe stands out straight over her white forehead; her bonnet is awry on the back of her head; her watch dangles from the end of a heavy gold chain, and the buttons of her jersey bodice gape open where the guard is passed through; she has a basket on her left arm. She clutches the wall and fumbles stupidly for the key, mumbling unintelligibly, and trying with all her might to keep her eyes open. The tall man watches her with ill-concealed disgust, and tosses a pretty coarse jest to her. The sandy man lays down his trowel and wipes his hands on his apron, and goes to her.

'Lookin' for yer key, missis? Let me 'elp yer; two 'eads is better nor one enny day!'

'Ca'an fin' it. M'm a bad wom—a bad wom—um,' she says, shaking her head solemnly at him, with heavy lids and distended pupils.

Meanwhile he has searched her pocket and opened the basket —nothing in it except a Family Novelette and a few gooseberries in a paper bag. He shakes his head, saying to himself: 'Dropped her marketing'.

'It ain't here, missis; sure you took it with ye?'

She nods stupidly and solemnly three times.

'Got the larchkey o' the fron' door?' queries the other.

She frowns, tries to pull up her skirt to get at her petticoat pocket, and lurches over.

''Old 'ard, missis, 'old 'ard. Throw them long legs o' yourn acrost the wall, maite, an' see if ye can't let 'er in!' says the little man, catching her deftly. The other agrees, and the key grates in the lock inside and he opens the door.

'She took the key an' lorst it, that's wot she did. She's a nice ole cup o' tea; she's a 'ot member for a mile, she iz, an' no mistaike!' and he takes up his trowel and a brick, singing with a sweet tenor.

The little man helps her into the house through the hall into the parlour. He unties her bonnet-strings, pulls off her jacket, and puts her into an arm-chair.

'Ye jist 'ave a sleep, an' ye'll be all right!'

She clutches at his hand in a foolish sort of way, and her eyes fill with tears.

''Ands orf, missis, 'ands orf, ye jist go to sleep!'

He halts in the kitchen and looks about him. It is very well furnished; the table is littered with unwashed breakfast things on trays—handsome china, plate and table-napkins, all in confusion. He shakes his head, puts some coal in the range, closes the door carefully, and goes back to his work.

'Well, did ye put beauty to bed?' laughs the big man. 'I'd rather Jones owned 'er nor me. 'E picked a noice mother fur iz kids 'e did! Yes, them three little nippers wot come out a wile ago is iz.'

''E must be pretty tidy orf,' says the little man; 'it looks very nice in there, an' seemin'ly the 'ole 'ouse is fitted up alike —pianner an' carpets an' chiffoneers.'

'Oh, Jones iz all right. 'E's a 'cute chap iz Jones. 'E's got a 'ell of a temper, that's all. 'E's bin barman at the Buckin'am for close twenty year; makes a book an' keeps iz eyes peeled. Bless ye, I know Jones since I woz a lad; iz first wife woz a sort o' cousin o' my missis—a clever woman too. 'E took this 'un 'cos 'e thort e'd maike a bit out o' gentlemen lorgers, she bein' a prize cook an' 'e 'avin' the 'ouse out of a buildin' society, an' be a mother to the kids as well. She'll keep no lorgers she won't, an' she's a fair beauty for the kids. If she woz mine'—tapping a brick—'I'd bash 'er 'ed in!'

'Maybe ye wouldn't!' says the little man; 'thet iz if ye understood. Wot if it ain't 'er fault?'

'Ain't 'er fault! Ooze iz it then?'

'That I ain't prepared to say, not knowin' circumstances; but it might be as it runs in 'er family.'

'Well, I'm blowed, I often 'eerd' (with a grin, showing all his white teeth) 'o' wooden legs runnin' that way, but I never 'eerd tell o' gin!'

'Ye ain't a readin' man I take it,' says the little man, with a touch of superiority, 'I thought that way onst meself. My ole woman drinks.' (He says it as if stating a casual fact that calls for no comment.) 'It woz then I came acrorst a book on "'ereditty", wot comes down from parents to children, ye know, an' I set to findin' all about 'er family. I took a 'eap o' trouble about it, I did, I wanted to do fair by 'er. An' then sez I to meself: 'Sam, she carn't 'elp it no more nor the colour of 'er 'air, an' that woz like a pine shavin' in sunshine. 'Er gran'father 'e drunk 'isself dead, an' then iz wife she reared my girl's mother for service—she woz cook at an 'otel in Aylesbury. Well, she married the boots; they 'ad a tidy bit saved, an' they took a country public with land an' orchard an' such like an' they did well for a long time. Then 'e took to liquor. I never could find out iz family 'istory; maybe as 'ow 'e couldn't 'elp it neither. 'E woz a Weller, an' she jined 'im arter a bit, which considerin' 'er father woz to be expected. My ole woman often told me 'ow she an' 'er brother used to 'ide out many a night in the orchard. Well they bust up an' 'e got notice to quit, an' wot does 'e do but goes an' 'angs 'isself to a willer next the well, an' she goes out to git a pail o' water an' finds 'im. That set 'er orf wuss nor ever, an' then she went orf sudden like with a parrylittic stroke. Some laidies took the children an' put 'em to school.' (He works steadily as he speaks.) 'Well, one bank 'olliday twenty-eight year come Whitsun' same date izzackly, I went down with a mate o' mine to an uncle of 'iz in Aylesbury; 'e 'ad a duck farm, an' I seed 'er. She woz as pretty as paint, an' there woz as much difference atween 'er an' city girls, as new milk an' chalk an' water. I woz doin' well, times woz better; I 'ave three trades, when one iz slack I works at another. I got work down there an' we kep' company, an' got our 'ome together, an' woz married, an' woz az 'appy az might be for six year. Then our eldest little lad 'e set 'isself afire one day she woz out, an' they took 'im to the infirmary, but 'e died in a 'our, a' wen we went to fetch 'im 'ome 'e woz rolled in wite bandages most like one o' them mummies in the British Museum. It went to my girl's 'eart like, for she couldn't seem to recognize 'im nohow. An' 'twoz arter that I begin to notice she took a drop. At fust I woz real mad, I gave 'er a black eye onst; but then I came acrorst that book—I woz allus a man for readin'—an' I found out about 'er folk, an' I see az 'ow she couldn't 'elp it. It got worser an' worser an' arter two years we come up to town; I couldn't stand the shame of it. Then I went down to my ole mother; she woz livin' with a widowed sister in Kent, an' I up an' told 'er: I sez, "Mother, ye got to take the kids. I ain't goin' to 'ave no more with the curse on 'em, an' I ain't goin' to 'ave 'em spoiled," an' I took 'em down an' sent 'er money regular, bad times same az good. She went on dreadful at first; I gave 'er a fair chance, I took 'er down to see 'em, and sez I: "Knock off the drink, ole girl, an' ye 'az 'em back!" She tried it, I really believe she did, but bless ye she couldn't, it woz in 'er blood same az the colourin' of 'er skin. I gave up 'ome then, wen she gets right mad she'd pawn everything in the show; I allus puts my own things in a Monday morning an' takes 'em out a Saturday night, it keeps 'em safe. The landlady looks arter 'er own, an' so she ain't got much to dispose on. I can't abide liquor meself, though I don't 'old with preachin' about it; an' that's wy they call me Seltzer Sam, and wy I gets my dinner in a cookshop.'

The little man is laying his bricks carefully one on top of the other.

'You spoke sort o' sharp to your missis today, cos she woz a bit laite, an' I thort as 'ow ye woz uncommon lucky to 'ave 'er come nice and tidy with it—it's twenty years since I woz brought me dinner in a basin.'

There's a silence. The big man looks thoughtful, then he says suddenly:

'Well I couldn't do it, I couldn't do it, that's all I sez. Wy don't ye put 'er away someweres?'

'I did, but lor, it woz no manner o' good. I allus fancied she'd set 'erself o' fire or fall in the street or somethink an' get took to the station on a stretcher with the boys a' callin' "meat" arter 'er, an' I couldn't sleep for thinkin' of it, so I fetched 'er back. We woz very 'appy for six year, an' thet's more nor some folk az in all their lives, an''—with a quaint embarrassment—'she were the only woman as ever I keered for, right from the fust minute I seed 'er 'oldin' a big bunch o' poppies an' that grass they call "wag wantons" down there, in 'er 'and, as pretty as a picture —an' I *didn't marry 'er cos she could cook*, that's no wearin' reason to marry a woman for, leastwise not for me. An' I wouldn't 'ave the children—I call 'em children, though, lor bless yer, they're grown up and doin' well—I wouldn't 'ave 'em think I'd turned their mother out o' doors—no'—with an emphatic dab of mortar—'no, 'er fate's my fate, an' I ain't the kind o' chap to turn the ole woman out for what she can by no manner o' means 'elp!' and he puts another brick neatly on the top of the last and scrapes the oozing mortar.

The big man rubs the back of his hand across his eyes, and says with a gulp:

'Shake 'ands, mate, damme if I know wot to call yer, a bloomin' archangel or a blasted softy.'

The woman lay as he left her, with her feet thrust out in her half-buttoned boots, and her hands hanging straight down. The sun crept round the room, and at length a clock chimed four strokes up on the drawing-room floor. A woman sitting writing at a table between the windows looks up with a sigh of relief, and moistens her lips; they are dry. A pile of closely written manuscript lies on the floor beside her; she drops each sheet as she finishes it.

She is writing for money, writing because she must, because it is the tool given to her wherewith to carve her way; she is nervous, overwrought, every one of her fingers seems as if it had a burning nerve-knot in its tip; she has thrust her slippers aside, for her feet twitch; she is writing feverishly now, for she has been undergoing the agony of a barren period for some weeks, her brain has seemed arid as a sand plain, not a flower of fancy has sprung up in it; she has felt in her despair as if she were hollowed out, honeycombed by her emotions, and she has cried over her mental sterility. Her measure of success has come to her, her public waits, what if she have nothing to give them? The thought has worn her, whispered to her in dreams at night, taken the savour out of her food by day. But this morning a little idea came and grew, grew so blessedly, and she has been working since early day. Her landlady has forgotten her luncheon; she never noticed the omission, but now she feels her frail body give way under the strain; she will finish this chapter and have some tea. She has heard steps below. She writes until the half-hour strikes, then drops the last sheet of paper with a sobbing sigh of relief. She pulls the bell sharply and sits waiting patiently. No one answers it. She rings again; there is a crash downstairs as of china falling with a heavy body, and a smothered groan. She trembles, listens, and then goes down.

The woman is lying in the doorway of the sitting-room, a small table with broken glass and wax flowers on the floor near her. She hides her face as she hears the light step.

'Did you hurt yourself? Can I help you?'

She drags her up, supports her into the bedroom and on to the unmade bed, and goes out into the kitchen. A look of weary disgust crosses her face as she sees the litter on the table. There is a knock at the back door, she opens it; three children peer cautiously in, keen-eyed London children with precocious knowledge of the darker sides of life. They enter holding one another's hands. The eldest signs to the others to sit down, steals up the passage, peers through the slit of the door, and returns with a satisfied look and nods to the others.

'Your mother is not well, I am afraid,' the woman says timidly, she is nervous with children. The three pairs of eyes examine her slowly to see if she is honest.

'Our mother is in heaven!' says the boy as if repeating a formula. 'That's our stepmother, and she's boozed!'

'Johnny!' calls the woman from the inner room. The boy's

face hardens into a sullen scowl, and she notices that he raises his hand involuntarily as if to ward off a blow, and that the smaller ones change colour and creep closer to one another. He goes to her—there is a murmur of voices.

'She sez I'm to get your tea!' he remarks as he comes out, and stirs up the dying fire. 'Ain't *you* 'ad nothin' since mornin'?'

She evades the question by asking: 'Have you children had anything?'

'We took some bread with us.' He opens a purse.

'There's nothin' in it, an' father gave 'er 'arf a sovereign this mornin'!'

'I will give you some money if you come upstairs, and then you can get my tea.'

The boy is deft-handed, prematurely 'cute, with a trick of peering under his lashes. It annoys her, and she is relieved when she has had her tea and got rid of him. She is restless, upset, she feels this means moving again. What a weary round a working woman's life is! She is so utterly alone. The silence oppresses her, the house seems filled with whispers; she cannot shake off this odd feeling, she felt it the first time she entered it; the rooms were pretty, and she took them, but this idea is always with her.

She puts on her hat and goes out, down the half-finished road and into a lighted thoroughfare. Costers' carts are drawn up alongside the pavement; husbands and wives with the inevitable perambulator are pricing commodities; girls are walking arm in arm, tossing back a look or a jest to the youths as they pass. The accents of the passers-by, the vociferous call of the vendors, the jostling of the people jar on her; she turns back with tears in her eyes. Her loneliness strikes doubly home to her, and she resolves to join a women's club; anything to escape it. She pauses near the door to get her latchkey, and notices the boy at the side entrance. He draws back into the shade as he sees her. She stands at her window and looks out into the murky summer night; a man comes whistling down the street; the boy runs to meet him, she sees him bend his head to catch the words better and then they turn back. She lights the gas and tries to read, she dreads the scenes she feels will follow, and she trembles when the door slams below and steps echo down the passage.

There is the low growl of the man's voice and the answers of the woman's, then both rise discordantly—a stifled scream and a heavy fall, footsteps down the passage, the bang of a door, and both voices raised in altercation, with the boy's voice striking shrilly in between—a blow, a crash of china and glass, then stillness. She is breathless with excitement; the quiet is broken by a sound of scuffling in the passage; he is going to put her out. Drag, and shove, and the scraping of feet, and the sullen 'you dare, you dare' of the woman, in reply to his muttered threats. She goes to the top of the stairs and cries:

'Don't hurt her, wait until morning to reason with her, don't hurt her!'

'Reason with *'er*, miss! There ain't no way of reasoning with the likes of 'er, chuck 'er out is the only way. Would ye, would ye? Ye drunken beast!—'

The woman and the man sway together in the passage and her bodice is torn open at the breast and her hair is loose, and she loses her footing and falls as he drags her towards the door. She clutches at the chairs and brass umbrella-stand and drags them down; and the woman, watching, rushes upstairs and buries her face in the sofa cushions. Then the door bangs to and the woman outside rings and knocks and screams; windows open and heads peer out; then the boy lets her in and there seems to be a truce.

A charwoman brings her breakfast next morning, and it is tea-time before she sees *her*. She has on a clean pink cotton gown and her hair is nicely done and her skin looks very pink and white; but her eyes are swollen, and there is a bruise on one temple and a bad scratch on her cheek. She hangs her head sullenly and loiters with the tea-things; then she goes over to her and stands with her eyes on the ground and her hair glittering like golden down on the nape of her thick neck in the light from the window at her back.

'I am sorry for yesterday, miss, it was bad of me, but you won't go away? I won't do it again. Take it off the rent, only forgive me, won't you, miss?'

She is flushing painfully; her face is working, perhaps it seems worse because it is a heavily moulded face and it does not easily express emotions. It has the attractive freshness of youth and vivid colouring.

'We won't say anything more about it. I am so sorry; I am not used to scenes and it made me quite ill; I was frightened, I thought you would be hurt.'

The woman's face changes and as she raises her heavy white lids her eyes seem to look crosswise with a curious gleam in them and her voice is hoarse.

'That little beast told him, the little sneak! But I'll pay him for it, I'll pay him!'

An uneasy dislike stirs in the woman; she says very quietly:

'But you can't expect a man to come home and find you so and then be pleased.'

'No, but he shouldn't—' she checks herself and passes her hand across her forehead. The other woman observes her closely as she does most things—as material. It is not that her sympathies are less keen since she took to writing, but that the habit of analysis is always uppermost. She sees a voluptuously made woman, with a massive milk-white throat rising out of the neck of her pink gown; her jaw is square and prominent, her nose short and straight, her brows traced distinctly; she is attractive and repellent in a singular way.

'You don't know what works in me, miss—' She says no more, but it is evident that something is troubling her and that she is putting restraint on herself. Late in the evening, when the children are in bed, she hears her go up to their room; there is a sound of quick blows and a frightened whimper; and the next morning she is roused from her sleep by a child's scream and the woman's voice uttering low threats:

'Will you be quiet?' (whimper) 'Will you be quiet? I'll teach you to make a row' (more stifled, frightened cries), and she feels in some subtle way that the woman is smothering the child in the bed-clothes. It worries her, and she never looks up at her when she brings her breakfast. The latter feels it and watches her furtively. At lunch time it strikes her that she has been drinking again; she musters heart of grace and says to her:

'You promised to be good, Mrs Jones. It seems to me to be

such a pity that you should drink, why do you? You are very young!'

Her voice is naturally tender, and her words have an unexpected effect; the woman covers her face with her hands and rocks her shoulders. Suddenly she cries:

'I don't know; I get thinkin'; I 'ave 'ad a trouble. I never knew a woman drink for the love of it like men, there's 'most always a cause. Don't think me a bad woman, miss, I ain't really, only I 'ave a trouble.' She talks hurriedly as if she can't help herself, as if the very telling is a necessity. 'I 'ad a little girl' (dropping her voice) 'before I was married—she's turned three, she's such a dear little thing, you never seen such 'air, miss, it's like floss silk an' 'er eyes are china blue, an' 'er lashes are that long'—measuring a good inch on her finger—'an' 'er skin is milk-white. I keep wantin' 'er all the time—' The tears fill her eyes and splash out. 'I was cook in a big business house, an' 'e was the 'ead of it—I was cruel fond of 'im. Then when my time came I went 'ome to my step-sister an' she nursed me. I paid 'er, an' then when I went out to service again she took 'er. I used to see 'er onst or twice a week. But she was fonder of 'er nor me, an' I couldn't bear it, it made me mad, I was jealous of every one as touched 'er. Then Jones, 'e woz always after me, 'e knew about it, an' 'e promised me that I could 'ave 'er if I married 'im. I didn't want to marry, I only wanted 'er, an' I couldn't 'ave 'er with me, an' 'e promised'—with resentful emphasis—''e swore as 'ow I could 'ave 'er. I took 'im on that an' 'e kep' puttin' me off, an' when I went to see 'er, 'e quarrelled, an' once when she was ill 'e wouldn't let me send 'er any money though 'e 'ad wot I saved when I married 'im—it just made me 'ate 'im—I see 'er so seldom, an' she calls '*er* mammy, it 'most kills me—I feel my 'ead burstin'—an' 'e laughed when I told 'im I wouldn't 'ave married 'im only for 'er sake!'

'Poor thing, it is hard, he ought to have kept his promise to you when he made it. Haven't you told him you wouldn't drink if you had her with you?'

'Where's the good? 'E says 'e never meant to keep it; as a man ain't such a fool as to keep a promise 'e makes a woman just to get 'er. 'E knows it sets me off, but 'e's that jealous that 'e can't abear 'er name. 'E says I would neglect 'is children, an' 'e called 'er names an' says 'e won't 'ave no bastard round with 'is children. That made me 'ate 'em first, nasty yellow things—'

'Yes, but the poor children are not to blame for it?'

'No, but they remind me of 'er, an' I 'ate the very sight of 'em.' There is such concentrated hatred in her voice that the woman shrinks. 'I ain't 'ad any money to send 'er this long time, but my sister's 'usband is as fond of 'er as 'is own; they 'ave seven of their own. I 'ate to see things in the shop windows, I used to keep 'er so pretty. I got a letter a while ago sayin' she wasn't very well, an' that set me off. You've spoken kind to me since you've been here, that's w'y I tell you, you won't think worse of me now than I deserve.'

She clears away the things sullenly, with her jaw set, and the strange oblique light flickering in her eyes. It oppresses the other woman; she feels as if she is facing one of those lurid tragedies that outsiders are powerless to prevent. This woman with her fierce devotion to the child of the man who betrayed her; her marriage, into which she has been cheated by a promise never meant to be kept; and the step-children fanning her fierce dislike by the very childish attributes that waken love in other circumstances. She stays a week longer, but every whimper of the children, every fresh outburst wears upon her, and she leaves, not without speaking with all the earnestness and sympathy of her nature to the woman of whose fate she has an oppressive, inexplicable presentiment.

The tears in her eyes at leaving have touched the girl, for she is little more, and she has promised to try and be better, as she childishly puts it. Things have gone pleasantly for some days, and she has been patient with the children. One of them has been ill and she has nursed it, and today she has made them an apple-cake and sent them to the park, and she is singing to herself over her work; she is cleaning out her bedroom. It is Derby Day. He has the day off, and has gone to the races. He gave her five shillings before he started in the morning, telling her she might send it to the 'young 'un.'

It touched her, and she brushed his coat and kissed him of her own accord. She has felt kindly to him all the morning for it. She notices a button dangling off his working coat and takes it out to the kitchen to sew it on; he seldom brings it home. There is nothing in the pockets except a slip of 'events' cut out of some sporting paper; but the lining of the breast-pocket is torn, and as she examines, it, the rustle of paper catches her ear. She smiles; what if it is a 'fiver'? She knows all about his betting. She slips two fingers down between the lining and works it up—a telegram. She still smiles, for she thinks she will find a clue to some of his winnings. She opens it, and reads, and her face changes; the blood rushes to it, until a triangular vein stands out on her forehead like a purple whipcord. Her throat looks as if it would burst; a pulse beats in her neck; her upper lip is completely sucked in by the set line of her under one, and her eyes positively squint. A fly that keeps buzzing on the pane rouses her to such a pitch, that she seizes a boot off the table and sends it crashing through the pane of glass into the yard, liberating the fly at the same time. Then she tries to reread it, but there is a red blaze before her eyes. She goes out, up the lane, towards the unfinished houses, to where the bricklayers are at work, and hands it to the little man, saying hoarsely:

'Read it, I'm dazed, I can't see it rightly.'

The big man stops whistling and looks curiously at her. She is perfectly sober; the flush has ceded to a lead-white pallor, and her face twitches convulsively. She stands absolutely still, with her hands hanging heavily down, though she is devoured with impatience. The little man wipes his hands, and takes out his spectacles, and reads slowly:

'Susie dying, come at once, no hope. Expecting you since Saturday, wrote twice.'

A minute's silence—then a hoarse scream that seems to come from the depths of her chest; it frightens both men, so that the big man drops a brick, and a carpenter in the house comes to the window and looks out.

'Since Saturday!' she cries, 'today is Wednesday. When was it sent, tell me!' she shakes the little man in her excitement, and he scans the form slowly, with the deliberation of his class:

'Stratford, 7.45.'

'But the date! the date, man!'

'The 20th.'

'Today,' with a groan, 'is the 22nd. So it come Monday, and today is Wednesday, an' they wrote twice. It must 'ave come when I fetched 'is beer, an' 'e kept it. But the letters?—that little cub, that sneak of 'ell! Aah, wait!' She calls down curses with such ferocity of expression, that the men shiver; then crushing the fateful paper inside the bosom of her gown, she rushes back, and in a few minutes they see her come out, tying on her bonnet as she runs.

'Well, this 'ere's a rum go, eh?' says the big man, regaining his colour, 'an' ooze Susie?'

The little man says nothing, only balances a brick in the palm of his hand before he fits it into its place, but his lips move silently.

In the parlour of one of a row of stiff two-storeyed houses, with narrow hall-doors in a poor street in Stratford, a little coffin painted white is laid on the table that is covered with a new white sheet.

There are plenty of flowers, from the white wreath sent by the grocer's wife, with a card bearing 'From a Sympathizer' in big silver letters, to the penny bunch of cornflowers of a playmate.

Susie has her tiny hands folded, and the little waxen face looks grey and pinched amongst the elaborately pinked-out glazed calico frills of her coffin lining. There is the unavoidable air of festivity that every holiday, even a sad one, imparts to a working-man's home. The children have their hair crimped and their Sunday clothes on, for they are going to the burial-ground in a grand coach with black horses and long tails, and they sit on the stairs and talk it over in whispers.

The men have come in at dinner-hour silently and stolidly, and looked at her, and gone out to the 'Dog and Jug' for a glass of beer to wash down whatever of sadness the sight of dead Susie may have roused in them.

Every woman in the row has had a cup of tea, and told of her own sorrows; related the death of every relative she has ever possessed, to the third and fourth degree, with the minuteness of irrelevant detail peculiar to her class. Every incident of Susie's death-struggle has been described with such morbid or picturesque addition as frequent rehearsals, or the fancy of the narrator, may suggest. Every corner of the house is crammed with people, for the funeral is to leave at three o'clock.

'Looks like satin it do, it's as pretty as ever I see!' pointing to the pinking, says one woman.

'Yes, Mr Triggs thought a 'eap o' Susie, an' 'e took extry pains. 'E's a beautiful undertaker, an' 'e's goin' to send the 'earse with the wite plumes! Don't she just look a little hangel?'

So they stream in and out, and in the kitchen a circle of matrons hold a Vehmgericht over the mother.

'She's an unfeelin' brute, even if she iz yer arf sister, Mrs Waters,' says a fat matron, 'to let that pretty, hinnocent hangel die without seein' 'er, not to speak o' buryin', I 'ave no patience with sich ways!'

The roll of wheels and the jingle of tyres cuts short her speech, and the knocker bangs dully. Heads crane out in every direction, and one of the children opens the door, and the woman steps in.

In her pink gown! when every one knows that not to pawn your bed or the washing-tubs, or anything available, to get a black skirt or crape bonnet, or at least a straw with bugles, is the greatest breach of propriety known to the poor, the greatest sticklers for mourning etiquette outside a German court. The half-sister is a quiet woman with smoothly parted hair and tender eyes, and a strong likeness to her about the underhung chin. She goes forward and leads her to the room; the women fall back and talk in whispers.

'W'y didn't you send?' she asks fiercely, turning from the coffin.

'We wrote Friday, an' then, when you didn't come, we wrote Sunday. Jim couldn't go, an' I never left 'er a minute, an' Tiny an' little Jim 'ad the measles, an' Katie 'ad to mind 'em; but a mate o' Jim's went to the 'Buckin'am' on Monday mornin' an' told '*im*, an' then we sent a tellygram, an' we couldn't do more, not if she were our own.'

There is a settled resignation in her voice; she has repeated it so often.

''E kep' the letters an' 'e never told me, an' I only found the tellygram this mornin' by accidin'. When's she to be buried?'

'At three o'clock,'—with a puzzled look at the set face.

'Leave me along of 'er then; go on!'—roughly.

The woman goes out, closes the door, and listens. Not a sound comes from the room, not one, not a sob nor cry. The women listen in silence when she tells them; they are used to the fierce passions of humanity, and jealousy is common amongst their men. After a while one of the children says, with an awe-struck face, 'Ma, she's singin'.' They go to the door and listen; she is crooning a nonsense song she used to sing to her when she was quite a baby, and the listening women pale, but fear to go in. For a long hour they hear her talking and singing to it; then the man comes to screw down the lid, and they find her on the sofa with the dead child on her lap, its feet, in their white cotton socks, sticking out like the legs of a great wax doll.

She lets them take it from her without a word, and watches them place it amongst the white frills, and lets them lead her out of the room. She sits bolt upright in the kitchen, with the same odd smile upon her lips and her hands hanging straight down. They go without her. When they return she is still sitting with her hands hanging, as if she has never stirred.

'Mother, w'y did they plant Susie in the ground? Mother, carn't you answer; will she grow?' queries one of the children, and something in the question rouses her. She starts up with a cry and a wild glare, and stares about as if in search of something—stands trembling in every limb, with the ugly flush on her face and the purple triangle on her forehead, and the pulse beating in her throat. The children cower away from her, and the sister watches her with frightened, pitying eyes.

'Sit down, Susan, there's a dear, sit down an' 'ave some tea!'

'No, I've got to go—I've got to go—I've got t—' she mutters, swaying unsteadily on her feet. The words come thickly, and the end of the sentence is lost.

'She'd be better if she could cry, poor thing!' says the fat matron.

'Give 'er somethink belonged to the young 'un!' says a little woman with a black eye. The sister goes to a drawer in the dresser and turns over some odds and ends and finds a necklet of blue beads with a brass clasp, and hands it to her. She takes it with a hoarse cry as of an animal in dire pain, and rocks and moans and kisses it, but no tears come; and then, before they can realize it, she is out through the passage, and the door slams. When they get to it and look out, she is hurrying wildly down the street, with her pink gown fluttering, and the roses nodding in her bonnet, through a drizzle of soft rain.

Six o'clock rings; the rain still falls steadily, and, through its dull beat, the splash of big drops on to the new boards in a roofless house, and the blows of a hammer, strike sharply.

'Comin', mate?' queries the big man. 'No? Well, so long!' He shoulders his straw kit and turns up the collar of his coat and goes off whistling. The little man puts his tools away, fastens a sack about his shoulders and creeps into a square of bricks —they had thrown some loose planks across the top earlier in the day as a sort of protection against the rain; he lights his pipe and sits patiently waiting for her return. He is hungry, and his wizened face looks pinched in the light of the match as he strikes it, but he waits patiently.

The shadows have closed in when she gets back, for she has walked all the way from Liverpool Street, unheeding the steady rain that has come with the south-west wind. The people maddened her. She felt inclined to strike them. A fierce anger surged up in her against each girl who laughed, each man who talked of the winner. She felt inclined to spit at them, make faces, or call them names. Her dress is bedrabbled, the dye of the roses has soaked through the gold of her fringe and runs down her forehead as if she has a bleeding wound there. The gas is lit in the kitchen, and her tea is laid and the kettle is singing on the stove; a yellow envelope is lying on the top of the cup; she opens it and turns up the gas and reads it:

'Been in luck to-day, going home with Johnson, back early to-morrow evening.'

She puts it down with a peculiar smile. She has the string of beads in her hand; she keeps turning them round her finger; then she steals to the foot of the stairs and listens.

The little man has watched her go in, and stands in the lane-way looking up at the house. A light appears in the top back window, but it must come from the stairs, it is too faint to be in the room itself. He bends his head as if to listen, but the steady fall of the rain and the drip of the roof on to some loose sheets of zinc dominate everything. He walks away a bit and watches a shadow cross the blinds; his step crunches on the loose bricks and stones; a woman rushes down the flagged path of the next house and opens the door.

'Is that Mr Sims?'

'No, ma'am, I'm one of the workmen.'

She has left her kitchen door open, and as the light streams out he can see she is a thin woman with an anxious look.

'I thought it was Mr Sims, the watchman. My baby is threatened with convulsions. I wanted him to run for the doctor at the end of the terrace; I daren't leave him, and my sister's lame. Will you go? It isn't far!'

She is listening, and though he hears nothing, she darts off calling, 'There he's off, do go, *do go*. Say Mrs Rogers' baby, Hawthorn House, number 23.'

He stands a moment irresolute; the shadow moves across the blind, and a second smaller shadow seems to wave across it; or was it only the rising wind flicking the blind? and is it fancy, or did not a stifled cry reach him; and was it from that room it came or from Mrs Rogers' baby? The little man is shaking with anxiety; he feels as if some malignant fate in the shape of Mrs Rogers' baby is playing tricks with him, to bring about a catastrophe he has stayed to avert. He is torn both ways; he can offer no excuse for not going; he dare not explain the secret dread that has kept him here supperless in the rain watching the house where the three motherless children sleep. He turns and runs stumbling over the rubbish into the side street and arrives breathless at the corner house where the red lamp burns at the gate—rings—what a time they keep him—it seems ages, and visions keep tumbling kaleidoscopically through his brain;

the very red of the light adds colour to the horrid tragedy he sees enacted in excited fancy.

'The doctor is out; won't be back for some time; there's a Dr Phillips round the corner,' explains the smart maid—the door slams to.

'Yes, Dr Phillips is in; you must wait a minute,' ushering him into a waiting-room. He sits on the edge of the chair with his wet hat in his hand. Two other people are waiting: a girl with a swelled face and a sickly-looking man.

A door opens, some one beckons, the man goes in. He looks at the clock—five minutes pass, seven, ten—each seems an hour—fifteen—and the woman's face as she went in, and the frightened children (his mate questioned them at tea-time), and the shadow on the blind of the room they slept in! Why should Mrs Rogers' baby go and get convulsions just this particular night? seems as though it were to be—seventeen; no, he won't wait any longer. The strange, inexplicable fear clutching the little man's soul gives him courage, though the well-furnished house awes him; he slips out into the hall, opens the door, and rings the bell. The same girl answers it.

'Well I never! W'y, I just let you in. Carn't you wait yer turn—the *idea*!'

A pale young man with spectacles coming down the stairs asks:

'What is it you want, my man?' The girl tosses her head and goes downstairs.

'I can't wait, sir; Mrs Rogers' baby, 'Awthorn 'Ouse, number 23 Pelham Road, round the corner, got the convulsions. She wants the doctor as soon as 'e can.'

'All right, I'll be round in a second.'

The little man hurries back, trying to add up the time he has been away—twenty-five minutes, it must be twenty-five, perhaps twenty-seven. The yard door of Mrs Rogers' house is open, and a girl peers out as he runs up the lane.

'The doctor woz out; Dr Phillips is comin' at onst!' His eyes rest on the window of the next house as he speaks. It is dark up there and silent. He pays no heed to the thanks of the girl, and he hears the tap of her crutch up the flagged path with a gasp of relief.

What has happened whilst he has been away on his errand of mercy? Has anything happened? After all, why should this ghastly idea of a tragedy possess him? He climbs on to a heap of loose bricks and peers over the wall—darkness and silence. He goes down the lane and round to the front of the house. A dim light shines through the stained glass over the door showing up the name 'Ladas', that is all, yet the little man shivers. The rain has soaked through his coat and is trickling down his neck; he scratches his head in perplexity, muttering to himself, 'I'm afear'd, an' I dunno wot I'm afear'd on. I meant to wotch; maybe arsk 'er for a light. It ain't my fault if Mrs Rogers' baby came atween—but twarn't no wearin' reason to marry for,' and he goes down the road and faces home. The rain ceases, and a tearful moon appears, and the water drips off the roof with a clucking sound. Upstairs in a back room in the silent house a pale strip of moonlight flickers over a dark streak on the floor, that trickles slowly from the pool at the bedside out under the door, making a second ghastly pool on the top step of the stairs—a thick sorghum red, blackening as it thickens, with a sickly serous border. Downstairs the woman sits in a chair with her arms hanging down. Her hands are crimson as if she has dipped them in dye. A string of blue beads lies on her lap, and she is fast asleep; and she smiles as she sleeps, for Susie is playing in a meadow, a great meadow crimson with poppies, and her blue eyes smile with glee, and her golden curls are poppy-crowned, and her little white feet twinkle as they dance, and her pinked-out grave frock flutters, and her tiny waxen hands scatter poppies, blood-red poppies, in handfuls over three open graves.

VIOLET

Frances Towers

THE ONLY person Violet couldn't handle was the mistress herself. From the very first, Mrs Titmus refused, in her obstinate way, to take to Violet; partly, perhaps, because Sophy had engaged her without taking up her references. So lazy of her, and dangerous. At her age, thought Mrs Titmus, I could have done the work of this house and thought nothing of it. I would have been glad to do something useful. Utterly selfish, thought Mrs Titmus, and bone-lazy, eager to grab at the first thing that offered to save herself a little effort.

But to Sophy, who had coped alone with the house for six weeks, it had become a monster that fed on the very marrow of her bones. So that Violet, stepping in and taking the reins in her absurdly small and fluttering hands, seemed like an angel of deliverance. From the beginning, the monster ate out of her hand. In less than no time it had resumed the orderly and polished look of former days. Skirtings acquired a dark glow, furniture a patina of port-wine richness, silver shone as if newly-minted. Any qualms that Sophy may have had that such a large house was too much for such a dot of a thing were quieted by her unruffled and competent air. But she had an effect in ways other than the merely physical.

It seemed to Sophy afterwards that it wasn't till Violet came to the house that the pattern of their lives emerged to her eyes. She was the focal point that related the different planes on which they lived to each other. She drew the design together, so that one became aware of values that had hitherto been submerged below the level of consciousness. With her smirks and the sudden gleam of light in her opaque eyes, her nods and becks, she illumined the hidden corners of their minds, she twitched aside curtains and revealed the fears and passions of their hearts, she smelt out their secrets, pounced on them and laid them out like dead mice, and she took a hand in their destinies.

On the first morning, when she brought the early tea into Sophy's room, in her neat pink dress with the turned-back white cuffs at the elbows, Sophy was aware of those dense black eyes taking in the rather tousled and puffy-eyed look which she knew only too well she presented on first awaking.

With an odd, humiliating feeling of being unworthy of the attentions of this crisp handmaid, she accepted the meticulously prepared tray.

'But you've given me the Queen Anne teapot,' she said, taken by surprise at the sight of this treasure reserved for guests of consequence.

'I like to be dainty first thing in the morning. It kind of sets the tone for the day,' said Violet, surprisingly. 'Madam's been down to see if I'd lighted the fire. When I saw her in her dressing-gown and her little plait sticking out, I didn't know she was the mistress. She fair frightened me. Must be nice to wake up in this room, miss, with flowers and that. They say you shouldn't sleep with flowers in the room; but I must say it's nice – ever so gentle and feminine. Makes you feel all glorious within, I expect. Madam said only toast for breakfast – is that right? But what about the master? Gentlemen like a couple of rashers and a fried egg. He looks a bit thin to me, kind of hungry-like. He was up ever so early catching slugs in the garden, and I took him out a cup of tea. He seemed ever so surprised. Poor old gentleman, ever so gentle and kind, he seemed. I think I'll do him a proper breakfast.'

'You must do as my mother says,' said Sophy, sipping her tea.

'Righty-ho!' Violet tripped out on her high heels.

But Sophy saw with dismay when she descended to breakfast that the girl had taken the law into her own hands.

Oh, dear! How tactless of her. And Mr Titmus must needs make it worse.

'Ho, ho, ho! It looks as if I'm going to be spoilt.'

Mrs Titmus looked down her nose. When her eyes had that

pale, blind look, as if all the blue had been withdrawn from them, Sophy, expert at interpreting signs and portents, knew that trouble was brewing. Her sisters swallowed their coffee and fled to catch the 8.15 to London. They had their careers and were apt to shelve domestic problems.

'Someone', said Mrs Titmus, fixing the old gentleman with that glazed fishy look, 'seemed to be creaking about the house all night, pulling the plugs. I couldn't sleep a wink.'

Sophy began to chatter wildly about the news in the morning paper. The year was 1938.

'How silly you are, getting all worked up! You don't know a thing about it,' Mrs Titmus said, with a venom that seemed quite unnecessary.

'Really, mother, I may be allowed to express an opinion, I suppose.'

'I don't know when', said Mr Titmus, seeking to throw oil on troubled waters, 'I've had a nicer breakfast.'

Was it possible, wondered Sophy, exasperated, that one so dense, so innocent, could have begotten her?

'I think there'll be war, and we shall all be blown to bits,' she said loudly and vindictively.

The prospect of war seemed a lesser calamity at the moment than the loss of Violet, which was probably imminent.

'Well, if we are, we are. It can't be helped, and there's nothing we can do about it,' said Mrs Titmus, with the bored manner of one who wished to hear no more of a tiresome subject.

She rose and pushed back her chair.

'Ring the bell', she said, 'for that girl to clear.'

'We must give her time to finish her own breakfast, poor little scrap,' remarked Mr Titmus, genially.

There was a hideous pause. Mrs Titmus stared at her husband, her eyes pale again with venom.

'What did you say? What term did you apply to the maid-of-all-work?'

'I know what father means, mother.' Sophy rushed in where no angel would have ventured so much as the tip of a toe. 'She really is the tiniest thing I've ever seen – like a little marmoset or something.'

'Well, I don't care for marmosets about *my* house,' was her mother's parting shot as she went out of the room.

'Dear, dear, dear! Your mother seems upset about something. You've not been cheeky to her, my dear, I hope. You girls are inclined to be cheeky, I've noticed.'

'Father,' said Sophy, 'you don't use a word like that about bitter females in their dim thirties.' She began to clear the breakfast plates with thin, nervous hands that shook a little.

'Now, what's the matter with her?' wondered Mr Titmus. Deep in the recesses of his consciousness, he asked himself why one should have married a shrew and become the father of shrews.

'I don't like 'em, not one of 'em,' he said wickedly to himself in the dark depths of his being. 'This yaller girl, she's as nugly as an 'orse,' he thought, regarding her sorrowfully with his innocent, filmy blue eyes.

Oh, what an old dog he was in his deep inwardness! How ugly and vicious! He had a private atrocious language of his own, when things got too much for him, to express the exasperation that boiled within him. They thought he was old Father Christmas, did they? They thought he was a gentle old pet? Ho! Sometimes he was shocked at his own wickedness. Sometimes he was afraid of God's punishment. Suppose He were to take one of the girls! When little Beatrice had pneumonia, he couldn't eat or sleep, he couldn't keep his food down. If God did a thing like that, it could break his heart.

But sometimes he knew such flashes of glory, it was like the gates of Heaven opening. Suddenly a line of poetry would come into his head – or he would hear the strings of his heart playing *Sheep may safely graze*, and he would feel as light and holy as a sainted spirit.

He looked so wistful that Sophy had a twinge of conscience.

'Sorry, father. It's because I'm so tired. This undercurrent of drama all the time . . . Do you ever wish you were dead?'

'No, no!' said Mr Titmus, shocked. '*With worms that are thy chambermaids*,' he said in a whisper, looking into vacancy, and stole away furtively, his shapeless slippers flapping at his heels.

Sophy's hands dropped to her sides. If she had opened a

cupboard and found a grinning skeleton inside, she could hardly have felt more chilled.

'I couldn't help hearing what you said,' said Violet, suddenly appearing from nowhere with a tray in her hands. 'If you wish evil, miss, you attract it to you. It would be more sensible, excuse me, to wish to get married. One never knows,' she added, darkly. Her soft black eyes fastened on Sophy's face and clung there, like persistent bees. They were so jetty dark, you couldn't tell if there were compassion in them, or brazen impudence.

Sophy gave her a quelling look, and stalked out of the room with a giraffe-like dignity.

Seeking refuge a few days later from domestic tension, she went to her room and took a leather-bound book out of the bookcase. It was tooled in gold, with the title '*Morte D'Arthur by Malory*', and its pages were blank except for such as were covered by her small pointed script.

'Notre domestique', wrote Sophy, in the green ink she affected, 'is no ordinary scullion. She might have washed up the wine-cups of the Borgias, or looked through the keyholes of the Medici. I have an idea that she can hear the mice scampering furtively behind the panels of our minds. I heard one the other day in an unaccustomed place. Father quoted Shakespeare and frightened me. I know now that he is a very lonely old man. La domestique knows it too. He loves his roses better than wife or daughters. It hurts him to have them picked by careless hands. Lalage is ruthless. She snips where she will and fills the vases. She comes into a room and stirs up flowers arranged by someone else, gritting her teeth, as though to say, How inartistic! What insensitiveness! She is a lazy, exquisite person, and, like a saint, exudes a delightful odour. It comes, of course, from a bottle and not from her bones; but is so much hers that the latter source seems the true one. She has the most charming hands and eyebrows, and is about the only person whose bath water one could use without distaste.

'I am deeply concerned about Bee. The other day a wedding-ring dropped out of her handbag. She swooped on it, and I pretended not to see. It was sinister, like finding a snake's egg in a drawer and knowing that strange rustlings must have occurred while one slept. A mouse behind the panels. And yet her small, rather cynical, face is quite untroubled, and she laughs still in her silent, inward way. It's the secrecy that hurts, so furtive. And yet, what would you, in our household? V., I fear, has heard that mouse. "There's something about Miss Beatrice that calls to mind a divorced lady – ever so worldly and stylish. A woman of the world, miss, if you know what I mean. Now, if you was to wear one of her hats, why, you'd look ridiculous!"

'I told Bee and she went into one of her silent convulsions of laughter. "Poor old Sophy!" she said. "Mind you keep her on the right side of mother! Your face was beginning to look like an old leather bag." She meant it kindly.

'Does mother hate Violet for some deep, intuitive reason?

'"Lord, madam. I never did see so many pill-boxes and medicine bottles. Makes one think of hospitals and death. It doesn't do to dwell so much on one's health – makes the end come all the quicker, I daresay."

'I heard mother's voice, with an edge in it. "You can leave my room. I prefer to do it myself." She didn't prefer it, when I was doing all the housework. She preferred to write her lectures for the Women's Institute.'

Sophy closed her book and returned it to the shelf. In that household, with such a title, it was safe from prying eyes. It was her consolation, her other self.

Lalage and Beatrice drew Violet out and compared notes. She was a source of infinite amusement to them.

Violet's young man had thrown her over. 'That's all right. I'm not breaking me heart,' she said. 'It wasn't love, it was lust.'

She cast a glance at a photograph on Lalage's mantelpiece.

'Excuse me, miss, but that gentleman's got ever such a nice face. I expect if he gives you flowers, they are real nice ones, gardenias and that. But he's not one to be kept dangling. He's got his pride. Never ask you twice, he wouldn't.' She sighed. 'I never had nothing from Bert, except a bit of dried heather he got off a gipsy. Mean he was. Everything for nothing was his motto. I suppose you'll be getting married, miss, before long?'

'What makes you think so?'

'Red hair and brown eyes, and then, your legs, miss . . . like champagne bottles. Miss Sophy, now, she's different. Only a very spiritual gentleman would single out Miss Sophy, and then he'd love her to the world's end. She's an acquired taste, as they say – and that kind's the most lasting.'

'The little devil,' said Sophy, when these remarks were repeated to her, and for some reason she looked at the same time disconcerted and gratified.

Bee might have noticed it. Her small green eyes might have peeped out of their lashes with a piercing glint. 'Spiritual . . . aha! So that accounts for all these attendances at St Petroc's.'

But Lalage was too lazy, too indifferent. One's heart might crack in two, and she would never guess.

It was a strange thing, but Christian Todmarsh did send her one day not gardenias, but orchids. She looked thoughtfully at his photograph. Yes, he had a proud face. He would easily be lost beyond recall. She rang him up, and their engagement was announced a few days later.

'Things always seem to happen when I come into a house,' remarked Violet, dropping her eyelids.

'The master and his roses,' she said one day, looking out of the window with a duster in her hand. 'It's as well to have a passion, even if it's only for flowers. My last gentleman had one for pictures. Ever so queer they were. You didn't hardly like to look at them. He said a thing I've never forgotten. He said there was some foreign painter that painted women as if they were roses, and roses as if they were women. That isn't a thing you'd be likely to forget. It makes a difference to your life . . . gives you ideas and that. Madam isn't a bit like a rose,' she added reflectively, almost under her breath; 'but Miss Lalage is. It comes out in her.'

Violet continued to skate blithely over thin ice. It seemed a shame that a gentleman with such a passion for roses should have no rose in his heart. Madam was like an east wind. She fair shrivelled one up. But she wasn't going to drive Violet away. So long as there were those that appreciated her, Violet would stay put. They needed her. Oh, but how desperately they needed her! How they had ever got on without her she didn't know.

She seemed to be moving all the time to some secret tune. Mrs

Titmus hated the way she laid the table, posturing and pirou-
etting like a ballet-dancer, setting down glasses and pepper-pots
with a turn of the wrist, as though she were miming to unheard
music, stepping back theatrically and regarding her handiwork
with her head on one side, waiting for the next beat of the
invisible baton. Even more irritating was it to hear her singing
below stairs, in raucous abandonment to emotion, with that
awful, vulgar scoop of the street singer who seeks to wring the
heart.

But there were other and worse things.

'I don't like the girl, and I never shall,' said Mrs Titmus. 'She
pesters your father. I caught her taking him a cup of cocoa in the
middle of the morning. He's so foolish that I've no doubt he
drank it.'

'But what harm in that? She meant it kindly. She isn't a bad
little thing,' said Sophy nervously, though she knew it was worse
than useless to attempt palliation of Violet's offences.

'Nonsense! You girls are idiotic about her. She's *evil*. She's
always *saying* things,' said Mrs Titmus, with a pinched look
about her mouth. 'Yesterday, she was putting clean sheets on my
bed, and she said, "Look, madam, diamonds all down the
middle fold."'

'Diamonds?' asked Sophy, blankly.

'Yes; the sheet had been badly folded, the way they do in this
laundry, and there were little squares. I wouldn't have noticed
them. "That means death," she said. I didn't like the look she
gave me. If I were ill and alone, I wouldn't care to be at the mercy
of that girl.'

Morbid, thought Sophy. It was a new aspect of her. Was there
to be no end to the discoveries one made about one's nearest and
dearest?

She looked at her mother as if she were seeing her for the first
time. The thin face, hooked nose and Greek knot at the back of
the head gave her the look of a teapot – was it? Or the Indian idol
of massive brass that had stood on the hall table ever since she
could remember, the head of Lakshmi, the goddess, brought
back by some ancestor and bearing on her forehead the red seal
of the Brahmin.

Teapot or goddess. She had something of both in her composition. She had comforted her children, and inspired them with fear. 'And now that one is middle-aged,' thought Sophy (who prided herself on facing unpleasant facts, to the extent of being guilty, more often than not, of overstatement) 'there is no longer need of comfort, but vestiges of the fear remain. I am still afraid sometimes that she can read my thoughts. I still tremble when her eyes go pale. This house, so shabby and so beautiful, is in part her creation, but she has long ceased to take any interest in it. She has become warped about money and won't spend a penny.'

Atmosphere is a mysterious thing. Like wallpapers superimposed to a thickness, maybe, of inches, atmosphere settles upon atmosphere with the succeeding tenants of an old house. The Titmus atmosphere, one felt (if one were a somewhat precious and fantastic creature like Sophy), owed something of its richness and duskiness to those others that it had absorbed since the days of Queen Anne. The sound of the harpsichord, she liked to think, had gone into the old wood. The scent of pomander balls was, perhaps, part of the peculiar Titmus smell . . . faintly peppery, with a hint of Russian leather and petal dust, that clung about the house and permeated all their belongings and even stole out of parcels sent across the seas. All their selves had left slimy invisible trails. The furniture knew it. It had that dumb but sentient look, as if something of their personalities had passed into it and fed and enriched it. Was it too fantastic, Sophy wondered, to imagine that lately it had taken on a darker, stranger glow, a glint as of the reflection of soft black eyes?

One sound had certainly haunted the house since the day it was first built, the sound of the bells of St Petroc's. They had a magical significance now for Sophy, like the aromatic poplars in the churchyard and the light that shone through the east window.

'The Vicar is in the drawing-room with Madam. But it's you he came to see, miss,' announced Violet, bursting in one afternoon when Sophy was communing with her book. Her heart turned over.

Violet fixed her with her soft black stare. There seemed to be the faintest trace of a smirk on her face.

'Did he ask for me?' enquired Sophy, turning away.

'Not to say, *asked*, but there are some things that are known without words. Madam doesn't go to his church, does she? Of course, this isn't his parish. You're St Matthew's, reelly. He preaches lovely, I think. Ever so deep. The silver tea service, I suppose, miss? And I'll soon make some scones.'

Sophy went slowly down the stairs. If she had been summoned to meet an archangel she could hardly have felt more frightened, more inadequate. Never had she sought the acquaintance of this man who had been so much hers in dreams that she could not bear to face the bleakness of reality. She could not rid herself of the feeling that unwanted love is the basest kind of treachery towards the beloved. She had made herself free of his mind and his heart without his knowledge. How could he ever forgive her? She had created a world in which he was her lover because she could not help herself. But she knew that one breath of reality would blow her world to smithereens, and dash her to pieces. And yet there was a terrible, painful excitement in her heart.

'I am the Rose of Sharon and the lily of the valleys,' she said to her reflection in the dim Venetian mirror in the hall, speaking out of her dream-world. For surely it must still be a dream. It couldn't be that he had intruded into the real world in which one shook hands and took tea and made conversation.

The odd thing was that when she came into the room, Mr Chandos's heart gave a sudden leap of recognition. A voice deep inside him said – 'This is the face I have been waiting for. This is the woman for me.'

But Sophy as she looked into the bright pale eyes that were the colour of the sea, that were as cold as aquamarines, was thinking – 'I shall not be able to endure the agony of loving this man.' The touch of his hand chilled her. There was something alien and terrifying in it, like the feel of a frog in her palm. Her mind felt cold and tingling, as though contact with the strange flesh of the beloved had frozen it. She rubbed it against the folds of her skirt, and still there was this queer, icy glow.

'Sophy,' thought Mrs Titmus, 'is behaving like a fool. If one could only *teach* them.' For in her reveries, she was still the girl she had once been; another Lalage, but much more vivid and vivacious. Lalage would never know the triumphs that had been hers. She remembered that dress she wore that everyone raved about at the Hunt Ball that year. He had kissed her shoulder in the dark. She could never hear the *Invitation to the Valse* without remembering. What a lover he was! But she had lost him a long time ago. She never identified him with old Mr Titmus, though they were one and the same person. It seemed strange that she should be married now to this old changeling. Once she had overheard him saying to himself in the bathroom – 'Now, where has she hidden my razor, the old . . . *puss!*' So treacherous! She had been shocked to the heart.

She came to the rescue of her awkward, helpless child.

'My daughter says the singing at St Petroc's is so beautiful. She is very musical, and has perfect pitch – which is quite uncommon, isn't it? So they tell me.'

Mr Chandos smiled and looked at Sophy. He couldn't take his eyes off that face. It made a pattern that fascinated him, like a map of olden times with its 'Here are dragons', and other strange indications. It was a unique face. New faces are seldom unfamiliar. They do not come upon us with a shock of strangeness, but are easily relegated to the different categories of faces which we draw up in our minds. Only out of history does a face sometimes look out with a hint of alien ineluctable charm. To Mr Chandos, the face of Sophy Titmus had that quality. Her soft mouse-like name enchanted him.

'You are not a communicant. I should have remembered you,' said Mr Chandos, making a pyramid with the joined tips of his fingers and resting his chin upon them.

'No, no. I am a lost sheep. I came in one evening to hear the anthem, and then you preached; and you quoted Donne. And then I had to join your congregation. But how did you know?'

'A member of your household, Violet Wilson, told me.' (That girl! thought Mrs Titmus with a little shiver as though a goose had walked over her grave, and thoughts of witchcraft came into the head of Sophy, already bemused and laid under a spell, so that her own voice, sounding out of the midst of the threefold circle that seemed to have been woven round her, was strange to her ears.) 'Did you like my sermon, Miss Titmus?'

'Have I not already told you? I see that priests have their vanities, like other artists.'

How hollow and far-away her voice sounded, like the voice of a stranger echoing in a cave.

A few weeks later, she was saying to herself amazedly – 'I had no idea it was as easy as this. I had no idea. I had no idea.'

For the unimaginable had come to pass. He was no longer an archangel, but her own Paul.

She had thought everyone must know it when she came into the house, when she floated in with the moon in her hair. But when she looked in at the drawing-room door, no one seemed aware that something tremendous had happened. They were doing silly, unimportant things, poor earthbound wretches, and glanced at her indifferently with lack-lustre eyes.

She retreated and caught Violet coming out of Mr Titmus's study. She was carrying a tea-tray. The old gentleman had been treated to his wife's best china and the silver muffin-dish, which still contained what was left of the forbidden dripping-toast he enjoyed so much. A little posy of wild flowers in a wine-glass added to the general effect of festivity and loving-kindness. Violet was playing her favourite game of circumventing the mistress. She was watering the withered old heart. She was shedding the beams of love upon it and re-awakening it. She was queering the old cat's pitch.

'Poor old gentleman!' she said, with a sidelong glance. 'He does like a little attention.' She smirked self-righteously, and then, catching sight of Sophy's face, nearly dropped the tray.

'Oh, miss! Whatever is it? Your heart's desire come true, that's what it is! I'm *ever* so glad.'

There was a strange look of triumph on her face.

After all, it was her doing, thought Sophy.

'Things always seem to happen when I come into a house,' said Violet, *sotto voce*. And suddenly Sophy remembered a greasy pack of cards she had found when looking for something in a drawer in the kitchen.

'Do you play patience alone down here in the evenings?' she had asked, with a spasm of pity.

'Not me,' Violet had replied. 'They fall for me the way I want them. It's wonderful what they tell you, if you have the gift.'

Sophy was moved now to put an arm about the girl. 'I shall never forget that I owe it to you,' she said softly.

'That's all right, miss,' said Violet, dropping her eyelids. There was an inscrutable expression on her face, as if she knew what she knew.

'And now there's Miss Beatrice. But the cards don't come out right for her. Not yet, they don't. A married man, I should think, miss.'

'What do you mean? You mustn't say such things. I've never heard such nonsense!' said Sophy, deeply alarmed.

'Oh, it's all right, miss! You can trust me. I'm as secret as the grave.' And she disappeared through the baize door to her own quarters. To the ace of spades and the mice, thought Sophy, with a little shiver. Love, she thought, and Death, dealt out on the kitchen table by those small, clever hands.

So that, in a way, she was prepared for that frightening moment when Mrs Titmus mounted the stairs to her room.

There was a look on her face, a sick and abject look, as if her pride had crumpled up in her, that hurt Sophy and shocked her.

She gave a backward look over her shoulder and closed the door furtively.

'Sophy,' she said, pitiably, in a strange whispering voice, 'that girl . . . I saw her. She was *pinching* diamonds into the table-cloth.'

'Oh, darling mother, she must go at once!' cried Sophy, flinging her arms round the gaunt figure.

For she knew now that Violet with a death-wish in her heart was about as safe to have in the house as a tame cheetah.

❁

THE PLUMS
Ama Ata Aidoo

SHE WAS a young mother pushing her baby in a pram. Later, she
was to tell Sissie that she did this quite often. She would come
and stand where Sissie stood, in the round sentry post, and look
at the town and the river.

> There was a castle
> Which the brochure tells you
> Was one of the largest in all
> Germany.
> Germany?
> The land of castles?
> So who was this
> Prince,
> This Lord and Master
> Who had built one of
> The largest castles of them all,
> Possessed the
> Biggest
> Land, the
> Greatest number of
> Serfs?
> And you wondered
> Looking at the river,
> How many
> Virgins had
> Our Sovereign Lord and Master
> Unvirgined on their nuptial nights
> For their young
> Husbands in

Red-eyed
Teeth-gnashing
Agony, their
Manhoods
Hurting . . .
But 'all the days are not equal', said the old
    village wall, and
The castle is now a youth hostel.

'Are you an Indian?' she asked Sissie.
  'No,' she replied —

Knowing she could be
Except for the hair.

She might have heard her answer. She might have not. But she was speaking on, the words tumbling out of her mouth as though she had planned out the meeting and even drafted the introductory remarks.

'Yes, I like zem weri much. The Indians. Zey verkt in ze supermarket. Zey ver weri nice.'
'Which Indians?'
'Ze two. It vas before last vinter. For a long time. And zen zey left. I like zem weri much.'
Sissie guessed they might have been male.

Fact dismissed.
Two Indians in a small town to house the
Serfs who
Slaved for the
Lord who
Owned one of the
Largest castles in all of
Germany . . .

It is a
Long way from
Calcutta to
Munich:

Aeroplanes brought you here.
But what else did
Migrant birds of the world,
Beginning with such
Few feathers too, which
                              drop
and
                              drop
and
                              drop
from
constant flights and
                    distances?
My
West Indian neighbour and his wife packed up
one morning to go to Canada, saying:

'They say that
Wages
There are quite
Handsome.'
So they went to Liverpool
To wait for a ship
That should have sailed the
Next day. Or so they had thought.
But it came to dock
Months
Later.

Don't
Ask
Me
How they managed with
Two kids.

But
All journeys
End at doorsteps – and
They too
Arrived in Canada,

Where
He, my neighbour,
Died
Soon enough:
Some silly accident in connection with
Underground chambers,
Oxygen supplies and
Computers that took a
Nap . . .
Before the
Contracts were signed.

She – my neighbour's widow,
Planned herself and the kids for a
Distant cousin who
Should have been
Living in
Newark
New Jersey.
'Cept they had not seen one another
In years
Not since
My neighbour's widow left the
Islands to go nursing in
UK,
While her
Distant cousin was bound for the
USA,
Where
We all know a
Nigger can make more money than
Any darkie
Anywhere in the
Commonwealth . . .
Yes?

But apart from
Keeping up correspondences with
Nursing distant cousins,

Other duties claim us:
West Indian neighbour's widow
Unknowing
Canadian Pacific
Rolling into
New England
Distant cousin
Gotten shot down . . .
'Any Negro can burn:
Potential snipers all
           and
Them is all alike.'

The feathers?
They
         drop
and
         drop
and
         drop, over
Many
Seas and
Lands,
Until the
Last wing
         falls: and
Skins bared to the
Cold winds or
Hot,
Frozen or
Scorched,
We
Die.

Sissie looked at the young mother and the thought came to her
that

Here,
Here on the edge of a pine forest in the

Heartland of
Bavaria, among the ruins of one of the
Largest
Castles in all
Germany,
IT CANNOT BE NORMAL
for a young
Hausfrau to
Like
Two Indians
Who work in
Supermarkets.

'My Mann is called
                ADOLF
And zo is our little zon.'

'Ver do you come from?' she asked Sissie.
   'Ghana.'
'Is that near Canada?'

Pre-Columbian South American with only a little
Stretch of imagination
Perhaps
But Eskimo?

No.
Too wide the
Disparity
In
Skin hue
Shape of eyes –
Thanks for the
Compliment, Madam,
But
No.

'I really like ze two Indians who verkt in ze supermarket,' she
insisted. 'Zo ver is Ghana?'

'West Africa. The capital is called Accra. It is . . .'

'Ah ja, ja, ja that is ze country zey have ze President Nuku-rumah, ja?'

'Yes.'

'My name is Marija. But me, I like ze English name Mary. Please call me Mary. Vas is your name?'

'My name? My name is Sissie. But they used to call me Mary too. In school.'

'Mary . . . Mary . . . Mary. Did you say in school zey call you Mary?'

'Yes.'

'Like me?'

'Yes.'

'Vai?'

'I come from a Christian family. It is the name they gave me when they baptised me. It is also good for school and work and being a lady.'

'Mary, Mary . . . and you an African?'

'Yes.'

'But that is a German name!' said Marija.

Mary?
But that is an English name, said Jane.
Maria . . . Marlene.
That is a Swedish name, said Ingrid.
Marie is a French name, said Michelle.
Naturally
Naturellement
Natürlich!

Mary is anybody's name but . . .

Small consolation that in some places,
The patient, long-suffering
Missionaries could not get as far
As
Calling up to the pulpit
A man and his wife who
Fight in the night

and
Whip them
Before the
Whole congregation of the
SAVED

But my brother,
They got
Far
Enough.

Teaching among other things,
Many other things,
That
For a child to grow up
To be a
Heaven-worthy individual,
He had
To have
Above all, a
Christian name.

And what shall it profit a native that
He should have
Systems to give
A boy
A girl
Two
Three names or
More?
Yaw Mensah Adu Preko Oboroampa Okotoboe

Ow, my brother . . .
Indeed there was a time when
Voices sang
Horns blew
Drums rolled to
Hail
Yaw
   – for getting born on Thursday

Preko
  — Just to extol Yaw
Mensah
  — Who comes third in a series of males
Adu
  — A name from father
  after venerable ancestor,
Okotoboe
  — For hailing the might of Adu.

No, my brother,
We no more
Care for
Such
Anthropological
Shit:

A man could have
Ten names.
They were all the same —
Pagan
Heathen
Abominable idolatry to the
Hearing of
God,
Who, bless his heart,
Is a rather
Nice
Old
European
Gentleman with a flowing white beard.
. . . And he sits
Flanked on either side by
Angels that take the roll-call for
The Elect.

Lord,
Let us Thy Servants depart in peace
Into our rest
Our oblivion and never

Dare expect
Angels who take roll-calls in
Latin – most likely –
To twist rather delicate tongues
Around names like
– Gyaemehara
Since, dear Lord, Your
Angels, like You, are
Western
White
English, to be precise.
Oh dear visionary Caesar!
There are no other kinds of
Angels, but
Lucifer, poor Black Devil.

Marija was warm.

Too warm for
Bavaria, Germany
From knowledge gained since.

She laughed easily. Her small buck teeth brilliantly white against
thin lips flaming red with lipstick.

White teeth –
Used to be one of the
Unfortunate characteristics of
Apes and
Negroes.
All that is
Changed now.
White teeth are in, my brother,
Because Someone is
Making
Money out of
White teeth.

'I like to be your friend, yes?' asked Marija wistfully.

'Yes.'

'And I call you Sissie, . . . please?'

'Sure.'

'Zo vas is zis name, "Sissie"?'

'Oh, it is just a beautiful way they call "Sister" by people who like you very much. Especially if there are not many girl babies in the family . . . one of the very few ways where an original concept from our old ways has been given expression successfully in English.'

'Yes?'

'Yes . . . Though even here, they had to beat in the English word, somehow.'

'Your people, they see many small things about people, yes?'

'Yes. Because a long time ago, people was all people had.'

'Ah zo. And you, you have many brothers and no sisters?'

'No. I mean, it is not like that for me. They call me Sissie because of something else. Some other reason . . . to do with school and being with many boys who treated me like their sister . . .'

'Oh yes?'

'Yes.'

'I really liked zose Indians. I sink of zem weri much as you speak English.'

> A common heritage. A
> Dubious bargain that left us
> Plundered of
> Our gold
> Our tongue
> Our life – while our
> Dead fingers clutch
> English – a
> Doubtful weapon fashioned
> Elsewhere to give might to a
> Soul that is already
> Fled.

ONCE UPON A TIME, she said,
I too had met an Indian
In Göttingen or thereabouts
My feelings were nebulous
Not liking or liking
Only hearing some other
Friend from some other place:

'We are the victims of our History and our
Present. They place too many obstacles in the
Way of Love. And we cannot enjoy even our
Differences in peace.'

D'accord
D'accord.

My Indian had been in
Germany 'for quite a number of years.'

Clearly for quite a number of
Years too, a Doctor, a
General Dispenser to the
Imaginary ailments of
Surburbia Germania.
I had looked at him
And switched on
Memory's images,
Pieced together from other
Travellers' tales of sick people in
Calcutta.
'Why did you remain
Here?'

'What do you mean?'
'Why did you not go back
Home?'
'Where?'
'Do they need you as a Doctor
Here,
As desperately?'

My voice rising hysterical,
Me on the verge of tears.
'Hm', he grunted,
'One of these Idealistic Ones, heh?'
Me on the defensive,
'Okay,
If I am idealistic
Let me be idealistic!'

'You say you come from
Ghana?'
'Yes!'
'Well,' he said,
Grinning most deliciously,
'There are as many Ghanaian doctors
practising here as there are Indians . . . more
in fact, counting population ratios at home.'

'I know.
I know.'
My foolish fears flowing,
He tut-tutting me.

But wondering at the same time what I would
Have him do.

Me not knowing what to say.
Though having to agree
'Going to work in a
State hospital is
Unnecessary
Slavery . . .'

Unless you are a smart one
Anxious to use
State beds,
State drugs
State time for civilized
Private patients,
Business tycoons,

Other clever public servants
Who only know how to
Lord-it-over the public,
Lodge-brothers and
Classmates,
Just any
Rascal who can pay for
Himself or his
Wife.

'500 for a boy,
400 for a girl.'

Why should it surprise
That it costs a little more
To make a baby boy?

Busy as we are
Building in earnest,
Firm, solid, foundations for
Our zombie dynasties?

But then,
'They would treat a doctor like shit
If they could get away with it.'

And he, my Indian, in a
Social order that
Froze a thousand years gone, would
Starve
Today
Should he 'open a
Private practice
Anywhere at
Home.'
A child-of-God ministering to the
Children-of-God, who, being
God's own babies
Cannot pay for
Medicare, but feed on

Air and the glory of rich men that
Come and go:
Excellent nourishment for the
Soul, no doubt:
Poor feed for the baby.

So, please,
Don't talk to me of the
Brain –
Drain –
Which of us stays in these days?
But those of us who fear
We cannot survive abroad,
One reason or another?

Gambian ophthalmologist in Glasgow
Filipino lung specialist in Boston
Brazilian cancer expert in
Brooklyn or
Basle or
Nancy.
While at home,
Wherever that may be,
Limbs and senses rot
Leaving
Clean hearts to be
Transplanted into
White neighbours' breasts . . .
    And
Peace Troops and other volunteers
Who in their home towns, might not
Get near patients with
Hayfever in league with
Local incompetence
Prepare
Rare cases for
Burial . . .

They agreed that Marija would come and collect Sissie from the ex-castle-youth-hostel at about five o'clock the following afternoon, and take her home.

Five o'clock was a good time to plan an outing for. Because usually, Sissie and the other campers returned from the pine nursery around one o'clock or two. By three, they had finished eating their lunch. Fresh potatoes, German goulash, cheese, sauerkraut, fish in some form or other, other food items. And always, three different types of bread: white bread, black bread, rye bread. Tons of butter. Pots of jam. Indeed, portions at each meal were heavy enough to keep a seven foot quarry worker on his feet for a month. All of which was okay by the campers. So that even after a riotous breakfast, each of them had to have one or two mammoth sandwiches for the mid-morning break.

> They stuffed themselves.
> Oh yes:
> Darling teenage pigs from
> Europe
> Africa
> Latin America
> The Middle East –
> Having realized as
> Quickly as only the young can,
> That perhaps here in
> Bavaria,
> By the softly flowing Salz,
> No one needed their work
> Not their brawn, anyway:

Certainly not in any of the ways that Sissie had known of, as a member of INVOLOU:

> Helping with missionary sense of gratification,
> A village build a school block,
> Dig a new-fangled well
> Straighten a
> seventh rate feeder road into a
> second rate feeder road . . .

And when you pass by,
Years later,
A warmth creeping inside your chest
As you see a new
Market
Where you had shared the
Unevenly cooked –
Hardly sufficient –
Meatless
Jolof rice.

From all around the Third World,
You hear the same story;
Rulers
Asleep to all things at
All times –
Conscious only of
Riches, which they gather in a
Coma –
Intravenously –

So that
You wouldn't know they were
Feeding if it was not for the
Occasional
Tell-tale trickle somewhere
Around the mouth.
And when they are jolted awake,
They stare about them with
Unseeing eyes, just
Sleepwalkers in a nightmare.

Therefore,
Nothing gets done in
Villages or towns,
If
There are no volunteers,
Local and half-hearted.
There are some other kinds:

> Imported,
> Eager,
> Sweet foreign aid
> Eventually to take a
> Thousand
> For every horse-power put in.

Sissie and her companions were required to be there, eating, laughing, singing, sleeping and eating. Above all eating.

> So
> They stuffed themselves
> With a certain calmness
> That passeth all understanding.

They felt no need to worry over who should want them to be there eating. Why should they? Even if the world is rough, it's still fine to get paid to have an orgasm . . . or isn't it? Of course, later on when we have become

> Diplomats
> Visiting Professors
> Local experts in sensitive areas
> Or
> Some such hustlers,

We would have lost even this small awareness, that in the first place, an invitation was sent . . .

Meanwhile, all that Sissie and her fellow campers had to do by way of work was at a pine nursery; to cover up the bases and stems of pine seedlings with ground turf or peat. To protect them from the coming chill of winter. As the boys shovelled up the turf and wheeled it down in barrows, the girls did the sprinkling.

There were Bavarian peasants too in the garden. Middle-aged women. At the beginning, the campers could not place them. Then they realized that they were in the employment of some public authority and that in fact it was their work the campers were doing. This peating-up of the little pines had some of the campers feeling bad. Especially the European kids. Unused as they were to being useful in their middle-class homes, they had become international volunteers in the hope of getting to the poverty-stricken multitudes of the earth. Rotten luck, there had been friends of theirs who couldn't even leave home. Too many applications. For some time, a few had been made to believe they would get to, at least, southern Italy. But now here they were, in southern Germany, nursing prospective Christmas trees!

The Bavarian dames came every day to supervise the work the campers were doing. Or more correctly, just to be with them, around them, chat them up. And when they felt '*die schönenkinder*' were taking the job too seriously, they would move up and pat each of them in turn, asking them to go slow. They probably knew for a fact what the campers could only guess at: that all that to-do was just an excuse to procure the voices of the children of the world to ring carefree through the old forests.

> After
> Each shocking experience
> Mother Earth recovers –
> That, of course, is true,
> But, with some effort
> Battered as she is.
> It is not bad if we help her
> Some of the time.

The Bavarian ladies wore black: each one of them, each day.

> Widows
> Widows
> Widows all –
> From knowledge gained since.
> The blood of their young men was
> Needed to mix the concrete for
> Building the walls of
> The Third Reich. But
> Its foundations collapsed before the walls
> were completed.

Dear Lord,
Dear Lord,
How this reminds me of the
Abome kings of Dahomey.

That's why
They wonder,
They wonder if, should they
Stop cultivating the little pine trees, would
Something else,
Sown there,
Many many years ago,
In
Those Bavarian woods
     SPROUT?

Marija went for Sissie and took her home, which turned out to be at the other end of the village. The house, a dainty new cottage, was the last in a row of several dainty new cottages, beautifully covered up by their summer foliage of creepers.

Like the rest, it had a backyard garden where Sissie saw several kinds of vegetables thriving. She recognized an old old friend. Tomato. Though in all their uniformity and richness, those tomatoes looked like some strange exotic fruits. Lush, crimson, perfected.

Anyhow, there were real fruit trees in the garden. Sissie asked Marija to walk around with her while she tried to identify apples, pears, plums, with her mind thrown back to textbook illustrations at home:

Known landscapes
Familiar territories
Pampas of Australia
Steppes of Eurasia
Prairies of America
Koumis
Conifers
Snow.

Though outside in the African sun,
Giant trees stood for centuries and
Little plants
Bloomed and
Died,
All unmentioned in
Geography notes.

They went indoors, sat down, chattered about this and that, then finally had coffee with cookies.

Marija was reluctant to let Sissie leave early. She told her that Big Adolf's shift ran the whole day and half the night. Therefore, there was no need to cook supper. She could scrounge up a small meal which the two of them would eat together. There was plenty of cheese, sausages, fruits and yes, yes, some cold flesh . . .

'Flesh?'

'Meat, yes?'
'Ah so . . .'

Yes, Big Adolf would come home certainly, but late, very late, and so tired he would not eat. They had not finished paying for the dainty new cottage, Marija informed Sissie, so Big Adolf had to do overtime, much overtime.

When Sissie managed to convince Marija that she had to return to the youth hostel, Marija immediately produced two brown paperbags filled with apples, pears, tomatoes and plums.

But
The plums.
What plums.
Such plums.

Sissie had never seen plums before she came to Germany. No, she had never seen real, living, plums. Stewed prunes, yes. Dried, stewed, sugared-up canned plums . . .

Praise the Lord for all dead things.

First course:
Cream of asparagus soup
Thirty months in an aluminium
Tin.

Second course:
Chicken moriturus under
Pre-mixed curry from
Shepherds Bush:
And since we are learning to take
Desserts – true mark of a leisured class –
Canned prunes
Canned pears
Canned apples
Apricots
Cherries.

Brother,
The internal logic is super-cool:
The only way to end up a cultural
Vulture
Is to feed on carrion all the way

You cannot achieve the
Moribund objectives of a
Dangerous education by using
Living forces.
Therefore, since
'Ghosts know their numbers,'
Dr Intellectual Stillborn
– with perfect reason –
Can break his neck to recruit
Academic corpses from Europe.
Wraith-like with age or
Just plain common.

Like pears, apricots and other fruits of the Mediterranean and
temperate zones, Sissie had seen plums for the first time in her life

only in Frankfurt. In the next few weeks, she was to see lots of them wherever she went, through the length and breadth of Germany. It was midsummer and the fruit stalls were overflowing. She had decided that being fruits, she liked them all, although her two loves were going to be pears and plums. And on those two she gorged herself. So she had good reason to feel fascinated by the character of Marija's plums. They were of a size, sheen and succulence she had not encountered anywhere else in those foreign lands. And which, unknown to her then, she would not be encountering again. What she was also not aware of, though, was that those Bavarian plums owed their glory in her eyes and on her tongue not only to that beautiful and black Bavarian soil, but also to other qualities that she herself possessed at that material time:

> Youthfulness
> Peace of mind
> Feeling free:
> Knowing you are a rare article,
> Being
> Loved.

So she sat, Our Sister, her tongue caressing the plump berries with skin-colour almost like her own, while Marija told her how she had selected them specially for her, off the single tree in the garden.

During the days that followed, Marija came to the castle every afternoon at five o'clock to take Sissie out. They avoided the main street and took a path through a park where they walked Little Adolf for a while before getting home. Sometimes they sat and talked. Or rather, Marija asked a few questions while Sissie, answering, told her friend about her

> Mad country and her
> Madder continent.

At other times, they just sat, each with her own thoughts. Occasionally, one of them would look up at the other. If their eyes met, they would smile. At the end of each day, she returned to the castle later than she had done the previous evening. And more heavily loaded too. For there was always a couple of brown paper bags, filled with delicacies, fruits and plums. Always, there were the plums. Sissie realized that Marija picked each lot about twenty-four hours ahead and kept them overnight in a polythene bag; a process that softened the plums and also rid them of their fresh tangy taste, preserving a soothing sweetness.

Yes,
Work is love made visible.

And so it was that Our Sister became known to her fellow campers in the ex-castle-youth-hostel as The-Bringer-of-Goodies-After-Lights-Out.

Supper was at seven. And what with the quantity of it, its overall density and nothing active to do afterwards but singing songs and rapping, most of the campers were ready to retire early to bed. Except that the environment was a sure sleep-breaker. For who knows of a better inspirer of puppy-love, European-style, than

An ancient ruined castle at the edge of a
Brooding pine forest, on the
Bank of a soft flowing river that
Sparkles silver
Under the late-night
Sun?

So there was a great deal of hand-holding, wet-kissing along ancient cobbled corridors. Pensive stares at the silvery eddies of the river.

The promises exchanged were not going to be kept. But who cared?

Love is always better when
Doomed . . .
If Sonja Simonian, Jewish,

Second generation immigrant from
Armenia to Jerusalem
Falls in love with Ahmed Mahmoud bin
Jabir from Algeria –
Then who dares to
Hope? Or not to hope?

On others, the great romanticism in the setting was completely lost. Most of Sissie's room-mates were such infants. However, even they stayed up. They might get into their bunks, but they played pillows, waiting for her to return, an hour or so before midnight. Nor was this surprising, it being midsummer and the day so long.

As soon as they heard the sound of her approaching figure, they would leap off their beds as one of their voices yelled: 'The plums!'

Screaming and yelping like baby hounds, they would jump on her, seize on the inevitable brown paper bags and devour their contents. And no one could go to sleep until the last plum had vanished.

There was Gertie from Bonn, free, light Gertie . . .

Jayne from East Putney, London, whose mother killed Sissie with

'Deeah, Jayn's been awai all dai,' . . .

Our Sister whose British-born and British-trained teachers had spent hours moulding her tongue around the nooks and crannies of the Received Pronunciation . . .

Marilyn. She took Sissie to visit her teacher training college one evening. Somewhere in the suburbs of London. And the first thing she did was to point out for Sissie the only black girl on campus. Triumph written over her face.

It happens all the time.

At nine a showpiece
At eighteen a darling
What shall you be
At thirty?

A dog among the masters, the
Most masterly of the
Dogs.

Father is the Minister of Education
At home. He knows where to get
Quality, so for
Education and other
Essentials, he orders straight from
Europe. And it's really
Better if we go
There for it.
Enrolled us at
Six months old,
You cannot rescue too early, you know . . .

Sissie in Lower Bavaria was something of a crowd-getter. It seemed as if any open function that was organized for the volunteers became an automatic success if she was present.

Since for those natives, the mere fact of the presence of the African girl was phenomenal.

Some among them had come across blacks on rare trips to Munich. Blacks who, whether they were American soldiers from NATO military bases or African students, always turned out to be men and fairly fluent speakers of German. And therefore not so exotic.

Whereas Our Sister was not only a female, but also spoke no German. They had heard she was fluent in English. That made no difference. English might be a familiar language but they neither spoke it nor understood it when it was spoken.

As for the African Miss, ah . . . h . . . h . . . look at her costume. How charming. And they gaped at her, pointing at her smile. Her nose. Her lips. Their own eyes shining. Not expecting her to feel embarrassed.

That's why, my brother,
You and I
Shall be
Impressed with

Aeronautics and all such
Acrobatics when they
Bring us a
Breathing Martian or a
Ten-eyed
Hairy drummer from the
Moon . . .

Meanwhile who was this Marija Sommer who was monopoliz-
ing the curiosity that provided such fun just by being? A little
housewife married to a factory hand?

And they fumed.

They raged. The thinned-out-end of the old aristocracy and
those traditional lickers of aristocratic arse, the pastor, the
burgomaster and the schoolteacher . . . Joined by the latest
newly-arrived.

The earliest of the new people had come in with the pre-war
National Construction that had expanded the size of the ancient
village. For in those pine forests, they say the Leader had had
built one of those massive chemical plants that served the
Empire. They say that in the very very big laboratories of the
chemical plant, experiments were done on herb, animal and
man. But especially on man, just hearing of which should get a
grown-up man urinating on himself, while seeing anything of
them should keep him screaming in his sleep for at least one
year.

After the war, they converted the structure into just another
chemical plant for producing pain-killing drugs. And more
people came into the village. And with the people the social
services, and their bosses. Most of these bosses, especially those
who had anything to do with money, considered themselves
important enough to be in the limelight.

So how was it that it was not them or their wives escorting the
African Miss? There must be something wrong with that Marija
Sommer!!

Why does she always walk with the black girl? asked the
director of the local branch of a bank.

Sommer does not speak English and the African speaks no

German. So who interprets for them? asked the manager of a supermarket.

What could they be talking about? wondered an insurance broker.

She must not take her to her house every day!

She must be getting neurotic!

It is perverse.

SOMEONE MUST TELL HER HUSBAND!!

And Marija's neighbours suddenly became important. For was it not they who were near the drama? And for once in their lives their afternoons were filled with meaning, as they sat and spied on the goings on between the two. A group of them would invariably find a reason to come and see Marija any time they knew Sissie was in, and yet pretend it was not because of her they came. Then hiding behind their language, they would slug Marija with questions, hang around for much more time than was reasonable in even their own eyes, and eventually leaving them alone, only when they sensed it would be too much to stay any longer.

Meanwhile Marija could tell Sissie of people whom she did not remember vaguely as ever meeting at all, now greeting her on the street and often stopping to ask her rather familiar questions as though they were lifelong friends. Marija was always calm.

But something of the commotion reached Marija so that the two women finally agreed to push up their meetings a couple of hours late.

That improved matters somewhat. Darkness did not come early, it being summer and the day so long. Yet by the normal hours of the evening, the creature man had responded to the workings of his body and succumbed to a feeling of tiredness. By eight o'clock, day activities had ended, giving way to those of night. The main street was deserted and the eerie quietness characteristic of night had enveloped human dwellings, even though the sun shone.

There was a certain strangeness about Marija the first time she came to fetch Sissie in the evening. Her eyes had a gleam in them that the African girl would have found unsettling if the smile that always seemed to be dancing around her lips had also not been more obviously there. She was flushed and hot. Sissie could feel the heat.

And there had always been formalities to go through before Sissie could leave the hostel. Like looking for one of the camp leaders to tell them she was going out. And also booking out, at the reception desk.

That evening, things turned out to be a little more difficult than usual. The camp leader thought it was rather late and the receptionist stated flatly that going out that late was against the rules.

Sissie stood and looked wistful, while Marija pleaded with them in their language and succeeded only in irritating them even more.

The receptionist was immovable. In the end, the camp leader gave in and then reluctantly explained to the receptionist that in spite of the rules, they obviously could not refuse the African Miss anything.

Outside, Marija heaved a sigh of relief declaring that she would not have been able to bear it if they had prevented Sissie from accompanying her home.

As for Our Sister, she didn't comment on that. What she was thinking was that the situation did not call for such panic. For as far as she was concerned, she could have gone back to her companions, after fixing an earlier date for the next day.

'I am zo glad vee are going home tonight, Sissie,' insisted Marija.

'I am too,' Sissie agreed.

A cool breeze was blowing. The river was a dark grey in the somewhat twilight and lapping quietly against the stone and concrete embankment. It was one of these moments in time when one feels secure, as though all of reality is made up of what can be seen, smelt, touched and explained.

'Sissie,' began Marija, with that special way she had for pronouncing the name. As though she was consciously making an effort to get the music in it not to die too soon but rather carry on into far distances.

'Yes, Marija?' she responded.

'I have baked a cake for you.'

'M-m-m,' Our Sister cooed; pretending to be more delighted at the news than she actually felt.

Indeed she was feeling uncomfortable.

She had already added about ten pounds to her weight since she arrived in that country. Therefore, she was no longer capable of feeling ecstasy at the news that any type of cake had been baked in her honour. Even if she was only an unconscious African schoolgirl?

> Who does not know that
> Plumpness and
> Ugliness are the
> Same, an
> Invitation for
> Coronary something or other?
> That
> Carbohydrates are debilitating
> Anyhow?

> Besides, my sister,
> If you want to believe the
> Brothers
> Telling
> You
> How Fat they
> Like their
> Women,
> Think of the
> Shapes of the ones they
> Marry;

> How
> Thin

> How
> Stringy
> Thin.

'It is a plum cake,' pursued Marija.

'Ah-h-h.' Our Sister cried softly. In anguish. For did she not remember that the cakes the natives of the land baked were very sweet and she herself did not like too many sweet things?

They walked on. Happy then, just to be alive. But soon, they came across an old man and an old woman, who stopped dead in their tracks. Two pairs of eyes popping out of their sockets. Old man talking his language; plenty of words: pointing first to his arm then to Sissie's arm, then to his, then to hers, back to his own arm then again to Sissie's arm. Poor old man breathing heavily and sweating. Old woman anxiously speaking her language. Plenty of words. Marija smiling, smiling, smiling. Sissie asking Marija for explanation of what is happening. Marija blushing R-E-D. Marija blushing but refusing to answer Sissie's question.

> Yes, my sister,
> Some things that
> Really
> Happen to us in our wanderings are
> Funnier than
> Travel jokes.

They walked on. Along the main thoroughfare of the town. Now their inner joys are gone, too aware of the sad ways of man.

Who was Marija Sommer?

> A daughter of mankind's
> Self-appointed most royal line,
> The House of Aryan —
>
> An heiress to some
> Legacy that would make you
> Bow
> Down
> Your head in
> Shame and
> Cry.

And Our Sister?

A Little
Black
Woman who
If things were what they should have been,
And time had not a way of
Making nonsense of Man's
Dreams, would
Not
Have been
There
Walking
Where the
Führer's feet had trod –
A-C-H-T-U-N-G!

They arrived at Marija's house. Just then Sissie realized that Little Adolf had not been with them.

'Where is Little Adolf, Marija?'

'He is in the house, sleeping . . .'

'Of course, of course,' said Sissie to herself. She had forgotten that it was much later than any safe hour to take a baby out. Marija was still talking.

'I wanted to be alone. To talk with you . . . you know, Sissie, sometimes one wants to be alone. Even from the child one loves so much. Just for a very little time . . . may be?'

She finished uncertainly, looking up to Sissie who did not have a child, as if for confirmation. A reassurance. That she was not speaking blasphemy.

It is
Heresy.

In
Africa
Europe,
Everywhere.

This is
Not a statement to come from a
Good mother's lips —

Touch wood.

Sissie was silent. Thinking that she did not know about babies.
But then, wasn't Marija too often by herself anyway?

Yet
Who also said that
Being alone is not like
Being
Alone?

They entered the house. It was as usual, very quiet. They turned
from the doorway into the kitchen which seemed to serve also as
the family sitting room. It was large and comfortable.

'Sit down, Sissie.'

The chairs were modernistic affairs in artificial fibre. And two
of them were placed companionably together as though Marija
had planned it that way. Sissie sat in one of them.

Marija relieved her of the sweater which she had taken along
with her although the day had been very warm. For it seemed not
to matter to Our Sister how warm the days were. She could never
trust this weather that changed so often and so violently, used as
she was to the eternal promise of tropical warmth.

Marija wondered if Sissie was ready for coffee.

Sissie said no, not for a little while. But was there water? Sissie
had noticed that for some reason, a request for water always
drew gasps from her hosts and hostesses; it didn't make a
difference in which part of the land they were. At any rate, they
appeared never to drink any water themselves.

'Yes,' said Marija, 'but perhaps blackcurrant juice?'

They grew in her mother's garden. The blackcurrants did.
Plenty, plenty. And every summer since she was little, her one
pleasure had been preserving blackcurrants — making its jam,
bottling its juices. And she still went home to help. Or rather, she
went to avail herself of the pleasure, the beauty, the happiness at

harvest time: of being with many people, the family. Working with a group. If they had met earlier, she could have taken Sissie home for that year's harvest. It was not far away. Her home. She was sure her mother would have liked Sissie very much.

Sissie was sipping the good drink . . . Marija asked her if she would like to see Little Adolf. Sissie said yes, getting up. But Marija said she could finish her drink. Later, they would go upstairs to see Little Adolf and Sissie would like to be shown around the upstairs of the house, since they had so far always remained downstairs?

Sissie agreed. Then she went on to say how beautiful she thought he was. The mother smiled, delighted. She had already informed Sissie that Adolf was going to be her only child. There had been complications with his birth and the Herr Doktor had advised her not to attempt to have another child. It might be unsafe for her. And now smiling even more broadly, she said that since Adolf was going to be the only child, she was very happy he was a boy.

> Any good woman
> In her senses
> With her choices
> Would say the
> Same
>
> In Asia
> Europe
> Anywhere:
>
> For
> Here under the sun,
> Being a woman
> Has not
> Is not
> Cannot
> Never will be a
> Child's game
>
> From knowledge gained since —

So why wish a curse on your child
Desiring her to be female
?
Beside, my sister,
The ranks of the wretched are
Full,
Are full.

Now Marija was saying that she was, oh so very, sorry, that she had no hope of ever visiting Sissie in Africa. But she prayed that one day, Little Adolf would go there, maybe.

And there is always
SOUTH AFRICA
   and
RHODESIA,
      you see.

'Sissie?'
'Yes, Marija?'
'You are from Africa. And oh, that is vonderful. Weri vunder-bar. And you trawel so much. But ver also did you say you vent?'
'Nigeria.'
'Oh yes?'
'Yes.'
'Neegeria. Ah-h, Nee-ge-ria. Vas did you go to do in Neegeria?'
Sissie opened her mouth to answer her. But it appeared there was something else Marija wanted to know first.
'Nee-ge-ria. What is Neegeria like?'
'Oh like my country. Only bigger. Or rather it has got bigger, everything that my country has.'
Sissie told Marija that she always persuaded friends from abroad who could only visit one country in Africa to make sure they went to Nigeria.
Marija was shocked because Sissie was sounding unpatriotic.
'Why, Sissie?'

Our Sister tried to explain herself. That as far as she was concerned, Nigeria not only has all the characteristics which nearly every African country has, but also presents these characteristics in bolder outlines. Therefore, what is the point in persuading a friend to see the miniature version of anything when the real stuff is there?

Nigeria.
Nigeria our love
Nigeria our grief.
Of Africa's offspring
Her likeness –

O Nigeria.
More of everything we all are,
More of our heat
   Our naiveté
   Our humanity
   Our beastliness
   Our ugliness
   Our wealth
   Our beauty

A big mirror to
   Our problems
   Our tragedies.
   Our glories.
Mon ami,
Household quarrels of
Africa become a
WAR in-
Nigeria:

'And Ghana?'
'Ghana?'

Ghana?
Just a
Tiny piece of beautiful territory in
Africa – had

Greatness thrust upon her
Once.
But she had eyes that saw not –
That was a long time ago . . .
Now she picks tiny bits of
Undigested food from the
Offal of the industrial world . . .
O Ghana.

Sissie shivered.
   'What is it?'
   'I am feeling cold.'
   'I bring you the sweater, yes?'
   'No, it is not the air that makes me cold. I shall feel better soon.'
   'Anywhere else you have been in Africa?'
   'Yes.'
   'Where?'
   'Upper Volta . . .'
   'And where is Upper Wolta?'
   'On top of Ghana.'
   'What did you go to do?'
   'Tourism.'
   Marija laughed.
Was Upper Wolta also beautiful?
   'Yes,' said Sissie. 'But in a poorer, drier, sadder way.'
   'Ja?'
   'Ja.'

She did not know she thought so then.
She was to know.

The bible talks of
Wilderness
Take your eyes to see
Upper Volta, my brother –
Dry land. Thorn trees. Stones.

The road from the Ghana border to
Ouagadougou was
Out-of-sight!

The French, with
Characteristic contempt and
Almost
Childish sense of
Perfidy had
A long time ago, tarred two
Narrow
Strips of earth for motor vehicles.
Each wide enough for
One tyre.

Result: When two vehicles passed one another, both of
them had to get off the tarred strips and on to the dust and
stones, or mud and stones according to the time of year. Three
friends travelled on it at a time when there was no difference
between the strips and the rest. The former being full of deathly
potholes and the latter just one long ditch. As they sped along,
the car fell into a pothole and caught fire. They were saved by
their fates. For between the three of them they had only enough
knowledge about automobiles to remove and fix a tyre after a
puncture, and no more. But groping around blindly in the
smoke, the smartest among them snapped some wires and the
smoking stopped. It was in the middle of nowhere and so all they
could do was sit by the roadside and wait for help. Presently a
Frenchman came by. The friends asked him why the country
permitted its international road to remain in such condition
years after independence.

'The President himself uses it every day.' The Frenchman said,
shrugged his shoulders and drove off.

A sickening familiar tale.
Poor Upper Volta too.

There are
Richer, much

Richer countries on this continent
Where
Graver national problems
Stay
Unseen while
Big men live their
Big lives
Within . . .

At the end of the day, the three friends came to a tiny French provincial town called Ouagadougou. Where between the heat of the Sahara and the heat of the Equator, they hang out cotton wool on window sills for snow, it being the Feast of Noël.

We have heard too,
Have we not? Of countries in
Africa where
Wives of
Presidents hail from
Europe.
Bringing their brothers or . . . who knows?
To run the
Economy.

Excellent idea . . .
How can a
Nigger rule well
Unless his
Balls and purse are
Clutched in
Expert White Hands?

And the Presidents and their
First Ladies
Govern from the North
Provençe, Geneva, Milan . . .
Coming south to Africa
Once a year
For holidays.

Meanwhile,
Look!

In the capitals,
Ex-convicts from European
Prisons drive the city buses, and
Black construction workers
Sweat under the tropical sun, making
Ice-skating rinks for
The Beautiful People . . .
While other Niggers sit
With vacant stares
    Or
Busy, spitting their lungs out.

JUST LIKE THE GOOD OLD DAYS
BEFORE INDEPENDENCE

Except –
The present is
S-o-o-o much
Better!
For
In these glorious times when
Tubercular illiterates
Drag yams out of the earth with
Bleeding hands,

Champagne-sipping
Ministers and commissioners
Sign away
Mineral and timber
Concessions, in exchange for
Yellow wheat which
The people can't eat.

And at noon,
The wives drive Mercedes-Benzes to
Hairdressers', making ready for
The evening's occasion
While on the market place,

The good yams rot for
Lack of transportation and
The few that move on,
Are shipped for
Paltry cents —
To foreign places as
Pretty decorations
On luxury tables.

We must sing and dance
Because some Africans made it.

EDUCATION HAS BECOME TOO
EXPENSIVE. THE COUNTRY CANNOT
AFFORD IT FOR EVERYBODY.
Dear Lord,
So what can we do about
Children not going to school,

When
Our representatives and interpreters,
The low-achieving academics
In low profile politics
Have the time of their lives
Grinning at cocktail parties and around
Conference tables?
At least, they made it, didn't they?

No,
Man does not live by
Gari or ugali alone —

Therefore
We do not complain about
Expensive trips to
Foreign 'Varsities' where
Honorary doctorate degrees
Come with afternoon teas and
Mouldy Saxon cakes from
Mouldier Saxon dames . . .

Nor do we mind
That when they come back here
Having mortgaged the country for a
Thousand and a year
To maintain themselves on our backs
With capitalist ships and fascist planes,
They
Tell
Us
How the water from their
Shit-bowls
Is better than what the villagers
Drink . . .

Ow, glory.
While
Able-bodied fishermen
Disappear in
Cholera, the rest, from under
Leaking roofs and unlit alleys
Shall drum,
and sing
dance
with
joy

This year of the pig-iron anniversary
Because
There is ecstasy
In dying from the hands of a
Brother
Who
Made
It.
. . .
Now we hear the road is
First class to Ouagadougou
Done-up with borrowed money from

Those who know where to sow
   – even in a wilderness –
To reap a millionfold.

'And now you come to Germany?' asked Marija.
'Yes,' Our Sister answered.
But before Bavaria, there had been France, Belgium, The Netherlands. One day in Salzburg, six in the two Berlins.

West Berlin –
As loud as a
Self-conscious whore at a
Gay last-night party
Aboard a sinking ship
East Berlin,
Quiet like a haunted house
On a Sunday afternoon.

With her neutral tastes, Sissie disliked both.
'Sissie, who pays for all the trawel?'
'Marija, there was a time when it was fashionable to be African. And it paid to be an African student. And if you were an African student with the wanderlust, you travelled.'

Young Christian Movements
Young Muslim Movements,
The Non-Believers' Conferences for Youth,
The Co-ordinated Committees for Students
of The Free World,
The First Internationals for Socialist Youth,
International Workcamping for
Non-Aligned Students . . .

'It is money well spent.
Nobody's fault that they do not know
How to make use of their
Staggering natural resources.

But first!

Their leaders must be wooed
For now and tomorrow.

And, it's quite in order
To procure
One
Or two of their sable countenances,
To garnish dull speeches and resolutions –

We
Know
What
We
Want:
The airlines profit a little too.'

And some of us paused and wondered
How long it would all last.

Marija's eyes were red. She was saying that since she had met Sissie, she had been wishing she was better educated to go places ... Not just like any tourist. Sissie said she was sorry. Not wanting pity, Marija smiled, saying it was good to have Little Adolf who would go to university, travel and come back to tell her all about his journeys.

'Yes,' said Sissie.

Remembering her own mother,
To whom she sent
Shamefully
Expurgated versions of
Her travel tales.
Letters?
Once a trip, even if a trip lasts
A lifetime.

They sat and time crept on. The false dusk had given way to proper night. Darkness had brought her gifts of silence and heaviness, making the most carefree of us wonder, when we are alone, about our place in all this.

Sissie had been unconsciously looking down, unaware that Marija had been watching her all the time. When Sissie lifted her head and their eyes met, red blood rushed into Marija's face. So deeply red.

Sissie felt embarrassed for no reason that she knew. The atmosphere changed.

Once or so, at the beginning of their friendship, Sissie had thought, while they walked in the park, of what a delicious love affair she and Marija would have had if one of them had been a man.

Especially if she, Sissie, had been a man. She had imagined and savoured the tears, their anguish at knowing that their love was doomed. But they would make promises to each other which of course would not stand a chance of getting fulfilled. She could see Marija's tears . . .

That was a game. A game in which one day, she became so absorbed, she forgot who she was, and the fact that she was a woman. In her imagination, she was one of these black boys in one of these involvements with white girls in Europe. Struck by some of the stories she had heard, she shivered, absolutely horrified.

> First Law:
> The Guest Shall Not Eat Palm-Nut Soup.
> Too intimate, too heavy.
>
> But my brothers do not know,
> Or knowing, forget.
>
> Yes?
>
> There are
> Exceptions
> Beautiful exceptions,
> Wonderful success?
>
> But the rest?
>
> I wail for
> Lost Black minds
> – Any lost Black mind –

Because
A tailor for the poor
Can ill afford to throw away his
Scraps:

Beautiful Black Bodies
Changed into elephant-grey corpses,
Littered all over the western world,
Thrown across railway tracks for
midnight expresses to mangle
just a little bit more –
Offered to cold flowing water
Buried in thickets and snow
Their penises cut.

Marija said quietly, 'You shall eat now, Sissie?'

'No. Marija, I am not hungry. It is very late, I think I should go back.'

'Me, I am also not hungry. But you said you want to look at Little Adolf, yes? And I also show you the upstairs of the house?'

'Okay,' said Sissie, slowly coming out of her misery into a world where the need to pay mortgages and go on holidays kept married chambers empty for strangers' inspection.

Both of them stood up and stretched. As they went up the stairs, all images of twentieth-century modernia escaped Sissie. Rather, what with the time of night, it seemed to her as though she was moving, not up, but down into some primeval cave. A turn to the right, a turn to the left, one more to the right, behold.

Sissie whistled.

'She is a bitch
Or a witch
Who whistles' the old ones had said.

Sissie whistled.

Displeasing gods she did not
Know – only heard of.

The room indeed looked as if it was cut out of a giant rock that must have existed in the architect's mind. All triangles and disappearing corners. White walls. A giant white bed, laid out smooth, waiting to be used.

> Speak softly
> Tread lightly
> It is a holy place
> A sanctuary for shrouded dreams.

Indeed, Sissie was convinced she had no right to be there. And Marija? Sissie could not associate her with the deserted looking chamber or its simple funereal elegance. And anyway, there she was, moving silently about, that strange Marija, touching this, touching that, as though for her too this was a first visit to the room.

On either side of the bed was a little chest. On one, there was nothing. On the other was one book, a handkerchief . . . Directly facing the bed was a built-in dressing table, a crescent-shaped shelf which projected out of the wall, making that side of the room look like a bar. On this shelf were bottled affairs from the beauty business. Fragile weapons for a ferocious war. There they stood, tall and elegant with slender necks and copious bottoms, their tops glittering golden over bodies that exuded delicate femaleness in their pastel delicacy. Pink and blue creams. More pink and blue lotions. Skin foods that were milky white or avocado green proclaiming impressive scientific origins.

There were some of them of whose uses Sissie did not have the vaguest idea. They all looked expensive. Yet with a number of them also still in their packaging, nothing looked over-used.

Sissie felt Marija's cold fingers on her breast. The fingers of Marija's hand touched the skin of Sissie's breasts while her other hand groped round and round Sissie's midriff, searching for something to hold on to.

It was the left hand that woke her up to the reality of Marija's embrace. The warmth of her tears on her neck. The hotness of her lips against hers.

As one does from a bad dream, impulsively, Sissie shook

herself free. With too much effort, unnecessarily, so that she unintentionally hit Marija on the right cheek with the back of her right hand.

It all happened within a second. Two people staring at one another. Two mouths wide open with disbelief.

Sissie thought of home. To the time when she was a child in the village. Of how she always liked to be sleeping in the bedchamber when it rained, her body completely-wrapped-up in one of her mother's akatado-cloths while mother herself pounded fufu in the anteroom which also served as a kitchen when it rained. Oo, to be wrapped up in mother's cloth while it rained. Every time it rained.

And now where was she? How did she get there? What strings, pulled by whom, drew her into those pinelands where not so long ago human beings stoked their own funeral pyres with other human beings, where now a young Aryan housewife kisses a young black woman with such desperation, right in the middle of her own nuptial chamber, with its lower middle-class cosiness? A love-nest in an attic that seems to be only a nest now, with love gone into mortgage and holiday hopes?

Marija's voice came from far away, thin, tremulous and full of old tears.

'This is our bedroom. Big Adolf and I.'

Who is Big Adolf?
What does he look like?
Big Adolf, the father of Little Adolf,
Naturally.

But then how can one believe in the existence of this being? You make friends with a woman. Any woman. And she has a child. And you visit the house. Invited by the woman certainly. Every evening for many days. And you stay many hours on each occasion but you still never see the husband and one evening the woman seizes you in her embrace, her cold fingers on your breasts, warm tears on your face, hot lips on your lips, do you go back to your village in Africa and say . . . what do you say even from the beginning of your story that you met a married woman? No, it would not be easy to talk of this white woman to just anyone at home . . . Look at how pale she suddenly is as she moves shakily, looking lost in her own house?

Marija was crying silently. There was a tear streaming out of one of her eyes. The tear was coming out of the left eye only. The right eye was completely dry. Sissie felt pain at the sight of that one tear. That forever tear out of one eye. Suddenly Sissie knew. She saw it once and was never to forget it. She saw against the background of the thick smoke that was like a rain cloud over the chimneys of Europe.

L
O
N
E
L
I
N
E
S
S

Forever falling like a tear out of a woman's eye.

And so this was it?

Bullying slavers and slave-traders.

Solitary discoverers.

Swamp-crossers and lion hunters.

Missionaries who risked the cannibal's pot to bring the
world to the heathen hordes.

Speculators in gold in diamond uranium and copper

Oil you do not even mention —

Preachers of apartheid and zealous educators.

Keepers of Imperial Peace and homicidal
plantation owners.

Monsieur Commandant and Madame the
Commandant's wife.

Miserable rascals and wretched whores whose only distinction in life was that at least they were better than the
Natives . . .

As the room began to spin around her, Sissie knew that she had to stop herself from crying. Why weep for them? In fact, stronger in her was the desire to ask somebody why the entire world has had to pay so much and is still paying so much for some folks' unhappiness. There it was. Still falling.

Once upon a time, many years ago, a missionary went to the Guinea coast. Not to find some of the legendary gold dust that made the sands on the shores glitter. Perhaps not. But to be headmistress of a girls' school . . . In the course of time, they say she turned into a panting tigress whose huge bosoms never suckled a cub. She gave first her youth, then the rest of her life, to educating and straightening out African girls. But one thing she could neither stand nor understand about them was that 'they never told the truth' and they were always giggling. They made her mad.

They say what broke her spirit was that one night, on one of her regular nocturnal inspections, she found two girls in bed together. Although the night was thick, they say they saw that first she turned white. Then she turned red.

'Good Heavens, girl!

Is your mother bush?'
'No, Miss.'
'Is your father bush?'
'No Miss.'

'Then
Why
Are
You
Bush?'
Giggles, giggles, giggles.

Naughty African girls
Cracking up
To hear, and
See
European single woman

Tearing up herself over
Two girls in a bed

But
Madam,
It is not
Just
Bush . . .
From knowledge gained since.

Hurrah for
The English wonder
The glorious
Understatement

Because
Madam,
It's not just b-u-s-h

But a
C-r-i-m-e
A Sin
S-o-d-o-m-y,

From knowledge gained since.

Sissie looked at the other woman and wished again that, at least, she was a boy. A man.

'So why are you crying?' she asked the other.

'It is nothing,' the other replied.

How then does one
Comfort her
Who weeps for
A collective loss?

They returned to the big kitchen. They must have done. And Marija must have laid the table for two. Brought out the cold cuts. Sliced cold ham. Sliced cold lamb. Pieces of cold chicken meat. Sliced cold sausages. Sliced cheese. Pickled olives. Pickled gherkins. Sauerkraut. Strange looking foods that tasted even stranger. Each of them stone cold. Yet all of them pulled out from the fridge or some corner of the kitchen with a loving familiarity.

Sissie would always puzzle over it. Cold food. Even after she had taught her tongue to accept them, she could never really understand why people ate cold food. To eat ordinary cooked food that has gone cold without bothering to heat it is unpleasant enough. But to actually chill food in order to eat it was totally beyond her understanding. In the end, she decided it had something to do with white skins, corn-silk hair and very cold weather.

Marija made coffee and then carried in the cake. Flat, fluffy and on top, the melting dark purple of jellied plums. Plums. It was altogether a feasty spread. Yet it was also clear that neither of them had a mouth for eating a plum cake. Or anything else for that matter. Breaking off little pieces after long intervals, putting them into their mouths, chewing, swallowing, chewing, swallowing.

Marija asked Sissie about her family.

'There are seven of us my mother's children and sixteen of us, my father's.' The two of them began to laugh. After the laughter, Sissie told Marija a little more about her family . . . about polygamy. What she always thought were some of its comforts, but admitting too that it was very unfair, basically.

When Sissie realized that the tension was broken, it occurred to her too that if Whoever created us gave us too much capacity for sorrow, He had, at the same time, built laughter into us to make life somewhat possible.

'When is your birthday?' Marija asked Sissie. The latter gave a reply.

> They had been twins.
> Their mother was three months pregnant
> Before the great earthquake, and
> They were ten months in the womb.

She too asked Marija's birth date. Just to be polite. Knowing she was going to forget that and many other things besides. She who never remembered the day on which she was born.

As usual, Marija took Sissie as far as the doorstep of the youth hostel. Then suddenly, as they were saying goodnight, Sissie remembered that she would be leaving within a week. In a few days she would be gone.

> Goodbye to
> One of the largest castles in all Germany
> To silent pomp and decayed miseries.

Goodbye to Marija. She knew she could not tell Marija about her imminent departure from the area. Not that evening. No, it was not an evening to give undue intimations of the passage of time, or of our mortality.

Seeing there are as many goodbyes as there are hellos, and we die with each separation. Sissie knew she did not possess the kind of courage it takes to have mentioned to Marija at that time the fact that she was leaving the area soon.

They split. When she entered her room, she discovered that every one of her room-mates was asleep. It was just as well, because neither she nor Marija had remembered the customary brown paper bag and its fruity contents.

During the next few days, the campers stopped going to the pine nursery. Instead, and as a rounding-off programme, they were being taken round the Bavarian countryside, seeing festivals and watching country dances. There was always an air of gaiety wherever they went. And they drank from famous shoe mugs, met country and district officials who talked to them about educational reforms and their country's contributions to international foreign aid to the developing nations. And peace . . .

> From knowledge gained since,
> One wonders if their
> Buxom wives had ever been
> Guinea pigs to test
> The pill and other
> Drugs

As they say
Happens to
Miners' wives to
Farmers' wives in
Remote corners of
Banana republics and other
So-called-developing countries?

Oh.
Let me wail for
The Man we betrayed
The Man we killed

For,
Which other man lives
Here
Who dare tell
These guardians of my peace, and
Those
Exploiting do-gooders
To forget
My problems of

Ignorance
Disease
Poverty –

To stop
Their mediocre human loans

To stuff
Their pills where
They want them?

I know of
A mad geo-political professor
Whom no one listens to:
Who says
The danger has never been
Over-population.

For
The Earth has land to hold
More than twice the exploding millions
And enough to feed them too.

But
We would rather
Kill
        than
Think
        or
Feel.

My brother,
The new game is so
Efficient,
Less messy —

A few withered limbs
        just
A few withered seeds.

Ah-h-h
Lord,
Only a Black woman
Can
'Thank
A suicidal mankind'
With her
Death.

Her last evening came. Soon after Sissie and her companions had returned from a trip to see the famous lakes and mountains of the area, she was told that Marija was waiting at reception for her. She changed quickly and went out to meet her.

Marija could see that Sissie was tired. Maybe not too tired to make talking to her unkind. But taking her through the town, all the way to her house would have been too much. So they agreed they would only go for a walk around the castle and look at the river. Marija had brought Little Adolf with her and Sissie could feel some excitement in her. Already, uncertain of how to tell the other that this was indeed her last evening in the town, she waited for her to speak first.

'Tomorrow you come to eat lunch at my house, yes? I am going to cook. Big Adolf will be home.'

Sissie said quietly to Marija, 'I cannot come. I am sorry.'

The other stopped in her tracks immediately, her hands flying away from the handle of the pram. Her reaction startled the young child in the carriage and he started to cry. His mother picked him up and tried to comfort him. She had turned very pale. Then she turned very red. Sissie was almost delighted with this magic, this blushing and blanching. Meeting Marija was her first personal encounter with the phenomenon.

'Why you cannot come?'

At this point, Sissie began to feel ashamed and unhappy, for apart from everything else, she was afraid that in her agitation, Marija would drop her child.

'Why you cannot come?'

'I should have told you this before now. Long before now, Marija.'

'What is it?' asked Marija, as she returned her somewhat pacified child into the carriage. Obviously, mothers do not go dropping their offspring just-like-that.

'I am leaving tomorrow.'

'Ver you are going?'

'Back to the north.'

'Which norz?'

'Frankfurt, Hanover and Göttingen, where I shall be in another camp on the eastern border. Then after the camp, I shall leave for my country.'

'And you must go now, to this camp? From here, tomorrow?'

'Yes, Marija. I must show my face there at least for a few days.'

'This is weri sad, Sissie.'

So it was. The sadness was not in her words but in her voice. Her eyes. A sudden gust of air blew across from the river as though a ghost had passed. And whatever remained of the day folded itself up and died.

Perhaps
There are certain meetings
Must not happen?
Babies not born?
Who come with nothing to enrich us,
Too brief their time here –

They leave us with
Only
The pains and aches for
What-could-have-been-but-
Was-not

Wasted time and energies that
Destroy our youth
Make us older but
Not wiser,
Poorer for all that?

'And anyway, in a month's time, they will reopen my university.'

'One monz, Sissie: and you leave now here?'

They could not be rooted in one stop forever so without being aware of what they were doing, Marija started pushing her baby's carriage again, while Sissie kept pace with her.

Sissie was feeling absolutely cornered.

'You know, a month is not too much when you are travelling,' she said defensively.

'Ja-a-a?'

'I also have to make two other stops on the way.'

'Vai?'

'I have to visit some people.'

'Here? Germany?'

'One here. In Hamburg.'

'Vas to do in Hamburg? Who is there?'

'She is a friend. A girl . . .'

'. . .'

'When I was leaving my country, her mother made me

promise that I shall not return home unless I go and see her daughter with my two eyes.'

'Vai?'

'So that I can tell her how she really is.'

'Ja?'

'Yes. You see, deep down, our people never feel good when their children come to Europe or go anywhere across the sea.'

'Vai?'

'Because anything can happen to them.'

'But people are in ze house. Something also happen there, nein?'

'Marija, it is not easy to be reasonable every time.'

'Ja,' Marija agreed, subdued, perhaps with some awareness that she too is sometimes unreasonable? Then she said gingerly: 'Ze students, zey write letters home to their volks?'

'Yes,' Sissie agreed. 'But unless you are looking deep into the eyes of somebody how can you know he is telling the truth?'

'You cannot,' agreed the other woman.

'And if he is speaking from beyond the seas?'

'It is impossible, yes?'

'Yes, Marija. So our people have a proverb which says that he is a liar who tells you that his witness is in Europe.'

'Vitness? Vas is Vitness?'

'Like in court, someone to speak for your side.'

'Zat is a lawyer.'

'No. Not necessarily. I refer to just anybody who can claim he is in a position to know that the accused person did not say or do what he is accused of saying or doing.'

'Ja-ja. And your people, vas do zey say about a Vitness?'

'That any man who insists that his witness is in Europe is a liar.'

Marija giggled, betraying something of her former self.

'And vas in London you go to do?'

'I am meeting a boyfriend.'

She turned flaming red again.

'Ah zo. Ah zo. Ah zo. You are meeting a boyfriend. It is weri important, ja? And you must leave here weri quickly, ja?'

Sissie was feeling a little sick with Marija and her excitement over that piece of information. Of course, it would be rather nice to meet Whoever. But as for it being so important, she was not really sure. Could Marija be feeling jealous?

Marija said, 'Why you don't tell me before?'

'I forgot. I am sorry, Marija.'

'It is weri sad you forgot.'

> Why should we
> Always imagine
> Others to be
> Fools,
> Just because they love us?

Sissie felt like a bastard. Not a bitch. A bastard.

Marija said quivering, 'You know vas I have done, Sissie?'

'No, what have you done?'

'Ja. From ze butcher's I make order for a rabbit. Ze man brought it today. It is all fresh and clean. I cook specially for you. Tomorrow I cook . . . Big Adolf he will be home . . . Vee all eat together. Me. Little Adolf. Big Adolf.'

'O God, Marija, I cannot come. Listen, you know how they schedule a foreign visitor like me? They have sent all sorts of tickets, train, air, everything with definite boarding times booked.'

' . . . '

'Marija, there is nothing I can do about it. I suspect that even the camp leader here . . .'

'But you did not tell me. And I said, Sunday I cook ze rabbit for Sissie.'

Suddenly, something exploded in Sissie like fire. She did not know exactly what it was. It was not painful. It did not hurt. On the contrary, it was a pleasurable heat. Because as she watched the other woman standing there, now biting her lips, now gripping at the handle of her baby's pram and looking so generally disorganized, she, Sissie wanted to laugh and laugh and laugh. Clearly, she was enjoying herself to see that woman hurt. It was nothing she had desired. Nor did it seem as if she could control it, this inhuman sweet sensation to see another human being squirming. It hit her like a stone, the knowledge that there is a pleasure in hurting. A strong three-dimensional pleasure, an exclusive masculine delight that is exhilarating beyond all measure. And this too is God's gift to man? She wondered.

'Why didn't you let me know before you went to make all those elaborate plans?' Sissie demanded of the other woman.

'It was for you a surprise,' replied Marija timidly.

'Well, too bad. You'll have to eat my share of the rabbit for me.'

Marija's confusion knew no bounds.

Sissie could see it all. In her uncertain eyes, on her restless hands and on her lips, which she kept biting all the time.

But oh, her skin. It seemed as if according to the motion of her emotions Marija's skin kept switching on and switching off like a two-colour neon sign. So that watching her against the light of the dying summer sun, Sissie could not help thinking that it must be a pretty dangerous matter, being white. It made you awfully exposed, rendered you terribly vulnerable. Like being born without your skin or something. As though the Maker had fashioned the body of a human, stuffed it into a polythene bag instead of the regular protective covering, and turned it loose into the world.

Lord, she wondered, is that why, on the whole, they have had to be extra ferocious? Is it so they could feel safe here on the earth, under the sun, the moon and the stars?

Then she became aware of the fact that she would do something quite crazy if she continued on that trail of mind . . . Luckily for her, Marija was speaking anyway.

'I say . . . I say, Sissie, when you are leaving tomorrow?'

'. . . I am sorry, I didn't hear you the first time . . . some terrible hour in the morning. Very early.'

'Six o'clock and thirty minutes – yes? Zer is only one train zat goes from here to Munich early in ze morning.'

'Yes . . . yes. It must be that one.'

'I come see you off.'

'Why bother? There's no need to waste your morning sleep . . . I hate last minute goodbyes, anyway.'

Marija just stared at her. And she knew the last statement was totally unnecessary. There was a long pause during which neither said a thing. Then Marija resumed her pursuit.

'I vas going to cook in French sauce, the rabbit, mit vine und garlic und käse . . . cheese. Ja, Sissie?'

And Sissie noted for the first time that all along in the brief time of their friendship, obviously the worse Marija felt, the more Germanic was her English.

'You see, Marija,' said Sissie, trying not to let her irritation show, 'you said Big Adolf will be home tomorrow.'

'Ja.'

'Hm. You sure the rabbit was not for him?'

'But no . . . yes . . . but . . . but . . .'

'Well, pretend it was for him and cheer up . . . Besides, it is not sound for a woman to enjoy cooking for another woman. Not under any circumstances. It is not done. It is not possible. Special meals are for men. They are the only sex to whom the Maker gave a mouth with which to enjoy eating. And woman the eternal cook is never so pleased as seeing a man enjoying what she has cooked; eh, Marija? So give the rabbit to Big Adolf and watch him enjoy it. For my sake. And better still, for your sake.'

This time too Marija watched Sissie with a curious concentration. Yet she did not understand a word of it. Because serious as it sounded, Sissie was only telling a rather precious joke.

> After inflicting pain,
> We try to be funny
> And fall flat on our faces,
> Unaware that for
> The sufferer,
> The Comedy is
> The Tragedy and
> That is the
> Answer to the
> Riddle.

They said goodbye and separated.

At the crack of dawn the following day, Sissie left the hostel with those few others from the group who also had to proceed to the north of the country.

> Left one of the greatest castles of all
> Germany . . .
> Its river
> Its dry moat
> Its silent screams in dungeons
> Gone into time –
> Greedy warring owners
>   and their
> Whitened bones.

They only had a few minutes to wait before the train came. Then Sissie saw Marija running towards them clutching a brown paper bag. It occurred to her rather irrelevantly, that Marija had had to wake up quite early.

Marija crashed into Sissie, hugging her, smiling, and the one suspicious tear already glistening on the lashes of the left eye.

'O Marija,' Sissie said. And that was all she could say anyway. Then the train was there. They stood staring at one another, not finding words, which would have been meaningless anyhow.

Finally, Marija bent her head a little and kissed Sissie on the cheek. Our Sister did not encourage a feeling of outrage from herself, recognizing in that gesture, a damned useful custom.

Meanwhile, her travel companions were beckoning Sissie to hurry up and board the train. Marija thrust the brown paper bag into her hands as she ran into the compartment. It was a local train and not crowded.

Sitting by the window, train whistling to warn of departure, Marija speaking hurriedly.

'Sissie, if you have time, in Munich, if your train have ze time, Sissie, before you go norz please don't miss it, stop in Munich, if only to spend a little time . . . please, Sissie, maybe for only two hours. Maybe zis morning. Zen you leave in ze afternoon. Yes?'

'Yes, Marija?'

'Because München, Sissie, is our city, Bavaria. Our own city . . . So beautiful you must see it, Sissie. I was going to take you zer. Ze two of us. To spend a day. Please, Sissie, see München. Zer is plenty music. Museums.'

The train moved. There on the platform stood Marija. To those for whom things were only what they seemed, a young Bavarian woman . . . not a teenager but not old either with dark brown hair cut short, very short, smiling, smiling, smiling, while one big tear trickled out of one of her eyes.

> München
> Marija
> Munich?
>
> No, Marija.
> She may promise
> But not fulfil –
>
> She shall not
> Waste a precious minute
> To see Munich and miss a train.
>
> Marija,
> There is nowhere in the
> Western world is a
> Must –
>
> No city is sacred,
> No spot is holy.
> Not Rome,
> Not Paris,
> Not London –
> Nor Munich, Marija
> And the whys and wherefores
> Should be obvious.
>
> Munich is just a place –
> Another junction to meet a
> Brother and compare notes.
>
> She said, 'Hi Brother.'
> He said, 'Hi Sister.'
> 'I am from Surinam.'
> 'I am from Ghana.'

They sat in a station restaurant
Ate with hefty German workers
Central European version of an
Afro-Spanish-Caribbean dish –
Chili-Corn-Carne
Dig?

And they talked of
Barcelona and bullfighting,
Spain –
Where an old man
Sits on a people's dreams –

Where they say there is no
Discrimination against BLACKS

Oh yeah?

When an empire decays,
Falls,
Its slaves are
Forgiven
Tolerated
Loved.
It might happen again, brother
It is happening now –
So let a Panther keep
Sharp
His claws and
His fangs . . .

Munich, Marija,
Is
The Original Adolf of the pub-brawls
and mobsters who were looking for
a
Führer –

Munich is
Prime Minister Chamberlain

Hurrying from his island home to
Appease,
While freshly-widowed
Yiddisher Mamas wondered
What Kosher pots and pans
Could be saved or not.

In 1965
Rhodesia declared herself independent
And the Prime Minister said, logically
From his island home –
'The situation remains
Unchanged,
We cannot fight
Our kith and kin.'

Or something to that effect.

Ach. München,
Marija,
Munich –
It is a pity, Marija,

But
Humans,
Not places,
Make memories.

Nein?

The train was determined to return Our Sister to her origins.
Soon the town disappeared from her sight. It was too early for
her to feel hungry, but out of curiosity, she opened up the brown
bag. There were sandwiches of liver sausages, a few pastries, a
slab of cheese, and some plums.

A WOMAN
YOUNG AND OLD
Grace Paley

MY MOTHER was born not too very long ago of my grandma, who named lots of others, girls and boys, all starting fresh. It wasn't love so much, my grandma said, but she never could call a spade a spade. She was imagination-minded, read stories all day and sighed all night, till my grandpa, to get near her at all, had to use that particular medium.

That was the basic trouble. My mother was sad to be so surrounded by brothers and sisters, none of them more good-natured than she. It's all part of the violence in the atmosphere is a theory – wars, deception, broken homes, all the irremediableness of modern life. To meet her problem my mother screams.

She swears she wouldn't scream if she had a man of her own, but all the aunts and uncles, solitary or wed, are noisy. My grandpa is not only noisy, he beats people up, that is to say – members of the family. He whacked my mother every day of her life. If anyone ever touched me, I'd reduce them to fall-out.

Grandma saves all her change for us. My uncle Johnson is in the nut house. The others are here and now, but Aunty Liz is seventeen and my mother talks to her as though she were totally grown up. Only the other day she told her she was just dying for a man, a real one, and was sick of raising two girls in a world just bristling with goddamn phallic symbols. Lizzy said yes, she knew how it was, time frittered by, and what you needed was a strong kind hand at the hem of your skirt. That's what the acoustics of this barn have to take.

My father, I have been told several hundred times, was a really stunning Latin. Full of *savoir-faire*, *joie de vivre*, and so forth. They were deeply and irrevocably in love till Joanna and I revoked everything for them. Mother doesn't want me to feel rejected, but she doesn't want to feel rejected herself, so she says *I* was too noisy and cried every single night. And then Joanna was the final blight and wanted titty all day *and* all night. '. . . a wife,' he said, 'is a beloved mistress until the children come and then . . .' He would just leave it hanging in French, but whenever I'd hear *les enfants*, I'd throw toys at him, guessing his intended slight. He said *les filles* instead, but I caught that petty evasion in no time. We pummelled him with noise and toys, but our affection was his serious burden is mother's idea, and one day he did not come home for supper.

Mother waited up reading *Le Monde*, but he did not come home at midnight to make love. He missed breakfast and lunch the next day. In fact, where is he now? Killed in the resistance, says Mother. A postcard two weeks later told her and still tells us all, for that matter, whenever it's passed around: 'I have been lonely for France for five years. Now for the rest of my life I must be lonely for you.'

'You've been conned, Mother,' I said one day while we were preparing dinner.

'Conned?' she muttered. 'You speak a different language than me. You don't know a thing yet, you weren't even born. You know perfectly well, misfortune aside, I'd take another Frenchman – Oh, Josephine,' she continued, her voice reaching strictly for the edge of the sound barrier, 'oh, Josephine, to these loathsomes in this miserable country I'm a joke, a real ha-ha. But over there they'd know me. They would just feel me boiling out to meet them. Lousy grammar and all, in French, I swear I could write Shakespeare.'

I turned away in despair. I felt like crying.

'Don't laugh,' she said, 'someday I'll disappear Air France and surprise you all with a nice curly Frenchman just like your daddy. Oh, how you would have loved your father. A growing-up girl with a man like that in the vicinity constantly. You'd thank me.'

'I thank you anyway, Mother dear,' I replied, 'but keep your taste in your own hatch. When I'm as old as Aunt Lizzy I might like American soldiers. Or a marine, I think. I already like some soldiers, especially Corporal Brownstar.'

'Is *that* your idea of a man?' asked Mother, rowdy with contempt.

Then she reconsidered Corporal Brownstar. 'Well, maybe you're right. Those powerful-looking boots . . . Very masculine.'

'Oh?'

'I know, I know. I'm artistic and I sometimes hold two views at once. I realize that Lizzy's going around with him and it does something. Look at Lizzy and you see the girl your father saw. Just like me. Wonderful carriage. Marvellous muscle tone. She could have any man she wanted.'

'She's already had some she wanted.'

At that very moment my grandma, the nick-of-time banker, came in, proud to have saved $4.65 for us. 'Whew, I'm so warm,' she sighed. 'Well, here it is. Now a nice dinner, Marvine, I beg of you, a little effort. Josie, run and get an avocado, and Marvine, please don't be small about the butter. And Josie dear, it's awful warm out and your mama won't mind. You're nearly a young lady. Would you like a sip of icy beer?'

Wasn't that respectful? To return the compliment I drank half a glass, though I hate that fizz. We broiled and steamed and sliced and chopped, and it was a wonderful dinner. I did the cooking and Mother did the sauces. We sicked her on with mouth-watering memories of another more gourmet time and, purely flattered, she made one sauce too many and we had it for dessert on saltines, with iced *café au lait*. While I cleared the dishes, Joanna, everybody's piece of fluff, sat on Grandma's lap telling her each single credible detail of her eight hours at summer day camp.

'Women,' said Grandma in appreciation, 'have been the pleasure and consolation of my entire life. From the beginning I cherished all the little girls with their clean faces and their listening ears . . .'

'Men are different than women,' said Joanna, and it's the only thing she says in this entire story.

'That's true,' said Grandma, 'it's the men that've always troubled me. Men and boys . . . I suppose I don't understand them. But think of it consecutively, all in a row, Johnson, Revere and Drummond . . . after all, where did they start from but me?

But all of them, all all all, each single one of them is gone, far away in heart and body.'

'Ah, Grandma,' I said, hoping to console, 'they were all so grouchy, anyway. I don't miss them a bit.'

Grandma gave me a miserable look. 'Everyone's sons are like that,' she explained. 'First grouchy, then gone.'

After that she sat in grieving sorrow. Joanna curled herself round the hassock at her feet, hugged it, and slept. Mother got her last week's copy of *Le Monde* out of the piano bench and calmed herself with a story about a farmer in Provence who had raped his niece and killed his mother and lived happily for thirty-eight years into respected old age before the nosy prefect caught up with him. She translated it into our derivative mother tongue while I did the dishes.

Night-time came and communication was revived at last by our doorbell, which is full of initiative. It was Lizzy and she did bring Corporal Brownstar. We sent Joanna out for beer and soft drinks and the dancing started right away. He co-operatively danced with everyone. I slipped away to my room for a moment and painted a lot of lipstick neatly on my big mouth and hooked a wall-eyed brassiere around my ribs to make him understand that I was older than Joanna.

He said to me, 'You're peaches and cream, you're gonna be quite a girl someday, Alice in Wonderland.'

'I am a girl already, Corporal.'

'Uh *huh*,' he said, squeezing my left bottom.

Lizzy passed the punch and handed out Ritz crackers and danced with Mother and Joanna whenever the corporal danced with me. She was delighted to see him so popular, and it just passed her happy head that he was the only man there. At the peak of the evening he said: 'You may all call me Browny.'

We sang air-force songs then until 2 a.m., and Grandma said the songs hadn't changed much since her war. 'The soldiers are younger though,' she said. 'Son, you look like your mother is still worried about you.'

'No reason to worry about me, I got a lot of irons in the fire. I get advanced all the time, as a matter of fact. Stem to stern,' he said, winking at Lizzy, 'I'm O.K. . . . . By the way,' he continued, 'could you folks put me up? I wouldn't mind sleeping on the floor.'

'The floor?' expostulated Mother. 'Are you out of your mind? A soldier of the Republic. My God! We have a cot. You know . . . an army cot. Set it up and sleep the sleep of the just, Corporal.'

'Oh, goodness,' Grandma yawned, 'talking about bed – Marvine, your dad must be home by now. I'd better be getting back.'

Browny decided in a courteous way to take Lizzy and Grandma home. By the time he returned, Mother and Joanna had wrapped their lonesome arms around each other and gone to sleep.

I sneakily watched him from behind the drapes scrubbing himself down without consideration for his skin. Then, shining and naked, he crawled between the sheets in totality.

I unshod myself and tiptoed into the kitchen. I poured him a cold beer. I came straight to him and sat down by his side. 'Here's a nice beer, Browny. I thought you might be hot after such a long walk.'

'Why, thanks, Alice Palace Pudding and Pie, I happen to be pretty damn hot. You're a real pal.'

He heaved himself up and got that beer into his gut in one gulp. I looked at him down to his belly button. He put the empty glass on the floor and grinned at me. He burped into my face for a joke and then I had to speak the truth. 'Oh, Browny,' I said, 'I just love you so.' I threw my arms around his middle and leaned my face into the golden hairs of his chest.

'Hey, pudding, take it easy. I like you too. You're a doll.'

Then I kissed him right on the mouth.

'Josephine, who the hell taught you that?'

'I taught myself. I practised on my wrist. See?'

'Josephine!' he said again. 'Josephine, you're a liar. You're one hell of a liar!'

After that his affection increased, and he hugged me too and kissed me right on the mouth.

'Well,' I kidded, 'who taught you that? Lizzy?'

'Shut up,' he said, and the more he loved me the less he allowed of conversation.

I lay down beside him, and I was really surprised the way a

man is transformed by his feelings. He loved me all over myself, and to show I understood his meaning I whispered: 'Browny, what do you want? Browny, do you want to do it?'

Well! He jumped out of bed then and flapped the sheet around his shoulders and groaned. 'Oh, Christ . . . Oh,' he said, 'I could be arrested. I could be picked up by MP's and spend the rest of my life in jail.' He looked at me. 'For God's sakes button your shirt. Your mother'll wake up in a minute.'

'Browny, what's the matter?'

'You're a child and you're too damn smart for your own good. Don't you understand? This could ruin my whole life.'

'But, Browny . . .'

'The trouble I could get into! I could be busted. You're a baby. It's a joke. A person could marry a baby like you, but it's criminal to lay a hand on your shoulder. That's funny, ha-ha-ha.'

'Oh, Browny, I would love to be married to you.'

He sat down at the edge of the cot and drew me to his lap. 'Gee, what a funny kid you are. You really like me so much?'

'I love you. I'd be a first-class wife, Browny – do you realize I take care of this whole house? When Mother isn't working, she spends her whole time mulling over Daddy. I'm the one who does Joanna's hair every day. *I* iron her dresses. I could even have a baby for you, Browny, I know just how to –'

'No! Oh no. Don't let anyone ever talk you into that. Not till you're eighteen. You ought to stay tidy as a doll and not strain your skin at least till you're eighteen.'

'Browny, don't you get lonesome in that camp? I mean if Lizzy isn't around and I'm not around . . . Don't you think I have a nice figure?'

'Oh, I guess . . .' he laughed, and put his hand warmly under my shirt. 'It's pretty damn nice, considering it ain't even quite done.'

I couldn't hold my desire down, and I kissed him again right into his talking mouth and smack against his teeth. 'Oh, Browny, I would take care of you.'

'OK, OK,' he said, pushing me kindly away. 'OK, now listen, go to sleep before we really cook up a stew. Go to sleep. You're a sweet kid. Sleep it off. You ain't even begun to see how wide the world is. It's a surprise even to a man like me.'

'But my mind is settled.'

'Go to sleep, go sleep,' he said, still holding my hand and patting it. 'You look almost like Lizzy now.'

'Oh, but I'm different. I know exactly what I want.'

'Go to sleep, little girl,' he said for the last time. I took his hand and kissed each brown finger tip and then ran into my room and took all my clothes off and, as bare as my lonesome soul, I slept.

The next day was Saturday and I was glad. Mother is a waitress all weekend at the Paris Coffee House, where she has been learning French from the waiters ever since Daddy disappeared. She's lucky because she really loves her work; she's crazy about the customers, the coffee, the décor, and is only miserable when she gets home.

I gave her breakfast on the front porch at about 10 a.m. and Joanna walked her to the bus. 'Cook the corporal some of those frozen sausages,' she called out in her middle range.

I hoped he'd wake up so we could start some more love, but instead Lizzy stepped over our sagging threshold. 'Came over to fix Browny some breakfast,' she said efficiently.

'Oh?' I looked her childlike in the eye. 'I think *I* ought to do it, Aunty Liz, because he and I are probably getting married. Don't you think I ought to in that case?'

'What? Say that slowly, Josephine.'

'You heard me, Aunty Liz.'

She flopped in a dirndl heap on the stairs. '*I* don't even feel old enough to get married and *I've* been seventeen since Christmas time. Did he really ask you?'

'We've been talking about it,' I said, and that was true. 'I'm in love with him, Lizzy.' Tears prevented my vision.

'Oh, love . . . I've been in love twelve times since I was your age.'

'Not me, I've settled on Browny. I'm going to get a job and send him to college after his draft is over . . . He's very smart.'

'Oh, smart . . . everybody's smart.'

'No, they are not.'

When she left I kissed Browny on both eyes, like the Sleeping Beauty, and he stretched and woke up in a conflagration of hunger.

'Breakfast, breakfast, breakfast,' he bellowed.

I fed him and he said, 'Wow, the guys would really laugh, me thiefin' the cradle this way.'

'Don't feel like that. I make a good impression on people, Browny. There've been lots of men more grown than you who've made a fuss over me.'

'Ha-ha,' he remarked.

I made him quit that kind of laughing and started him on some kisses, and we had a cheerful morning.

'Browny,' I said at lunch, 'I'm going to tell Mother we're getting married.'

'Don't she have enough troubles of her own?'

'No, no,' I said. 'She's all for love. She's crazy about it.'

'Well, think about it a minute, baby face. After all, I might get shipped out to some troubled area and be knocked over by a crazy native. You read about something like that every day. Anyway, wouldn't it be fun to have a real secret engagement for a while? How about it?'

'Not me,' I said, remembering everything I'd ever heard from Liz about the opportunism of men, how they will sometimes dedicate with seeming goodwill thirty days and nights, sleeping and waking, of truth and deceit to the achievement of a moment's pleasure. 'Secret engagement! Some might agree to a plan like that, but not me.'

Then I knew he liked me, because he walked around the table and played with the curls of my home permanent a minute and whispered, 'The guys would really laugh, but I get a big bang out of you.'

Then I wasn't sure he liked me, because he looked at his watch and asked it: 'Where the hell is Lizzy?'

I had to do the shopping and put off some local merchants in a muddle of innocence, which is my main Saturday chore. I ran all the way. It didn't take very long, but as I rattled up the stairs and into the hall, I heard the thumping tail of a conversation. Browny was saying, 'It's your fault, Liz.'

'I couldn't care less,' she said. 'I suppose you get something out of playing around with a child.'

'Oh no, you don't get it at all . . .'

'I can't say I want it.'

'Goddamit,' said Browny, 'you don't listen to a person. I think you stink.'

'Really?' Turning to go, she smashed the screen door in my face and jammed my instep with the heel of her lavender pump.

'Tell your mother we will,' Browny yelled when he saw me. 'She stinks, that Liz, goddamnit. Tell your mother tonight.'

I did my best during that passing afternoon to make Browny more friendly. I sat on his lap and he drank beer and tickled me. I laughed, and pretty soon I understood the game and how it had to have variety and ran shrieking from him till he could catch me in a comfortable place, the living-room sofa or my own bedroom.

'You're OK,' he said. 'You are. I'm crazy about you, Josephine. You're a lot of fun.'

So that night at nine-fifteen when mother came home I made her some iced tea and cornered her in the kitchen and locked the door. 'I want to tell you something about me and Corporal Brownstar. Don't say a word, Mother. We're going to be married.'

'What?' she said. 'Married?' she screeched. 'Are you crazy? You can't even get a job without working papers yet. You can't even get working papers. You're a baby. Are you kidding me? You're my little fish. You're not fourteen yet.'

'Well, I decided we could wait until next month when I will be fourteen. Then, I decided, we can get married.'

'You can't, my God! Nobody gets married at fourteen, nobody, nobody. I don't know a soul.'

'Oh, Mother, people do, you always see them in the paper. The worst that could happen is it would get in the paper.'

'But I didn't realize you had much to do with him. Isn't he Lizzy's? That's not nice – to take him away from her. That's a rotten sneaky trick. You're a sneak. Women should stick together. Didn't you learn anything yet?'

'Well, she doesn't want to get married and I do. And it's essential to Browny to get married. He's a very clean-living boy, and when his furlough's over he doesn't want to go back to those camp followers and other people's wives. You have to appreciate that in him, Mother – it's a quality.'

'You're a baby,' she droned. 'You're my slippery little fish.'

Browny rattled the kitchen doorknob ten minutes too early.

'Oh, come in,' I said, disgusted.

'How's stuff? Everything settled? What do you say, Marvine?'

'I say shove it, Corporal! What's wrong with Lizzy? You and she were really beautiful together. You looked like twin stars in the summer sky. Now I realize I don't like your looks much. Who's your mother and father? I never even heard much about them. For all I know, you got an uncle in Alcatraz. And your teeth are in terrible shape. I thought the Army takes care of things like that. You just don't look so hot to me.'

'No reason to be personal, Marvine.'

'But she's a baby. What if she becomes pregnant and bubbles up her entire constitution? This isn't India. Did you ever read what happened to the insides of those Indian child brides?'

'Oh, he's very gentle, Mother.'

'What?' she said, construing the worst.

That conference persisted for about two hours. We drank a couple of pitcherfuls of raspberry Kool-Aid we'd been saving for Joanna's twelfth birthday party the next day. No one had a dime, and we couldn't find Grandma.

Later on, decently before midnight, Lizzy showed up. She had a lieutenant (j.g.) with her and she introduced him around as Sid. She didn't introduce him to Browny, because she has stated time and time again that officers and enlisted men ought not to mix socially. As soon as the lieutenant took Mother's hand in greeting, I could see he was astonished. He began to perspire visibly in long welts down his back and in the gabardine armpits of his summer uniform. Mother was in one of those sullen, indolent moods which really put a fire under some men. She was just beady to think of my stubborn decision and how my life contained the roots of excitement.

'France is where I belong,' she murmured to him. 'Paris, Marseilles, places like that, where men like women and don't chase little girls.'

'I have a lot of sympathy with the Gallic temperament and I do like a real woman,' he said hopefully.

'Sympathy is not enough.' Her voice rose to the requirements of her natural disposition. 'Empathy is what I need. The empathy of a true friend is what I have lived without for years.'

'Oh yes, I feel all that, empathy too,' he fell deeply into his heart, from which he could scarcely be heard . . . 'I like a woman who's had some contact with life, cradled little ones, felt the pangs of birth, known the death of loved ones . . .'

'. . . and of love,' she added sadly. 'That's unusual in a young good-looking man.'

'Yet that's my particular preference.'

Lizzy, Browny, and I borrowed a dollar from him while he sat in idyllic stupor and we wandered out for some ice cream. We took Joanna because we were sorry to have drunk up her whole party. When we returned with a bottle of black-raspberry soda, no one was in sight. 'I'm beginning to feel like a procurer,' said Lizzy.

That's how come Mother finally said yes. Her moral turpitude took such a lively turn that she gave us money for a Wassermann. She called Dr Gilmar and told him to be gentle with the needles. 'It's my own little girl, Doctor. Little Josie that you pulled right out of me yourself. She's so headstrong. Oh, Doctor, remember me and Charles? She's a rough little customer, just like me.'

Due to the results of this test, which is a law, and despite Browny's disbelief, we could not get married. Grandma, always philosophical with the advantage of years, said that young men sowing wild oats were often nipped in the bud, so to speak, and that modern science would soon unite us. Ha-ha-ha, I laugh in recollection.

Mother never even noticed. It passed her by completely, because of large events in her own life. When Browny left for camp drowned in penicillin and damp with chagrin, she gave him a giant jar of Loft's Sour Balls and a can of walnut rum tobacco.

Then she went ahead with her own life. Without any of the disenchantment Browny and I had suffered, the lieutenant and Mother got married. We were content, all of us, though it's common knowledge that she has never been divorced from Daddy. The name next to hers on the marriage licence is Sidney LaValle, Jr, Lieut. (j.g.), USN. An earlier, curlier generation of LaValles came to Michigan from Quebec, and Sid has a couple of usable idioms in Mother's favourite tongue.

I have received one card from Browny. It shows an aerial view of Joplin, Mo. It says: 'Hi, kid, chin up, love, Browny. P. S. Health improved.'

Living as I do on a turnpike of discouragement, I am glad to hear the incessant happy noises in the next room. I enjoyed hugging with Browny's body, though I don't believe I was more to him than a hope for civilian success. Joanna has moved in with me. Though she grinds her teeth well into daylight, I am grateful for her company. Since I have been engaged, she looks up to me. She is a real cuddly girl.

THE LONG TRIAL
Andrée Chedid

SOMEONE was scratching at the door. Amina put her last nursling on the ground and got up. Left alone, the little one shook with rage while one of his young sisters – half naked, moving on all fours – hurried towards him.

All at once the baby girl stopped still; fascinated by the tiny face of her younger brother, by his reddened cheeks and forehead. She probed his fragile eyelids, squashed with her index finger one of the baby's tears and carried it to her own mouth to taste the salt. Then she broke out sobbing, covering with her cries the wailing of the baby.

At the other end of the room – tiny, with mud walls and a low ceiling – which constituted the entire dwelling, two older children, their clothes in tatters, their hair straggling, their lips covered with flies, were beating upon each other for possession of a melon rind. Samyra, a seven-year-old, armed with a soup ladle, was chasing the chickens which scattered every which way. Her younger brother, Osman, was struggling to climb upon the back of a capering goat.

Before opening the door, Amina turned, annoyed, towards her string of children: 'Be quiet! If you wake your father, he'll beat the lot of you.' Her threats were in vain; among the nine children there were always some engaged in complaining or crying. She shrugged her shoulders and prepared to draw the bolt.

'Who knocked?' the sleepy voice of Zekr, her husband, asked.

It was the hour when the men dozed in their huts, those hardened and cracked cubes of mud, before returning to the fields. But the women, they remained watchful, always.

Amina disengaged the bolt from its cradle – the unscrewed

crampons held poorly to the wood – the hinges grated, making her gnash her teeth. How many times had she asked Zekr to oil those hinges! She pulled back the door and cried with joy:

'It's Hadj Osman!'

Hadj Osman had several times made the holy pilgrimage to Mecca; his virtue was widely known. For many years he had wandered about the country, begging his bread and freely giving his blessings. When he passed by, maladies disappeared, the growing crops took on a new vigour. Villagers recognized him from a great distance by his long black robe, topped with a sash of khaki wool with which he wrapped his chest and head.

'You honour our house, holy man. Enter!'

At a single visit prayers were answered. One told that at the village of Suwef, thanks to the putting on of hands, a young man who had made only throat sounds since birth was suddenly made to articulate. Amina had herself been witness to the miracle of Zeinab, a girl just at puberty who terrified her neighbours with her frequent fits – rolling about in the sand, her legs wild and her lip pulled up. Hadj Osman was called in; he said a few words; ever since that time Zeinab had remained calm. One was even speaking now of finding a husband for her.

Amina opened the door more widely. Light inundated the room.

'Enter, holy man. Our home is your home.'

The man excused himself, preferring to remain outside.

'Bring me some bread and water. I have made a long journey; my strength has left me.'

Awake with a start, Zekr recognized the voice. He hastened to put on his calotte and, grasping the water jug by the handle, he got up, bleary, advanced rubbing his eyes.

When her husband reached the threshold and saluted the old man, the woman retired.

The door closed, Amina turned toward her stove of pressed earth. No amount of fatigue could bend her back. She had that sovereign carriage of Egyptian peasants which makes the head seem always to balance and carry a fragile and heavy burden.

Was she young? Hardly thirty! But what good is youth, if no care is taken for it?

At the stove, the woman leaned forward to draw from a nook the bread for the week, rolled in jute cloth. A few dried olives lying in a bowl, two strings of onions hanging on the wall. The woman counted the flatcakes, hefted them; she placed them against her cheek to test their freshness. Having chosen the two best, she dusted them with the back of her sleeve, blew upon them. Then, taking them as an offering, between her open hands, she advanced again to the door.

The presence of the visitor delighted her. Her hut seemed less wretched, her children less squalling, and the voice of Zekr more lively, more animated.

On the way she bumped into two of her children. One hung upon her skirts, stretching up to seize a flatcake:

'Give me. I'm hungry.'

'Go away, Barsoum. It's not for you. Let go!'

'I'm not Barsoum. I'm Ahmed.'

The darkness of the room obscured their faces.

'I'm hungry!'

She shoved him back. The child slipped, fell, rolled upon the earth and howled.

Feeling herself at fault, she hastened forward, pushed the door open quickly, crossed the threshold. She closed the door immediately and leaned back against it with all her weight. Her face sweaty, her mouth pressed shut, she stood motionless, facing the old man and her husband, and drew breath deeply into her lungs.

'The eucalyptus under which I repose, which grows in the midst of a field of oats . . .' began Hadj Osman.

'It is still there,' sighed the woman.

'The last time, it seemed very sickly.'

'It's still there,' she replied. 'Here, nothing ever changes. Nothing at all.'

What she had just said gave her a sudden wish to cry and to complain. The old man could hear her; he might console her, perhaps? But for what? She didn't know exactly. 'For everything' she thought to herself.

'Take these cakes. They are for you!'

The empty water jug lay upon the ground. Hadj Osman took the flatcakes from the hands of the woman and thanked her. He slipped one of the cakes between his robe and the skin of his chest; he bit into the other. He chewed diligently, making each mouthful last a long time.

Pleased to see him regain strength because of her bread, Amina smiled once again. Then, remembering that her husband objected severely to her remaining any length of time outside the house, she took leave of the two men, bowing to them.

'May Allah heap blessings upon you!' the old man exclaimed. 'May he bless you and grant you seven more children!'

The woman pressed against the wall to keep from staggering, she shrank into her large, black clothing, she hid her face.

'What's the matter? Are you ill?' the old man asked.

She was unable to form the words. At last she blurted out:

'I have nine children already, holy man, I beg you withdraw your benediction.'

He thought he must have misunderstood; she articulated so poorly.

'What did you say? Repeat.'

'Take back your benediction, I beg you.'

'I don't understand you,' interrupted the old man. 'You don't know what you are saying.'

Her face still buried in her hands, the woman shook her head from right to left, from left to right:

'No! No! . . . Enough! . . . It is enough!'

All around children metamorphosed into grasshoppers, bounded against her, encircled her, transformed her into a clod of earth, inert. Their hundreds of hands became claws, nettles twitching her clothes, tearing her flesh.

'No, no! . . . I can't endure any more!'

She choked:

'Take back the benediction!'

Zekr, petrified by her aplomb, stood facing her, not opening his mouth.

'The benedictions come from the hand of God, I can change nothing in them.'

'You can . . . You *must* take them back!'

With a smirk of disdain, Hadj Osman turned his head away.

But she continued to harass him:

'Take back the benediction! Speak to me. You must take back the benediction.'

She clenched her fists and advanced towards him:

'You must reply to me!'

The old man pushed her back with both hands:

'Nothing. I withdraw nothing.'

She reared, advanced again. Was she the same woman of but a few moments ago?

'Take back the benediction,' she hurled.

From what source had she got that look, that voice?

'What use is it to tame the waters? What good are the promised harvests? Here, everywhere there will be thousands of other mouths to feed! Have you looked at our children? What do they look like to you! If you only looked at them!'

Opening wide the door of her hovel, she called in:

'Barsoum, Fatma, Osman, Naghi! Come. Come, all of you. The bigger ones carry the smaller ones in their arms. Come out, all nine. Show yourselves!'

'You are mad!'

'Show your arms, your shoulders! Lift your dress, show your stomachs, your thighs, your knees!'

'You deny life!' the old man sneered.

'Don't talk to me about life! You know nothing about life!'

'Children – they are life!'

'Too many children – they are death!'

'Amina, you blaspheme!'

'I call upon God!'

'God will not hear you.'

'He will hear me!'

'If I were your husband, I'd chastize you.'

'No one, today, no one will lift a hand to me. No one!' She seized the moving arm of Hadj Osman:

'Not even you! . . . Take back the benediction or I will not let loose.'

She shook him to force him to recall his words:

'Do what I tell you: take back the benediction!'

'You are possessed! Get back; don't touch me again. I withdraw nothing!'

Even though the old man had several times called upon him to speak, Zekr remained mute and immobile. Then, brusquely, he moved. Would he hurl himself upon Amina and beat her, as he usually did?

'You Zekr, on your knees! Now you! You make him understand. Beg him! With me.'

The words had come from her! How had she dared to say them? and with such an imperious tone? Suddenly, seized with a trembling, strangled with old fears, she unclenched her fists; her limbs grew soft as cotton. Elbows raised to protect herself from blows, she shrivelled against the wall.

'The woman is right, holy man. Take back the benediction.'

She couldn't believe her ears. Nor her eyes. Zekr had heard her. Zekr was there on his knees at the feet of the old man.

Alerted by the clamour, neighbours came running in from all sides. Zekr sought the eye of Amina kneeling beside him; the woman was overwhelmed with gratitude.

'Holy man, take back the benediction,' the two implored together.

A tight circle formed about them. Feeling himself supported by that crowd, the old man stretched up on his toes and raised a menacing index finger:

'This man, this woman reject the work of God. They sin! Drive them out. Else an evil will fall upon the village!'

'Seven children! He has ordained seven more children upon us! What can we do?' groaned Amina.

Fatma, her cousin, already had eight. Soad, six. Fathia, who always accompanied her younger sister of the rotten teeth and the wild eyes, had four sons and three daughters. And the others? It was the same story ... Yet, each of the women, fearful, hesitant, looked mistrustfully at Amina.

'Births are in God's hands,' said Fatma, seeking the approbation of the old man – and of the other men.

'It's up to us to decide whether we want children,' proclaimed Zekr, leaping up.

'That's blasphemy,' protested Khalifé, a young man with protruding ears. 'Something bad will happen to us!'

'Drive them out!' the old man insisted. 'They profane the place.'

Amina put her hand fraternally upon her husband's shoulder.

'We must listen to Hadj Osman; he's a holy man,' murmured a few disturbed voices.

'No, it is I you must listen to!' cried Zekr, 'I who am like all of you. It's Amina you must listen to, Amina who is a woman like other women. How could she bear seven more children? What could we do?'

His cheeks were aflame. From way back someone made a timid echo:

'What will they do?'

From mouth to mouth those words swelled:

'What will they do?'

'No more children!' suddenly uttered a blind little girl clinging to her mother's skirts.

What was happening to this village, to these people, to this valley? Hadj Osman sadly shook his head.

'No more children!' the voices repeated.

Swinging between his crutches, Mahmoud the one-legged, approached the old man and whispered to him:

'Take back your benediction.'

'I withdraw nothing!'

Pushing with his elbows to disengage himself from the crowd, the holy man spat out curses; and with an angry motion he upset the cripple, who lost hold of his crutches and rolled to the ground.

That was the signal.

Fikhry threw himself upon the old man. To avenge the one-legged man, Zekr struck also. Salah, whipping the air with his bamboo cane, approached. It was a sarabande of motion and cries. Hoda ran in with a piece of garden hose. A little boy pulled up a boundary stake. An elderly man broke a branch from a weeping willow and entered into the melée.

'No more children!'

'Take back your benediction!'

'We won't endure any more!'

'We want to live.'

'Live!'

Towards evening the police found Hadj Osman stretched out, face down, next to a trampled flatcake and a water jug broken into bits. They raised him up, brushed off his garments, and took him to the nearest dispensary.

The next day, a police raid took place in the village. The men who had taken part in the melée were driven off in a paddy wagon. The vehicle bounced off, down the long tow-path which led to the police station.

Eyes shining, Amina and her companions gathered at the edge of the village, stared a long while down the road. Clouds of dust rose and spread.

Their husbands weren't really going away, leaving them behind . . . never had they felt themselves so close together. Never.

That day was not a day like all other days.

That day, the long trial had reached its end.

THE LOVES OF LADY PURPLE

Angela Carter

INSIDE the pink-striped booth of the Asiatic Professor only the marvellous existed and there was no such thing as daylight.

The puppet-master is always dusted with a little darkness. In direct relation to his skill, he propagates the most bewildering enigmas for, the more life-like his marionettes, the more god-like his manipulations and the more radical the symbiosis between inarticulate doll and articulating fingers. The puppeteer speculates in a no-man's-limbo between the real and that which, although we know very well it is not, nevertheless seems to be real. He is the intermediary between us, his audience, the living, and they, the dolls, the undead, who cannot live at all and yet who mimic the living in every detail since, though they cannot speak or weep, still they project those signals of signification we instantly recognize as language.

The master of marionettes vitalizes inert stuff with the dynamics of his self. The sticks dance, make love, pretend to speak and, finally, personate death; yet, so many Lazaruses out of their graves they spring again in time for the next performance and no worms drip from their noses nor dust clogs their eyes. All complete, they once again offer their brief imitations of men and women with an exquisite precision which is all the more disturbing because we know it to be false; and so this art, if viewed theologically, may, perhaps, be subtly blasphemous.

Although he was only a poor travelling showman, the Asiatic Professor had become a consummate virtuoso of puppetry. He transported his collapsible theatre, the cast of his single drama and a variety of properties in a horse-drawn cart and, after he played his play in many beautiful cities which no longer exist, such as Shanghai, Constantinople and St Petersburg, he and his small entourage arrived at last in a country in Middle Europe where the mountains sprout jags as sharp and unnatural as those a child outlines with his crayon, a dark, superstitious Transylvania where they wreathed suicides with garlic, pierced them through the heart with stakes and buried them at crossroads while warlocks continually practised rites of immemorial beastliness in the forests.

He had only the two assistants, a deaf boy in his teens, his nephew, to whom he taught his craft, and a foundling dumb girl no more than seven or eight they had picked up on their travels. When the Professor spoke, nobody could understand him for he knew only his native tongue, which was an incomprehensible rattle of staccato k's and t's, so he did not speak at all in the ordinary course of things and, if they had taken separate paths to silence, all, in the end, signed a perfect pact with it. But, when the Professor and his nephew sat in the sun outside their booth in the mornings before performances, they held interminable dialogues in sign language punctuated by soft, wordless grunts and whistles so that the choreographed quiet of their discourse was like the mating dance of tropic birds. And this means of communication, so delicately distanced from humanity, was peculiarly apt for the Professor, who had rather the air of a visitant from another world where the mode of being was conducted in nuances rather than affirmatives. This was due partly to his extreme age, for he was very old although he carried his years lightly even if, these days, in this climate, he always felt a little chilly and so wrapped himself always in a moulting, woollen shawl; yet, more so, it was caused by his benign indifference to everything except the simulacra of the living he himself created.

Besides, however far the entourage travelled, not one of its members had ever comprehended to any degree the foreign. They were all natives of the fairground and, after all, all fairs are the same. Perhaps every single fair is no more than a dissociated fragment of one single, great, original fair which was inexplicably scattered long ago in a diaspora of the amazing. Whatever its location, a fair maintains its invariable, self-consistent atmosphere. Hieratic as knights in chess, the painted horses on the roundabouts describe perpetual circles as immutable as those of the planets and as immune to the drab world of here and now whose inmates come to gape at such extraordinariness, such freedom from actuality. The huckster's raucous invitations are made in a language beyond language, or, perhaps, in that ur-language of grunt and bark which lies behind all language. Everywhere, the same old women hawk glutinous candies which seem devised only to make flies drunk on sugar and, though the outward form of such excessive sweets may vary from place to place, their nature, never. A universal cast of two-headed dogs, dwarfs, alligator men, bearded ladies and giants in leopard-skin loin cloths reveal their singularities in the side-shows and, wherever they come from, they share the sullen glamour of deformity, an internationality which acknowledges no geographic boundaries. Here, the grotesque is the order of the day.

The Asiatic Professor picked up the crumbs that fell from this heaping table yet never seemed in the least at home there for his affinities did not lie with its harsh sounds and primary colouring although it was the only home he knew. He had the wistful charm of a Japanese flower which only blossoms when dropped in water for he, too, revealed his passions through a medium other than himself and this was his didactic vedette, the puppet, Lady Purple.

She was the Queen of Night. There were glass rubies in her head for eyes and her ferocious teeth, carved out of mother o' pearl, were always on show for she had a permanent smile. Her face was as white as chalk because it was covered with the skin of supplest white leather which also clothed her torso, jointed limbs and complication of extremities. Her beautiful hands seemed more like weapons because her nails were so long, five inches of pointed tin enamelled scarlet, and she wore a wig of black hair arranged in a chignon more heavily elaborate than any human neck could have endured. This monumental *chevelure* was stuck through with many brilliant pins tipped with pieces of broken mirror so that, every time she moved, she cast a multitude of scintillating reflections which danced about the theatre like mice of light. Her clothes were all of deep, dark, slumbrous colours – profound pinks, crimson and the vibrating purple with which she was synonymous, a purple the colour of blood in a love suicide.

She must have been the masterpiece of a long-dead, anonymous artisan and yet she was nothing but a curious structure until the Professor touched her strings, for it was he who filled her with necromantic vigour. He transmitted to her an abundance of the life he himself seemed to possess so tenuously and, when she moved, she did not seem so much a cunningly simulated woman as a monstrous goddess, at once preposterous and magnificent, who transcended the notion she was dependent on his hands and appeared wholly real and yet entirely other. Her actions were not so much an imitation as a distillation and intensification of those of a born woman and so she could become the quintessence of eroticism, for no woman born would have dared to be so blatantly seductive.

The Professor allowed no one else to touch her. He himself looked after her costumes and jewellery. When the show was over, he placed his marionette in a specially constructed box and carried her back to the lodging house where he and his children shared a room, for she was too precious to be left in the flimsy theatre and, besides, he could not sleep unless she lay beside him.

The catchpenny title of the vehicle for this remarkable actress was: *The Notorious Amours of Lady Purple, the Shameless Oriental Venus*. Everything in the play was entirely exotic. The incantatory ritual of the drama instantly annihilated the rational and imposed upon the audience a magic alternative in which nothing was in the least familiar. The series of tableaux which illustrated her story were in themselves so filled with meaning that when the Professor chanted her narrative in his impenetrable native tongue, the compulsive strangeness of the spectacle was enhanced rather than diminished. As he crouched above the stage directing his heroine's movements, he recited a verbal recitative in a voice which clanged, rasped and swooped up and down in a weird duet with the stringed instrument from which the dumb girl struck peculiar intervals. But it was impossible to mistake him when the Professor spoke in the character of Lady Purple herself for then his voice modulated to a thick, lascivious murmur like fur soaked in honey which sent unwilling shudders of pleasure down the spines of the watchers. In the iconography of the melodrama, Lady Purple stood for passion and all her movements were calculations in an angular geometry of sexuality.

The Professor somehow always contrived to have a few handbills printed off in the language of the country where they played. These always gave the title of his play and then they used to read as follows:

> *Come and see all that remains of Lady Purple, the famous prostitute and wonder of the East!*

A unique sensation. See how the unappeasable appetites of Lady Purple turned her at last into the very puppet you see before you, pulled only by the strings of *lust*. Come and see the very doll, the only surviving relic of the shameless Oriental Venus herself.

The bewildering entertainment possessed almost a religious intensity for, since there can be no spontaneity in a puppet drama, it always tends towards the rapt intensity of ritual, and, at its conclusion, as the audience stumbled from the darkened booth, it had almost suspended disbelief and was more than half convinced, as the Professor assured them so eloquently, that the bizarre figure who had dominated the stage was indeed the petrification of a universal whore and had once been a woman in whom too much life had negated life itself, whose kisses had withered like acids and whose embrace blasted like lightning. But the Professor and his assistants immediately dismantled the scenery and put away the dolls who were, after all, only mundane wood and, next day, the play was played again.

This is the story of Lady Purple as performed by the Professor's puppets to the delirious *obbligato* of the dumb girl's samisen and the audible click of the limbs of the actors.

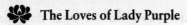 **The Loves of Lady Purple**

The Notorious Amours of Lady Purple
The Shameless Oriental Venus

WHEN she was only a few days old, her mother wrapped her in a tattered blanket and abandoned her on the doorstep of a prosperous merchant and his barren wife. These respectable *bourgeois* were to become the siren's first dupes. They lavished upon her all the attentions which love and money could devise and yet they reared a flower which, although perfumed, was carnivorous. At the age of twelve, she seduced her foster-father. Utterly besotted with her, he trusted to her the key of the safe where he kept all his money and she immediately robbed it of every farthing.

Packing his treasure in a laundry basket together with the clothes and jewellery he had already given her, she then stabbed her first lover and his wife, her foster mother, in their bellies with a knife used in the kitchen to slice fish. Then she set fire to their house to cover the traces of her guilt. She annihilated her own childhood in the blaze that destroyed her first home and, springing like a corrupt phoenix from the pyre of her crime, she rose again in the pleasure quarters, where she at once hired herself out to the madame of the most imposing brothel.

In the pleasure quarters, life passed entirely in artificial day for the bustling noon of those crowded alleys came at the time of drowsing midnight for those who lived outside that inverted, sinister, abominable world which functioned only to gratify the whims of the senses. Every rococo desire the mind of man might, in its perverse ingenuity, devise found ample gratification here, amongst the hall of mirrors, the flagellation parlours, the cabarets of nature-defying copulations and the ambiguous soirées held by men-women and female men. Flesh was the speciality of every house and it came piping hot, served up with all the garnishes imaginable. The Professor's puppets dryly and perfunctorily performed these tactical manœuvres like toy soldiers in a mock battle of carnality.

Along the streets, the women for sale, the mannequins of desire, were displayed in wicker cages so that potential customers could saunter past inspecting them at leisure. These exalted prostitutes sat motionless as idols. Upon their real features had been painted symbolic abstractions of the various aspects of allure and the fantastic elaboration of their dress hinted it covered a different kind of skin. The cork heels of their shoes were so high they could not walk but only totter and the sashes round their waists were of brocade so stiff the movements of the arms were cramped and scant so they presented attitudes of physical unease which, though powerfully moving, derived partly, at least, from the deaf assistant's lack of manual dexterity, for his apprenticeship had not as yet reached even the journeyman stage. Therefore the gestures of these *hetaerae* were as stylized as if they had been clockwork. Yet, however fortuitously, all worked out so well it seemed each one was as absolutely circumscribed as a figure in rhetoric, reduced by the rigorous discipline of her vocation to the nameless essence of the idea of woman, a metaphysical abstraction of the female which could, on payment of a specific fee, be instantly translated into an oblivion either sweet or terrible, depending on the nature of her talents.

Lady Purple's talents verged on the unspeakable. Booted, in leather, she became a mistress of the whip before her fifteenth birthday. Subsequently, she graduated in the mysteries of the torture chamber, where she thoroughly researched all manner of ingenious mechanical devices. She utilized a baroque apparatus of funnel, humiliation, syringe, thumbscrew, contempt and spiritual anguish; to her lovers, such severe usage was both bread and wine and a kiss from her cruel mouth was the sacrament of suffering.

Soon she became successful enough to be able to maintain her own establishment. When she was at the height of her fame, her slightest fancy might cost a young man his patrimony and, as soon as she squeezed him dry of fortune, hope and dreams, for she was quite remorseless, she abandoned him; or else she might, perhaps, lock him up in her closet and force him to watch her while she took for nothing to her usually incredibly expensive bed a beggar encountered by chance on the street. She was no malleable, since frigid, substance upon which desires might be executed; she was not a true prostitute for she was the object on which men prostituted themselves. She, the sole perpetrator of desire, proliferated malign fantasies all around her and used her lovers as the canvas on which she executed boudoir masterpieces of destruction. Skins melted in the electricity she generated.

Soon, either to be rid of them or, simply, for pleasure, she took to murdering her lovers. From the leg of a politician she poisoned she cut out the thighbone and took it to a craftsman who made it into a flute for her. She persuaded succeeding lovers to play tunes for her on this instrument and, with the supplest and most serpentine grace, she danced for them to its unearthly music. At this point, the dumb girl put down her samisen and took up a bamboo pipe from which issued weird cadences and, though it was by no means the climax of the play, this dance was the apex of the Professor's performance for the numinous pavane progressed like waves of darkness and, as she stamped, wheeled and turned to the sound of her malign chamber music, Lady Purple became entirely the image of irresistible evil.

She visited men like a plague, both bane and terrible enlightenment, and she was as contagious as the plague. The final condition of all her lovers was this: they went clothed in rags held together with the discharge of their sores, and their eyes held an awful vacancy, as if their minds had been blown out like candles. A parade of ghastly spectres, they trundled across the stage, their passage implemented by medieval horrors for, here, an arm left its socket and whisked up out of sight into the flies and, there, a nose hung in the air after a gaunt shape that went tottering noseless forward.

So foreclosed Lady Purple's pyrotechnical career, which ended as if it had been indeed a firework display, in ashes, desolation and silence. She became more ghastly than those she had infected. Circe at last became a swine herself and, seared to the bone by her own flame, walked the pavements like a dessicated shadow. Disaster obliterated her. Cast out with stones and oaths by those who had once adulated her, she was reduced to scavenging on the seashore, where she plucked hair from the heads of the drowned to sell to wigmakers who catered to the needs of more fortunate since less diabolic courtesans.

Now her finery, her paste jewels and her enormous superimposition of black hair hung up in the green room and she wore a drab rag of coarse hemp for the final scene of her desperate decline, when, outrageous nymphomaniac, she practised extraordinary necrophilies on the bloated corpses the sea tossed contemptuously at her feet for her dry rapacity had become entirely mechanical and still she repeated her former actions though she herself was utterly other. She abrogated her humanity. She became nothing but wood and hair. She became a marionette herself, herself her own replica, the dead yet moving image of the shameless Oriental Venus.

THE PROFESSOR was at last beginning to feel the effects of age and travel. Sometimes he complained in noisy silence to his nephew of pains, aches, stiffening muscles, tautening sinews, and shortness of breath. He began to limp a little and left to the boy all the rough work of mantling and dismantling. Yet the balletic mime of Lady Purple grew all the more remarkable with the passage of the years, as though his energy, channelled for so long into a single purpose, refined itself more and more in time and was finally reduced to a single, purified, concentrated essence which was transmitted entirely to the doll; and the Professor's mind attained a condition not unlike that of the swordsman trained in Zen, whose sword is his soul, so that neither sword nor swordsman has meaning without the presence of the other. Such swordsmen, armed, move towards their victims like automata, in a state of perfect emptiness, no longer aware of any distinction between self or weapon. Master and marionette had arrived at this condition.

Age could not touch Lady Purple for, since she had never aspired to mortality, she effortlessly transcended it and, though a man who was less aware of the expertise it needed to make her so much as raise her left hand might, now and then, have grieved to see how she defied ageing, the Professor had no fancies of that kind. Her miraculous inhumanity rendered their friendship entirely free from the anthropomorphic, even on the night of the Feast of All Hallows when, the mountain-dwellers murmured, the dead held masked balls in the graveyards while the devil played the fiddle for them.

The rough audience received their copeck's worth of sensation and filed out into a fairground which still roared like a playful tiger with life. The foundling girl put away her samisen and swept out the booth while the nephew set the stage afresh for next day's matinée. Then the Professor noticed Lady Purple had ripped a seam in the drab shroud she wore in the final act. Chattering to himself with displeasure, he undressed her as she swung idly, this way and that way, from her anchored strings and then he sat down on a wooden property stool on the stage and plied his needle like a good housewife. The task was more difficult than it seemed at first for the fabric was also torn and required an embroidery of darning so he told his assistants to go home together to the lodging house and let him finish his task alone.

A small oil-lamp hanging from a nail at the side of the stage cast an insufficient but tranquil light. The white puppet glimmered fitfully through the mists which crept into the theatre from the night outside through all the chinks and gaps in the tarpaulin and now began to fold their chiffon drapes around her as if to decorously conceal her or else to render her more translucently enticing. The mist softened her painted smile a little and her head dangled to one side. In the last act, she wore a loose, black wig, the locks of which hung down as far as her softly upholstered flanks, and the ends of her hair flickered with her random movements, creating upon the white blackboard of her back one of those fluctuating optical effects which make us question the veracity of our vision. As he often did when he was alone with her, the Professor chatted to her in his native language, rattling away an intimacy of nothings, of the weather, of his rheumatism, of the unpalatability and expense of the region's coarse, black bread, while the small winds took her as their partner in a scarcely perceptible *valse triste* and the mist grew minute by minute thicker, more pallid and more viscous.

The old man finished his mending. He rose and, with a click or two of his old bones, he went to put the forlorn garment neatly on its green room hanger beside the glowing, winey purple gown splashed with rosy peonies, sashed with carmine, that she wore for her appalling dance. He was about to lay her, naked, in her coffin-shaped case and carry her back to their chilly bedroom when he paused. He was seized with the childish desire to see her again in all her finery once more that night. He took her dress off its hanger and carried it to where she drifted, at nobody's volition but that of the wind. As he put her clothes on her, he murmured to her as if she were a little girl for the vulnerable flaccidity of her arms and legs made a six-foot baby of her.

'There, there, my pretty; this arm here, that's right! Oops a daisy, easy does it . . .'

Then he tenderly took off her penitential wig and clicked his tongue to see how defencelessly bald she was beneath it. His arms cracked under the weight of her immense chignon and he had to stretch up on tiptoe to set it in place because, since she was as large as life, she was rather taller than he. But then the ritual of apparelling was over and she was complete again.

Now she was dressed and decorated, it seemed her dry wood had all at once put out an entire springtime of blossoms for the old man alone to enjoy. She could have acted as the model for the most beautiful of women, the image of that woman whom only memory and imagination can devise, for the lamplight fell too mildly to sustain her air of arrogance and so gently it made her long nails look as harmless as ten fallen petals. The Professor had a curious habit; he always used to kiss his doll good night.

A child kisses its toy before he pretends it sleeps although, even though he is only a child, he knows its eyes are not constructed to close so it will always be a sleeping beauty no kiss will waken. One in the grip of savage loneliness might kiss the face he sees before him in the mirror for want of any other face to kiss. These are kisses of the same kind; they are the most poignant of caresses, for they are too humble and too despairing to wish or seek for any response.

Yet, in spite of the Professor's sad humility, his chapped and withered mouth opened on hot, wet, palpitating flesh.

The sleeping wood had wakened. Her pearl teeth crashed against his with the sound of cymbals and her warm, fragrant breath blew around him like an Italian gale. Across her suddenly moving face flashed a whole kaleidoscope of expression, as though she were running instantaneously through the entire repertory of human feeling, practising, in an endless moment of time, all the scales of emotion as if they were music. Crushing vines, her arms, curled about the Professor's delicate apparatus of bone and skin with the insistent pressure of an actuality by far more authentically living than that of his own, time-desiccated flesh. Her kiss emanated from the dark country where desire is objectified and lives. She gained entry into the world by a mysterious loophole in its metaphysics and, during her kiss, she sucked his breath from his lungs so that her own bosom heaved with it.

So, unaided, she began her next performance with an apparent improvisation which was, in reality, only a variation upon a theme. She sank her teeth into his throat and drained him. He did not have the time to make a sound. When he was empty, he slipped straight out of her embrace down to her feet with a dry rustle, as of a cast armful of dead leaves, and there he sprawled on the floorboards as empty, useless and bereft of meaning as his own tumbled shawl.

She tugged impatiently at the strings which moored her and out they came in bunches from her head, her arms and her legs. She stripped them off her fingertips and stretched out her long, white hands, flexing and unflexing them again and again. For the first time for years, or, perhaps, for ever, she closed her blood-stained teeth thankfully, for her cheeks still ached from the smile her maker had carved into the stuff of her former face. She stamped her elegant feet to make the new blood flow more freely there.

Unfurling and unravelling itself, her hair leapt out of its confinements of combs, cords and lacquer to root itself back into her scalp like cut grass bounding out of the stack and back again into the ground. First, she shivered with pleasure to feel the cold, for she realized she was experiencing a physical sensation; then either she remembered or else she believed she remembered that the sensation of cold was not a pleasurable one so she knelt and, drawing off the old man's shawl, wrapped it carefully about herself. Her every motion was instinct with a wonderful, reptilian liquidity. The mist outside now seemed to rush like a tide into the booth and broke against her in white breakers so that she looked like a baroque figurehead, lone survivor of a shipwreck, thrown up on a shore by the tide.

But whether she was renewed or newly born, returning to life or becoming alive, awakening from a dream or coalescing into the form of a fantasy generated in her wooden skull by the mere repetition so many times of the same invariable actions, the brain beneath the reviving hair contained only the scantiest notion of the possibilities now open to it. All that had seeped into the wood was the notion that she might perform the forms of life not so much by the skill of another as by her own desire that she did so, and she did not possess enough equipment to comprehend the complex circularity of the logic which inspired her for she had only been a marionette. But, even if she could not perceive it, she could not escape the tautological paradox in which she was trapped; had the marionette all the time parodied the living or was she, now living, to parody her own performance as a marionette? Although she was now manifestly a woman, young and extravagantly beautiful, the leprous whiteness of her face gave her the appearance of a corpse animated solely by demonic will.

Deliberately, she knocked the lamp down from its hook on the wall. A puddle of oil spread at once on the boards of the stage. A little flame leapt across the fuel and immediately began to eat the curtains. She went down the aisle between the benches to the little ticket booth. Already, the stage was an inferno and the corpse of the Professor tossed this way and that on an uneasy bed of fire. But she did not look behind her after she slipped out into the fairground although soon the theatre was burning like a paper lantern ignited by its own candle.

Now it was so late that the sideshows, gingerbread stalls and liquor booths were locked and shuttered and only the moon, half obscured by drifting cloud, gave out a meagre, dirty light, which sullied and deformed the flimsy pasteboard façades, so the place, deserted with curds of vomit, the refuse of revelry, underfoot, looked utterly desolate.

She walked rapidly past the silent roundabouts, accompanied only by the fluctuating mists, towards the town, making her way like a homing pigeon, out of logical necessity, to the single brothel it contained.

❀

THE EARTH

Djuna Barnes

UNA AND LENA were like two fine horses, horses one sees in the early dawn eating slowly, swaying from side to side, horses that plough, never in a hurry, but always accomplishing something. They were Polish women who worked a farm day in and day out, saying little, thinking little, feeling little, with eyes devoid of everything save a crafty sparkle which now and then was quite noticeable in Una, the elder. Lena dreamed more, if one can call the silences of an animal dreams. For hours she would look off into the skyline, her hairless lids fixed, a strange metallic quality in the irises themselves. She had such pale eyebrows that they were scarcely visible, and this, coupled with her wide-eyed silences, gave her a half-mad expression. Her heavy peasant face was fringed by a bang of red hair like a woollen table-spread, a colour at once strange and attractive, an obstinate colour, a colour that seemed to make Lena feel something alien and bad-tempered had settled over her forehead; for, from time to time, she would wrinkle up her heavy white skin and shake her head.

Una never showed her hair. A figured handkerchief always covered it, though it was pretty enough, of that sullen blonde type that one sees on the heads of children who run in the sun.

Originally the farm had been their father's. When he died he left it to them in a strange manner. He feared separation or quarrel in the family, and therefore had bequeathed every other foot to Una, beginning with the first foot at the fence, and every other foot to Lena, beginning with the second. So the two girls ploughed and furrowed and transplanted and garnered a rich harvest each year, neither disputing her inheritance. They worked silently side by side, uncomplaining. Neither do orchards complain when their branches flower and fruit and become heavy. Neither does the earth complain when wounded with the plough, healing up to give birth to flowers and to vegetables.

After long months of saving, they had built a house, into which they moved their furniture and an uncle, Karl, who had gone mad while gathering the hay.

They did not evince surprise nor show regret. Madness to us means reversion; to such people as Una and Lena it meant progression. Now their uncle had entered into a land beyond them, the land of fancy. For fifty years he had been as they were, silent, hard-working, unimaginative. Then all of a sudden, like a scholar passing his degree, he had gone up into another form, where he spoke of things that only people who have renounced the soil speak of – strange, fanciful, unimportant things, things to stand in awe of, because they discuss neither profits nor loss.

When Karl would strike suddenly into his moaning, they would listen awhile in the field as dogs listen to a familiar cry, and presently Lena would move off to rub him down in the same hard-palmed way she would press the long bag that held the grapes in preserving time.

Una had gone to school just long enough to learn to spell her name with difficulty and to add. Lena had somehow escaped. She neither wrote her name nor figured; she was content that Una could do 'the business'. She did not see that with addition comes the knowledge that two and two make four and that four are better than two. That she would some day be the victim of knavery, treachery or deceit never entered her head. For her, it was quite settled that here they would live and here they would die. There was a family graveyard on the land where two generations had been buried. And here Una supposed she, too, would rest when her wick no longer answered to the oil.

The land was hers and Una's. What they made of it was shared, what they lost was shared, and what they took to themselves out of it was shared also. When the pickle season went well and none of the horses died, she and her sister would drive into town to buy new boots and a ruffle for the Sabbath. And if everything shone upon them and all the crops brought good prices, they added a few bits of furniture to their small supply, or bought more silver to hide away in the chest that would go to the sister that married first.

Which of them would come in for this chest Lena never troubled about. She would sit for long hours after the field was cleared, saying nothing, looking away into the horizon, perhaps tossing a pebble down the hill, listening for its echo in the ravine.

She did not even speculate on the way Una looked upon matters. Una was her sister; that was sufficient. One's right arm is always accompanied by one's left. Lena had not learned that left arms sometimes steal while right arms are vibrating under the handshake of friendship.

Sometimes Uncle Karl would get away from Lena and, striding over bog and hedge, dash into a neighbouring farm, and there make trouble for the owner. At such times, Lena would lead him home, in the same unperturbed manner in which she drove the cows. Once a man had brought him back.

This man was Swedish, pale-faced, with a certain keenness of glance that gave one a suspicion that he had an occasional thought that did not run on farming. He was broad of shoulder, standing some six feet three. He had come to see Una many times after this. Standing by the door of an evening, he would turn his head and shoulders from side to side, looking first at one sister and then at the other. He had those pale, well-shaped lips that give the impression that they must be comfortable to the wearer. From time to time, he wetted them with a quick plunge of his tongue.

He always wore brown overalls, baggy at the knee, and lighter in colour where he leaned on his elbows. The sisters had learned the first day that he was 'help' for the owner of the adjoining farm. They grunted their approval and asked him what wages he got. When he said a dollar and a half and board all through the winter season, Una smiled upon him.

'Good pay,' she said, and offered him a glass of mulled wine.

Lena said nothing. Hands on hips, she watched him, or looked up into the sky. Lena was still young and the night yet appealed to her. She liked the Swede too. He was compact and big and 'well bred'. By this she meant what is meant when she said the same thing of a horse. He had quality – which meant the same thing through her fingers. And he was 'all right' in the same way soil is all right for securing profits. In other words, he was healthy and was making a living.

At first he had looked oftenest at Lena. Hers was the softer face of two faces as hard as stone. About her chin was a pointed excellence that might have meant that at times she could look kindly, might at times attain sweetness in her slow smile, a smile that drew lips reluctantly across very large fine teeth. It was a smile that in time might make one think more of these lips than of the teeth, instead of more of the teeth than the lips, as was as yet the case.

In Una's chin lurked a devil. It turned in under the lower lip secretively. Una's face was an unbroken block of calculation, saving where, upon her upper lip, a little down of hair fluttered.

Yet it gave one an uncanny feeling. It made one think of a tassel on a hammer.

Una had marked this Swede for her own. She went to all the trouble that was in her to give him the equivalent of the society girl's most fetching glances. Una let him sit where she stood, let him lounge when there was work to be done. Where she would have set anyone else to peeling potatoes, to him she offered wine or flat beer, black bread and sour cakes.

Lena did none of these things. She seemed to scorn him, she pretended to be indifferent to him, she looked past him. If she had been intelligent enough, she would have looked through him.

For him her indifference was scorn, for him her quietness was disapproval, for him her unconcern was insult. Finally he left her alone, devoting his time to Una, calling for her often of a Sunday to take a long walk. Where to and why, it did not matter. To a festival at the church, to a pig killing, if one was going on a Sunday. Lena did not seem to mind. This was her purpose; she was by no means generous, she was by no means self-sacrificing. It simply never occurred to her that she could marry before her sister, who was the elder. In reality it was an impatience to be married that made her avoid Una's lover. As soon as Una was off her hands, then she, too, could think of marrying.

Una could not make her out at all. Sometimes she would call her to her and, standing arms akimbo, would stare at her for a good many minutes, so long that Lena would forget her and look off into the sky.

One day Una called Lena to her and asked her to make her mark at the bottom of a sheet of paper covered with hard cramped writing, Una's own.

'What is it?' asked Lena, taking the pen.

'Just saying that every other foot of this land is yours.'

'That you know already, eh?' Lena announced, putting the pen down. Una gave it back to her.

'I know it, but I want you to write it – that every other foot of land is mine, beginning with the second foot from the fence.'

Lena shrugged her shoulders. 'What for?'

'The lawyers want it.'

Lena signed her mark and laid down the pen. Presently she began to shell peas. All of a sudden she shook her head.

'I thought', she said, that second foot was mine – what?' She thrust the pan down toward her knees and sat staring at Una with wide, suspicious eyes.

'Yah,' affirmed Una, who had just locked the paper up in a box.

Lena wrinkled her forehead, thereby bringing the red fringe a little nearer her eyes.

'But you made me sign it that it was you, hey?'

'Yah,' Una assented, setting the water on to boil for tea.

'Why?' inquired Lena.

'To make more land,' Una replied, and grinned.

'More land?' queried Lena, putting the pan of peas upon the table and standing up. 'What do you mean?'

'More land for me,' Una answered complacently.

Lena could not understand and began to rub her hands. She picked up a pod and snapped it in her teeth.

'But I was satisfied,' she said, 'with the land as it was. I don't want more.'

'I do,' answered Una.

'Does it make me more?' Lena asked suspiciously, leaning a little forward.

'It makes you,' Una answered, 'nothing. Now you stay by me as helper –'

Then Lena understood. She stood stock still for a second. Suddenly she picked up the breadknife and, lurching forward, cried out: 'You take my land from me–'

Una dodged, grasped the hand with the knife, brought it down, took it away placidly, pushed Lena off and repeated: 'Now you work just the same, but for me – why you so angry?'

No tears came to Lena's help. And had they done so, they would have hissed against the flaming steel of her eyeballs. In a level tone thick with a terrible and sudden hate, she said: 'You know what you have done – eh? Yes, you have taken away the fruit trees from me, you have taken away the place where I worked for years, you have robbed me of my crops, you have stolen the harvest – that is well – but you have taken away from me the grave, too. The place where I live you have robbed me of and the place where I go when I die. I would have worked for you perhaps – but', she struck her breast, 'when I die I die for myself.' Then she turned and left the house.

She went directly to the barn. Taking the two stallions out, she harnessed them to the carriage. With as little noise as possible she got them into the driveway. Then climbing in and securing the whip in one hand and the reins fast in the other, she cried aloud in a hoarse voice: 'Ahya you little dog. Watch me ride!' Then as Una came running to the door, Lena shouted back, turning in the trap: 'I take from you too.' And flinging the whip across the horses, she disappeared in a whirl of dust.

Una stood there shading her eyes with her hand. She had never seen Lena angry, therefore she thought she had gone mad as her uncle before her. That she had played Lena a dirty trick, she fully realized, but that Lena should realize it also, she had not counted on.

She wondered when Lena would come back with the horses. She even prepared a meal for two.

Lena did not come back. Una waited up till dawn. She was more frightened about the horses than she was about her sister; the horses represented six hundred dollars, while Lena only represented a relative. In the morning, she scolded Karl for giving mad blood to the family. Then towards the second evening, she waited for the Swede.

The evening passed as the others. The Swedish working man did not come.

Una was distracted. She called in a neighbour and set the matter before him. He gave her some legal advice and left her bewildered.

Finally, at the end of that week, because neither horses nor Lena had appeared, and also because of the strange absence of the man who had been making love to her for some weeks, Una reported the matter to the local police. And ten days later they located the horses. The man driving them said that they had been sold to him by a young Polish woman who passed through his farm with a tall Swedish man late at night. She said that she had tried to sell them that day at a fair and had been unable to part with them, and finally let them go to him at a low price. He added that he had paid three hundred dollars for them. Una bought them back at the figure, from hard-earned savings, both of her own and Lena's.

Then she waited. A sour hatred grew up within her and she moved about from acre to acre with her hired help like some great thing made of wood.

But she changed in her heart as the months passed. At times she almost regretted what she had done. After all, Lena had been quiet and hard-working and her kin. It had been Lena, too, who had best quieted Karl. Without her he stormed and stamped about the house, and of late had begun to accuse her of having killed her sister.

Then one day Lena appeared carrying something on her arms, swaying it from side to side while the Swede hitched a fine mare to the barn door. Up the walk came Lena, singing, and behind her came her man.

Una stood still, impassible, quiet. As Lena reached her, she uncovered the bundle and held the baby up to her.

'Kiss it,' she said. Without a word, Una bent at the waist and kissed it.

'Thank you,' Lena said as she replaced the shawl. 'Now you have left your mark. Now you have signed.' She smiled.

The Swedish fellow was a little browned from the sun. He took his cap off, and stood there grinning awkwardly.

Lena pushed in at the door and sat down.

Una followed her. Behind Una came the father.

Karl was heard singing and stamping overhead. 'Give her some molasses water and little cakes,' he shouted, putting his head down through the trap door, and burst out laughing.

Una brought three glasses of wine. Leaning forward, she poked her finger into the baby's cheek to make it smile. 'Tell me about it,' she said.

Lena began: 'Well, then I got him,' she pointed to the awkward father. 'And I put him in behind me and I took him to town and I marry him. And I explain to him. I say: "She took my land from me, the flowers and the fruit and the green things. And she took the grave from me where I should lie —"'

And in the end they looked like fine horses, but one of them was a bit spirited.

OKE OF OKEHURST

Vernon Lee

I

THAT SKETCH up there with the boy's cap? Yes; that's the same woman. I wonder whether you could guess who she was. A singular being, is she not? The most marvellous creature, quite, that I have ever met: a wonderful elegance, exotic, far-fetched, poignant; an artificial perverse sort of grace and research in every outline and movement and arrangement of head and neck, and hands and fingers. Here are a lot of pencil-sketches I made while I was preparing to paint her portrait. Yes; there's nothing but her in the whole sketch-book. Mere scratches, but they may give some idea of her marvellous, fantastic kind of grace. Here she is leaning over the staircase, and here sitting in the swing. Here she is walking quickly out of the room. That's her head. You see she isn't really handsome; her forehead is too big, and her nose too short. This gives no idea of her. It was altogether a question of movement. Look at the strange cheeks, hollow and rather flat; well, when she smiled she had the most marvellous dimples here. There was something exquisite and uncanny about it. Yes; I began the picture, but it was never finished. I did the husband first. I wonder who has his likeness now? Help me to move these pictures away from the wall. Thanks. This is her portrait; a huge wreck. I don't suppose you can make much of it; it is merely blocked in, and seems quite mad. You see my idea was to make her leaning against a wall – there was one hung with yellow that seemed almost brown – so as to bring out the silhouette.

It was very singular I should have chosen that particular wall. It does look rather insane in this condition, but I like it; it has something of her. I would frame it and hang it up, only people would ask questions. Yes; you have guessed quite right – it is Mrs Oke of Okehurst. I forgot you had relations in that part of the country; besides, I suppose the newspapers were full of it at the time. You didn't know that it all took place under my eyes? I can scarcely believe now that it did: it all seems so distant, vivid but unreal, like a thing of my own invention. It really was much stranger than any one guessed. People could no more understand it than they could understand her. I doubt whether any one ever understood Alice Oke besides myself. You mustn't think me unfeeling. She was a marvellous, weird, exquisite creature, but one couldn't feel sorry for her. I felt much sorrier for the wretched creature of a husband. It seemed such an appropriate end for her; I fancy she would have liked it could she have known. Ah! I shall never have another chance of painting such a portrait as I wanted. She seemed sent me from heaven or the other place. You have never heard the story in detail? Well, I don't usually mention it, because people are so brutally stupid or sentimental; but I'll tell it you. Let me see. It's too dark to paint any more to-day, so I can tell it you now. Wait; I must turn her face to the wall. Ah, she was a marvellous creature!

II

You remember, three years ago, my telling you I had let myself in for painting a couple of Kentish squireen? I really could not understand what had possessed me to say yes to that man. A friend of mine had brought him one day to my studio – Mr Oke of Okehurst, that was the name on his card. He was a very tall, very well-made, very good-looking young man, with a beautiful fair complexion, beautiful fair moustache, and beautifully fitting clothes; absolutely like a hundred other young men you can see any day in the park, and absolutely uninteresting from the crown of his head to the tip of his boots. Mr Oke, who had been a lieutenant in the Blues before his marriage, was evidently extremely uncomfortable on finding himself in a studio. He felt misgivings about a man who could wear a velvet coat in town, but at the same time he was nervously anxious not to treat me in the very least like a tradesman. He walked round my place, looked at everything with the most scrupulous attention, stammered out a few complimentary phrases, and then, looking at his friend for assistance, tried to come to the point, but failed. The point, which the friend kindly explained, was that Mr Oke was desirous to know whether my engagements would allow of my painting him and his wife and what my terms would be. The poor man blushed perfectly crimson during this explanation, as if he had come with the most improper proposal; and I noticed – the only interesting thing about him – a very odd nervous frown between his eyebrows, a perfect double gash – a thing which usually means something abnormal: a mad-doctor of my acquaintance calls it the maniac-frown. When I had answered, he suddenly burst out into rather confused explanations: his wife – Mrs Oke – had seen some of my – pictures – paintings – portraits – at the – the – what d'you call it? Academy. She had – in short, they had made a very great impression upon her. Mrs Oke had a great taste for art; she was, in short, extremely desirous of having her portrait and his painted by me, *etcetera*.

'My wife,' he suddenly added, 'is a remarkable woman. I don't know whether you will think her handsome – she isn't exactly, you know. But she's awfully strange,' and Mr Oke of Okehurst gave a little sigh and frowned that curious frown, as if so long a speech and so decided an expression of opinion had cost him a great deal.

It was a rather unfortunate moment in my career. A very influential sitter of mine – you remember the fat lady with the crimson curtain behind her? – had come to the conclusion or been persuaded that I had painted her old and vulgar, which, in fact, she was. Her whole clique had turned against me, the newspapers had taken up the matter, and for the moment I was considered as a painter to whose brushes no woman would trust her reputation. Things were going badly. So I snapped but too gladly at Mr Oke's offer, and settled to go down to Okehurst at the end of a fortnight. But the door had scarcely closed upon my future sitter when I began to regret my rashness; and my disgust at the thought of wasting a whole summer upon the portrait of a totally uninteresting Kentish squire, and his doubtless equally uninteresting wife, grew greater and greater as the time for execution approached. I remember so well the frightful temper in which I got into the train for Kent, and the even more frightful temper in which I got out of it at the little station nearest to Okehurst. It was pouring floods. I felt a comfortable fury at the thought that my canvases would get nicely wetted before Mr Oke's coachman had packed them on the top of the waggonette. It was just what served me right for coming to this confounded place to paint these confounded people. We drove off in the steady downpour. The roads were a mass of yellow mud; the endless flat grazing-grounds under the oak-trees, after having been burnt to cinders in a long drought, were turned into a hideous brown sop; the country seemed intolerably monotonous.

My spirits sank lower and lower. I began to meditate upon the modern Gothic country-house, with the usual amount of Morris furniture, Liberty rugs, and Mudie novels, to which I was doubtless being taken. My fancy pictured very vividly the five or six little Okes – that man certainly must have at least five children – the aunts, and sisters-in-law, and cousins; the eternal routine of afternoon tea and lawn-tennis; above all, it pictured Mrs Oke, the bouncing, well-informed, model housekeeper, electioneering, charity-organizing young lady, whom such an individual as Mr Oke would regard in the light of a remarkable woman. And my spirit sank within me, and I cursed my avarice in accepting the commission, my spiritlessness in not throwing it over while yet there was time. We had meanwhile driven into a large park, or rather a long succession of grazing-grounds, dotted about with large oaks, under which the sheep were huddled together for shelter from the rain. In the distance, blurred by the sheets of rain, was a line of low hills, with a jagged fringe of bluish firs and a solitary windmill. It must be a good mile and a half since we had passed a house, and there was none to be seen in the distance – nothing but the undulation of sere grass, sopped brown beneath the huge blackish oak-trees, and whence arose, from all sides, a vague disconsolate bleating. At last the road made a sudden bend, and disclosed what was evidently the home of my sitter. It was not what I had expected. In a dip in the ground a large red-brick house, with the rounded gables and high chimney-stacks of the time of James I – a forlorn, vast place, set in the midst of the pasture-land, with no trace of garden before it, and only a few large trees indicating the possibility of one to the back; no lawn either, but on the other side of the sandy dip, which suggested a filled-up moat, a huge oak, short, hollow, with wreathing, blasted, black branches, upon which only a handful of leaves shook in the rain. It was not at all what I had pictured to myself the home of Mr Oke of Okehurst.

My host received me in the hall, a large place, panelled and carved, hung round with portraits up to its curious ceiling – vaulted and ribbed like the inside of a ship's hull. He looked even more blond and pink and white, more absolutely mediocre in his tweed suit; and also, I thought, even more good-natured and duller. He took me into his study, a room hung round with whips and fishing-tackle in place of books, while my things were being carried upstairs. It was very damp, and a fire was smouldering. He gave the embers a nervous kick with his foot, and said, as he offered me a cigar –

'You must excuse my not introducing you at once to Mrs Oke. My wife – in short, I believe my wife is asleep.'

'Is Mrs Oke unwell?' I asked, a sudden hope flashing across me that I might be off the whole matter.

'Oh no! Alice is quite well; at least, quite as well as she usually is. My wife,' he added, after a minute, and in a very decided tone, 'does not enjoy very good health – a nervous constitution. Oh no! not at all ill, nothing at all serious, you know. Only nervous, the doctors say; mustn't be worried or excited, the doctors say; requires lots of repose – that sort of thing.'

There was a dead pause. This man depressed me, I knew not why. He had a listless, puzzled look, very much out of keeping with his evident admirable health and strength.

'I suppose you are a great sportsman?' I asked from sheer despair, nodding in the direction of the whips and guns and fishing-rods.

'Oh no! not now. I was once. I have given up all that,' he answered, standing with his back to the fire, and staring at the polar bear beneath his feet. 'I – I have no time for all that now,' he added, as if an explanation were due. 'A married man – you know. Would you like to come up to your rooms?' he suddenly interrupted himself. 'I have had one arranged for you to paint in. My wife said you would prefer a north light. If that one doesn't suit, you can have your choice of any other.'

I followed him out of the study, through the vast entrance-hall. In less than a minute I was no longer thinking of Mr and Mrs Oke and the boredom of doing their likeness; I was simply overcome by the beauty of this house, which I had pictured modern and philistine. It was, without exception, the most perfect example of an old English manor-house that I had ever seen; the most magnificent intrinsically, and the most admirably preserved. Out of the huge hall, with its immense fireplace of delicately carved and inlaid grey and black stone, and its rows of family portraits, reaching from the wainscoting to the oaken ceiling, vaulted and ribbed like a ship's hull, opened the wide, flat-stepped staircase, the parapet surmounted at intervals by heraldic monsters, the wall covered with oak carvings of coats-of-arms, leafage, and little mythological scenes, painted a faded red and blue, and picked out with tarnished gold, which harmonized with the tarnished blue and gold of the stamped leather that reached to the oak cornice, again delicately tinted and gilded. The beautifully damascened suits of court armour looked, without being at all rusty, as if no modern hand had ever touched them; the very rugs under foot were of sixteenth-century Persian make; the only things of today were the big bunches of flowers and ferns, arranged in majolica dishes upon the landings. Everything was perfectly silent; only from below came the chimes, silvery like an Italian palace fountain, of an old-fashioned clock.

It seemed to me that I was being led through the palace of the Sleeping Beauty.

'What a magnificent house!' I exclaimed as I followed my host through a long corridor, also hung with leather, wainscoted with carvings, and furnished with big wedding coffers, and chairs that looked as if they came out of some Van Dyck portrait. In my mind was the strong impression that all this was natural, spontaneous – that it had about it nothing of the picturesqueness which swell studios have taught to rich and aesthetic houses. Mr Oke misunderstood me.

'It is a nice old place,' he said, 'but it's too large for us. You see, my wife's health does not allow of our having many guests; and there are no children.'

I thought I noticed a vague complaint in his voice; and he evidently was afraid there might have seemed something of the kind, for he added immediately –

'I don't care for children one jackstraw, you know, myself; can't understand how any one can, for my part.'

If ever a man went out of his way to tell a lie, I said to myself, Mr Oke of Okehurst was doing so at the present moment.

When he had left me in one of the two enormous rooms that were allotted to me, I threw myself into an armchair and tried to focus the extraordinary imaginative impression which this house had given me.

I am very susceptible to such impressions; and besides the sort of spasm of imaginative interest sometimes given to me by certain rare and eccentric personalities, I know nothing more subduing than the charm, quieter and less analytic, of any sort of complete and out-of-the-common-run sort of house. To sit in a room like the one I was sitting in, with the figures of the tapestry glimmering grey and lilac and purple in the twilight, the great bed, columned and curtained, looming in the middle, and the embers reddening beneath the overhanging mantelpiece of inlaid Italian stonework, a vague scent of rose-leaves and spices, put into the china bowls by the hands of ladies long since dead, while the clock downstairs sent up, every now and then, its faint silvery tune of forgotten days, filled the room; – to do this is a special kind of voluptuousness, peculiar and complex and indescribable, like the half-drunkenness of opium or hashish, and which, to be conveyed to others in any sense as I feel it, would require a genius, subtle and heady, like that of Baudelaire.

After I had dressed for dinner I resumed my place in the armchair, and resumed also my reverie, letting all these impressions of the past – which seemed faded like the figures in the arras, but still warm like the embers in the fireplace, still sweet and subtle like the perfume of the dead rose-leaves and broken spices in the china bowls – permeate me and go to my head. Of Oke and Oke's wife I did not think; I seemed quite alone, isolated from the world, separated from it in this exotic enjoyment.

Gradually the embers grew paler; the figures in the tapestry more shadowy; the columned and curtained bed loomed out vaguer; the room seemed to fill with greyness; and my eyes wandered to the mullioned bow-window, beyond whose panes, between whose heavy stonework, stretched a greyish-brown expanse of sere and sodden park grass, dotted with big oaks; while far off, behind a jagged fringe of dark Scotch firs, the wet sky was suffused with the blood-red of the sunset. Between the falling of the raindrops from the ivy outside, there came, fainter or sharper, the recurring bleating of the lambs separated from their mothers, a forlorn, quavering, eerie little cry.

I started up at a sudden rap at my door.

'Haven't you heard the gong for dinner?' asked Mr Oke's voice.

I had completely forgotten his existence.

III

I FEEL that I cannot possibly reconstruct my earliest impressions of Mrs Oke. My recollection of them would be entirely coloured by my subsequent knowledge of her; whence I conclude that I could not at first have experienced the strange interest and admiration which that extraordinary woman very soon excited in me. Interest and admiration, be it well understood, of a very unusual kind, as she was herself a very unusual kind of woman; and I, if you choose, am a rather unusual kind of man. But I can explain that better anon.

This much is certain, that I must have been immeasurably surprised at finding my hostess and future sitter so completely unlike everything I had anticipated. Or no – now I come to think of it, I scarcely felt surprised at all; or if I did, that shock of surprise could have lasted but an infinitesimal part of a minute. The fact is, that, having once seen Alice Oke in the reality, it was quite impossible to remember that one could have fancied her at all different: there was something so complete, so completely unlike every one else, in her personality, that she seemed always to have been present in one's consciousness, although present, perhaps, as an enigma.

Let me try and give you some notion of her: not that first impression, whatever it may have been, but the absolute reality of her as I gradually learned to see it. To begin with, I must repeat and reiterate over and over again, that she was, beyond all comparison, the most graceful and exquisite woman I have ever seen, but with a grace and an exquisiteness that had nothing to do with any preconceived notion or previous experience of what goes by these names: grace and exquisiteness recognized at once as perfect, but which were seen in her for the first, and probably, I do believe, for the last time. It is conceivable, is it not, that once in a thousand years there may arise a combination of lines, a system of movements, an outline, a gesture, which is new, unprecedented, and yet hits off exactly our desires for beauty and rareness? She was very tall; and I suppose people would have called her thin. I don't know, for I never thought about her as a body – bones, flesh, that sort of thing; but merely as a wonderful series of lines, and a wonderful strangeness of personality. Tall and slender, certainly, and with not one item of what makes up our notion of a well-built woman. She was as straight – I mean she had as little of what people call figure – as a bamboo; her shoulders were a trifle high, and she had a decided stoop; her arms and her shoulders she never once wore uncovered. But this bamboo figure of hers had a suppleness and a stateliness, a play of outline with every step she took, that I can't compare to anything else; there was in it something of the peacock and something also of the stag; but, above all, it was her own. I wish I could describe her. I wish, alas! – I wish, I wish, I have wished a hundred thousand times – I could paint her, as I see her now, if I shut my eyes – even if it were only a silhouette. There! I see her so plainly, walking slowly up and down a room, the slight highness of her shoulders just completing the exquisite arrangement of lines made by the straight supple back, the long exquisite neck, the head, with the hair cropped in short pale curls, always drooping a little, except when she would suddenly throw it back, and smile, not at me, nor at any one, nor at anything that had been said, but as if she alone had suddenly seen or heard something, with the strange dimple in her thin, pale cheeks, and the strange whiteness in her full, wide-opened eyes: the moment when she had something of the stag in her movement. But where is the use of talking about her? I don't believe, you know, that even the greatest painter can show what is the real beauty of a very beautiful woman in the ordinary sense: Titian's and Tintoretto's women must have been miles handsomer than they have made them. Something – and that the very essence – always escapes, perhaps because real beauty is as much a thing in time – a thing like music, a succession, a series – as in space. Mind you, I am speaking of a woman beautiful in the conventional sense. Imagine, then, how much more so in the case of a woman like Alice Oke; and if the pencil and brush, imitating each line and tint, can't succeed, how is it possible to give even the vaguest notion with mere wretched words – words possessing only a wretched abstract meaning, an impotent conventional association? To make a long story short, Mrs Oke of Okehurst was, in my opinion, to the highest degree exquisite and strange – an exotic creature, whose charm you can no more describe than you could bring home the perfume of some newly discovered tropical flower by comparing it with the scent of a cabbage-rose or a lily.

That first dinner was gloomy enough. Mr Oke – Oke of Okehurst, as the people down there called him – was horribly shy, consumed with a fear of making a fool of himself before me and his wife, I then thought. But that sort of shyness did not wear off; and I soon discovered that, although it was doubtless increased by the presence of a total stranger, it was inspired in Oke, not by me, but by his wife. He would look every now and then as if he were going to make a remark, and then evidently restrain himself, and remain silent. It was very curious to see this big, handsome, manly young fellow, who ought to have had any amount of success with women, suddenly stammer and grow crimson in the presence of his own wife. Nor was it the consciousness of stupidity; for when you got him alone, Oke, although always slow and timid, had a certain amount of ideas, and very defined political and social views, and a certain child-like earnestness and desire to attain certainty and truth which was rather touching. On the other hand, Oke's singular shyness was not, so far as I could see, the result of any kind of bullying on his wife's part. You can always detect, if you have any observation, the husband or the wife who is accustomed to be snubbed, to be corrected, by his or her better-half: there is a self consciousness in both parties, a habit of watching and fault-finding, of being watched and found fault with. This was clearly not the case at Okehurst. Mrs Oke evidently did not trouble herself about her husband in the very least; he might say or do any amount of silly things without rebuke or even notice; and he might have done so, had he chosen, ever since his wedding-day. You felt that at once. Mrs Oke simply passed over his existence. I cannot say she paid much attention to any one's, even to mine. At first I thought it an affectation on her part – for there was something far-fetched in her whole appearance, something suggesting study, which might lead one to tax her with affectation at first; she was dressed in a strange way, not according to any established aesthetic eccentricity, but individually, strangely, as if in the clothes of an ancestress of the seventeenth century. Well, at first I thought it a kind of pose on her part, this mixture of extreme graciousness and utter indifference which she manifested towards me. She always seemed to be thinking of something else; and although she talked quite sufficiently, and with every sign of superior intelligence, she left the impression of having been as taciturn as her husband.

In the beginning, in the first few days of my stay at Okehurst, I imagined that Mrs Oke was a highly superior sort of flirt; and that her absent manner, her look, while speaking to you, into an invisible distance, her curious irrelevant smile, were so many means of attracting and baffling adoration. I mistook it for the somewhat similar manners of certain foreign women – it is beyond English ones – which means, to those who can understand, 'pay court to me.' But I soon found I was mistaken. Mrs Oke had not the faintest desire that I should pay court to her; indeed she did not honour me with sufficient thought for that; and I, on my part, began to be too much interested in her from another point of view to dream of such a thing. I became aware, not merely that I had before me the most marvellously rare and exquisite and baffling subject for a portrait, but also one of the most peculiar and enigmatic of characters. Now that I look back upon it, I am tempted to think that the psychological peculiarity of that woman might be summed up in an exorbitant and absorbing interest in herself – a Narcissus attitude – curiously complicated with a fantastic imagination, a sort of morbid day-dreaming, all turned inwards, and with no outer character- istic save a certain restlessness, a perverse desire to surprise and shock, to surprise and shock more particularly her husband, and thus be revenged for the intense boredom which his want of appreciation inflicted upon her.

I got to understand this much little by little, yet I did not seem to have really penetrated the something mysterious about Mrs Oke. There was a waywardness, a strangeness, which I felt but could not explain – a something as difficult to define as the peculiarity of her outward appearance, and perhaps very closely connected therewith. I became interested in Mrs Oke as if I had been in love with her; and I was not in the least in love. I neither dreaded parting from her, nor felt any pleasure in her presence. I had not the smallest wish to please or to gain her notice. But I had her on the brain. I pursued her, her physical image, her psycho- logical explanation, with a kind of passion which filled my days, and prevented my ever feeling dull. The Okes lived a remarkably solitary life. There were but few neighbours, of whom they saw but little; and they rarely had a guest in the house. Oke himself seemed every now and then seized with a sense of responsibility towards me. He would remark vaguely, during our walks and after-dinner chats, that I must find life at Okehurst horribly dull; his wife's health had accustomed him to solitude, and then also his wife thought the neighbours a bore. He never questioned his wife's judgment in these matters. He merely stated the case as if resignation were quite simple and inevitable; yet it seemed to me, sometimes, that this monotonous life of solitude, by the side of a woman who took no more heed of him than of a table or chair, was producing a vague depression and irritation in this young man, so evidently cut out for a cheerful, commonplace life. I often wondered how he could endure it at all, not having, as I had, the interest of a strange psychological riddle to solve, and of a great portrait to paint. He was, I found, extremely good – the type of the perfectly conscientious young Englishman, the sort of man who ought to have been the Christian soldier kind of thing; devout, pure-minded, brave, incapable of any baseness, a little intellectually dense, and puzzled by all manner of moral scruples. The condition of his tenants and of his political party – he was a regular Kentish Tory – lay heavy on his mind. He spent hours every day in his study, doing the work of a land agent and a political whip, reading piles of reports and newspapers and agricultural treatises; and emerging for lunch with piles of letters in his hand, and that odd puzzled look in his good healthy face, that deep gash between his eyebrows, which my friend the mad-doctor calls the maniac-frown. It was with this expression of face that I should have liked to paint him; but I felt that he would not have liked it, that it was more fair to him to represent him in his mere wholesome pink and white and blond conventionality. I was perhaps rather unconscientious about the likeness of Mr Oke; I felt satisfied to paint it no matter how, I mean as regards character, for my whole mind was swallowed up in thinking how I should paint Mrs Oke, how I could best transport on to canvas that singular and enigmatic personality. I began with her husband, and told her frankly that I must have much longer to study her. Mr Oke couldn't understand why it should be necessary to make a hundred and one pencil-sketches of his wife before even determining in what attitude to paint her; but I think he was rather pleased to have an opportunity of keeping me at Okehurst; my presence evidently broke the monotony of his life. Mrs Oke seemed perfectly indifferent to my staying, as she was perfectly indifferent to my presence. Without being rude, I never saw a woman pay so little attention to a guest; she would talk with me sometimes by the hour, or rather let me talk to her, but she never seemed to be listening. She would lie back in a big seventeenth-century armchair while I played the piano, with that strange smile every now and then in her thin cheeks, that strange whiteness in her eyes; but it seemed a matter of indifference whether my music stopped or went on. In my portrait of her husband she did not take, or pretend to take, the very faintest interest; but that was nothing to me. I did not want Mrs Oke to think me interesting; I merely wished to go on studying her.

The first time that Mrs Oke seemed to become at all aware of my presence as distinguished from that of the chairs and tables, the dogs that lay in the porch, or the clergyman or lawyer or stray neighbour who was occasionally asked to dinner, was one day – I might have been there a week – when I chanced to remark to her upon the very singular resemblance that existed between herself and the portrait of a lady that hung in the hall with the ceiling like a ship's hull. The picture in question was a full length, neither very good nor very bad, probably done by some stray Italian of the early seventeenth century. It hung in a rather dark corner, facing the portrait, evidently painted to be its companion, of a dark man, with a somewhat unpleasant expression of resolution and efficiency, in a black Van Dyck dress. The two were evidently man and wife; and in the corner of the woman's portrait were the words, 'Alice Oke, daughter of Virgil Pomfret, Esq., and wife to Nicholas Oke of Okehurst', and the date 1626 – 'Nicholas Oke' being the name painted in the corner of the small portrait. The lady was really wonderfully like the present Mrs Oke, at least so far as an indifferently painted portrait of the early days of Charles I can be like a living woman of the nineteenth century. There were the same strange lines of figure and face, the same dimples in the thin cheeks, the same wide-opened eyes, the same vague eccentricity of expression, not destroyed even by the feeble painting and conventional manner of the time. One could fancy that this woman had the same walk, the same beautiful line of nape of the neck and stooping head as her descendant; for I found that Mr and Mrs Oke, who were first cousins, were both descended from that Nicholas Oke and that Alice, daughter of Virgil Pomfret. But the resemblance was heightened by the fact that, as I soon saw, the present Mrs Oke distinctly made herself up to look like her ancestress, dressing in garments that had a seventeenth-century look; nay, that were sometimes absolutely copied from this portrait.

'You think I am like her,' answered Mrs Oke dreamily to my

remark, and her eyes wandered off to that unseen something, and the faint smile dimpled her thin cheeks.

'You are like her, and you know it. I may even say you wish to be like her, Mrs Oke,' I answered, laughing.

'Perhaps I do.'

And she looked in the direction of her husband. I noticed that he had an expression of distinct annoyance besides that frown of his.

'Isn't it true that Mrs Oke tries to look like that portrait?' I asked, with a perverse curiosity.

'Oh, fudge!' he exclaimed, rising from his chair and walking nervously to the window. 'It's all nonsense, mere nonsense. I wish you wouldn't, Alice.'

'Wouldn't what?' asked Mrs Oke, with a sort of contemptuous indifference. 'If I am like that Alice Oke, why I am; and I am very pleased any one should think so. She and her husband are just about the only two members of our family – our most flat, stale, and unprofitable family – that ever were in the least degree interesting.'

Oke grew crimson, and frowned as if in pain.

'I don't see why you should abuse our family, Alice,' he said. 'Thank God, our people have always been honourable and upright men and women!'

'Excepting always Nicholas Oke and Alice his wife, daughter of Virgil Pomfret, Esq.,' she answered, laughing, as he strode out into the park.

'How childish he is!' she exclaimed when we were alone. 'He really minds, really feels disgraced by what our ancestors did two centuries and a half ago. I do believe William would have those two portraits taken down and burned if he weren't afraid of me and ashamed of the neighbours. And as it is, these two people really are the only two members of our family that ever were in the least interesting. I will tell you the story some day.'

As it was, the story was told to me by Oke himself. The next day, as we were taking our morning walk, he suddenly broke a long silence, laying about him all the time at the sere grasses with the hooked stick that he carried, like the conscientious Kentish-man he was, for the purpose of cutting down his and other folk's thistles.

'I fear you must have thought me very ill-mannered towards my wife yesterday,' he said shyly; 'and indeed I know I was.'

Oke was one of those chivalrous beings to whom every woman, every wife – and his own most of all – appeared in the light of something holy. 'But – but – I have a prejudice which my wife does not enter into, about raking up ugly things in one's own family. I suppose Alice thinks that it is so long ago that it has really got no connection with us; she thinks of it merely as a picturesque story. I daresay many people feel like that; in short, I am sure they do, otherwise there wouldn't be such lots of discreditable family traditions afloat. But I feel as if it were all one whether it was long ago or not; when it's a question of one's own people, I would rather have it forgotten. I can't understand how people can talk about murders in their families, and ghosts, and so forth.'

'Have you any ghosts at Okehurst, by the way?' I asked. The place seemed as if it required some to complete it.

'I hope not,' answered Oke gravely.

His gravity made me smile.

'Why, would you dislike it if there were?' I asked.

'If there are such things as ghosts,' he replied, 'I don't think they should be taken lightly. God would not permit them to be, except as a warning or a punishment.'

We walked on some time in silence, I wondering at the strange type of this commonplace young man, and half wishing I could put something into my portrait that should be the equivalent of this curious unimaginative earnestness. Then Oke told me the story of those two pictures – told it me about as badly and hesitatingly as was possible for mortal man.

He and his wife were, as I have said, cousins, and therefore descended from the same old Kentish stock. The Okes of Okehurst could trace back to Norman, almost to Saxon times, far longer than any of the titled or better-known families of the neighbourhood. I saw that William Oke, in his heart, thoroughly looked down upon all his neighbours. 'We have never done anything particular, or been anything particular – never held any office,' he said; 'but we have always been here, and apparently always done our duty. An ancestor of ours was killed in the Scotch wars, another at Agincourt – mere honest captains.' Well, early in the seventeenth century, the family had dwindled to a single member, Nicholas Oke, the same who had rebuilt Okehurst in its present shape. This Nicholas appears to have been somewhat different from the usual run of the family. He had, in his youth, sought adventures in America, and seems, generally speaking, to have been less of a nonentity than his ancestors. He married, when no longer very young, Alice, daughter of Virgil Pomfret, a beautiful young heiress from a neighbouring county. 'It was the first time an Oke married a Pomfret,' my host informed me, 'and the last time. The Pomfrets were quite different sort of people – restless, self-seeking; one of them had been a favourite of Henry VIII.' It was clear that William Oke had no feeling of having any Pomfret blood in his veins; he spoke of these people with an evident family dislike – the dislike of an Oke, one of the old, honourable, modest stock, which had quietly done its duty, for a family of fortune-seekers and Court minions. Well, there had come to live near Okehurst, in a little house recently inherited from an uncle, a certain Christopher Lovelock, a young gallant and poet, who was in momentary disgrace at Court for some love affair. This Lovelock had struck up a great friendship with his neighbours of Okehurst – too great a friendship, apparently, with the wife, either for her husband's taste or her own. Anyhow, one evening as he was riding home alone, Lovelock had been attacked and murdered, ostensibly by highwaymen, but as was afterwards rumoured, by Nicholas Oke, accompanied by his wife dressed as a groom. No legal evidence had been got, but the tradition had remained. 'They used to tell it us when we were children,' said my host, in a hoarse voice, 'and to frighten my cousin – I mean my wife – and me with stories about Lovelock. It is merely a tradition, which I hope may die out, as I sincerely pray to heaven that it may be false.' 'Alice – Mrs Oke – you see,' he went on after some time, 'doesn't feel about it as I do. Perhaps I am morbid. But I do dislike having the old story raked up.'

And we said no more on the subject.

IV

FROM that moment I began to assume a certain interest in the eyes of Mrs Oke; or rather, I began to perceive that I had a means of securing her attention. Perhaps it was wrong of me to do so; and I have often reproached myself very seriously later on. But after all, how was I to guess that I was making mischief merely by chiming in, for the sake of the portrait I had undertaken, and of a very harmless psychological mania, with what was merely the fad, the little romantic affectation or eccentricity, of a scatter-brained and eccentric young woman? How in the world should I have dreamed that I was handling explosive substances? A man is surely not responsible if the people with whom he is forced to deal, and whom he deals with as with all the rest of the world, are quite different from all other human creatures.

So, if indeed I did at all conduce to mischief, I really cannot blame myself. I had met in Mrs Oke an almost unique subject for a portrait-painter of my particular sort, and a most singular, *bizarre* personality. I could not possibly do my subject justice so long as I was kept at a distance, prevented from studying the real character of the woman. I required to put her into play. And I ask you whether any more innocent way of doing so could be found than talking to a woman, and letting her talk, about an absurd fancy she had for a couple of ancestors of hers of the time of Charles I, and a poet whom they had murdered? – particularly as I studiously respected the prejudices of my host, and refrained from mentioning the matter, and tried to restrain Mrs Oke from doing so, in the presence of William Oke himself.

I had certainly guessed correctly. To resemble the Alice Oke of the year 1626 was the caprice, the mania, the pose, the whatever you may call it, of the Alice Oke of 1880; and to perceive this resemblance was the sure way of gaining her good graces. It was the most extraordinary craze, of all the extraordinary crazes of childless and idle women, that I had ever met; but it was more than that, it was admirably characteristic. It finished off the strange figure of Mrs Oke, as I saw it in my imagination – this *bizarre* creature of enigmatic, far-fetched exquisiteness – that she should have no interest in the present, but only an eccentric passion in the past. It seemed to give the meaning to the absent look in her eyes, to her irrelevant and far-off smile. It was like the words to a weird piece of gypsy music, this that she, who was so different, so distant from all women of her own time, should try and identify herself with a woman of the past – that she should have a kind of flirtation – But of this anon.

I told Mrs Oke that I had learnt from her husband the outline of the tragedy, or mystery, whichever it was, of Alice Oke, daughter of Virgil Pomfret, and the poet Christopher Lovelock. That look of vague contempt, of a desire to shock, which I had noticed before, came into her beautiful, pale, diaphanous face.

'I suppose my husband was very shocked at the whole matter,' she said – 'told it you with as little detail as possible, and assured you very solemnly that he hoped the whole story might be a mere dreadful calumny? Poor Willie! I remember already when we were children, and I used to come with my mother to spend Christmas at Okehurst, and my cousin was down here for his holidays, how I used to horrify him by insisting upon dressing up in shawls and waterproofs, and playing the story of the wicked Mrs Oke; and he always piously refused to do the part of Nicholas, when I wanted to have the scene on Cotes Common. I didn't know then that I was like the original Alice Oke; I found it out only after our marriage. You really think that I am?'

She certainly was, particularly at that moment, as she stood in a white Van Dyck dress, with the green of the park-land rising up behind her, and the low sun catching her short locks and surrounding her head, her exquisitely bowed head, with a pale-yellow halo. But I confess I thought the original Alice Oke, siren and murderess though she might be, very uninteresting compared with this wayward and exquisite creature whom I had rashly promised myself to send down to posterity in all her unlikely wayward exquisiteness.

One morning while Mr Oke was despatching his Saturday heap of Conservative manifestoes and rural decisions – he was justice of the peace in a most literal sense, penetrating into cottages and huts, defending the weak and admonishing the ill-conducted – one morning while I was making one of my many pencil-sketches (alas, they are all that remain to me now!) of my future sitter, Mrs Oke gave me her version of the story of Alice Oke and Christopher Lovelock.

'Do you suppose there was anything between them?' I asked – 'that she was ever in love with him? How do you explain the part which tradition ascribes to her in the supposed murder? One has heard of women and their lovers who have killed the husband; but a woman who combines with her husband to kill her lover, or at least the man who is in love with her – that is surely very singular.' I was absorbed in my drawing, and really thinking very little of what I was saying.

'I don't know,' she answered pensively, with that distant look in her eyes. 'Alice Oke was very proud, I am sure. She may have loved the poet very much, and yet been indignant with him, hated having to love him. She may have felt that she had a right to rid herself of him, and to call upon her husband to help her to do so.'

'Good heavens! what a fearful idea!' I exclaimed, half laughing. 'Don't you think, after all, that Mr Oke may be right in saying that it is easier and more comfortable to take the whole story as a pure invention?'

'I cannot take it as an invention,' answered Mrs Oke contemptuously, 'because I happen to know that it is true.'

'Indeed!' I answered, working away at my sketch, and enjoying putting this strange creature, as I said to myself, through her paces; 'how is that?'

'How does one know that anything is true in this world?' she replied evasively; 'because one does, because one feels it to be true, I suppose.'

And, with that far-off look in her light eyes, she relapsed into silence.

'Have you ever read any of Lovelock's poetry?' she asked me suddenly the next day.

'Lovelock?' I answered, for I had forgotten the name. 'Lovelock, who –' But I stopped, remembering the prejudices of my host, who was seated next to me at table.

'Lovelock who was killed by Mr Oke's and my ancestors.'

And she looked full at her husband, as if in perverse enjoyment of the evident annoyance which it caused him.

'Alice,' he entreated in a low voice, his whole face crimson, 'for mercy's sake, don't talk about such things before the servants.'

Mrs Oke burst into a high, light, rather hysterical laugh, the laugh of a naughty child.

'The servants! Gracious heavens! do you suppose they haven't heard the story? Why, it's as well known as Okehurst itself in the neighbourhood. Don't they believe that Lovelock has been seen about the house? Haven't they all heard his footsteps in the big corridor? Haven't they, my dear Willie, noticed a thousand times that you never will stay a minute alone in the yellow drawing-room – that you run out of it, like a child, if I happen to leave you there for a minute?'

True! How was it I had not noticed that? or rather, that I only now remembered having noticed it? The yellow drawing-room was one of the most charming rooms in the house: a large, bright room, hung with yellow damask and panelled with carvings, that opened straight out on to the lawn, far superior to the room in which we habitually sat, which was comparatively gloomy. This time Mr Oke struck me as really too childish. I felt an intense desire to badger him.

'The yellow drawing-room!' I exclaimed. 'Does this interesting literary character haunt the yellow drawing-room? Do tell me about it. What happened there?'

Mr Oke made a painful effort to laugh.

'Nothing ever happened there, so far as I know,' he said, and rose from the table.

'Really?' I asked incredulously.

'Nothing did happen there,' answered Mrs Oke slowly, playing mechanically with a fork, and picking out the pattern of the tablecloth. 'That is just the extraordinary circumstance, that, so far as any one knows, nothing ever did happen there; and yet that room has an evil reputation. No member of our family, they say, can bear to sit there alone for more than a minute. You see, William evidently cannot.'

'Have you ever seen or heard anything strange there?' I asked of my host.

He shook his head. 'Nothing,' he answered curtly, and lit his cigar.

'I presume you have not,' I asked, half laughing, of Mrs Oke, 'since you don't mind sitting in that room for hours alone? How do you explain this uncanny reputation, since nothing ever happened there?'

'Perhaps something is destined to happen there in the future,' she answered, in her absent voice. And then she suddenly added, 'Suppose you paint my portrait in that room?'

Mr Oke suddenly turned round. He was very white, and looked as if he were going to say something, but desisted.

'Why do you worry Mr Oke like that?' I asked, when he had gone into his smoking-room with his usual bundle of papers. 'It is very cruel of you, Mrs Oke. You ought to have more consideration for people who believe in such things, although you may not be able to put yourself in their frame of mind.'

'Who tells you that I don't believe in *such things*, as you call them?' she answered abruptly.

'Come,' she said, after a minute, 'I want to show you why I believe in Christopher Lovelock. Come with me into the yellow room.'

V

WHAT Mrs Oke showed me in the yellow room was a large bundle of papers, some printed and some manuscript, but all of them brown with age, which she took out of an old Italian ebony inlaid cabinet. It took her some time to get them, as a complicated arrangement of double locks and false drawers had to be put in play; and while she was doing so, I looked round the room, in which I had been only three or four times before. It was certainly the most beautiful room in this beautiful house, and, as it seemed to me now, the most strange. It was long and low, with something that made you think of the cabin of a ship, with a great mullioned window that let in, as it were, a perspective of the brownish green park-land, dotted with oaks, and sloping upwards to the distant line of bluish firs against the horizon. The walls were hung with flowered damask, whose yellow, faded to brown, united with the reddish colour of the carved wainscoting and the carved oaken beams. For the rest, it reminded me more of an Italian room than an English one. The furniture was Tuscan of the early seventeenth century, inlaid and carved; there were a couple of faded allegorical pictures, by some Bolognese master, on the walls; and in a corner, among a stack of dwarf orange-trees, a little Italian harpsichord of exquisite curve and slenderness, with flowers and landscapes painted upon its cover. In a recess was a shelf of old books, mainly English and Italian poets of the Elizabethan time; and close by it, placed upon a carved wedding-chest, a large and beautiful melon-shaped lute. The panes of the mullioned window were open, and yet the air seemed heavy, with an indescribable heavy perfume, not that of any growing flower, but like that of old stuff that should have lain for years among spices.

'It is a beautiful room!' I exclaimed. 'I should awfully like to paint you in it'; but I had scarcely spoken the words when I felt I had done wrong. This woman's husband could not bear the room, and it seemed to me vaguely as if he were right in detesting it.

Mrs Oke took no notice of my exclamation, but beckoned me to the table where she was standing sorting the papers.

'Look!' she said, 'these are all poems by Christopher Love-lock'; and touching the yellow papers with delicate and reverent fingers, she commenced reading some of them out loud in a slow, half-audible voice. They were songs in the style of those of Herrick, Waller and Drayton, complaining for the most part of the cruelty of a lady called Dryope, in whose name was evidently concealed a reference to that of the mistress of Okehurst. The songs were graceful, and not without a certain faded passion; but I was thinking not of them, but of the woman who was reading them to me.

Mrs Oke was standing with the brownish yellow wall as a background to her white brocade dress, which, in its stiff seventeenth-century make, seemed but to bring out more clearly the slightness, the exquisite suppleness, of her tall figure. She held the papers in one hand, and leaned the other, as if for support, on the inlaid cabinet by her side. Her voice, which was delicate, shadowy, like her person, had a curious throbbing cadence, as if she were reading the words of a melody, and restraining herself with difficulty from singing it; and as she read, her long slender throat throbbed slightly, and a faint redness came into her thin face. She evidently knew the verses by heart, and her eyes were mostly fixed with that distant smile in them, with which harmonized a constant tremulous little smile in her lips.

'That is how I would wish to paint her!' I exclaimed within myself; and scarcely noticed, what struck me on thinking over the scene, that this strange being read these verses as one might fancy a woman would read love-verses addressed to herself.

'Those are all written for Alice Oke – Alice the daughter of Virgil Pomfret,' she said slowly, folding up the papers. 'I found them at the bottom of this cabinet. Can you doubt of the reality of Christopher Lovelock now?'

The question was an illogical one, for to doubt of the existence of Christopher Lovelock was one thing, and to doubt of the mode of his death was another; but somehow I did feel convinced.

'Look!' she said, when she had replaced the poems, 'I will show you something else.' Among the flowers that stood on the upper storey of her writing-table – for I found that Mrs Oke had a writing-table in the yellow room – stood, as on an altar, a small black carved frame, with a silk curtain drawn over it: the sort of thing behind which you would have expected to find a head of Christ or of the Virgin Mary. She drew the curtain and displayed a large-sized miniature, representing a young man, with auburn curls and a peaked auburn beard, dressed in black, but with lace about his neck, and large pear-shaped pearls in his ears: a wistful melancholy face. Mrs Oke took the miniature religiously off its stand, and showed me, written in faded characters upon the back, the name 'Christopher Lovelock', and the date 1626.

'I found this in the secret drawer of that cabinet, together with the heap of poems,' she said, taking the miniature out of my hand.

I was silent for a minute.

'Does – does Mr Oke know that you have got it here?' I asked; and then wondered what in the world had impelled me to put such a question.

Mrs Oke smiled that smile of contemptuous indifference. 'I have never hidden it from any one. If my husband disliked my having it, he might have taken it away, I suppose. It belongs to him, since it was found in his house.'

I did not answer, but walked mechanically towards the door. There was something heady and oppressive in this beautiful room; something, I thought, almost repulsive in this exquisite woman. She seemed to me, suddenly, perverse and dangerous.

I scarcely know why, but I neglected Mrs Oke that afternoon. I went to Mr Oke's study, and sat opposite to him smoking while he was engrossed in his accounts, his reports, and electioneering papers. On the table, above the heap of paper-bound volumes and pigeon-holed documents, was, as sole ornament of his den, a little photograph of his wife, done some years before. I don't know why, but as I sat and watched him, with his florid, honest, manly beauty, working away conscientiously, with that little perplexed frown of his, I felt intensely sorry for this man.

But this feeling did not last. There was no help for it: Oke was not as interesting as Mrs Oke; and it required too great an effort to pump up sympathy for this normal, excellent, exemplary young squire, in the presence of so wonderful a creature as his wife. So I let myself go to the habit of allowing Mrs Oke daily to talk over her strange craze, or rather of drawing her out about it. I confess that I derived a morbid and exquisite pleasure in doing so: it was so characteristic in her, so appropriate to the house! It completed her personality so perfectly, and made it so much easier to conceive a way of painting her. I made up my mind little by little, while working at William Oke's portrait (he proved a less easy subject than I had anticipated, and, despite his conscientious efforts, was a nervous, uncomfortable sitter, silent and brooding) — I made up my mind that I would paint Mrs Oke standing by the cabinet in the yellow room, in the white Van Dyck dress copied from the portrait of her ancestress. Mr Oke might resent it, Mrs Oke even might resent it; they might refuse to take the picture, to pay for it, to allow me to exhibit; they might force me to run my umbrella through the picture. No matter. That picture should be painted, if merely for the sake of having painted it; for I felt it was the only thing I could do, and that it would be far away my best work. I told neither of my resolution, but prepared sketch after sketch of Mrs Oke, while continuing to paint her husband.

Mrs Oke was a silent person, more silent even than her husband, for she did not feel bound, as he did, to attempt to entertain a guest or to show any interest in him. She seemed to spend her life – a curious, inactive, half-invalidish life, broken by sudden fits of childish cheerfulness – in an eternal day-dream, strolling about the house and grounds, arranging the quantities of flowers that always filled all the rooms, beginning to read and then throwing aside novels and books of poetry, of which she always had a large number; and, I believe, lying for hours, doing nothing, on a couch in that yellow drawing-room, which, with her sole exception, no member of the Oke family had ever been known to stay in alone. Little by little I began to suspect and to verify another eccentricity of this eccentric being, and to understand why there were stringent orders never to disturb her in that yellow room.

It had been a habit at Okehurst, as at one or two other English manor-houses, to keep a certain amount of the clothes of each generation, more particularly wedding-dresses. A certain carved oaken press, of which Mr Oke once displayed the contents to me, was a perfect museum of costumes, male and female, from the early years of the seventeenth to the end of the eighteenth century – a thing to take away the breath of a *bric-a-brac* collector, an antiquary, or a *genre* painter. Mr Oke was none of these, and therefore took but little interest in the collection, save in so far as it interested his family feeling. Still he seemed well acquainted with the contents of that press.

He was turning over the clothes for my benefit, when suddenly I noticed that he frowned. I know not what impelled me to say, 'By the way, have you any dresses of that Mrs Oke whom your wife resembles so much? Have you got that particular white dress she was painted in, perhaps?'

Oke of Okehurst flushed very red.

'We have it,' he answered hesitatingly, 'but – it isn't here at present – I can't find it. I suppose,' he blurted out with an effort, 'that Alice has got it. Mrs Oke sometimes has the fancy of having some of these old things down. I suppose she takes ideas from them.'

A sudden light dawned in my mind. The white dress in which I had seen Mrs Oke in the yellow room, the day that she showed me Lovelock's verses, was not, as I had thought, a modern copy; it was the original dress of Alice Oke, the daughter of Virgil Pomfret – the dress in which, perhaps, Christopher Lovelock had seen her in that very room.

The idea gave me a delightful picturesque shudder. I said nothing. But I pictured to myself Mrs Oke sitting in that yellow room – that room which no Oke of Okehurst save herself ventured to remain in alone, in the dress of her ancestress, confronting, as it were, that vague, haunting something that seemed to fill the place – that vague presence, it seemed to me, of the murdered cavalier poet.

Mrs Oke, as I have said, was extremely silent, as a result of being extremely indifferent. She really did not care in the least about anything except her own ideas and day-dreams, except when, every now and then, she was seized with a sudden desire to shock the prejudices or superstitions of her husband. Very soon she got into the way of never talking to me at all, save about Alice and Nicholas Oke and Christopher Lovelock; and then, when the fit seized her, she would go on by the hour, never asking herself whether I was or was not equally interested in the strange craze that fascinated her. It so happened that I was. I loved to listen to her, going on discussing by the hour the merits of Lovelock's poems, and analysing her feelings and those of her two ancestors. It was quite wonderful to watch the exquisite, exotic creature in one of these moods, with the distant look in her grey eyes and the absent-looking smile in her thin cheeks, talking as if she had intimately known these people of the seventeenth century, discussing every minute mood of theirs, detailing every scene between them and their victim, talking of Alice, and Nicholas, and Lovelock as she might of her most intimate friends. Of Alice particularly, and of Lovelock. She seemed to know every word that Alice had spoken, every idea that had crossed her mind. It sometimes struck me as if she were telling me, speaking of herself in the third person, of her own feelings – as if I were listening to a woman's confidences, the recital of her doubts, scruples and agonies about a living lover. For Mrs Oke, who seemed the most self-absorbed of creatures in all other matters, and utterly incapable of understanding or sympathizing with the feelings of other persons, entered completely and passionately into the feelings of this woman, this Alice, who, at some moments, seemed to be not another woman, but herself.

'But how could she do it – how could she kill the man she cared for?' I once asked her.

'Because she loved him more than the whole world!' she exclaimed, and rising suddenly from her chair, walked towards the window, covering her face with her hands.

I could see, from the movement of her neck, that she was sobbing. She did not turn round, but motioned me to go away.

'Don't let us talk any more about it,' she said. 'I am ill today, and silly.'

I closed the door gently behind me. What mystery was there in this woman's life? This listlessness, this strange self-engrossment and stranger mania about people long dead, this indifference and desire to annoy towards her husband – did it all mean that Alice Oke had loved or still loved some one who was not the master of Okehurst? And his melancholy, his preoccupation, the something about him that told of a broken youth – did it mean that he knew it?

VI

THE following days Mrs Oke was in a condition of quite unusual good spirits. Some visitors – distant relatives – were expected, and although she had expressed the utmost annoyance at the idea of their coming, she was now seized with a fit of housekeeping activity, and was perpetually about arranging things and giving orders, although all arrangements, as usual, had been made, and all orders given, by her husband.

William Oke was quite radiant.

'If only Alice were always well like this!' he exclaimed; 'if only she would take, or could take, an interest in life, how different things would be! But,' he added, as if fearful lest he should be supposed to accuse her in any way, 'how can she, usually, with her wretched health? Still, it does make me awfully happy to see her like this.'

I nodded. But I cannot say that I really acquiesced in his views. It seemed to me, particularly with the recollection of yesterday's extraordinary scene, that Mrs Oke's high spirits were anything but normal. There was something in her unusual activity and still more unusual cheerfulness that was merely nervous and feverish; and I had, the whole day, the impression of dealing with a woman who was ill and who would very speedily collapse.

Mrs Oke spent her day wandering from one room to another, and from the garden to the greenhouse, seeing whether all was in order, when, as a matter of fact, all was always in order at Okehurst. She did not give me any sitting, and not a word was spoken about Alice Oke or Christopher Lovelock. Indeed, to a casual observer, it might have seemed as if all that craze about Lovelock had completely departed, or never existed. About five o'clock, as I was strolling among the red-brick round-gabled outhouses – each with its armorial oak – and the old-fashioned espaliered kitchen and fruit garden, I saw Mrs Oke standing, her hands full of York and Lancaster roses, upon the steps facing the stables. A groom was currycombing a horse, and outside the coach-house was Mr Oke's little high-wheeled cart.

'Let us have a drive!' suddenly exclaimed Mrs Oke, on seeing me. 'Look what a beautiful evening – and look at that dear little cart! It is so long since I have driven, and I feel as if I must drive again. Come with me. And you, harness Jim at once and come round to the door.'

I was quite amazed; and still more so when the cart drove up before the door, and Mrs Oke called to me to accompany her. She sent away the groom, and in a minute we were rolling along, at a tremendous pace, along the yellow-sand road, with the sere pasture-lands, the big oaks, on either side.

I could scarcely believe my senses. This woman, in her mannish little coat and hat, driving a powerful young horse with the utmost skill, and chattering like a schoolgirl of sixteen, could not be the delicate, morbid, exotic, hot-house creature, unable to walk or to do anything, who spent her days lying about on couches in the heavy atmosphere, redolent with strange scents and associations, of the yellow drawing-room. The movement of the light carriage, the cool draught, the very grind of the wheels upon the gravel, seemed to go to her head like wine.

'It is so long since I have done this sort of thing,' she kept repeating; 'so long, so long. Oh, don't you think it delightful, going at this pace, with the idea that any moment the horse may come down and we two be killed?' and she laughed her childish laugh, and turned her face, no longer pale, but flushed with the movement and the excitement, towards me.

The cart rolled on quicker and quicker, one gate after another swinging to behind us, as we flew up and down the little hills, across the pasture – lands, through the little red-brick gabled villages, where the people came out to see us pass, past the rows of willows along the streams, and the dark-green compact hop-fields, with the blue and hazy tree-tops of the horizon getting bluer and more hazy as the yellow light began to graze the ground. At last we got to an open space, a high-lying piece of common-land, such as is rare in that ruthlessly utilized country of grazing-grounds and hop-gardens. Among the low hills of the Weald, it seemed quite preternaturally high up, giving a sense that its extent of flat heather and gorse, bound by distant firs, was really on the top of the world. The sun was setting just opposite, and its lights lay flat on the ground, staining it with the red and black of the heather, or rather turning it into the surface of a purple sea, canopied over by a bank of dark-purple clouds – the jet-like sparkle of the dry ling and gorse tipping the purple like sunlit wavelets. A cold wind swept in our faces.

'What is the name of this place?' I asked. It was the only bit of impressive scenery that I had met in the neighbourhood of Okehurst.

'It is called Cotes Common,' answered Mrs Oke, who had slackened the pace of the horse, and let the reins hang loose about his neck. 'It was here that Christopher Lovelock was killed.'

There was a moment's pause; and then she proceeded, tickling the flies from the horse's ears with the end of her whip, and looking straight into the sunset, which now rolled, a deep purple stream, across the heath to our feet –

'Lovelock was riding home one summer evening from Appledore, when, as he had got halfway across Cotes Common, somewhere about here – for I have always heard them mention the pond in the old gravel-pits as about the place – he saw two men riding towards him, in whom he presently recognized Nicholas Oke of Okehurst accompanied by a groom. Oke of Okehurst hailed him; and Lovelock rode up to meet him. "I am glad to have met you, Mr Lovelock," said Nicholas, "because I have some important news for you"; and so saying, he brought his horse close to the one that Lovelock was riding, and suddenly turning round, fired off a pistol at his head. Lovelock had time to move, and the bullet, instead of striking him, went straight into the head of his horse, which fell beneath him. Lovelock, however, had fallen in such a way as to be able to extricate himself easily from his horse; and drawing his sword, he rushed upon Oke, and seized his horse by the bridle. Oke quickly jumped off and drew his sword; and in a minute, Lovelock, who was much the better swordsman of the two, was having the better of him. Lovelock had completely disarmed him, and got his sword at Oke's throat, crying out to him that if he would ask forgiveness he should be spared for the sake of their old friendship, when the groom suddenly rode up from behind and shot Lovelock through the back. Lovelock fell, and Oke immediately tried to finish him with his sword, while the groom drew up and held the bridle of Oke's horse. At that moment the sunlight fell upon the groom's face, and Lovelock recognized Mrs Oke. He cried out, 'Alice, Alice! it is you who have murdered me!' and died. Then Nicholas Oke sprang into his saddle and rode off with his wife, leaving Lovelock dead by the side of his fallen horse. Nicholas Oke had taken the precaution of removing Lovelock's purse and throwing it into the pond, so the murder was put down to certain highwaymen who were about in that part of the country. Alice Oke died many years afterwards, quite an old woman, in the reign of Charles II; but Nicholas did not live very long, and shortly before his death got into a very strange condition, always brooding, and sometimes threatening to kill his wife. They say that in one of these fits, just shortly before his death, he told the whole story of the murder, and made a prophecy that when the head of his house and master of Okehurst should marry another Alice Oke, descended from himself and his wife, there should be an end of the Okes of Okehurst. You see, it seems to be coming true. We have no children, and I don't suppose we shall ever have any. I, at least, have never wished for them.'

Mrs Oke paused, and turned her face towards me with the absent smile in her thin cheeks: her eyes no longer had that distant look; they were strangely eager and fixed. I did not know what to answer; this woman positively frightened me. We remained for a moment in that same place, with the sunlight dying away in crimson ripples on the heather, gilding the yellow banks, the black waters of the pond, surrounded by thin rushes, and the yellow gravel-pits; while the wind blew in our faces and bent the ragged warped bluish tops of the firs. Then Mrs Oke touched the horse, and off we went at a furious pace. We did not exchange a single word, I think, on the way home. Mrs Oke sat with her eyes fixed on the reins, breaking the silence now and then only by a word to the horse, urging him to an even more furious pace. The people we met along the roads must have thought that the horse was running away, unless they noticed Mrs Oke's calm manner and the look of excited enjoyment in her face. To me it seemed that I was in the hands of a mad-woman, and I quietly prepared myself for being upset or dashed against a cart. It had turned cold, and the draught was icy in our faces when we got within sight of the red gables and high chimney-stacks of Okehurst. Mr Oke was standing before the door. On our approach I saw a look of relieved suspense, of keen pleasure come into his face.

He lifted his wife out of the cart in his strong arms with a kind of chivalrous tenderness.

'I am so glad to have you back, darling,' he exclaimed – 'so glad! I was delighted to hear you had gone out with the cart, but as you have not driven for so long, I was beginning to be frightfully anxious, dearest. Where have you been all this time?'

Mrs Oke had quickly extricated herself from her husband,

who had remained holding her, as one might hold a delicate child who has been causing anxiety. The gentleness and affection of the poor fellow had evidently not touched her – she seemed almost to recoil from it.

'I have taken him to Cotes Common,' she said, with that perverse look which I had noticed before, as she pulled off her driving-gloves. 'It is such a splendid old place.'

Mr Oke flushed as if he had bitten upon a sore tooth, and the double gash painted itself scarlet between his eyebrows.

Outside, the mists were beginning to rise, veiling the parkland dotted with big black oaks, and from which, in the watery moonlight, rose on all sides the eerie little cry of the lambs separated from their mothers. It was damp and cold, and I shivered.

VII

THE next day Okehurst was full of people, and Mrs Oke, to my amazement, was doing the honours of it as if a house full of commonplace, noisy young creatures, bent upon flirting and tennis, were her usual idea of felicity.

The afternoon of the third day – they had come for an electioneering ball, and stayed three nights – the weather changed; it turned suddenly very cold and began to pour. Every one was sent indoors, and there was a general gloom suddenly over the company. Mrs Oke seemed to have got sick of her guests, and was listlessly lying back on a couch, paying not the slightest attention to the chattering and piano-strumming in the room, when one of the guests suddenly proposed that they should play charades. He was a distant cousin of the Okes, a sort of fashionable artistic Bohemian, swelled out to intolerable conceit by the amateur-actor vogue of a season.

'It would be lovely in this marvellous old place,' he cried, 'just to dress up, and parade about, and feel as if we belonged to the past. I have heard you have a marvellous collection of old costumes, more or less ever since the days of Noah, somewhere, Cousin Bill.'

The whole party exclaimed in joy at this proposal. William

Oke looked puzzled for a moment, and glanced at his wife, who continued to lie listless on her sofa.

'There is a press full of clothes belonging to the family,' he answered dubiously, apparently overwhelmed by the desire to please his guests; 'but – but – I don't know whether it's quite respectful to dress up in the clothes of dead people.'

'Oh, fiddlestick!' cried the cousin. 'What do the dead people know about it? Besides,' he added, with mock seriousness, 'I assure you we shall behave in the most reverent way and feel quite solemn about it all, if only you will give us the key, old man.'

Again Mr Oke looked towards his wife, and again met only her vague, absent glance.

'Very well,' he said, and led his guests upstairs.

An hour later the house was filled with the strangest crew and the strangest noises. I had entered, to a certain extent, into William Oke's feeling of unwillingness to let his ancestors' clothes and personality be taken in vain; but when the masquerade was complete, I must say that the effect was quite magnificent. A dozen youngish men and women – those who were staying in the house and some neighbours who had come for lawn-tennis and dinner – were rigged out, under the direction of the theatrical cousin, in the contents of that oaken press: and I have never seen a more beautiful sight than the panelled corridors, the carved and escutcheoned staircase, the dim drawing-rooms with their faded tapestries, the great hall with its vaulted and ribbed ceiling, dotted about with groups or single figures that seemed to have come straight from the past. Even William Oke, who, besides myself and a few elderly people, was the only man not masqueraded, seemed delighted and fired by the sight. A certain schoolboy character suddenly came out in him; and finding that there was no costume left for him, he rushed upstairs and presently returned in the uniform he had worn before his marriage. I thought I had really never seen so magnificent a specimen of the handsome Englishman; he looked, despite all the modern associations of his costume, more genuinely old-world than all the rest, a knight for the Black Prince or Sidney, with his admirably regular features and beautiful fair hair and complexion. After a minute, even the elderly people had got costumes of some sort – dominoes arranged at the moment, and hoods and all manner of disguises made out of pieces of old embroidery and Oriental stuffs and furs; and very soon this rabble of masquers had become, so to speak, completely drunk with its own amusement – with the childishness, and, if I may say so, the barbarism, the vulgarity underlying the majority even of well-bred English men and women – Mr Oke himself doing the mountebank like a schoolboy at Christmas.

'Where is Mrs Oke? Where is Alice?' some one suddenly asked.

Mrs Oke had vanished. I could fully understand that to this eccentric being, with her fantastic, imaginative, morbid passion for the past, such a carnival as this must be positively revolting; and, absolutely indifferent as she was to giving offence, I could imagine how she would have retired, disgusted and outraged, to dream her strange day-dreams in the yellow room.

But a moment later, as we were all noisily preparing to go in to dinner, the door opened and a strange figure entered, stranger than any of these others who were profaning the clothes of the dead: a boy, slight and tall, in a brown riding-coat, leathern belt, and big buff boots, a little grey cloak over one shoulder, a large grey hat slouched over the eyes, a dagger and pistol at the waist. It was Mrs Oke, her eyes preternaturally bright, and her whole face lit up with a bold, perverse smile.

Every one exclaimed, and stood aside. Then there was a moment's silence, broken by faint applause. Even to a crew of noisy boys and girls playing the fool in the garments of men and women long dead and buried, there is something questionable in the sudden appearance of a young married woman, the mistress of the house, in a riding-coat and jack-boots; and Mrs Oke's expression did not make the jest seem any the less questionable.

'What is that costume?' asked the theatrical cousin, who, after a second, had come to the conclusion, that Mrs Oke was merely a woman of marvellous talent whom he must try and secure for his amateur troop next season.

'It is the dress in which an ancestress of ours, my namesake Alice Oke, used to go out riding with her husband in the days of

Charles I,' she answered, and took her seat at the head of the table. Involuntarily my eyes sought those of Oke of Okehurst. He, who blushed as easily as a girl of sixteen, was now as white as ashes, and I noticed that he pressed his hand almost convulsively to his mouth.

'Don't you recognize my dress, William?' asked Mrs Oke, fixing her eyes upon him with a cruel smile.

He did not answer, and there was a moment's silence, which the theatrical cousin had the happy thought of breaking by jumping upon his seat and emptying off his glass with the exclamation –

'To the health of the two Alice Okes, of the past and the present!'

Mrs Oke nodded, and with an expression I had never seen in her face before, answered in a loud and aggressive tone –

'To the health of the poet, Mr Christopher Lovelock, if his ghost be honouring this house with its presence!'

I felt suddenly as if I were in a madhouse. Across the table, in the midst of this room full of noisy wretches, tricked out red, blue, purple, and parti-coloured, as men and women of the sixteenth, seventeenth, and eighteenth centuries, as improvised Turks and Eskimos and dominoes, and clowns, with faces painted and corked and floured over, I seemed to see that sanguine sunset, washing like a sea of blood over the heather, to where, by the black pond and the wind-warped firs, there lay the body of Christopher Lovelock, with his dead horse near him, the yellow gravel and lilac ling soaked crimson all around; and above emerged, as out of the redness, the pale blond head covered with the grey hat, the absent eyes, and strange smile of Mrs Oke. It seemed to me horrible, vulgar, abominable, as if I had got inside a madhouse.

VIII

From that moment I noticed a change in William Oke; or rather, a change that had probably been coming on for some time got to the stage of being noticeable.

I don't know whether he had any words with his wife about

her masquerade of that unlucky evening. On the whole I decidedly think not. Oke was with every one a diffident and reserved man, and most of all so with his wife; besides, I can fancy that he would experience a positive impossibility of putting into words any strong feeling of disapprobation towards her, that his disgust would necessarily be silent. But be this as it may, I perceived very soon that the relations between my host and hostess had become exceedingly strained. Mrs Oke, indeed, had never paid much attention to her husband, and seemed merely a trifle more indifferent to his presence than she had been before. But Oke himself, although he affected to address her at meals from a desire to conceal his feeling, and a fear of making the position disagreeable to me, very clearly could scarcely bear to speak to or even see his wife. The poor fellow's honest soul was quite brimful of pain, which he was determined not to allow to overflow, and which seemed to filter into his whole nature and poison it. This woman had shocked and pained him more than was possible to say, and yet it was evident that he could neither cease loving her nor commence comprehending her real nature. I sometimes felt, as we took our long walks through the monotonous country, across the oak-dotted grazing-grounds, and by the brink of the dull-green, serried hop-rows, talking at rare intervals about the value of the crops, the drainage of the estate, the village schools, the Primrose League, and the iniquities of Mr Gladstone, while Oke of Okehurst carefully cut down every tall thistle that caught his eye – I sometimes felt, I say, an intense and impotent desire to enlighten this man about his wife's character. I seemed to understand it so well, and to understand it well seemed to imply such a comfortable acquiescence; and it seemed so unfair that just he should be condemned to puzzle for ever over this enigma, and wear out his soul trying to comprehend what now seemed so plain to me. But how would it ever be possible to get this serious, conscientious, slow-brained representative of English simplicity and honesty and thoroughness to understand the mixture of self-engrossed vanity, of shallowness, of poetic vision, of love of morbid excitement, that walked this earth under the name of Alice Oke?

So Oke of Okehurst was condemned never to understand; but

he was condemned also to suffer from his inability to do so. The poor fellow was constantly straining after an explanation of his wife's peculiarities; and although the effort was probably unconscious, it caused him a great deal of pain. The gash – the maniac-frown, as my friend calls it – between his eyebrows, seemed to have grown a permanent feature of his face.

Mrs Oke, on her side, was making the very worst of the situation. Perhaps she resented her husband's tacit reproval of that masquerade night's freak, and determined to make him swallow more of the same stuff, for she clearly thought that one of William's peculiarities, and one for which she despised him, was that he could never be goaded into an outspoken expression of disapprobation; that from her he would swallow any amount of bitterness without complaining. At any rate she now adopted a perfect policy of teasing and shocking her husband about the murder of Lovelock. She was perpetually alluding to it in her conversation, discussing in his presence what had or had not been the feelings of the various actors in the tragedy of 1626, and insisting upon her resemblance and almost identity with the original Alice Oke. Something had suggested to her eccentric mind that it would be delightful to perform in the garden at Okehurst, under the huge ilexes and elms, a little masque which she had discovered among Christopher Lovelock's works; and she began to scour the country and enter into vast correspondence for the purpose of effectuating this scheme. Letters arrived every other day from the theatrical cousin, whose only objection was that Okehurst was too remote a locality for an entertainment in which he foresaw great glory to himself. And every now and then there would arrive some young gentleman or lady, whom Alice Oke had sent for to see whether they would do.

I saw very plainly that the performance would never take place, and that Mrs Oke herself had no intention that it ever should. She was one of those creatures to whom realization of a project is nothing, and who enjoy plan-making almost the more for knowing that all will stop short at the plan. Meanwhile, this perpetual talk about the pastoral, about Lovelock, this continual attitudinizing as the wife of Nicholas Oke, had the further attraction to Mrs Oke of putting her husband into a condition of frightful though suppressed irritation, which she enjoyed with the enjoyment of a perverse child. You must not think that I looked on indifferent, although I admit that this was a perfect treat to an amateur student of character like myself. I really did feel most sorry for poor Oke, and frequently quite indignant with his wife. I was several times on the point of begging her to have more consideration for him, even of suggesting that this kind of behaviour, particularly before a comparative stranger like me, was very poor taste. But there was something elusive about Mrs Oke, which made it next to impossible to speak seriously with her; and besides, I was by no means sure that any interference on my part would not merely animate her perversity.

One evening a curious incident took place. We had just sat down to dinner, the Okes, the theatrical cousin, who was down for a couple of days, and three or four neighbours. It was dusk, and the yellow light of the candles mingled charmingly with the greyness of the evening. Mrs Oke was not well, and had been remarkably quiet all day, more diaphanous, strange, and far-away than ever; and her husband seemed to have felt a sudden return of tenderness, almost of compassion, for this delicate, fragile creature. We had been talking of quite indifferent matters, when I saw Mr Oke suddenly turn very white, and look fixedly for a moment at the window opposite to his seat.

'Who's that fellow looking in at the window, and making signs to you, Alice? Damn his impudence!' he cried, and jumping up, ran to the window, opened it, and passed out into the twilight. We all looked at each other in surprise; some of the party remarked upon the carelessness of servants in letting nasty-looking fellows hang about the kitchen, others told stories of tramps and burglars. Mrs Oke did not speak; but I noticed the curious, distant-looking smile in her thin cheeks.

After a minute William Oke came in, his napkin in his hand. He shut the window behind him and silently resumed his place.

'Well, who was it?' we all asked.

'Nobody. I — I must have made a mistake,' he answered, and turned crimson, while he busily peeled a pear.

'It was probably Lovelock,' remarked Mrs Oke, just as she

might have said, 'It was probably the gardener,' but with that faint smile of pleasure still in her face. Except the theatrical cousin, who burst into a loud laugh, none of the company had ever heard Lovelock's name, and, doubtless imagining him to be some natural appanage of the Oke family, groom or farmer, said nothing, so the subject dropped.

From that evening onwards things began to assume a different aspect. That incident was the beginning of a perfect system – a system of what? I scarcely know how to call it. A system of grim jokes on the part of Mrs Oke, of superstitious fancies on the part of her husband – a system of mysterious persecutions on the part of some less earthly tenant of Okehurst? Well, yes, after all, why not? We have all heard of ghosts, had uncles, cousins, grand-mothers, nurses, who have seen them; we are all a bit afraid of them at the bottom of our soul; so why shouldn't they be? I am too sceptical to believe in the impossibility of anything, for my part! Besides, when a man has lived throughout a summer in the same house with a woman like Mrs Oke of Okehurst, he gets to believe in the possibility of a great many improbable things, I assure you, as a mere result of believing in her. And when you come to think of it, why not? That a weird creature, visibly not of this earth, a reincarnation of a woman who murdered her lover two centuries and a half ago, that such a creature should have the power of attracting about her (being altogether superior to earthly lovers) the man who loved her in that previous existence, whose love for her was his death – what is there astonishing in that? Mrs Oke herself, I feel quite persuaded, believed or half believed it; indeed she very seriously admitted the possibility thereof, one day that I made the suggestion half in jest. At all events, it rather pleased me to think so; it fitted in so well with the woman's whole personality; it explained those hours and hours spent all alone in the yellow room, where the very air, with its scent of heady flowers and old perfumed stuffs, seemed redolent of ghosts. It explained that strange smile which was not for any of us, and yet was not merely for herself – that strange, far-off look in the wide pale eyes. I liked the idea, and I liked to tease, or rather to delight her with it. How should I know that the wretched husband would take such matters seriously?

He became day by day more silent and perplexed-looking; and, as a result, worked harder, and probably with less effect, at his land-improving schemes and political canvassing. It seemed to me that he was perpetually listening, watching, waiting for something to happen: a word spoken suddenly, the sharp opening of a door, would make him start, turn crimson, and almost tremble; the mention of Lovelock brought a helpless look, half a convulsion, like that of a man overcome by great heat, into his face. And his wife, so far from taking any interest in his altered looks, went on irritating him more and more. Every time that the poor fellow gave one of those starts of his, or turned crimson at the sudden sound of a footstep, Mrs Oke would ask him, with her contemptuous indifference, whether he had seen Lovelock. I soon began to perceive that my host was getting perfectly ill. He would sit at meals never saying a word, with his eyes fixed scrutinizingly on his wife, as if vainly trying to solve some dreadful mystery; while his wife, ethereal, exquisite, went on talking in her listless way about the masque, about Lovelock, always about Lovelock. During our walks and rides, which we continued pretty regularly, he would start whenever in the roads or lanes surrounding Okehurst, or in its grounds, we perceived a figure in the distance. I have seen him tremble at what, on nearer approach, I could scarcely restrain my laughter on discovering to be some well-known farmer or neighbour or servant. Once, as we were returning home at dusk, he suddenly caught my arm and pointed across the oak-dotted pastures in the direction of the garden, then started off almost at a run, with his dog behind him, as if in pursuit of some intruder.

'Who was it?' I asked. And Mr Oke merely shook his head mournfully. Sometimes in the early autumn twilights, when the white mists rose from the park-land, and the rooks formed long black lines on the palings, I almost fancied I saw him start at the very trees and bushes, the outlines of the distant oast-houses, with their conical roofs and projecting vanes, like gibing fingers in the half light.

'Your husband is ill,' I once ventured to remark to Mrs Oke, as she sat for the hundred-and-thirtieth of my preparatory sketches (I somehow could never get beyond preparatory sketches with her). She raised her beautiful, wide, pale eyes, making as she did so that exquisite curve of shoulders and neck and delicate pale head that I so vainly longed to reproduce.

'I don't see it,' she answered quietly. 'If he is, why doesn't he go to town and see the doctor? It's merely one of his glum fits.'

'You should not tease him about Lovelock,' I added, very seriously. 'He will get to believe in him.'

'Why not? If he sees him, why, he sees him. He would not be the only person that has done so'; and she smiled faintly and half perversely, as her eyes sought that usual distant indefinable something.

But Oke got worse. He was growing perfectly unstrung, like a hysterical woman. One evening that we were sitting alone in the smoking-room, he began unexpectedly a rambling discourse about his wife; how he had first known her when they were children, and they had gone to the same dancing-school near Portland Place; how her mother, his aunt-in-law, had brought her for Christmas to Okehurst while he was on his holidays; how finally, thirteen years ago, when he was twenty-three and she was eighteen, they had been married; how terribly he had suffered when they had been disappointed of their baby, and she had nearly died of the illness.

'I did not mind about the child, you know,' he said in an excited voice; 'although there will be an end of us now, and Okehurst will go to the Curtises. I minded only about Alice.' It was next to inconceivable that this poor excited creature, speaking almost with tears in his voice and in his eyes, was the quiet, well-got-up, irreproachable young ex-Guardsman who had walked into my studio a couple of months before.

Oke was silent for a moment, looking fixedly at the rug at his feet, when he suddenly burst out in a scarce audible voice –

'If you knew how I cared for Alice – how I still care for her. I could kiss the ground she walks upon. I would give anything – my life any day – if only she would look for two minutes as if she liked me a little – as if she didn't utterly despise me'; and the poor fellow burst into a hysterical laugh, which was almost a sob. Then he suddenly began to laugh outright, exclaiming, with a

sort of vulgarity of intonation which was extremely foreign to
him –

'Damn it, old fellow, this *is* a queer world we live in!' and rang
for more brandy and soda, which he was beginning, I noticed, to
take pretty freely now, although he had been almost a blue-
ribbon man – as much so as is possible for a hospitable country
gentleman – when I first arrived.

IX

IT BECAME clear to me now that, incredible as it might seem, the
thing that ailed William Oke was jealousy. He was simply madly
in love with his wife, and madly jealous of her. Jealous – but of
whom? He himself would probably have been quite unable to
say. In the first place – to clear off any possible suspicion –
certainly not of me. Besides the fact that Mrs Oke took only just
a very little more interest in me than in the butler or the
upper-housemaid, I think that Oke himself was the sort of man
whose imagination would recoil from realizing any definite
object of jealousy, even though jealousy might be killing him
inch by inch. It remained a vague, permeating, continuous
feeling – the feeling that he loved her, and she did not care a
jackstraw about him, and that everything with which she came
into contact was receiving some of that notice which was refused
to him – every person, or thing, or tree, or stone: it was the
recognition of that strange far-off look in Mrs Oke's eyes, of that
strange absent smile on Mrs Oke's lips – eyes and lips that had
no look and no smile for him.

Gradually his nervousness, his watchfulness, suspiciousness,
tendency to start, took a definite shape. Mr Oke was for ever
alluding to steps or voices he had heard, to figures he had seen
sneaking round the house. The sudden bark of one of the dogs
would make him jump up. He cleaned and loaded very carefully
all the guns and revolvers in his study, and even some of the old
fowling-pieces and holster-pistols in the hall. The servants and
tenants thought that Oke of Okehurst had been seized with a
terror of tramps and burglars. Mrs Oke smiled contemptuously
at all these doings.

'My dear William,' she said one day, 'the persons who worry you have just as good a right to walk up and down the passages and staircase, and to hang about the house, as you or I. They were there, in all probability, long before either of us was born, and are greatly amused by your preposterous notions of privacy.'

Mr Oke laughed angrily. 'I suppose you will tell me it is Lovelock – your eternal Lovelock – whose steps I hear on the gravel every night. I suppose he has as good a right to be here as you or I.' And he strode out of the room.

'Lovelock – Lovelock! Why will she always go on like that about Lovelock?' Mr Oke asked me that evening, suddenly staring me in the face.

I merely laughed.

'It's only because she has that play of his on the brain,' I answered; 'and because she thinks you superstitious, and likes to tease you.'

'I don't understand,' sighed Oke.

How could he? And if I had tried to make him do so, he would merely have thought I was insulting his wife, and have perhaps kicked me out of the room. So I made no attempt to explain psychological problems to him, and he asked me no more questions until once – But I must first mention a curious incident that happened.

The incident was simply this. Returning one afternoon from our usual walk, Mr Oke suddenly asked the servant whether any one had come. The answer was in the negative; but Oke did not seem satisfied. We had hardly sat down to dinner when he turned to his wife and asked, in a strange voice which I scarcely recognized as his own, who had called that afternoon.

'No one,' answered Mrs Oke; 'at least to the best of my knowledge.'

William Oke looked at her fixedly.

'No one?' he repeated, in a scrutinizing tone; 'no one, Alice?'

Mrs Oke shook her head. 'No one,' she replied.

There was a pause.

'Who was it, then, that was walking with you near the pond, about five o'clock?' asked Oke slowly.

His wife lifted her eyes straight to his and answered contemptuously –

'No one was walking with me near the pond, at five o'clock or any other hour.'

Mr Oke turned purple, and made a curious hoarse noise like a man choking.

'I – I thought I saw you walking with a man this afternoon, Alice,' he brought out with an effort; adding, for the sake of appearances before me, 'I thought it might have been the curate come with that report for me.'

Mrs Oke smiled.

'I can only repeat that no living creature has been near me this afternoon,' she said slowly. 'If you saw any one with me, it must have been Lovelock, for there certainly was no one else.'

And she gave a little sigh, like a person trying to reproduce in her mind some delightful but too evanescent impression.

I looked at my host; from crimson his face had turned perfectly livid, and he breathed as if some one were squeezing his windpipe.

No more was said about the matter. I vaguely felt that a great danger was threatening. To Oke or to Mrs Oke? I could not tell which; but I was aware of an imperious inner call to avert some dreadful evil, to exert myself, to explain, to interpose. I determined to speak to Oke the following day, for I trusted him to give me a quiet hearing, and I did not trust Mrs Oke. That woman would slip through my fingers like a snake if I attempted to grasp her elusive character.

I asked Oke whether he would take a walk with me the next afternoon, and he accepted to do so with a curious eagerness. We started about three o'clock. It was a stormy, chilly afternoon, with great balls of white clouds rolling rapidly in the cold blue sky, and occasional lurid gleams of sunlight, broad and yellow, which made the black ridge of the storm, gathered on the horizon, look blue-black like ink.

We walked quickly across the sere and sodden grass of the park, and on to the highroad that led over the low hills, I don't know why, in the direction of Cotes Common. Both of us were silent, for both of us had something to say, and did not know how to begin. For my part, I recognized the impossibility of starting the subject: an uncalled-for interference from me would merely indispose Mr Oke, and make him doubly dense of comprehension. So, if Oke had something to say, which he evidently had, it was better to wait for him.

Oke, however, broke the silence only by pointing out to me the condition of the hops, as we passed one of his many hop-gardens. 'It will be a poor year,' he said, stopping short and looking intently before him – 'no hops at all. No hops this autumn.'

I looked at him. It was clear that he had no notion what he was saying. The dark-green bines were covered with fruit; and only yesterday he himself had informed me that he had not seen such a profusion of hops for many years.

I did not answer, and we walked on. A cart met us in a dip of the road, and the carter touched his hat and greeted Mr Oke. But Oke took no heed; he did not seem to be aware of the man's presence.

The clouds were collecting all round; black domes, among which coursed the round grey masses of fleecy stuff.

'I think we shall be caught in a tremendous storm,' I said; 'hadn't we better be turning?' He nodded, and turned sharp round.

The sunlight lay in yellow patches under the oaks of the pasture-lands, and burnished the green hedges. The air was heavy and yet cold, and everything seemed preparing for a great storm. The rooks whirled in black clouds round the trees and the conical red caps of the oast-houses which give that country the look of being studded with turreted castles; then they descended – a black line – upon the fields, with what seemed an unearthly loudness of caw. And all round there arose a shrill quavering bleating of lambs and calling of sheep, while the wind began to catch the topmost branches of the trees.

Suddenly Mr Oke broke the silence.

'I don't know you very well,' he began hurriedly, and without turning his face towards me; 'but I think you are honest, and you have seen a good deal of the world – much more than I. I want you to tell me – but truly, please – what do you think a man should do if –' and he stopped for some minutes.

'Imagine,' he went on quickly, 'that a man cares a great deal – a very great deal for his wife, and that he finds out that she – well, that – that she is deceiving him. No – don't misunderstand me; I mean – that she is constantly surrounded by some one else and will not admit it – some one whom she hides away. Do you understand? Perhaps she does not know all the risk she is running, you know, but she will not draw back – she will not avow it to her husband –'

'My dear Oke,' I interrupted, attempting to take the matter lightly, 'these are questions that can't be solved in the abstract, or by people to whom the thing has not happened. And it certainly has not happened to you or me.'

Oke took no notice of my interruption. 'You see,' he went on, 'the man doesn't expect his wife to care much about him. It's not that; he isn't merely jealous, you know. But he feels that she is on the brink of dishonouring herself – because I don't think a woman can really dishonour her husband; dishonour is in our own hands, and depends only on our own acts. He ought to save her, do you see? He must, must save her, in one way or another. But if she will not listen to him, what can he do? Must he seek out the other one, and try and get him out of the way? You see it's all the fault of the other – not hers, not hers. If only she would trust in her husband, she would be safe. But that other one won't let her.'

'Look here, Oke,' I said boldly, but feeling rather frightened; 'I know quite well what you are talking about. And I see you don't understand the matter in the very least. I do. I have watched you and watched Mrs Oke these six weeks, and I see what is the matter. Will you listen to me?'

And taking his arm, I tried to explain to him my view of the situation – that his wife was merely eccentric, and a little theatrical and imaginative, and that she took a pleasure in teasing him. That he, on the other hand, was letting himself get into a morbid state; that he was ill, and ought to see a good doctor. I even offered to take him to town with me.

I poured out volumes of psychological explanations. I dissected Mrs Oke's character twenty times over, and tried to show him that there was absolutely nothing at the bottom of his suspicions beyond an imaginative *pose* and a garden-play on the brain. I adduced twenty instances, mostly invented for the nonce, of ladies of my acquaintance who had suffered from similar fads. I pointed out to him that his wife ought to have an outlet for her imaginative and theatrical over-energy. I advised him to take her to London and plunge her into some set where every one should be more or less in a similar condition. I laughed at the notion of there being any hidden individual about the house. I explained to Oke that he was suffering from delusions, and called upon so conscientious and religious a man to take every step to rid himself of them, adding innumerable examples of people who had cured themselves of seeing visions and of brooding over morbid fancies. I struggled and wrestled, like Jacob with the angel, and I really hoped I had made some impression. At first, indeed, I felt that not one of my words went into the man's brain – that, though silent, he was not listening. It seemed almost hopeless to present my views in such a light that he could grasp them. I felt as if I were expounding and arguing at a rock. But when I got on to the tack of his duty towards his wife and himself, and appealed to his moral and religious notions, I felt that I was making an impression.

'I daresay you are right,' he said, taking my hand as we came in sight of the red gables of Okehurst, and speaking in a weak, tired, humble voice. 'I don't understand you quite, but I am sure what you say is true. I daresay it is all that I'm seedy. I feel sometimes as if I were mad, and just fit to be locked up. But don't think I don't struggle against it. I do, I do continually, only sometimes it seems too strong for me. I pray God night and morning to give me the strength to overcome my suspicions, or to remove these dreadful thoughts from me. God knows, I know what a wretched creature I am, and how unfit to take care of that poor girl.'

And Oke again pressed my hand. As we entered the garden, he turned to me once more.

'I am very, very grateful to you,' he said, 'and, indeed, I will do my best to try and be stronger. If only,' he added, with a sigh, 'if only Alice would give me a moment's breathing-time, and not go on day after day mocking me with her Lovelock.'

X

I HAD begun Mrs Oke's portrait, and she was giving me a sitting. She was unusually quiet that morning; but, it seemed to me, with the quietness of a woman who is expecting something, and she gave me the impression of being extremely happy. She had been reading, at my suggestion, the *Vita Nuova*, which she did not know before, and the conversation came to roll upon that, and upon the question whether love so abstract and so enduring was a possibility. Such a discussion, which might have savoured of flirtation in the case of almost any other young and beautiful woman, became in the case of Mrs Oke something quite different; it seemed distant, intangible, not of this earth, like her smile and the look in her eyes.

'Such love as that,' she said, looking into the far distance of the oak-dotted park-land, 'is very rare, but it can exist. It becomes a person's whole existence, his whole existence, his whole soul; and it can survive the death, not merely of the beloved, but of the lover. It is unextinguishable, and goes on in the spiritual world until it meet a reincarnation of the beloved; and when this happens, it jets out and draws to it all that may remain of that lover's soul, and takes shape and surrounds the beloved one once more.'

Mrs Oke was speaking slowly, almost to herself, and I had never, I think, seen her look so strange and so beautiful, the stiff white dress bringing out but the more the exotic exquisiteness and incorporealness of her person.

I did not know what to answer, so I said half in jest –

'I fear you have been reading too much Buddhist literature, Mrs Oke. There is something dreadfully esoteric in all you say.'

She smiled contemptuously.

'I know people can't understand such matters,' she replied, and was silent for some time. But, through her quietness and silence, I felt, as it were, the throb of a strange excitement in this woman, almost as if I had been holding her pulse.

Still, I was in hopes that things might be beginning to go better in consequence of my interference. Mrs Oke had scarcely once alluded to Lovelock in the last two or three days; and Oke had been much more cheerful and natural since our conversation. He no longer seemed so worried; and once or twice I had caught in him a look of great gentleness and loving-kindness, almost of pity, as towards some young and very frail thing, as he sat opposite his wife.

But the end had come. After that sitting Mrs Oke had complained of fatigue and retired to her room, and Oke had driven off on some business to the nearest town. I felt all alone in the big house, and after having worked a little at a sketch I was making in the park, I amused myself rambling about the house.

It was a warm, enervating, autumn afternoon; the kind of weather that brings the perfume out of everything, the damp ground and fallen leaves, the flowers in the jars, the old woodwork and stuffs; that seems to bring on to the surface of one's consciousness all manner of vague recollections and expectations, a something half pleasurable, half painful, that makes it impossible to do or to think. I was the prey of this particular, not at all unpleasurable, restlessness. I wandered up and down the corridors, stopping to look at the pictures, which I knew already in every detail, to follow the pattern of the carvings and old stuffs, to stare at the autumn flowers, arranged in magnificent masses of colour in the big china bowls and jars. I took up one book after another and threw it aside; then I sat down to the piano and began to play irrelevant fragments. I felt quite alone, although I had heard the grind of the wheels on the gravel, which meant that my host had returned. I was lazily turning over a book of verses – I remember it perfectly well, it was Morris's *Love is Enough* – in a corner of the drawing-room, when the door suddenly opened and William Oke showed himself. He did not enter, but beckoned to me to come out to him. There was something in his face that made me start up and follow him at once. He was extremely quiet, even stiff, not a muscle of his face moving, but very pale.

'I have something to show you,' he said, leading me through the vaulted hall, hung round with ancestral pictures, into the gravelled space that looked like a filled-up moat, where stood the big blasted oak, with its twisted, pointing branches. I followed him on to the lawn, or rather the piece of park-land that ran up to the house. We walked quickly, he in front, without exchanging a word. Suddenly he stopped, just where there jutted out the bow-window of the yellow drawing-room, and I felt Oke's hand tight upon my arm.

'I have brought you here to see something,' he whispered hoarsely; and he led me to the window.

I looked in. The room, compared with the outdoor, was rather dark; but against the yellow wall I saw Mrs Oke sitting alone on a couch in her white dress, her head slightly thrown back, a large red rose in her hand.

'Do you believe now?' whispered Oke's voice hot at my ear. 'Do you believe now? Was it all my fancy? But I will have him this time. I have locked the door inside, and, by God! he shan't escape.'

The words were not out of Oke's mouth. I felt myself struggling with him silently outside that window. But he broke loose, pulled open the window, and leapt into the room, and I after him. As I crossed the threshold, something flashed in my eyes; there was a loud report, a sharp cry, and the thud of a body on the ground.

Oke was standing in the middle of the room, with a faint smoke about him; and at his feet, sunk down from the sofa, with her blond head resting on its seat, lay Mrs Oke, a pool of red forming in her white dress. Her mouth was convulsed, as if in that automatic shriek, but her wide-open white eyes seemed to smile vaguely and distantly.

I know nothing of time. It all seemed to be one second, but a second that lasted hours. Oke stared, then turned round and laughed.

'The damned rascal has given me the slip again!' he cried; and quickly unlocking the door, rushed out of the house with dreadful cries.

That is the end of the story. Oke tried to shoot himself that evening, but merely fractured his jaw, and died a few days later, raving. There were all sorts of legal inquiries, through which I went as through a dream; and whence it resulted that Mr Oke had killed his wife in a fit of momentary madness. That was the end of Alice Oke. By the way, her maid brought me a locket which was found round her neck, all stained with blood. It contained some very dark auburn hair, not at all the colour of William Oke's. I am quite sure it was Lovelock's.

GIRL
Jamaica Kincaid

WASH the white clothes on Monday and put them on the stone heap; wash the colour clothes on Tuesday and put them on the clothes-line to dry; don't walk barehead in the hot sun; cook pumpkin fritters in very hot sweet oil; soak your little cloths right after you take them off; when buying cotton to make yourself a nice blouse, be sure that it doesn't have gum on it, because that way it won't hold up well after a wash; soak salt fish overnight before you cook it; is it true that you sing benna in Sunday school?; always eat your food in such a way that it won't turn someone else's stomach; on Sundays try to walk like a lady and not like the slut you are so bent on becoming; don't sing benna in Sunday school; you mustn't speak to wharf-rat boys, not even to give directions; don't eat fruits on the street – flies will follow you; *but I don't sing benna on Sundays at all and never in Sunday school*; this is how to sew on a button; this is how to make a buttonhole for the button you have just sewed on; this is how to hem a dress when you see the hem coming down and so to prevent yourself from looking like the slut I know you are so bent on becoming; this is how you iron your father's khaki shirt so that it doesn't have a crease; this is how you iron your father's khaki pants so that they don't have a crease; this is how you grow okra – far from the house, because okra tree harbours red ants; when you are growing dasheen, make sure it gets plenty of water or else it makes your throat itch when you are eating it; this is how you sweep a corner; this is how you sweep a whole house; this is how you sweep a yard; this is how you smile to someone you don't like too much; this is how you smile to someone you don't like at all; this is how you smile to someone you like completely; this is how you set a table for tea; this is how you set a table for dinner; this is how you set a table for dinner with an important guest; this is how you set a table for lunch; this is how you set a table for breakfast; this is how to behave in the presence of men who don't know you very well, and this way they won't recognize immediately the slut I have warned you against becoming; be sure to wash every day, even if it is with your own spit; don't squat down to play marbles — you are not a boy, you know; don't pick people's flowers — you might catch something; don't throw stones at blackbirds, because it might not be a blackbird at all; this is how to make a bread pudding; this is how to make doukona; this is how to make pepper pot; this is how to make a good medicine for a cold; this is how to make a good medicine to throw away a child before it even becomes a child; this is how to catch a fish; this is how to throw back a fish you don't like, and that way something bad won't fall on you; this is how to bully a man; this is how a man bullies you; this is how to love a man, and if this doesn't work there are other ways, and if they don't work don't feel too bad about giving up; this is how to spit up in the air if you feel like it, and this is how to move quick so that it doesn't fall on you; this is how to make ends meet; always squeeze bread to make sure it's fresh; *but what if the baker won't let me feel the bread?*; you mean to say that after all you are really going to be the kind of woman who the baker won't let near the bread?

AUNT LIU

Luo Shu

I WAS awakened that day not by the songs the cowherds sang as they drove their oxen up the slope, nor by one of our household speaking loudly to my mother who was hard of hearing. A strange, rough voice exclaiming: 'Why, she's grown up now!' woke me.

Rather annoyed I opened my eyes to see who was in the room. Standing by my bed was a shabbily-dressed middle-aged woman with a somewhat flat, pock-marked face under wispy hair. Her lips parted in a fearful toothless smile.

I felt I had seen this unattractive, ugly face before. But I could not place her.

I gazed at her silently, trying to find some record of her filed in my mind.

'I'm Aunt Liu . . . I knew you'd have forgotten Aunt Liu,' she said as if reading my thoughts. 'It's eight years since I saw you last. And how you have grown! I wouldn't have recognized you if I had met you on the street.'

'What? You're Aunt Liu? The Aunt Liu who took care of me?'

I jumped down from my bed, my face flushed with excitement.

A child easily remembers trifles but is apt to forget what ought to be remembered. How could I have forgotten this woman who had once been so good to me? What an ungrateful little creature!

She backed away as I went up to her. Behind her was a desk where I did my lessons when I came home at week-ends. Bumping against it, she upset the vase of bright summer daisies on it. Quite put out, she hastily tried to repair the damage while I did my best to stop her.

'You . . .'

I meant to say something to put her at ease but my mind was in a whirl too. I had no idea whether to say 'you used to be' or 'you are'. Maybe what I meant was, 'You are entirely different from before!'

Yes, she had certainly changed. She used to feel uneasy only in the presence of my father and mother. Why should she behave like this now in front of me? Wasn't I the little girl she loved and cared for like a mother? Nevertheless, I knew if she had sat down on a stool and offered to hold me on her knee, so that she could croon the ballads my mother had forbidden, tell blood-curdling stories that might mark a young mind, or ask me to hug her and kiss her red pock-marked face, I would have refused without a moment's hesitation.

She was not to blame. Neither was I. Time and hateful conventions had made a wide gap between us.

It was awkward staring at each other in utter silence. I felt I must find something appropriate to say. Mother's arrival saved the situation.

She was in a good mood that day and chuckled as she walked in.

'What a hostess . . . Why don't you ask Liu to sit down?'

I didn't realize until then that I was sitting on my bed while Liu stood in the middle of the room.

'Look, she has grown taller than I,' said Mother. Pointing at the two plaited knots on the back of my head, she continued, 'These seem to be the craze with middle-school students! They look quite nice, don't they?'

Liu had not forgotten that she needed only to nod, whatever Mother said. But perhaps she had not noticed what Mother was saying. Her eyes scrutinized me from head to toe. Was she looking for some trace of the little girl of eight years ago?

'You hardly know each other now!' Liu's scrutiny made Mother smile. 'One of you has grown up while the other is getting old. How time flies!' Then she said to me, 'You ought to be glad. You never expected Liu to turn up in this valley hidden in the mountains, did you? She must have had a time of it finding us. Do you remember the day I fired her? She had just bought you a lot of water-chestnuts and some lotus roots. I sent her away because she was too fond of drinking.'

Mother's bluntness amazed me. Fancy coming out openly like that with the ill turn she had done Aunt Liu!

The mention of water-chestnuts and lotus roots did something to me. I tried to avoid the two pairs of eyes fastened on me.

A gust of wind swept the palm leaves against my window. I pulled one off, tore it to shreds and scattered them over the floor.

Suddenly I thought of a question.

'How did you find out that we had moved to this place?'

'I asked! You hadn't crossed the country – it was easy to find you.'

She was still so outspoken and sharp.

I was going to ask more questions when Mother sent for a bottle of wine which she held out to Liu.

'I know this is what you like best,' she said. 'Go and have a drink in the kitchen. This is good seasoned wine, so don't overdo it. Leave some to take home and share with your husband.'

When she was gone Mother told me that Liu had married a man who had seven-tenths of a *mu* of land in the hills and who worked as a sedan-chair carrier. She didn't remember where Liu was living now but she sympathized with this ill-fated woman.

I knew very little of Liu's past. Someone might have told me, but it had left no impression. Now Mother told me the whole story again.

When she was fifteen, Liu was tricked into leaving her home and sold as a maid to a rich family. One night, she had too much to drink and was raped by her master, a man of over forty. When she was found to be pregnant, they drove her out of the black gate flanked on both sides by stone lions. The baby was born in a privy by the street and died three days after birth. A good-hearted scavenger cleared away the grubs around the little corpse, wrapped it up in a tattered mat and buried it for her. Thereafter she had managed by mending and taking in washing or by standing at the outskirts of the town and stretching out her hand for alms. Sometimes she sold porridge in the lanes. In the end she contrived to be taken on by us as a servant. This was a remarkable opportunity for her. How good life must have seemed!

If she had not been so fond of tippling, Mother wouldn't have sent her away.

This fondness for drink was her only fault. And my mother was a kind-hearted woman, I knew . . . But I recalled the day before Liu left us eight years ago.

It was a summer day just like this one. Thunder was rumbling in the distance. I was watching the yellow ants fight the black ants under a Judas tree. Behind the bamboo door curtain Mother was talking to some woman and her voice sounded angry.

Just then Liu came through the gate. You could see at a glance that she had been drinking again. In her hands were two thick white lotus roots and a package wrapped in a lotus leaf. The pitcher hanging from her arm obviously contained rice wine.

Giving the package to me she said:

'I have brought you something good. Eat the water-chestnuts first while I wash and slice the lotus roots for you.'

Mother told me not to eat the water-chestnuts.

When Liu returned with a plate for me, the woman who had been speaking with my mother rushed up to her, jabbed at her forehead and said fiercely:

'You're fired. Pack your things and look for another job. I've done all I could to help you but you just don't try to make good. You never stop drinking that stinking yellow liquor! You've brought this on your own head.'

Liu said nothing, just urged me to eat the lotus roots.

I could do nothing but accept the plate which I offered to my mother. She was embroidering a white silk pillow-case. The bright flower made her angry face look much sterner than usual. She slammed the plate down on a table and froze me with a look. Although she didn't lay any blame on me I was already trembling. More for Liu's sake than my own.

That night at dinner Liu didn't wait on us and the strange thing was Mother didn't send for her either.

I sneaked to the kitchen as soon as Mother's back was turned. The kitchen door was closed. I dared not knock. Peeping in through a crack, I called Liu softly.

All the servants were sitting round the table, a winecup in ftont of each. The pitcher Liu had brought was in the middle.

They were eating and drinking merrily, unaware that outside the door a little girl was gazing so lovingly at one among them. Liu's face was red, her sleeves were rolled up high and her tunic was unbuttoned, her throat bare. This was the first time I had seen her in such a state and I was puzzled by her strange behaviour. Later on I realized that since she would be eating our rice no longer she felt she could let herself go. To hell with the rules that had bound her for three whole years! She would do as she pleased on the eve of her departure.

'Ask someone to put in a word for you. The mistress may let you stay,' suggested one.

'Working for others, you have to do as they say.'

'There's no need. No sense in trying to stay when you're not wanted. Servants have one foot inside the door and the other one out. You can step in if things go well or out if they don't. If one family doesn't want you, go to another. With able hands and feet you can make a living anywhere. I've begged for my food before now, what have I to fear?'

Afraid Mother might be looking for me, I hurried back and tugged at the hem of her coat.

'What do you want?' she asked.

'Mother! . . . Aunt Liu! . . .' I had to repeat myself twice before she understood.

'I have told her to go tomorrow. I don't want to leave you in the care of a woman like that. I'll find someone else to look after you, someone kind.' Then she remarked, half to herself: 'As a matter of fact, she's a good honest creature. The only trouble is the way she drinks. I'm sorry for her, though . . . I'll cancel what she owes us, give her an extra month's pay and a suit of clothes.'

Next morning I woke up to find Liu gone. And since then eight years had passed.

I had never dreamt that she would come to see us. I was pleasantly surprised and rather touched.

If Mother had not dismissed her, she would not have become so bedraggled and haggard-looking. But I could not lay the blame entirely on Mother.

I hoped that Mother would let her stay with us.

When Liu came back after her meal I asked her, 'Did you have enough?'

'A very good meal, thank you. It's two years since I've had white rice.'

'Are you doing all right?'

'Well, I manage somehow. Whether you get on well or badly, it's all the same. Even if you don't get on well you must go on living.'

I was silent for some time and then explained, 'I mean, do you have enough to eat?'

'Of course not! He brings home barely enough to feed himself. I live on that plot we have in the hills. I gather firewood every day to make ends meet. When there's no firewood I sometimes do coolie work. I can manage a load of seventy or eighty catties.'

'Is your husband good to you?'

'Not bad . . . Since I left you I have had three men. Every one of them beat me. When I found I could not hold my own with the last of them I ran away and married this one . . .'

'Does he beat you?' I asked quickly.

'What do you think? All men beat their wives!' She smiled at me as if to say, 'Doesn't your father beat your mother too?' Then she said, 'I can always run away when it gets too much for me or I can't hold my own.'

It was growing dark and she seemed anxious to go.

'It's getting dark and it looks like rain. I still have more than five *li* to go. I'm going to raise two fat hens when I get back; I want you and the mistress to come for a meal in the autumn when it's cooler.' Then she shook her head. 'But my place is no better than a pigsty – you won't come.'

'Stay a bit longer. I've something else to ask you. Do you mean to go on like this? Why not find a job?'

'What job can I find? Even your family doesn't want a beggar like me. Besides, I'm used to running wild and my hands are too rough for delicate work. It's better this way . . . Just take life as it comes. After all, I won't starve.'

I had nothing more to say.

Unable to make her stay longer, Mother gave her a peck of white rice and what remained of the bottle of wine.

Soon after that I went to study in the provincial town. Mother never told me whether she visited Liu or ate the fat hens specially raised for us.

When I went home the following year, I was told that Liu had left her husband again. No one knew where she had drifted.

I believe she is living still and with all my heart I wish her well, for she understands life.

NOTES ON THE AUTHORS

Ama Ata Aidoo (1942–   ).   Playwright, writer of fiction and teacher, born in the Gold Coast before it became Ghana, she now shuttles between West and East Africa, Europe and the USA as visiting scholar and lecturer. 'The Plums' comes from her fictional memoir or set of meditations, *Our Sister Killjoy: Reflections from a Black-Eyed Squint*, published in 1977. Her collection of short stories, *No Sweetness Here*, came out in 1970.

Djuna Barnes (1892–1982).   Daughter of a writer mother and a painter father, Djuna Barnes was born into the Bohemia of turn-of-the-century New York, and herself became both writer and illustrator. 'The Earth' is a story from her early days, when she worked as a feature writer for the Brooklyn *Daily Eagle* between 1913 and 1919. She travelled to Paris in 1919 with letters of introduction to Ezra Pound and James Joyce. Her novel, *Nightwood*, published in 1936, is an authentic modern classic.

Jane Bowles (1917–73).   A native of New York, she settled more or less permanently in Tangiers in 1947 with her husband, the writer and composer Paul Bowles. Her work includes a novel, *Two Serious Ladies*, a play, *In the Summerhouse*, and short stories, some of which were collected in the volume, *Plain Pleasures*, from which 'A Guatemalan Idyll' is taken. Her writing is characterized by strangeness, surprise and disenchantment. At the age of forty, she suffered a cerebral haemorrhage and wrote no more, dying in Malaga, Spain, in 1973. Like Djuna Barnes, her fiction demonstrates how certain women writers appropriated the alienation of modernism to express some aspects of women's lives.

Leonora Carrington (1917–   ).   Painter and writer; born in Lancashire, she now lives and works in Mexico and New York. Her first stories, of which 'The Débutante' is one, were written in French in her early twenties, when she was a close associate of the Surrealists. Her writing includes one of the most gripping of all accounts of an experience of madness, *Down There* (1940).

Angela Carter (1940–   ).   Novelist, short story writer, scriptwriter and journalist. Born in England but has lived in Japan, Australia and the USA for short periods. Her longest novel is *Nights at the Circus* (1984). 'The Loves of Lady Purple' comes from the second of her three collections of short stories, *Fireworks* (1974).

Andrée Chedid (1929–   ).   Born in Egypt, she has lived mainly in France since 1946, although she took her BA degree in Cairo at the American University. She writes in French and has published both poetry and fiction. In 1975 she received the Belgian Academy's Grand Prize; in 1976, the Mallarmé Prize; and the Goncourt Award in 1979.

Colette (1873–1954).   One of the great writers of this century, Colette (born Sidonie Gabrielle Colette in Burgundy) was novelist, short story writer, journalist, beautician, music hall performer, actress – a woman who forged an entire literary identity out of 'knowing about life', and a fiction out of her enormously wide range of experience of the world. Her collected writing runs to fifteen volumes. She was the first woman President of the Academie Goncourt and when she died she was given a state funeral. 'The Rainy Moon' is the title story of a collection published in English in 1958; in it, Colette herself appears as a working writer.

George Egerton (1859–1945).   Real name, Mary Chavelita Dunne; born in Australia, her nomadic childhood was followed by life in New York, London and Norway, where she encountered the harsh realism in the work of Ibsen and Strindberg and met and was influenced by Knut Hamsen. In 1893 she published a volume of short stories, *Keynotes*, followed by a second, *Discords*, the next year, from which 'Wedlock' is taken. The sexual and emotional honesty of her stories remains undiminished by time and still shocks.

Rocky (Raquel) Gámez. She was born and brought up in the lower Rio Grande Valley of Texas. At present she lives and works in the San Francisco Bay area. Her short stories are featured in the anthology, *Cventos: Stories By Latinas* (New York, 1983).

Bessie Head (1937–86). Bessie Head left South Africa, where she was born, to live the rest of her life in Botswana; as she put it, she returned 'to ancient Africa'. The tragic circumstances of her life, child of the illicit union of a white mother and a black father, raised in institutions, suffering the full force of apartheid, are reflected in her novel, *A Question of Power* (1973). The story of 'Life' comes from her collection of stories of village life in her adopted country, *The Collector of Treasures* (1977). She is the finest of all the women writers who have emerged from South Africa, and is shamefully little known in Britain.

Elizabeth Jolley (1923–). Child of a Viennese mother and an English father, she was brought up in a German-speaking household in the industrial Midlands of England. She moved to Western Australia with her husband and three children in 1959. She cultivates a small orchard and goose farm and conducts writing workshops in prisons and community centres. Over the last decade, she has published a number of novels – including *Mr Scobie's Riddle* and *Miss Peabody's Inheritance* – and many short stories that have established her an international reputation with extraordinary rapidity.

Jamaica Kincaid (1941–). Born in St John's, Antigua, she now lives in New York, where she is a staff writer for the *New Yorker* magazine. She has published a novel, and a collection of short stories, *At the Bottom of the River*.

Vernon Lee (1856–1935). Real name, Violet Paget; novelist, short story writer and essayist, with a special talent for the supernatural and the grotesque; an original. Like many of her generation, she loved Italy and spent much of her life there.

In a letter, she succinctly defined 'man's love' as 'acquisitive, possessive and BESTIAL.'

Katherine Mansfield (1888–1923). Born in Wellington, New Zealand, she came to live in London in 1908. She travelled frequently in Europe, dying of tuberculosis in France after a lengthy illness. She turned the short story in English into the perfect instrument for the reflection of sensibility. Her collected stories are published in one volume by Oxford University Press in a definitive edition.

Suniti Namjoshi (1941–). Born in India, Suniti Namjoshi now teaches in the Department of English at the University of Toronto. She has published poetry, fables, articles and reviews in literary and Women's Studies journals in India, Canada, the USA and Britain. Her novel, *The Conversations of Cow*, was published in 1985. These three fables come from *Feminist Fables*, published in 1981; her writing combines lightness of heart with seriousness of intent.

Grace Paley (1922–). Of Russian–Jewish immigrant stock, her work is the pure product of New York City. Due to her stated conviction that 'Art is long, life is short,' she has produced only three slim volumes of short stories over the past three decades, *The Little Disturbances of Man* (1959), *Enormous Changes at the Last Minute* (1974) and *Later the Same Day* (1985). These alone have been sufficient to establish her as one of America's most important writers of fiction, although it is possible that Grace Paley's work in the protest movement against American involvement in Vietnam in the 1960s, and her current work in the anti-nuclear movement, seem to her more important in human terms; and, besides, what is the point of writing stories if there is nobody left to read them?

Luo Shu (1903–38). Born in Sichuan Province, she travelled to France in 1929 to study, returning to China four years later, where she translated works by Romain Rolland and others into Chinese before herself beginning to write fiction. Her first work, *Twice-Married Woman*, was published in 1936. In 1937, she began work on a novel depicting the life of salt-workers but a year later she died in child-birth.

Frances Towers was born in Calcutta, India, but grew up in England. She worked, first, for the Bank of England and subsequently as a teacher. She died on New Year's Day, 1948 and her short stories were collected together and published the next year, under the title of one of them, *Tea With Mr Rochester*.